LOOKING THROUGH GLASS

LOOKING THROUGH GLASS

MUKUL KESAVAN

Farrar, Straus and Giroux

New York

For Papa, Ma and Arun

ACKNOWLEDGEMENTS
Hari Sen, Amitav Ghosh, Gautam Mukhopadhyaya,
Rukun Advani, Radhika Chopra, Shalini Advani,
Partho Dutta, Sanjeev Saith, Ishwari Bajpai, Chandrakanta Das,
Alok Sarin, Gaiti Hasan, Ashok Ganju, Shukla Pulin
and Sudhakar Kesavan.
Many thanks.

Library of Congress Cataloging-in-Publication Data
Kesavan, Mukul.
Looking through glass / Mukul Kesavan.
p. cm.
I. Title.
PR9499.3.K38L66 1995 823—dc20 94-24172 CIP

Contents

LOOKING
THROUGH
GLASS

Deathbed Guilt

ALL THAT WAS left of her when we returned the next morning was ash and bone grit. Dadi was eighty-eight when her heart failed and she burned like brittle paper. She would have been pleased, I thought, leaning over the extinguished pyre to sift the dust for bits of bone. She had hated leftovers. Mealtimes in her Kashmiri Gate house were grimly policed. The grandchildren were served measured portions and she stood over us till we had picked our plates clean. Malingerers were reminded of the red-hot kitchen tongs buried in the choolha. She never needed to show them to us – we knew, just as the adults did, that Dadi was a woman of her word.

When her husband died, she continued to live in the Kashmiri Gate house, attended by a single maid, refusing the half-hearted hospitality of her children: my father had planned to share her on a half-yearly basis with his younger brother. I grew up hearing relatives routinely marvelling at her self-sufficiency, at that iron independence undented by age. No leftover food, no unpaid dues: herself a social worker in the field of fallen women, she was determined not to become an object of charity.

My parents didn't visit her much in the decade after Dadaji's death, and I became close to her only after I discovered my school's darkroom. Mr D'Mello, the teacher-in-charge, was fond of saying that black-and-white photography was about texture and grain. Texture and grain, he would say, holding up an enormous blow-up of a thumbprint, texture and grain. This seemed a substantial insight to me at eighteen, so that when the *Illustrated Weekly of India* announced a competition for photo-portraits, I borrowed my father's Rolleiflex and hurried down the road from Ludlow Castle to Kashmiri Gate, shuffling angles in my mind, greedy for the wrinkles and pouches of Dadi's oldness.

I didn't win a prize for my picture of her sitting behind the blurred wheel of a charkha, spinning, but my visits continued, once a month on an average till she died. In the beginning it was the house that drew me . . . its flaking whitewashed walls, the latticed shadows of its window-grilles, its mosaic floors erratically lit by sunlight sloping down from high ventilators. It wasn't a house – it was a box of pictures waiting to be taken.

I took them and the cumulative result – which I learnt to call a portfolio – gave me a start in life as a freelance photographer. But there was a price I paid for those pictures; an hour of every visit was spent listening patiently to Dadi's first-person account of the struggle for independence. In the early days it was an epic tale; she gave me a wide-angle picture of the Gandhian decades, but after the first few visits she zoomed in on the great Salt Satyagraha led by the Mahatma in 1930. There, in the high theatre of civil disobedience, Dadi replayed, with ever more detailed props, the single scene of which she was the heroine.

Actually, I knew that scene in outline well before Dadi relived it for me; it was part of family folklore. With my unweaned father at her breast, Dadi had answered Gandhi's call by picketing the liquor shop in the Kashmiri Gate arcade. She lay on its threshold daring customers to step over her. No one did but the police finally dragged the picketers away – so Dadi and my father spent six months in a colonial jail.

I knew the story in all its hundred versions by the time my black-and-white phase came to an end. The repetition didn't mean that she was senile or crazed with loneliness. Retelling that story was a strong woman's single self-indulgence. It was also her way of teaching me that I, like the rest of her grandchildren, was among the first citizens of free India – because she had paid my dues. In her mind there was an absolute distinction between the status of her descendants and those of women who had suffered nothing in the cause of freedom. The others were independent India's charity children, orphans sustained by the benevolence of the state,

2

whereas we, by birthright, were shareholders in the nation. Dadi was dedicated to balancing books and it gave her huge satisfaction that her family was solidly in the black.

It was a terrible irony, then, that this hard-won sense of self was destroyed when the Republic officially recognized her patriotic credentials. One Independence Day, the government decided to honour a lengthy roll of freedom fighters. This meant a copper citation and a pension of four hundred rupees a month. My father was proud of her and a little relieved: he thought it was appropriate and useful that his mother's sacrifices for freedom should underwrite her own independence in old age.

My visits had tapered off around that time because I had just switched to colour photography and moved away from Dadi and her Kashmiri Gate house to other subjects. Breaking into the colour supplements was hard work because the commissions went to elaborately equipped professionals and all I had was my father's Rolleiflex, state-of-the-art circa 1957. I needed money. My parents had none to give me because every rupee of their savings had gone into building a house before my father retired. So, nine months after my last visit, I returned to Kashmiri Gate, for reasons more material than inspiration in black-and-white.

Dadi was sitting at her charkha – but she wasn't spinning. She was staring at it as if she had never seen a spinning wheel before. Her hair, normally scraped back, had escaped its neat little knot, to straggle around her face in dirty white tendrils. She was looking ill and inches thinner. Why, I thought, taken aback, she's just an old woman now. Then she did something completely out of character.

I need your help, she said.

There was something seriously wrong if she could bring herself to ask, so I went and sat by her side.

Wait, she said, struggling to her feet, using my shoulder willingly to push herself up. She disappeared into her little store room and came out holding something that looked like a necklace box. I want you to find the office that sent me this and return it to the officer concerned. Painfully, she settled down behind the spinning wheel again. And tell him, she continued in the mechanical tone of a lawyer reading a will, to stop sending me money. She took a tired breath . . . Make sure he crosses my name off his ledger.

I opened the box and saw my face distorted in still-untarnished copper. It was Dadi's citation. It was this that she wanted to return; this and the pension that came with it.

I have the three thousand six hundred rupees they've sent me so far, she said. I haven't spent any of it. You must take it to the accountant in that office and give it back to him . . . don't forget to get a receipt for it.

But why was she doing this? It was a government honour, a government pension; there was no taint to either. She had fought for freedom, she had been jailed, she had risked the well-being of her family, she was entitled –

No I am not, she interrupted vehemently. Her rigid upright-ness sagged a little and she allowed herself to lean against the takht behind her. Then she explained her unworthiness . . .

She had been pleased when the official letter announcing the recognition first arrived. Pleased and only a little sad that her husband wasn't alive to share her joy as she had shared his when he was made a Companion of the Indian Empire in 1942. 1942. She hadn't thought of that date in forty years.

And yet, it had been a year to remember, a sacred year in the memory of the Nation, the year of the Quit India rebellion.

For two weeks that August, said Dadi, her eyes filling with long-ago pride, the Raj didn't exist in north India. There were republics inaugurated in Ballia and Azamgarh . . . they didn't last, of course, because the British had whole armies in India to fight the Japanese and they won in the end. But the Empire trembled. That's why the British left five years later, explained Dadi. They had been taught their lesson in 1942.

But Dadi hadn't been one of the teachers and that was the root of it all. When the rebellion began, twelve years had passed since the passion of the Salt Satyagraha, and Dadi's world had changed. She was older, her husband was a Judge now and her sons were at a new but promising boarding school in the hills. She had grown used to paying her tithe to the Nation in the coin of social work – so when the call came to man the barricades, she looked away.

4

I still didn't understand. Why this anguish now? After forty years?

She tried to explain. There had been guilt even then, but her family, her home for fallen women and her spinning had crowded it out. Then freedom came and it was easy to forget the past because there was a future to think about.

It wasn't until she reached Rashtrapati Bhavan, where she and a hundred others were to be given their citations in a public ceremony, that the guilt stirred again. Sitting in her red plush chair, waiting her turn, listening to the master of ceremonies call out their names and summarize their sacrifices, she realized that everyone there had been beaten, wounded or jailed in 1942. Every patriot of her generation seemed to have participated in both the Satyagraha of '30 and the rebellion of '42. Everyone except her. That was when the guilt returned.

Had I done what she asked of me that afternoon – returned the citation and the uncashed pension cheques – she might have made her peace with the past. But I didn't. I didn't because I needed her money to pay for a zoom lens that would bring me close to horizons otherwise unreachable. I played upon her love for me and took from her the three thousand six hundred rupees that she hadn't spent. That was the down payment. But the rest of the money had to be paid in instalments, so in the end, for my sake, Dadi kept her stipend on, always in the hope of eventually returning every paisa . . . when I paid her back as I swore I would but never did.

I thought she was being silly but the guilt consumed her. Every month I found her thinner and more obsessed than before. She agonized about the debit mounting against her name each time the pension cheque arrived. She wasn't a shareholder in the Republic any more, just a debtor, a drain on the Nation's resources, accepting money which she hadn't earned.

After the first eighteen months of the pension, she couldn't think on any other subject for more than ten minutes continuously. She got a reader's ticket to the public library and went there every day to look through their newspaper archives. She went through every paper of the time to catch up with those heroic days in August that she had missed out on. Then, when I visited her for the money, she would relate in awful detail some aspect of the insurrection she had just read up . . . to highlight the enormity of what she had not done. She never spoke of what she actually did in '42, of her children, her husband, their life together. The August rebellion became a black hole in her memory that sucked in everything that ever happened to her afterwards, that collapsed her entire life into a single non-event.

She didn't lose her mind, though. Till the end, with the help of Jumna, her maid, she coped with the present well enough to live on her own. It was her terror of becoming dependent on her sons that kept her this side of sanity; her legendary self-sufficiency was all she had left. She died as she would have wanted to, in her home in Kashmiri Gate, sitting by her old charkha, spinning.

She had told us all and written it in her will that we weren't to burn her in the ovens of the electric crematorium – she wanted to burn in the open air. So we took her to Nigambodh Ghat by the Jamuna, less than a mile away, where she burned briskly and well.

After I finished scrabbling through the ashes, what was left of her filled less than a third of the little clay urn I had been given. I covered the mouth of the urn with a cloth and carried it to the temple across the road. The brahmin there tied a sling around its neck and hung it on a branch of the huge peepul that grew in the temple's courtyard. It would hang there till I retrieved it the next evening, before setting off on a journey that would take me via Lucknow to Banaras, where on the steps of Dasashwamedh Ghat, I would tip her ashes into the Ganga.

It was nine hours to Lucknow by the overnight Mail and, having managed to avoid an aisle berth, I knew I would sleep well. The camera bag was my pillow because it was my first time out with the zoom and I was looking out for thieves. It was the kind of assignment I would never have got without the long lens. I had been commissioned by the *India Magazine* to illustrate an essay on 'The Use of Lime Plaster and Stucco in Nawabi Lucknow' and the author wanted blown-up details of moulding and ornament and glaze. And since these details lived on column capitals or unclimbable domes, the only way of getting close enough was a zoom. I owned every inch of its potent length – Dadi's last pension cheque had closed that chapter neatly.

Her ashes were travelling in a thermos flask which (on my mother's advice) I wore strapped across my body, even in sleep. She had transferred the ashes from the urn because she was afraid it would break during the two train journeys. I was taking the ashes to Banaras because Dadi had written it in her will that she wanted them tipped into the Ganga at Kashi. Everyone in the family thought they understood why but they didn't. Dadi's wish had nothing to do with the holiness of Banaras; it was her salaam-in-death to the martyrs of 1942, many of whom had come from Banaras and its neighbourhood, her last attempt to be part of the Quit India rebellion. She died at a convenient time because I was already headed east for the Lucknow commission. I volunteered to take the ashes – I owed her a debt and this was a good way of squaring the books.

The night went well. For once the purple nightlight didn't stir up ugly dreams and the tea-boy's chai-chai rasp at echoing midnight halts didn't wake me up. I woke to the rhythms of summer's loveliest sound – rain, drumming on the roof of my carriage as the train chugged through the uneventful flatness of the Ganga's plain. My watch showed five; there was still an hour for Lucknow. I reached for the camera bag and felt about . . . the lens was there, reassuring in its solid length. On the other side of me was the flask. I touched them both again and stretched contentedly. Between the exciting nearness of magnified horizons and the tidy prospect of sinking Dadi's leftovers, I was happy.

It seemed wrong to taste this happiness through unbrushed teeth, so I climbed down from my bunk and made my way to the washbasin at the end of the aisle. It was awkward standing there, waiting my turn, with the others looking curiously at the camera bag and flask, but I couldn't risk being separated from them. Embarrassment was a small price to pay for secure possession. In the lavatory, afterwards, I bent my rule and hung the flask on the door peg before squatting.

7

The aisle seats by the window were unoccupied when I returned to the compartment and I settled down on one of them to watch the rain outside without the distraction of company. I lifted the glass shutter without getting soaked because the rain was slanting away from the window in a crosswise gale. After fifteen minutes of breathing in the damp freshness, fifteen minutes of the breeze glancing off my face, I was within a heartbeat of bliss. And then, as if to flag off my just-brushed teeth, a sketchily uniformed attendant appeared, selling tea. I let it cool in the saucer and wondered if someone was fine-tuning the world to my frequency. I should have touched wood.

The train halted at the last station before Lucknow. The card-players threw in their hands and rushed out on to the platform to buy things to eat. I kept to my seat and day-dreamed about the magical properties of my new lens. I hadn't taken a single picture with it yet – it would be blooded on this trip. The power of it . . . The world close-up from an invulnerable distance! the grimace of a straining rick-shaw-wallah, the graffiti on a peeling dome – it was mine in all the detail I wanted, mine without the risks of proximity.

A whistle blew and the train started to move. The platform slid away and wet greenness filled my window again. On impulse I unzipped the camera bag and took out the lens. Ignoring the interested stares of the card-players, who had stopped playing on this last lap to Lucknow, I fitted its length to the camera body. Then, remembering the rain and what it might do to the surface of the virgin lens, I capped it and sat back, and tried to be inconspicuous. The others in the compartment probably thought that I'd been showing off and who could blame them. Fiddling with the camera case, I looked determinedly out of the window, sick of rain and vegetation now, longing for the journey to end.

But half an hour short of Lucknow, as we were going over a bridge, the train slowed and stopped. Immediately the compartment began rustling with restlessness as everyone went to the doors and peered out. Then, down the long, running aisle that linked the carriages crept the explanatory rumour – line not clear – and people settled down again.

The train had stopped on the bridge, just short of land. Through the girders of the bridge I could see the sluggish green surface of the river and the brown of its gently sloping bank on which tiny figures were moving metronomically. When I looked at them through my magic eye, they became dhobis, slapping clothes on washing stones.

Dhobis? What were they doing in the rain? I looked through the lens again and saw it wasn't in fact raining on the riverbank – there were sharply cast shadows miming the movements of the washermen. Looking up at the sky, I saw a great fault in the massed cloud above us through which watery sunlight was shining down on the river. I stuck my head out of the window and surveyed the bank we had left behind. That was sunlit too, though beyond it the landscape was still curtained off by rain. Just the river, its banks, the bridge and the train stuck on it were being shone upon.

It was slanted, enigmatic light, the kind that limns photographers' frames with easy mystery. I took aim through the window again but from inside the train there was no clean angle on the dhobis: the girders kept getting in the way.

There was a look-out point, though, in line with my window, where the straight lines of the bridge were broken by an observation platform which jutted further out over the river. It was less than six feet from my compartment; already a nonchalant passenger had crossed the single girder joining the observation platform to the track and smoked a cigarette there. Then, as casually, he strolled over it again and resumed his place in the revived card game. It made me dizzy to watch him – there was nothing for his hands to hold on to; just emptiness on either side, all the way down to the river.

I wouldn't have dared if it hadn't been for the rainbow. Suddenly it was there, spanning cloudbank and riverbank in a great gaudy arc. The card-players peered through the windows again and smiled – for them it was only a spectacle; for me, with Kodachrome in my camera and a lens to blood, it was a sign.

The train hadn't whistled yet, so I had time. Taking a deep breath, I walked down the aisle to the door and strode over the girder without once looking down or exhaling. My heart thudded with daring and excitement, as I leaned on the platform's railing to steady the lens. But in the five minutes I was there, I took no photographs because there wasn't after all a great picture to be taken. I managed to section the dhobis off into several worthy frames but turbaned heads and saris spread to dry on sand had been done to death: for the inaugural use of this hard-won lens I needed an exceptional subject. I straightened up reluctantly and nerved myself to return to the train – the girder had to be risked again. I steadied myself; first by pushing the flask, which I still had slung round me, till it rested against my buttocks and then by wedging the camera under one arm so that it didn't dangle and tip me off balance. Approaching that narrow walkway, cross-eyed with the effort of concentrating on its eighteen-inch breadth, I was distracted by a figure in my peripheral vision.

It, or rather he, was standing where the bridge's last column sank into the riverbank, knee deep in water . . . looking up. I stepped back from the girder and tried to train the camera on him, but he had now disappeared from view, cut off by the platform's edge. So, crouching, I inched up to the girder till he came into frame again. I pushed the lens out and zoomed in on him. I would have laughed out loud if my perch had been more secure, because a man in a white kurta much like mine was looking up at the train through a little telescope. Man-with-a-lens – here was the picture I had been looking for. I broadened the frame to take in his rolled-up pajamas and the water but just then he moved two steps to his left and spoilt it all. Made brave by the lens (which exorcised vertigo by eliminating distance), I moved up a foot and braced my left leg on the girder. For a few seconds as I focused and set aperture, we stared at each other through layers of ground glass and I felt a quick affection for this unidentical twin. If nothing else, he would make a good, eccentric study.

And then . . . well, it wasn't any one thing. It was the whistle going as I made to click; that clap of thunder in the distance, the flask rolling round my behind – it was all of these. But most of all it was the weight of the lens. I had braced myself and allowed for its weight, but as I tensed to shoot, it suddenly became twice as heavy and in the nanosecond that it

10

took to squeeze the shutter button, ten times its normal weight and more, as it dragged me downwards. Then I was falling, hurtling towards the green river, the downswinging dhobis, the man with the telescope – and just before I knew nothing I saw my free-falling ten-ton lens beat me to the water. It made a big splash.

I woke to the sound of someone choking. It was me. Breathing wasn't automatic any more; I had to be awake to think it through. After a minute of frightening vacuum sounds, the rhythm returned and I fell back on the couch to weep gratefully. It took me a minute to recover enough to smell the frying liver and see the grimy chandelier hanging over me. There was a large bolster-like thing under my head. I was lying under a white sheet. Nothing felt wet.

But my chest felt raw and my forehead was pulsing like a skinned sinus. My hand obeyed when I made it wipe my eyes though it worked in slow motion. Then I heard a door open, the smell of liver grew stronger and assorted footsteps approached me. Two women appeared at the foot of the couch, two men by its side.

I asked after my camera but what came out was a strangled rattle. The older woman shook her head and put a finger to her lips. The younger man and the girl were clearly related: they were both good-looking in a light-skinned, sharp-featured way. The fat woman trying to keep me quiet was their mother, I decided, because even with dark glasses on, she looked like the boy. The odd one out was the sallow man with bristling moustaches, who propped me up with cushions and gave me a cup of tea. He was the one who explained.

I had been saved from the river by Masroor. The fine-looking son smiled reassuringly and I knew him at once – he was the man with the telescope. I had fallen close to the bank and he had pulled me out quickly. But the shock and the sucked-in water had kept me unconscious right through the resuscitation on the riverbank and the rickshaw-ride. You're in a state of shock, said Moustaches severely. He obviously thought that I was suicidal. Rest, he commanded, then they backed off and left me alone again, without a word to explain why Masroor had been peering up at a train through a telescope.

But the advice was good. I needed sleep. Only I still wasn't sure about the breathing, so I rubbed my eyes and stayed propped up on the cushions. It was an old house. The room I was in looked into a courtyard through three green-painted metal arches fitted with doors – these had been left open to let in the air. Though the chandelier needed cleaning, the furniture and fittings were nicely period and the whole interior was of a piece with the age of the house: nothing plastic – every object was wood metal glass leather wool. The rugs seemed worn enough to be ancestral and the doors had panes of orange and green glass of a kind not used any more. The mantel clock on a side table was an unnecessary touch, but the other pieces in the living room seemed to belong there, better than the junk that had cluttered Dadi's house.

Dadi. My heart stopped and my breathing broke down again. I coughed great tearing coughs till strings of mucus dribbled from my mouth on to the sheet. I wiped my face and looked about wildly – then cried real tears when I saw the flask on a little table by the head of the couch. Fumbling, I unscrewed the cap and looked inside; the ashes were there, dry as the day she was burnt. I stood the flask on the floor this time, within arm's reach. Then I lay back on the cushions and concentrated on the problem of unselfconscious breathing.

Thinking of other things was useless because tiredness wouldn't let me think. So I tried reading: if what I read was dull enough there was a chance that I'd fall asleep without my lungs noticing. They had left newspapers on the couchside table. The Urdu ones were no good for me but under them was one called the *Pioneer*. I could tell that it was a provincial paper from its masthead; no metropolitan broadsheet had used a Gothic face in years. Even the layout was primitive, with headlines compressed into two columns. Soviets Bomb Nazi Shipping on the Volga: they had used three lines to cram it in. And the Million Men Mobilized in Manchukuo had been stuffed into a single column. Manchukuo? Sleep vanished; my eyes focused on the date under the masthead. It matched . . . It matched the Gothic masthead and the headlines and the period furniture. 4 August 1942.

For the second time that morning I saw the end of the world and then knew nothing.

Inside

I DIDN'T ASK after the camera again. Or about Masroor's telescope, though I worked that out for myself, later, without being told. Amnesia had its rules and I kept to them. Once 1942 became undeniable, I chose to lose my memory. I didn't have a choice; any other course would have meant impossible explanations. So I didn't stint – I even lost my name.

Masroor's sister, Asharfi, found me another but that was later. It was strange managing without a name. Masroor cleared his throat at me; Asharfi called me bhaisahib; Ammi, their mother, just shouted 'arrey' when she wanted my attention and the whiskered man, whose name was Haasan, called me Chinna. He took my amnesia hardest. Till you remember your family, he said worriedly, I am your uncle.

I met no one else for the first five days so namelessness wasn't a real embarrassment. It may even have helped; it turned me from a grown man into a homeless waif. This was probably one reason for Ammi's unwary hospitality. There were others: Masroor felt proprietorial about me in the absence of other claimants – he had, after all, breathed new life into me. Later, when Asharfi renamed me, I became her handiwork as well.

But for that first week I didn't care why they kept me, so long as they left me alone. Ammi had put me in a room on the upper floor. It was a large house built before the 1857 Mutiny, stuccoed and plastered to no purpose in the absence of my camera. I spent my mornings sitting in the verandah that overlooked the courtyard, drinking tea and not reading the newspaper. The courtyard was roofed over by a grid of thin metal rods, strong enough to be walked upon but fine enough to let the sunlight through. I spent whole days looking through this metal grille at the bustle in the courtyard below. On the days that it was impossible to accept that this was 1942, I felt I was watching a command performance of some endless period play.

When it wasn't raining, unfurled black umbrellas lolled by the entrance to the hall, drying. Mother and daughter didn't go out much; the umbrellas belonged to Masroor or his friends. He lived in a room across the courtyard on the ground floor, from which he emerged every morning at six, passed under the grille and went through the door into Massaldan Lane. I knew it was called that because Asharfi once tried to explain the location of the house in case I ever got lost. Since I didn't intend stepping out of the house till the morning of the ninth (and then never to return), her directions were wasted on me. I tried not to listen; my fate hinged on perfect insulation from everything around me – even to learn directions was to let this world leak in.

But Massaldan Lane stuck in my mind as did other bits of dangerous information because Asharfi was both too kind and too beautiful to be easily ignored. Masroor visited me too – after lunch sometimes, or in between the long huddled conversations he had with his friends, all of them sitting in the courtyard if the weather was fine, in the hall if it was raining. He didn't say much to me; he just asked after my health or my memory and occasionally he would offer to buy me anything I needed from the shops outside. And when I refused (always more vehemently than I meant to) he would nod and smile and return to whispered conversations with his indefinably covert friends.

I wasn't curious. He was none of my business. Nothing in this world was. There was a desolate sort of comfort in that certainty. Six days from the day I had fallen into the river, the Mail would run again and take me home. I planned to board it at Charbagh station so that when it passed through that time warp on the bridge, I'd find my time again. Once again there would be sun on the river and gloom on land, men playing cards and dhobis on the banks. And me . . . without a haunted camera lens to tip me over. This time, when the train drew into Delhi station, I would step out into the real world of colour television and people I knew.

If I stayed indoors as quietly and deafly and indifferently as possible, I would return to a present unchanged by its past. In the gigantic surge of history, the tiny splash I had made would pass unnoticed. Not everything that happened in the past was history and when the facts of this rewound time were sifted by historians, I wanted to be sifted out. So I had decided to be more rigorously detached from August 1942 than even poor Dadi had been.

Indifference was easiest between eight and lunch when Asharfi was away at college and Masroor pedalled off to La Martinière where he taught history. Every day after they left, I climbed down the stairs and crept into one of the huge armchairs in the hall. The room doubled as a library, so there was plenty to read. Most mornings I had Ammi for company but she was so busy that it was safe being with her.

Once she had supervised the cleaning of the house and told Moonis the lunch menu, the mornings belonged to the magazine which she edited and published each quarter, *Khatoon*. *Khatoon* was ten years old, it had two hundred and eleven subscribers and nothing in common with other women's journals like *Tahzib-un-Niswan* or *Ismat*, which relentlessly strove to rescue Muslim women from ignorance through home hints and homilies. We have no interest in these matters, she was fond of saying grandly. What can I tell a woman about babies and recipes that she won't discover for herself? My khatoons, she would say, need to live, not learn. It was living that they couldn't do in their homes, tied down as they were by the domestic round . . . so four times a year, she mailed them other lives.

She wrote the entire magazine – every article, sometimes even the letters to the editor when her readers failed her. In fact the first time she mentioned *Khatoon* to me was because she wanted me to read the July issue and to write her a letter. She wanted it to be three hundred words long and signed by Waheed Jahan, who was one of her regular proxies, but she didn't have time for her in this issue. I was so obliged to Ammi for refuge that I agreed. But when she gave the relevant issue of *Khatoon* to me it was in Urdu, written in the Persian script, as barred to me as a Martian cipher. After this, she used me for the heavy work; I carried great stacks of newsprint to the old zenana. The zenana was connected to the hall by a steep spiral stairway and the first time I went there I discovered that its rooms looked into the hall, through screened windows. From where secluded women had once peeped at male festivity, I had a top view of Ammi writing a brisk account of the Haj. As soon as it was finished it would be rushed to the press, which lived in the zenana and was worked by Masroor.

Ammi tried out bits of the Haj piece on me by reading them out. It was in the first person. All the articles in *Khatoon* were in the first person; it was one of Ammi's rules. There was nothing like the first person to help readers live other lives. She had stopped accepting articles from outsiders because they tended to peddle information in the third person. Now she wrote whole issues under half-a-dozen pen-names, so that the readers got exactly what she wanted.

The current issue, which was running behind schedule, featured a walking tour of Moorish Granada (including a description in cinematic detail of the Alhambra and its unparalleled stucco and plaster ornamentation), a memoir of the great and bloody Moplah rebellion of 1921 in Kerala by a Gentlewoman of Calicut, a letter about a rail journey from Istanbul to Paris by an emancipated Turkish lady and, of course, the Haj pilgrimage to Mecca by the widowed Shakila Rahman of Mymensingh, who, Ammi declared in her editorial introduction, was an inspiration to us all.

Great chunks of each of these were read out to me and I was happy to listen because all the accounts were made up by Ammi; the I in each case was pseudonymous, the narratives were imaginary, the geography impressionistic (the gentle-woman from Calicut remembered a Malabar lapped by the Bay of Bengal) and such facts as she worked in were randomly cribbed from books and newspapers. The articles were so removed from the reality of 1942 that there was no risk of them infecting me with the present.

Ammi didn't mind admitting that nothing in *Khatoon* grew out of real-life experience. The Haj story, for example; Lucknow was the furthest west she had been. But the absence of first-hand knowledge didn't worry her. If I start waiting on experience, she said to me once, I'll have to fill *Khatoon* with recipes. She was sceptical about the relevance of real life: till women re-invent the world, she said to me, who will let them live in it? This suited me; until the tenth when the Mail came round to take me back to my own time, I wanted no dealings with reality.

Detachment got harder at lunchtime because Masroor came home to eat and he seemed to bring the world in with him. He was often accompanied by unannounced friends, but even when he came by himself the cushioned peace of the house was given restless edges. After three days of sharing lunch with him, I knew that he was worried about something. Fortunately his preferred mealtime manner was troubled taciturnity and for this I was grateful. Ignorance is best cultivated in silence. Through the fourth, fifth and sixth of August, then, I managed to ignore his boding quiet, Ammi's mute concern for her edgy son and Masroor's savagely bitten fingernails. I would eat as quickly as decency permitted and retire on grounds of weakness to my room. Here, like a wintering bear, I built myself a den of sleep.

But on the seventh I was denied both sleep and innocence. The morning had passed restfully and at two, Ammi, Asharfi and I had sat down to lunch after waiting half an hour for Masroor. It had been raining hard in the courtyard, so Ammi finally decided that he was waiting it out and instructed Moonis to serve the meal. But barely had we begun than the courtyard door was flung open and Masroor, with Haasan close behind him, rushed in. They dropped their umbrellas in the courtyard when they made the shelter of the hall's arches and remembered to slip their shoes off before walking into the eating area. They joined us at the table in less time than it took to swallow a mouthful, so though I sensed there was trouble brewing, I was trapped in the procedures of lunch.

The days-old dam of pent-up feeling burst immediately.

You wouldn't believe me, Masroor accused his mother. Just a rumour, you said, when I told you about the match. Well it isn't a rumour. I know for certain now because they're playing the match on our school's cricket field. The head-master's agreed – he wants to be knighted.

Ammi looked worriedly at Haasan, who nodded and confirmed the story. Aligarh Muslim University was playing Banaras Hindu University at cricket over three days, starting on the eleventh. It was the U.P. Governor's scheme for raising money for the War Fund. Tickets were eight annas and one rupee.

Having recited the salient facts, Haasan stopped, without explaining why a cricket match had so upset Masroor.

They're putting up stands, said Haasan angrily. The Governor wants four thousand spectators on the school ground on the eleventh, watching eleven Hindus play eleven Muslims.

He did a quick circuit of the room, biting his lips in fury.

What a splendid idea, he said throatily. Cricket, healthy competition and a collection for our lovely war. Lovely, lovely . . . marquees, sunshine, lemonade, whites on the field and rupees in the war chest. Masroor stopped pacing. Hallett's gone mad; one bad decision and we'll have short legs and long legs lying lopped off in the stands.

Rubbish, protested Haasan. There's never been a Hindu-Muslim riot in Lucknow.

That's what they said in Allahabad till 1938, snapped Masroor sarcastically. And in Banaras till 1939 – but the riots happened anyway. There's always a first time.

Haasan shook his head. Nothing will happen, he said. There have been crowds in Lucknow before. I've been here twenty years and lived through dozens of huge, mixed gatherings.

Masroor took a deep breath.

That was then. It's different now. In the United Provinces of 1942, he said with savage deliberation, there are still occasions when large numbers of Hindus and Muslims gather in public, and mix uninhibitedly, without restraint or any thought for normal social distance . . . we call them riots.

That's ridiculous, said Haasan, unamused. I tell you nothing will happen.

And when it does, you'll spend hours in your coffee house, discussing whether it was inevitable or just an accident, said Masroor cuttingly. Well, there's been enough killing in the last five years for a riot on the eleventh to be a real possibility. I'm going to make sure that the possibility doesn't arise.

He strode out of the house as impetuously as he had entered it. Ammi called after him but he had gone. She looked imploringly at Haasan who sighed and, more slowly than Masroor had done, followed him out of the courtyard. Asharfi shut the door after him and now it was Ammi's turn to sigh. I bent over my plate and began eating at a tremendous rate. I wanted neither explanations nor confidences. No doubt Masroor had his reasons, but these, like everything else in this world, had no claim on me.

Do you know what your brother plans to do? she asked her daughter. Asharfi shook her head. There was silence for a while as Ammi stared across the courtyard at the bolted door.

I wish he could talk to Intezar, she whispered to no one in particular. There was such sadness in those words that I looked up from my plate. Tears were running unwiped down her round face; even in my willed ignorance I could tell that she wasn't weeping for Masroor. Asharfi walked round the table and cradled her mother's head; I bolted my meal and fled upstairs.

That evening, after my nap, I was sitting in bed, wondering if it was wise to risk new names and fresh disclosures by going down for tea, when Haasan, who generally came round after finishing work at the coffee house, walked into my room. He was carrying a tray of tea things. Even as he poured, I had the uneasy feeling that in his role as uncle he was going to give me the context of this household's afternoon crisis.

From the day I had made it clear that I was amnesiac, Haasan had taken upon himself the job of refurnishing my emptied mind. Until now his strategy had been to lure me outside the house so that I could accumulate new memories at first hand. Every day, he invited me to lunch with him at the coffee house near Hazrat Ganj where he was the manager, and every day I refused. But today was different. He handed me a cup of tea and started talking. Having failed to draw me out, he had decided, instead, to fill me in.

Intezar, he explained, was one of the names of Ammi's lost husband. The other one, the one he had answered to for the

20

first twenty-four years of his life, was Charandass, Charandass Ganjoo. Charandass into Intezar: the story of this mutation was the key to Ammi's tears and Masroor's crusading rage.

Masroor's father was born to Kalidass Ganjoo, a brahmin of Kashmiri descent domiciled in Lucknow. Kalidass' grandfather, Makhandass (just Makhandass, surnames were optional in 1825), the founder of the Lucknow line, had migrated from Srinagar to find employment in the court of the Nawab of Awadh. Makhandass, and later his son Purshottamdass, rose modestly to become serishtadars in the Nawab's service.

Vital to the continued prosperity of their line was their ability to read the direction of the prevailing wind. In the confusion of 1857, they fled mutinous Lucknow and headed unerringly for the British encampment in Meerut. They returned with the redcoat army and played a crucial supporting role by (here Haasan pulled out a battered leather-bound book and read from it) 'procuring towards the close of the siege, tolerable, constant and trustworthy information from their contacts in the city'.

Upon this weathercock agility, unreasonably called traitorous (for where was the Nation then) were the family fortunes founded. Haasan riffled through the pages of the book, which was titled *The History and Destiny of the Ganjoos*, and read out the text of the grant that Makhandass had received as his reward:

> The Right Hon. the Governor-General of India on the 25th October 1858, in consideration of such loyal conduct was pleased to confer on Makhandass and the lineal heirs lawfully begotten of his body, a plot of land 125 Acres, 2 Roods and 25 Poles in area, situated in Malihabad near Lucknow, being the confiscated property of the rebel Syed Hussain, as also the aforementioned rebel's haveli or town house in the locality of Lal Baugh in Lucknow, rent free in perpetuity during the pleasure of the British Government.

Apart from the dead rebel's lands, all his dependants,

including the women in his zenana, fell to the share of Makhandass and those lawfully sprung from his loins. Hussain's women didn't protest overmuch: being kept by a comfortable kafir in those troubled times was better than making ends meet on the street. So Purshottamdass' new, expanded household (Makhandass was taken by the 'flu the same year that the grant was made) functioned smoothly . . . so smoothly that when a boy was born to his long-barren wife, the city's gossips credited the child to Ummehani Begum, the youngest and most exquisite relict of the expended Hussain. But the begum lived out her span in the seclusion of the zenana, now home to the *Khatoon*'s press, and the rumour died unconfirmed. The boy grew to manhood and assumed his inheritance as the rightful heir.

As soon as he inherited the family's estate, Kalidass helped tradition along by taking on and maintaining at great expense two Muslim mistresses. One of them, in fact, died in unexplained circumstances soon after Intezar was born; there might have been a scandal if Kalidass hadn't become so impregnably successful.

The secret of his success lay in his pushfulness. When he left St Stephen's College after finishing his B.A. in 1897, the year of his father's death, he made sure he left with recommendations from the Principal, S.S. Allnutt, who was white, and A.C. Maitland, M.A., the Professor of English Literature, who was white as well. He had copies made of these and of every other testimonial his family had collected since turning its coat in '57 and enclosed them in his applications to every civil servant of the rank of Commissioner and above, petitioning for a sinecure. Sometimes in addition to the commendations of his teachers and the certificates of unrelenting loyalty, he would enclose rhymed eulogies to the officer concerned, and, occasionally, a Bokhara rug.

After appearing twice for tehsildari examinations and failing both times, he took to enclosing evidence of his failure. He respectfully argued that since the avenue of merit had been exhausted, it was the more needful that he be nominated to a job. Not just any job, but one commensurate with the social standing of his family, its pioneering role in female education

22

(he had endowed a small primary school for girls) and, since with Kalidass nothing went without saying, its loyalty to the Raj.

It worked. Pandit Kalidass Ganjoo was made not a mere tehsildar – which was what his father had managed with similar importuning – but an E.A.C., the highest rank to which a native Indian could aspire. Or, as Appendix XIV of the family history compiled by the great man himself put it:

(Revenue Secretary to Senior Secretary Finance Commission, Letter No. 229, 14 August 1897) . . . I am directed to say that the Lt. Governor is pleased to accept Pandit Kalidass Ganjoo s/o Pandit Purshottamdass Ganjoo as a candidate for the post of Extra Assistant Commissioner under Rule 160 of the rules under the Land Revenue Act 1887. The original enclosures of your letter are returned.

Well, not all the enclosures – at least no one returned the Bokhara rug – but Kalidass was pleased to get his certificates back which he inserted as appendices into his history of the clan Ganjoo. The last chapter of the first volume of this work (the second was about the family's destiny) was Kalidass' account of the naming of his son.

According to Kalidass, when the bustle and whispering in the zenana were drowned by the shrieks of his crumpled son, he turned to the picture of Victoria enthroned, hung prominently in the hall, kissed the gathered hem roughly where her feet might have been, and resolved to call his new-born Charandass. Never one to waste a good story, he had the chronicle printed and bound – with a footnote explaining that Charandass meant 'slave at the feet of' – and sent it with his Christmas greetings to his English superiors – a humble saga of unstinting service to Mallika Victoria.

Blessed like all the Ganjoos with a keen nose for the coming thing, Kalidass had planned for his son a career in the law. He had decided that at age fifteen, Charandass would take the P&O steamer to Dover. Once in England, he would acquire some public school starch, go up to Oxford and then eat his way through the Inns of Court. Money was no consideration: the orchards at Malihabad were yielding well and their revenues, when added to his salary and topped off by honest graft, made him a wealthy man. But for reasons beyond his control, none of this came to be; on Charandass' fifteenth birthday came the Great War.

But not everything was lost. Kalidass put his son through worthy Indian substitutes: La Martinière (white founder); St Stephen's College (fledgling child of the Cambridge Mission); the University of Allahabad (cradle of lawyers, Oxford of the East); and Charandass set up practice in Lucknow, as English as India could make him.

I didn't know him then, said Haasan. The first time we met was in 1924. In 1921 I had troubles of my own in Malabar. But others who knew him around that time always said that he was remarkably pukka for someone who wasn't really foreign returned. But under that shell of starch, something had changed, and his father sensed this. It wasn't politics, though Kalidass knew that his son was a closet Congressman. He didn't mind: long-sighted as ever, he was impressed by the force of Gandhi's non-cooperation movement, raging around him at that time, and he recognized it as the coming thing. A patriot in the family was useful insurance; so he indulged Charandass when he obeyed Gandhi's call to boycott the law courts when he should have been building his practice.

But it wasn't nationalism that was churning Charandass' insides; it was a more dangerous obsession: the deadly worm of Urdu verse was nibbling at his soul. It had been feeding some years, ever since the first mushaira he had attended while still at college in Delhi. The first inkling Kalidass had of his son's secret passion was when Charandass organized a reading of militantly anti-British verse at the Lalbagh house.

Kalidass raised no objection. Himself schooled in Urdu and Persian, he could, like any educated man, turn a rhyme or quote the telling couplet. So when the mushaira began, he good-naturedly took his place in the audience. It was a good time for political verse in Urdu and Kalidass enjoyed it all in a remote sort of way, at a great ideological distance. Then, at the end, everyone insisted that Charandass read something of his own to round the mushaira off – that's when unease first stirred.

Charandass got to his feet reluctantly, blushing with embarrassment, and took his place at the centre of the ragged semi-circle of listeners. He had nothing of his own to offer, he said nervously, so he would recite some passages from a poem by Hali that was close to his heart. Then he began.

Kalidass knew it at once, as who would not – it was Hali's *Musaddas*, his legendary lament on the decline of Islam. At a time when politically minded Indians were agitating against the move by the victorious Allies to abolish Islam's last caliphate, it was a good poem with which to complete an evening of rousing declamation.

So it wasn't the poem but the manner of its recitation that worried Kalidass. Less than half a minute after he had begun, tears stood large and bright in Charandass' eyes, and then, as his father watched in horror, rolled down his face. And it went on like that. Though he knew the passages by heart, Charandass never managed to say ten lines continuously, because his voice would quiver, or he would stop to wipe his eyes. For ten minutes, undeterred by emotion, he soldiered on while his father cringed in embarrassment and alarm. When he finished, the gathering was profoundly silent . . . whether out of shock, grief or good manners, it was impossible to say.

Afterwards, when the guests had left, Kalidass gingerly questioned his son about his performance.

What happened to you? he asked. Was it something in the poem?

No, answered Charandass, and his father breathed again – it wasn't some eccentric nostalgia for the glories of Islam.

According to Charandass his tears had nothing to do with what *Musaddas* said. No, it was just the words of it, those rustling, throaty, half-learnt words that raised a lump of unrefined emotion and made him choke. It happened to him a lot – and not only with *Musaddas*. The tears had first come in middle school while reading a poem in English class: 'When they shot him down on the highway,/Down like a dog on the highway,/And he lay in his blood on the highway,/With a bunch of lace at his throat.' He had forgotten everything about

25

the poem except this verse because when his turn to read had come, his lips trembled and his voice tripped over every second syllable. It wasn't so much what the poem said as the sound of it, he told his father, the heart-squeezing beat of those lines.

With that Kalidass had to be content because it was the only explanation Charandass gave. He was even a little relieved – at least his son wasn't infatuated with Islam, even if he seemed a little touched in respect to other things. But no premonition, no second sight warned him where Charandass' aural passion was going to lead him. Yet, when it happened, it seemed predictable: in the course of rushing from one mushaira to another, Charandass met Kamran Gulmargi, a poet as old as his father – with a daughter as young as him. Kulsum.

Kulsum? I wondered aloud.

Yes, Kulsum, said Haasan irritably, peeved at being interrupted in full flow. Ammi has a name, you know.

They got married, Kulsum and Charandass. She was a Muslim, of course, but that wasn't why he married her. He wasn't suddenly consumed by some apostate passion for Islam. He married her for a perfectly secular reason: love.

You didn't need a reason for falling in love with Kulsum, said Haasan, shaking his head in remembered wonder. She was prettier than Ruby Myers.

He married her after the necessary preliminary of becoming a Muslim and here, certainly, *Musaddas* and the magic of Urdu helped in making Islam a painless prospect. Painless for Charandass, that is, not for his father – who in one fell evening heard that besides marrying the ultimate non-Hindu, his son had turned Muslim and changed his name.

He didn't really change his name. Charandass had invented the mushaira persona of Intezar long before he ever met Kulsum. Intezar was his nom de plume, his takhallus. He had chosen it because it staked his claim to poethood and simultaneously accounted for the absence of poems. Intezar. Waiting. Stern, silent poet waiting for the Muse. So after marriage he didn't take on a second name – he simply discarded the first one.

But his father was too devastated to worry about such nice

distinctions. For him it was the end of the world, or, at the very least, of history. He, Kalidass, whose ancestors had moved to Kashmir from the clean Aryan climes of Jalalabad in the third century before Christ, whose ancestor Kalhana was the first to write India into history, whose forebears had, for a thousand years, affirmed old Aryan gods even as lesser tribes all round them embraced Islam, he, of all men, had in the wink of an eye acquired a Semite son who knelt to the west, never bathed and washed his bum with a beak-spout kettle.

It meant that the *Destiny of the Ganjoos* would never be completed. His son, a Muslim! Anything else he could have reconciled with his vision of the family's future. He had accommodated divergences with reality before. After all, in the *Destiny of the Ganjoos*, he had predicted an English education for his son. When that didn't come to pass he had extemporized a good Indian approximation, without altering the original chapter because he believed that destinies were vindicated by the unfolding truth of their essence, not by trifling matters of detail. But this marriage . . . this marriage wasn't a hiccup in the life of the Ganjoos – it was a heart attack. No son called Intezar could be grafted on to the family tree. In fact now there wasn't a family left . . . just a severed lineage dangling in time. Intezar was his only son.

Face to face with oblivion, Kalidass sent the servants away, locked the doors and shut out the meaningless world. A week later when they battered down the courtyard door and rushed into the soundless house, he was slumped over his desk with a pen in his hand and his face in a pool of blue ink.

He had been trying to write his way out of his destiny's dead end. The table was piled high with scored-out sheets, the waste-basket crammed with crumpled desperation. Some of them were half-hearted schemes to prolong just anyhow the future of his family so that his blighted opus, the *Destiny of the Ganjoos*, could come to a dignified end. One of the twists of paper in the basket revealed that he had considered adoption then rejected it on the principled view that the future of any family worth its salt unfolded on its own without gerrymandering. Remarriage and a natural heir had held him longer: the pros and cons spilled over many sheets. Eligible widower, just turned fifty, wealthy, fair-complexioned, sound of mind – he wouldn't lack offers. But in the end this route was pot-holed by too many ifs: a fecund woman; a male child who would live to manhood, immune to epidemics and disease; who would be a filial son and steer the charted course, deaf to the siren sounds of love and poetry. The things he might have taken for granted as a young man were Chinese walls in late middle-age. So he scored it out – remarriage was an act of faith he couldn't sustain. The armour of hope was made for younger men.

There were other plans, few of which went past the second sentence, and those that did tailed off a little later. By the time he died, he had forsaken the future; he was merely trying to write himself an end. The last few sheets, the papers that he lay slumped on, were full of closely written penance. He saw that he had been punished for hubris, for his presumption in trying to prescribe his family's destiny, and with proper contrition he submitted himself to fate. He remembered an older prescription that bade the householder with adult children to forsake his family and eke out his remaining years in mendicant wandering. A saffron dhoti, beads, a begging bowl, some ash . . . he would get Kashinath to take the old Stonely out and drive him down to Banaras, which, he knew, was the best place for renouncers to be. And then . . . and then he died; not quite having writ, moved on – with his nose in royal blue ink.

Fortunately for Intezar and Kulsum, in all those heaps of scribbled paper, there was no will. This meant that the erstwhile Charandass came into the house and everything else besides in the normal way, without litigation or other trouble. One of the more problematic articles that he inherited was Kalidass' corpse. It wasn't smelling or anything like that – in fact for a body some days dead, it was remarkably preserved, almost as if time had stopped in the house through the days of the dead man's brooding. But it had to be cremated and Intezar after his conversion couldn't do it and there was no one else. Eventually it was Kashinath, the driver, who offered to light his master's pyre. Afterwards, he drove his ashes down to Kashi in the old Stonely, so Kalidass had his last wish fulfilled, though only after a fashion. Then he returned the car

28

and gave in his notice. Having seen off the old master, he abandoned the new one – like Kalidass he had strong views on apostasy.

By the time Intezar and Kulsum moved into the house, the Khilafat movement was ebbing and when Kemal Pasha abolished the caliphate in Turkey, it whimpered out. It was time to think about work again, so Intezar lined the hall with law reports and began a desultory practice. But he didn't really need to earn a living, so most of his time was spent being instructed in the Koran. He was a conscientious convert; if he never achieved the pinnacle of belief, he managed the foothills of literal understanding.

His main interest in the Koran, however, was other than theological; it was, in effect, an extension of his passion for Urdu verse. He had often wondered why poetry in Urdu, wonderful and stirring as it was, sounded so banal in translation. Where did its magic lie? Not in its grammar, that much was certain because it shared its syntax with Hindi and verse in that prosy language had all the potency of a bullock. Which left its vocabulary, nourished by Persian and Arabic, where Hindi had fed off Sanskrit. It was the resonance of Urdu's words that was untranslatable. So he groped through the Koran to find the fountainhead of Urdu's genius.

Each day the maulvi came and led him like a child through the verses, paraphrasing them in Urdu till, after an eternity of lessons, Intezar decided that this was folly. When mortal inspiration rhymed in Urdu fared so badly in another language, how could translation cope with the subtlety and grandeur of God's revelation in the chosen tongue? It was not for nothing that the Koran in translation wasn't allowed the authority of revelation.

Suddenly, the way seemed clear to him. It was Arabic he needed to learn first, if he wanted to come to grips with Urdu. For it struck him that if Arabic words spliced on to an alien grammar could give Urdu such force, what undreamt magic must they work embedded in their native syntax, in the land of the revealed version.

So with Kulsum's amused consent he planned a year-long stay in Mecca. Perhaps Arabic, he said half-jokingly to his wife, as they were packing his bags for the Haj, perhaps Arabic will finally push me into poetry. Kulsum smiled. You'll need a new pen-name then, she said, because then the waiting will be over.

The terrible irony of that reply came back to haunt her in the years of shrinking hope that followed his departure. I had known him for four years then, said Haasan, introducing himself into the plot in a minor role. And I knew he meant to return within a year of leaving. In that last month, he used to come to the coffee house every day and worry aloud about the children and how his absence would affect them. There was no question that he meant to come back. But he never did. Never once in nearly eleven years. Not a letter or a message, not even a rumour. He just disappeared.

Haasan stopped . . . just as it was getting interesting. I wanted to kick him. A story couldn't end with the main character vanishing. Not that I had any stake in Intezar's fate, but in my role as audience I was entitled to an ending.

Then he started again.

For the first year, Masroor didn't sleep for missing his father. In the normal course, he would have got over his loss and Intezar would have become a set of happy memories. But then, one winter's day in 1932, the restless ghost of Kalidass ambushed Masroor. He had been pulling quilts out of a cabin trunk stored in the old zenana, when he found a mothballed copy of his grandfather's incomplete epic: *The History and Destiny of the Ganjoos.*

Like all chroniclers of the relatively recent past, Kalidass ran out of history when he ran up against the present. But since he had a very developed sense of chosenness, he solved the problem by commencing a history of his family's future. Being ambitious for his descendants, he merged the destiny of the Ganjoos with the triumph of Indian nationalism. It began with Charandass' return from England, the equal of any Englishman in Englishry, a pukka barrister. But instead of making money out of English law, he adopted the cause of the Nation. And in spite of his privileged growing up, and despite the fact that he had never earned an honest day's wages, the masses took him to their hearts. The people danced to his commands, the British yielded to his arguments, and finally he plucked the flame of liberty from Westminster and set it burning among his people somewhere under India Gate. The grateful citizens of the sovereign Nation made him their ruler and he ruled them till he died, after which his children ruled and then his children's children.

That's how it went, finished Haasan hurriedly, anxious to keep my attention. All rubbish of course, just fantasy, but you have to remember that when he read it, Masroor was only fourteen, very young. His father's life had diverged cruelly from his prescribed destiny; far from helping India find her way, he had managed to lose himself. Worse still, the future predicted for his father had actually come to pass for someone else; Intezar's destiny had been hijacked by a Kashmiri contemporary farther east, Allahabad's Nehru, the younger one.

Worst of all, Masroor read his grandfather's book just after the second civil disobedience campaign of '32 led by Gandhi with Nehru as his right-hand man. Jawaharlal's face figured on the front pages every day around that time. While Masroor's father, for whom this part had been written, had disappeared. Once that fatal comparison was made, Masroor remembered Intezar not as a gentle father or a vanished pilgrim, but as a barren poet, an absurd adult who went around losing himself, a dilettante who had failed to live up to his future.

Since then, Masroor had spent every waking minute of his life making sure that the same would never be said of him. There wasn't a cause or a party that he didn't make his own. He joined the Congress, he joined the Muslim League. In the elections of 1937 he ran errands for both. When the two fell out, he stayed with the Congress because Nehru should have been his father. Now he distrusted all the parties; he just wanted to help keep the peace. That's why he was so worked up about the cricket match.

He's too intense, said Haasan. It's too much feeling for a little cricket match.

He shook his head. In an earlier time, this intensity would have made him a leader of men, but by 1942 it was too late.

Between Gandhi, Jinnah and the man who had stolen his father's future, all the shares in India's liberation were taken.

Haasan stopped again and this time it wasn't a pause – he was done. He still hadn't satisfactorily explained Intezar's disappearance but he had done what he had set out to do: paraphrase the family's history to explain Masroor. He was looking at me expectantly, waiting for a reaction to his family saga.

He didn't get it. I said instead that I wanted to wash my hair and excused myself. It was true – I did. My scalp had been itching right through the tale. I turned on the bathroom tap and scratched my head as the bucket filled. It had prickled all day. Was it premonition?

No. It was lice.

Outside

L ICE. CRAWLING.

This sank in properly only after I had smeared three on the bathroom wall. Then the day's food vaulted out of my insides without notice once, twice and endlessly. I lay in bed and let my head hang over the edge to help the beasts drop off. Lice belonged in the orange hair of traffic-light urchins. What did they have to do with me?

Whose were they? Not Ammi's or Asharfi's. Because (a) my head had never been close enough to theirs and (b) they didn't show the guilt or shame that nits and eggs must bring. Ditto with Moonis the cook and Uncle Haasan. That left nobody; there was no one else I had met in 1942. Perhaps the lice had boarded on the train, then hatched and multiplied in the time that I had been convalescing in the house. This was the theory that I favoured; it allowed me to be infested by my contemporaries. I didn't want to be assimilated to 1942 by lice.

But what was I to do with them? I didn't think that they could be combed out. And I couldn't ask my hosts to pick them out. If I soaked my head in a disinfectant there would be questions about the smell and I couldn't tell them the truth – even Ammi would baulk at a lousy house-guest. No one gave vermin the benefit of the doubt. Instead of going down for dinner that night, I tied on a bath-towel turban to quarantine the beasts and went to bed.

I was troubled all night by bookish nightmares. In the morning I counted my feet, examined the inside of the towel, brushed my teeth and went down the stairs for breakfast. Masroor didn't flinch when I took the chair next to his at the dining table; Moonis poured me a cup of tea without comment; Ammi read out for my benefit the final instalment

33

of Shakila Rahman's intrepid pilgrimage – as if nothing had happened, as if my hair wasn't alive with crawling filth. The kind are blind.

Haasan suddenly emerged from the kitchen carrying a large frying pan with an omelette in it. He transferred it on to his plate and said:

And you'll never be able to unscrew the fishplates.

Masroor left the table to stand defiantly framed in one of the three arched doorways that opened on to the courtyard.

I had arrived in the middle of an argument.

Haasan cut the omelette into two squares and called to Moonis to hurry up with the toast.

Masroor stayed where he was.

Even if Bhukay gets a spanner the right size and gauge, continued Haasan, deaf to Masroor's silence. Even then.

He stopped again and worked his jaws till his mouth was half empty. Then he held out his thumb and forefinger, half an inch apart, and said:

The nuts will be rusted that deep into the washers. That deep. You'll need King Kong or Gama to turn those screws. Which one do you have?

The question was rhetorical but Masroor answered it.

Bhukay, Bihari and me, he said, in the even tones of a patient man goaded to the limit.

So there are three of you, said Haasan, pretending to count. Let's be optimistic. We'll assume that someone has been oiling the fishplate screws every week since the lines were laid and that they open at the first turn of the spanner. Fifteen minutes of unscrewing and all four fishplates are free and there's nothing holding that section of track down any more. There's just one small job left – shifting that section. Not removing it completely – just enough to disturb the alignment of the track. Because if you leave it as it is, it's likely that the free rail will stay in place under the weight of the train . . . and the Mail will get to Charbagh station with the Aligarh team in time for the match.

Masroor, in an armchair now, with his head thrown back and his face organized into a look of beleaguered disdain, stared at the ceiling in silence.

Haasan sectioned his second toast-and-omelette into square mouthfuls. Do you know, have you any idea, how much a ten-foot section of rail line weighs? The three of you had better start lifting weights at the Kaisarbagh akhara if you're serious about sabotage.

Masroor refused to rise. In fact he became progressively more casual and nonchalant as Haasan strove to shock him out of his ardent lunacy by pointing up the absurdity of his plan. Haasan succeeded only in persuading Ammi that no one, not even her passionate son, could be serious about such an idiotic scheme. Once Haasan had established the impossibility of the whole idea, she looked relieved and instructed a harassed-looking Moonis to make up a batch of shami kababs by way of thanksgiving. By the time breakfast ended Haasan had given up and the argument seemed laid to rest. Ammi had gone back to being preoccupied with the next issue of *Khatoon*. As Masroor left for work, she called out a reminder: he was to help her with the printing of the next issue tomorrow. Masroor said something in reply as he lifted his bicycle over the threshold of the courtyard door, which Ammi seemed to understand. Then Haasan and Asharfi left for the coffee house and I.T. College respectively, and it became a normal day again.

That evening, I took advantage of the calm to confide in Masroor. He had disappeared into his room after dinner, where I followed him, weak with shame and nervousness. When he opened his door I saw that he was working. In the wash of angle-poised light on his table, a book lay open. It was a Bradshaw, a railway timetable. But he seemed pleased to see me, so instead of muttering that I'd come later, I let him sit me down. Then I told him.

I have lice. Like that. Straight. I'd have liked to lead up to it but nothing, no path-clearing preliminaries occurred to me. What is that book? I have lice; or Do you smoke? I do but I have lice, sounded silly, so I just told him.

Then, to pre-empt silence, I kept talking. I had only just found out, I explained desperately. The bed sheets were free of the infestation and I could stay in my room if he felt there was any danger of my giving it to others. All I wanted was advice on killing them.

35

He heard me out without horror or amusement. Even more reassuring was the way he listened. He didn't steeple his fingers or sit back, or watch the ceiling . . . that is, he didn't seem or look to be considering. He sat leaning forward in his chair, elbows on knees, hands knit in a double-fist . . . he looked interested in the story of my lice. So when I ran out of things to say, I felt bold enough to ask in a forlorn way if he could keep the story to himself because I didn't want Ammi and Asharfi to know.

It was a lot to ask. He had brought me home and now his house-guest was host to vermin. He would have been within his rights to consult his mother. But my instinct was true.

Don't worry, he said. We don't have to worry Ammi with this. He thought for a while. I had lice in Class IX, he said finally, forehead wrinkling as he strenuously called up his past for a guiding precedent. I think Ammi . . . wait a minute, he said, walking up to a shelf. Reaching up, he brought down a dusty horizontal book. It was a photograph album made up of stiff black sheets interleaved with cobwebby tracing paper. He found what he was looking for in the last ten pages, which were pasted with group photographs of Masroor and his classmates as they worked their way up the ten-rung ladder of school. They looked like ten copies of the same print – the class was always arranged on a set of steps, the background was always filled by a mad-looking building that looked like something assembled from the leftovers of assorted ruins, the boys were always wearing blazers and ties, and there was always an adult in the middle. This central seated adult was the only variable – the other faces stayed the same.

Masroor riffled through the pages for a bit, then grunted. In the relevant picture a completely bald Masroor is standing in the tall row, grinning hugely into the camera. The shutter has caught the boy on his left with his head turned and his hand raised to stroke Masroor's baldness. Masroor grinned again across the distance of a dozen years. Gaya got caned for spoiling the picture, he said.

There it was in black-and-white: Masroor had had lice in Class IX and Ammi had got his hair shaved off. Right here, in the courtyard, he explained. The barber used to come home

36

every Saturday till I refused to have my hair cut in front of the family because it was childish. I wanted it done at a barber's like a man.

So he began cycling off to the barbershop, which was miles away in Aminabad. It used to take him half an hour to get there. Ammi wanted him to go to a barbershop in Lalbagh, but Masroor enjoyed the ride because setting off early on Sunday morning was independence and adventure. He still went there every other week.

We could go there early tomorrow if you want, he said. Unless you want to have it done in the house. I could send word and he'll bring his scissors here.

I shook my head in silent horror at the prospect of being deloused in full view of Ammi and Asharfi.

We'll leave at seven tomorrow morning, then, said Masroor.

I nodded.

Can you cycle?

I nodded again.

Good, said Masroor encouragingly. You can take Moonis' bicycle. Don't worry about your hair. We'll be back by breakfast and you'll be clean.

Thanks, I whispered, fighting the grateful urge to tell him everything. I climbed the stairs to my room and settled into bed.

Hours later, just as I was finally drifting into sleep, I heard the muffled chimes of the mantel clock downstairs. It was striking twelve. Drowsily it came to me that the eighth day of August 1942 was done. The inaugural date of the movement that had haunted my grandmother's last years had come and gone and nothing had happened.

Early morning on the ninth of August. I woke to the sound of radio static and the breathless thought that this was my last whole day in 1942. By 7 a.m. tomorrow I would be sitting in the Mail, headed back to Delhi and my own time.

I brushed my teeth and gingerly combed my hair and hurried down the steps to Masroor's room. When I walked in, Masroor was twiddling the knob of a large radio in a round cabinet. The room was filled with amplified gabble as the impatiently spun needle glanced off unwanted frequencies. He turned the volume down and poured me a glass of tea. It was the third pot he had brewed; he had been through the first two in the past hour, trying to catch the news.

News of what, I asked timidly, cradling the too hot tea.

For a second his brows knit in irritation, then he looked contrite.

I'm sorry, he said. I keep forgetting that you don't remember anything. I'm trying to get news of what was decided in the Congress session at Bombay. They were debating the Quit India resolution last night.

Then he began to explain, not knowing that, thanks to Dadi, I probably knew the Quit India resolution better than the Congressmen who had discussed it.

Masroor was against it. Not because of what the resolution said: it wanted the British to hand over the government of India to Indians. He was for that. But there was a war on. And there were Muslims who didn't trust the Congress. Only six months ago Gandhi himself had said that he wouldn't start a civil disobedience movement without a settlement of the Hindu–Muslim question. But now, said Masroor, agitatedly pouring himself another cup, he's asking us to do or die! He shook his head and drank the tea. If they go ahead with this Quit India business, he said more quietly, Jinnah will have his Pakistan by the end of the decade.

I didn't have to take his word for it. I knew. Jinnah had got his Pakistan well before the decade was out. On 14 August 1947, to be precise, which made Pakistan one day older than my Republic. My armies had fought three wars with that upstart state and here was Masroor hoping that the resolution wouldn't be passed, that the August movement wouldn't happen, that Partition wouldn't come to pass. For a moment I felt the joyless superiority of a ninety-year-old listening to the enthusiasms of a child. Masroor, who would stop trains for his cause, who crept out of the house after dark, like a turn-of-the-century anarchist off to kill the Czar, seemed suddenly as absurd as the canteen radicals I had known on campus. Hindsight makes cartoonists of all.

38

After a minute more of useless twiddling, Masroor remembered the barbershop and switched the set off. Toothbrush in one hand and toothpowder in the other, he tiptoed to the washbasin stuck on the wall in a corner of the courtyard and then rent the morning calm by hawking and spitting and blowing his nose and gagging as he scraped the root of his tongue and dredged up ancient deposits of phlegm. All the while the lice were digging in.

By the time we were ready to leave I was smelling of mothballs because Masroor had found me clothes to go out in from a trunk in his room in which Ammi had preserved his old school uniforms. He must have been a large schoolboy because the trousers had to be lashed to my waist with a knotted belt, and the short-sleeved shirt hung over my elbows. But his feet were only two sizes larger and the brick-brown canvas shoes almost fitted. He had thought of everything – he gave me a sola topi to cover my baldness with on the way back. He was wearing one too. The leather on its chin-strap was cracked and it looked older than Masroor. Pushing our bicycles over the threshold, I wondered if the topis had belonged to his father, and shivered. It felt strange, wearing the hat of a disappeared man.

When we set off it was half-past six and pleasant, but our cycle ride took so long that by the time we reached Aminabad the early morning cool was a memory in the wet heat of an August day. Masroor wanted to revisit his memories, because he was due to stop a train and didn't know what the future held, so we meandered past the G.P.O., his old school, La Martinière, Haasan's coffee house, the ruined Residency, the lunatic asylum in Kaisarbagh, the Bara Imambara . . . everywhere, he dismounted, stood quietly in what looked like a two-minute silence in memoriam, and set off again.

After forty minutes of this tour by tangents, I became nervous. I had thought that this once-only exposure to the world outside the Lalbagh house would be a quick sortie. But here I was, drifting promiscuously through this alien time, infecting more and more of it with my presence and being lathered by its dust in return.

We finally entered Aminabad through a narrow lane shared

out in little shops. They hadn't opened for business yet, so the lane was still except for the creaking of a large black machine being fed bunched sticks of sugarcane by a sweating man. Just as we turned left into the main street of the bazaar, a tonga passed us, piled high with baskets, bedrolls, one man in a grey sherwani, two women in obscuring burqas and some children. Its wheels and hooves sounded clearly in the decrepit silence. It reminded me of a troubling film I couldn't name.

But the barber's name was clear at once because Masroor called out to him as soon as we entered the shop. It was a large saloon with six high-backed chairs with cushioned head-rests, each drawn up to a washbasin and a mirror, arranged two to a wall along three walls. One chair was occupied by an enormously fat man who was red in the face with the effort of tucking his chin in as the barber did the back of his head.

Bhukay, the proprietor, had a proper name according to Masroor but an enormous adolescent appetite founded on stomach worms had forever lumbered him with Bhukay. Masroor had a whispered word with Bhukay, who nodded and waved me into the chair next to the fat man, while he finished with the subtly Anglo-Indian head he was working on. I settled in feeling nervous and ashamed, hoping that Masroor would stay in the saloon for the duration of the haircut. I could watch him in the mirror, sitting on a bench, rummaging through an untidy heap of magazines. He knocked his sola topi off the bench with his elbow, then picked it up and jammed it on his head for safe-keeping and resumed his search. Where's today's paper? he asked Bhukay. It hadn't yet arrived.

The barber on my left had finished with the fat man's hair. He was now giving him a massage, slapping and kneading his head with his fingers, knuckles and the heels of his palms. His customer's piggy little features had relaxed to the point where his face looked like a happy round of creaseless fat. When the massage was done, the barber powdered his neck and whisked unwanted hair away. He untied the sheet that did duty as a giant bib and stood to one side solicitously as the fat man heaved himself out of the chair, covered his haircut with a black topi and waddled out of the shop.

Bhukay completed a short back-and-sides on the Anglo-Indian and made his way to my chair. He undid the buttons of my shirt, wrapped a flat strip of cotton wool round my neck and knotted a clean sheet around it. With a bottle-pump he sprayed my hair with water. Then he pushed my head over the washbasin and squeezed and cuffed the surplus water out. That done, he slicked my hair back with a comb and set to work. His scissors chattered like a bird by my ear; I sighed and closed my eyes. For the first time since falling into the Gomti, I relaxed. I was in good hands: a professional was taking care of my troubles.

In less than ten minutes he had cropped my hair into a ragged poll. He discarded the scissors and gave my lice a shower again. Then he stropped his razor. I watched timidly in the mirror – cut-throats made me nervous. But he was an artist. A few absent passes over my head and then a series of unhurried strokes which peeled off running strips of hair till there was nothing. He wasn't finished; he poured a little disinfecting spirit into an enamel bowl and with swabs of cotton he rubbed it into my shaven head, making it tingle. There was more. Before I could stop him, he picked up a yellow flannel, the kind most often used for cleaning cars, and polished my scalp till it glowed. In the end I didn't really care: I was relieved and tired and the chair was comfortable. So I just lay there, slumped and drowsy, gleaming like a copper doorknob.

He hated hair. Hated it. He said it seriously, credo-wise. Dandruff, scurf, dirt, smells, lice, dead-alive parasite feeding off our heads. Thick thin long short straight curly oily dry – the disorder of it. The skull was the perfect form, just as the egg was. Hair was pointless. It had been a pleasure, shaving me bald. Most days he compromised his art and his principles to make a living. He trimmed whiskers, shaped sideburns, helped balding men cover their goodness with lank threads of shame. But even with material like me, he sculpted on sand. His was a hopeless cause. Already my hair was invisibly growing; no matter how close he shaved me, the ugly black stubble would surface again. Like shaving faces: every victory was an admission of defeat. Nothing stayed still – time and life kept crawling in.

41

When Bhukay finished with me, Masroor was still darting in and out of the saloon looking for a newspaper boy. We left the saloon and stepped into the heat of a sunrisen summer morning. My back prickled because of the heat and the tiny hair that had sneaked through the cordon of the bib-sheet down my neck. I was walking towards our bicycles parked in the shade a few yards away from the barber's when Masroor caught me by the elbow and steered me in the opposite direction – there was one stop left in this morning's tour of his life and times in Lucknow.

We didn't have far to go. Less than a furlong down the road Masroor stopped in front of a mostly shuttered sweet-shop. Only one part of its façade, on the extreme left, was open for business, where a man in a fraying vest was making jalebis. This was Bihari Halvai. Masroor knew him well from the time he had been a boy, helping his father out at the same shop. Masroor seemed on first-name terms with most of Lucknow.

The shop was old – its right wall was jammed against the crumbling whitewashed brick of a tiny tomb. And that was exactly how the sweet-shop styled itself: The Famous Old Sweet-Shop Hard by the Tomb. Apart from some brick and half a hollow dome, not much was visible. From where I was standing I couldn't see the door into the monument because the tomb was smothered by an enormous banyan. The parent stem had long since vanished; now there was a whole grove of interconnected trunks which had once been aerial roots that had reached the ground and burrowed in. Some hadn't got that far; they had simply grown into another branch or trunk on the way down and there they remained, fixed in ambiguity, at once branch, root and thwarted trunk. Every-day monkeys peered through the obscuring mass of its rain-green leaves at the sweet-shop.

Bihari bobbed his head when he saw Masroor and motioned us towards the wooden benches scattered on the broad pavement in front of the shop. He was sitting cross-legged on a low takht, deftly squeezing spirals of white flour paste into a vat of simmering oil which alchemized them into a translucent yellow gold. When his bag of paste was done, he pushed the newly inscribed batch about with a perforated iron ladle and watched the whorls change colour. His customers at this early hour were mainly servants sent to make milk and jalebi breakfasts possible for their masters.

But after making two batches he turned to serve a bent old man whose skullcap and beard declared he was Muslim. He was obviously an old customer because Bihari began making up his order without a word being exchanged. Bag in hand he began writing from right to left on the smoking oil. By the time he'd spanned the diameter of that massive vat, even I, illiterate as I was, could recognize the loops and curves of the Arabic script. He laid another strip of script below the first and then another and so on until one hemisphere was dense with words and the other, nakedly bubbling. He sat back, still frowning with concentration, and looked at the old man standing quietly by.

Here, Jamal Mian, he said. Your lines.

Jamal Mian gazed reverently at the letters of gold trembling on the oil and nodded. Bihari broke the strips up into manageable words and syllables, then wrapped them in newspaper. The old man tucked his stick under his arm, the better to hold the parcel, and began walking carefully in the direction of the overgrown tomb.

What was all that for? asked Masroor curiously, watching Jamal Mian as he disappeared into the mystery of the banyan and the tomb.

That is Haji Jamaluddin, said Bihari affectionately. And he's carrying lines from the Koran.

You've never done that before, said Masroor.

That's because you don't usually visit at this hour, answered the jalebi maker. I've done it every day for five years now. But only for him.

Was it any verse from the Koran or did Jamal Mian choose? This was Masroor again, endlessly curious about the world around him. We had been outdoors for an hour and a half now, knocking around in a time that didn't belong to me. The longer I loitered and the more people I met, the greater was the possibility of my being there making a difference. With a train to catch to my mislaid present early next morning, I wasn't going to tempt fate. I didn't care who chose the verse. I just wanted to kick Masroor for asking.

Bihari smiled and shook his head. Jamal Mian's illiterate. He can't even read Urdu, let alone the Koran. There's no choosing business. We just follow the book in sequence, one line after the other.

So you could write anything, I said offensively, hoping to cut this exchange short, and he wouldn't know the difference.

It didn't work. Bihari disarmed me by admitting that he had done just that, three years ago, in '39. This was a daily visit Jamal Mian made; he had been coming since the winter of 1936, the year he went to Mecca on the Haj. On his way back in the boat, Baba Farid – the saint in the tomb – who had been dead three hundred years, came to him in a vision. He complained that his rest had of late been disturbed by the rising tide of violence in the land. The Word had been forgotten. So he wanted Jamal, who was a Haji, to read him the Koran verse by verse from beginning to end and then start up again from the beginning. And the apparition promised that as long as Jamal kept this up, the violence that stalked the world would never reach Lucknow.

Jamal Mian didn't know what to do. He couldn't have read the book aloud because he couldn't read. His family was originally from the east, weavers from Banaras, illiterate from the beginning of time. Then one day he put his problem to Bihari, who suggested the way out. The Koran inscribed in jalebi, a line each day. This way he could simultaneously be true to his vision and make the edible offering that was customary at Baba Farid's graveside.

How had he learnt enough of the Koran to write it in jalebi? What I meant, of course, was how did a cook come by a working knowledge of classical Arabic?

Again he took no offence, though I must have overdone the scepticism because Masroor frowned at my tone. My father, he said, had a maulvi teach me the Koran for two hours every early morning till I was fourteen. Bihari Halvai is what my friends call me but I was named Omar, Omar Qureishi.

I flushed to the roots of my shaven hair. I hadn't thought he was Muslim because I'd never come upon a Muslim halvai before. I made no further attempts to speed matters up.

Then one day, resumed Bihari, two and a half years after Jamal Mian had started doing this morning round, I gave him, instead of the usual line from the Koran, the headlines from an old newspaper that I used to wrap the jalebis in. I don't know what made me do it – boredom, I suppose; we had been through the Koran once already and we were more than half-way through it the second time round. Perhaps it was the heat . . . it was around the middle of June. In fact it was the nineteenth day of June. I remember the date because the next morning's newspaper carried two-inch headlines on the riot in Kanpur. It was the biggest communal riot in years; there were four hundred dead and twice as many injured. And Kanpur was less than seventy miles away from Lucknow.

I'm not a superstitious man, said Bihari grimly, but sometimes it's hard to ignore a sign. I never dishonoured Jamal Mian's pledge again.

He gave us a second serving of the jalebis. Eating the first batch had turned my hands and mouth into flypaper, airports for every coasting fleck. He squeezed in another lot and settled back, wiping the sweat off his face with a shoulder cloth. He pointed at the tomb:

One day, just one day I gave Jamal Mian the wrong words and the killing came as close as Kanpur. If I fry the right verses till the Day of Judgement I still won't bring the Kanpur dead to life. That's why I'm coming with you to stop the Aligarh train. I want to help Baba Farid keep his promise to Jamal Mian – the killing mustn't come to Lucknow.

With a flourish he laid two parallel lines of paste on the oil's surface and before they could drift apart, he joined them with short horizontal strokes at equal intervals. When he finished it looked like a ladder, but it wasn't. Given the context it was plainly meant to be a length of railway track. When it was the right colour, Bihari picked it out and snapped it in two. Casually. Only Masroor wasn't there to applaud his bravado because he had spotted a newspaper boy at last and rushed across the road, without a thought for the traffic. Not that there was much motor traffic at eight on a Sunday morning in 1942 . . . just the odd khaki jeep or camouflaged truck, headed for some distant cantonment.

45

Masroor paid the newspaper boy and spread the paper out. I could have told him what it said; Dadi had rehearsed the headlines of the ninth of August for years. Do or Die Says Gandhi; Congress Passes Quit India Resolution; Gandhi and Others Arrested; Congress Banned; Jinnah Condemns Congress Blackmail; Attack On Public Buildings. Not all of these, of course, but depending on the paper Masroor had bought, at least a mix of two or three.

So I wasn't surprised when Masroor sank hopelessly to his knees on the farther pavement to read on all fours this confirmation of everything he had feared. I wasn't surprised but I wanted to cross the road and put an arm around him and offer the comfort of hindsight. I wanted to tell him that there would be no communal riots for the duration of the civil disobedience movement that had just begun. There would be tracks blown up, telegraph wires cut, police stations attacked, townships machine-gunned from the air, thousands jailed and many killed, but the violence would be between the Raj and the rebels, not Hindus and Muslims. The killing he thought would result from a unilateral declaration of independence by the Congress didn't actually happen. I got to my feet to reassure him . . . then stopped and settled back on the bench. How would I say it? Don't worry, the movement will be dead in a couple of months and there won't be any riots in that time? Don't worry, there is a time and place for everything, even your despair, and the time for that is not now but five years from now, when the British quit India in fact and the killings begin in earnest.

I stayed on the bench and left him alone to cope with the news. Properly speaking, it was his future he was agonized about, not mine; having mislaid my present, I could hardly start counselling him on his. Besides, my train was due at seven the next morning and I was on parole.

Just as I had decided not to get involved, Masroor got to his feet, leaving the newspaper lying on the ground. He turned and began walking towards us, grim-faced, tipping his sola topi back, shirtsleeves flapping, shoulders braced against the worst the world could do. For many months afterwards, that was how I remembered Masroor each time I thought of him.

46

He had paused on the edge of the pavement before stepping on the road when I heard the engine sound to my left. I turned to look and saw a military lorry hurtling down the road. Masroor had stopped to let a knot of cyclists pass, so he must have seen the lorry because it was coming from the same direction. But inexplicably he made to cross as soon as the cyclists passed; he hadn't taken two steps when the lorry was upon him. Brakes shrieked, I jerked my head away, hands clenched, eyes tightly shut.

When I opened them, the lorry had squealed to a halt. I surged towards the accident where, amazingly, no crowd had gathered. Fearfully I ran round the back of the truck to the farther pavement. I steeled myself to look at the front wheel and the bumper. No blood, no mangled Masroor. With a huge effort I kept myself from retching and squatted lower to get a sight of the underside of the lorry. He wasn't mixed into its innards or smeared on the road.

Abruptly, the lorry began moving and, half-squatting still, I stumbled backwards to the safety of the pavement. As the lorry gathered speed, a recruiting advertisement painted right across its side passed slowly before my eyes. Take the King's Commission, read the caption, The Noblest Life on Earth. Where the letters ended, two moustachioed men in epauletted khaki gazed sternly into my eyes. Next to them, not front-on but in profile, was a figure in loose khaki trousers and a white short-sleeved shirt. His feet, shod in red-brown Home Guard shoes, were in the air – or off the lower edge of the advertisement – in a painterly study of motion. One half-raised hand was either sketching a salute or tipping back a sola topi. As the truck pulled away, I raced alongside, trying to keep the advertisement in view, till I couldn't breathe, till I was gagging on the thick cloud of its exhaust. Well after the smoke had cleared and the truck was lost in the distance, I stood rooted in the middle of the road, frozenly trying to work out how a three-dimensional man could be ironed on to a flat surface: because that third figure on the side of the lorry wasn't a soldier – it was Masroor.

★

I forget how long it took me to get to the Lalbagh house but I ran all the way. Without a thought for our bicycles parked by the barbershop or for Bihari, who had also seen the truck run Masroor over, I raced through unknown streets, losing my way at every turn until I found myself on the road by the G.P.O.'s spire, from where I turned left and sprinted home. The morning wore on as I ran and the roads filled up with rickshaws and cycles and people but the animation flashing past me seemed contrived and remote, like the back-projected traffic whizzing past the windows of a studio car. Guru Dutt in *Aar Paar* driving a stationary Buick with the streets of Bombay worked carefully into his rear windscreen. No one was taken in but nobody complained because what mattered were the stars and they were real. I laughed hysterically (still running) at the thought that I was the hero of this one. By the time I reached the lane which led to the Lalbagh house, I was light-headed and breathless. I knew there was nothing real or substantial about my surroundings so I didn't bother to knock on the courtyard door, I just ran through it.

I must have fainted with the pain. I remember an explosion in my nose as it burst and another in my crotch as the groin-level bolt on the door rebuffed it. I dropped to the ground, holding myself in both hands, unable to breathe or scream. And just as Asharfi's worried voice asked Kaun? from behind the door, a second before I fainted, I felt a surge of irritation at the inconsistency of this film. It was like letting a studio car actually run into Flora Fountain. You have to make up your mind, director-sahib, I thought crossly. Things can't be make-believe at random and real when they choose to be.

Haasan Takes Over

W HEN HAASAN CAME around that evening, I was sitting in the courtyard with Ammi and Asharfi, tense with not knowing how to begin. Shocked by Masroor's disappearance and dazed after the collision, I had offered no explanation for my baldness and they hadn't inquired. Masroor's comings and goings were so eccentric that Ammi and Asharfi didn't even ask after him. Ammi dabbed Mercurochrome over my nose and shooed me up to my room to recover. At lunchtime Asharfi brought me a tray of food and left me to sleep through the afternoon. Sometime during this troubled siesta I dreamed that Bihari had visited and told them everything, so that was taken care of, I wouldn't be the one to break it to them, I didn't need a beginning.

But when I went down for tea, they were so cheerful that I knew it was up to me. Asharfi handed me a cup and grinned encouragingly.

You're part of the family now, she said, looking at my shaven head. Proper baldy you look – every inch a Ganjoo!

The pun unnerved me. How could I tell her that she had lost a Ganjoo, not found one. That her brother was riding the side of a five-ton truck, selling the army in two dimensions. Why not just say that I had dropped from the future without a parachute.

Not that I had to tell them anything. I was leaving this world and its improbabilities early next morning. But I wanted to. Partly because I owed them the truth for their goodness to me, but mainly to purge myself of the intolerable absurdity of the morning's happenings. I didn't want to carry the morning like a solitary secret into my own time. It had to be handed over in the here and now; if it was unfinished business, it was the unfinished business of 1942 and its residents: they could have it.

49

Haasan came in looking grim and asked what had happened. That made it easy. The fact that he knew or seemed to know there was something wrong meant that I wouldn't have to start from scratch. No sooner had he asked than I told them everything. For nearly an hour I bore unstopped witness to the morning's events. It was a good story and I told it recklessly, so I told it well. When I described the vanishing, Ammi and Asharfi gasped – a minute later they didn't believe me but the telling took their breath away.

Still, the comfort of disbelief came easily because I was the storyteller: an amnesiac baldy from nowhere who ran full tilt into bolted doors. Oh, nobody said as much but Ammi asked for another round of tea and worried aloud if Masroor would be back in time that evening to finish printing the *Khatoon*'s August run. I was hurt by that, which was silly, because I had expected disbelief. But when it came, I resented it.

By the time we finished tea, I decided not to care. Even if they believed every word, what difference would it make to me? I'd be gone in the morning to a time where news of Masroor would never reach me. Even if I went looking for them in the Lucknow of my time, Ammi would be very likely dead, Asharfi would be seventy and Masroor – if he wasn't peeling off the side of an ancient lorry – would be a grandfather, not the dauntless man I knew. So I returned to the room upstairs without pressing the truth of my story and put together the few things that I would need early the next morning: a change of clothes (another of Masroor's khaki-and-white school uniforms); money for the fare (lent me by Masroor); Home Guard shoes (Masroor's), and the only thing there that was truly mine: the thermos flask that was my grandmother's urn. Then I went downstairs for one last meal in the Lalbagh house.

For one breathless moment when I walked into the hall, I wondered if they knew I was leaving because the long dark table was aglow with the dancing light of a branched candelabra. It looked like the setting for a valedictory dinner. Only it wasn't – a fuse had blown, dousing the lights on the ground floor. But fuse or not, it felt grand sitting around one end of the table as Moonis served up the food, turning our poshly shadowed faces this way and that like a bunch of old paintings in conversation. Haasan had stayed on for dinner, so there were four of us in that dining room.

I was so excited by the thought of going home the next morning that it wasn't until I had mopped up the first serving of korma with my second roti that I realized the faces around me were strained and worried in the kindly candlelight. Of course – Masroor hadn't returned for dinner. He had been gone twelve hours now and Ammi was looking edgy.

It was Haasan who broke the building silence. I've just been to Bihari's shop, he said quietly. He said he had been bending over the vat squeezing in a new lot of jalebis when he heard the brakes shriek. When he looked up he thought he saw a glimpse of Masroor (at least, it was a man wearing a sola topi, the kind Masroor had on that morning) and then the truck was upon him. It took him a few seconds to get off his perch, but when he got to the road, the truck was still standing there. He squatted and looked under it but Masroor wasn't there; the only face he saw was yours, doing the same thing from the other side of the lorry. Then the driver crashed the gears and it moved off, with you running alongside. He says he shouted after you to stop but you didn't and that was the last he saw of either you or the truck or Masroor.

Haasan cleared his throat. I asked him about the picture you saw, he said carefully, glancing at Ammi, who was staring at me. He didn't see anything like that . . . at least not on the side of the truck that he could see.

So we don't know what to think, said Ammi to me, anxiously. All I know is that he never misses dinner without telling me – and he isn't home. Tell me, couldn't it have been a window in the truck that you saw him through . . . or a door?

Perversely, I felt vindicated by the anxiety all round me. This would teach them not to dismiss the improbable. I had been living with the improbable for a week now. They had just lost a relative – I had lost a world.

Then I remembered that my salvation was at hand, that at seven tomorrow morning I'd be on my way home. The thought made me more generous, benign. I was warmed by pity, not only because they had lost Masroor but because the end of the world they knew was due. In less than five years there would be murder, arson, rape, flight-migration, butchered trains, refugees, dispossession, enemy aliens . . . in short, Partition. And here they were, Asharfi, Ammi and Haasan, living in the lull and thinking it the storm. It made me feel omniscient: I felt like a historian brought up face to face with some lost cause, some extinct line that he had chronicled.

So I gave them hope.

I pleaded a state of shock, I cited the time-lag between the truck screeching to a stop and my reaching it, I even invoked the obscuring smoke of its exhaust. The truck had been moving quite fast and keeping up had taken all my energy, so yes, it might have been Masroor in a window, briefly, or, why not, a door. And then there was the delirium of exhaustion, the treachery of recall and, of course, my amnesia which might selectively extend to the immediate past. Concussion had to be considered too: my head had been bashed by the courtyard door. Already a red and purple bruise disfigured my head, right where the forehead receded into the scalp.

I don't know if they swallowed this revised version, because all of them, including Ammi (who wanted desperately to be persuaded), still looked troubled when I finished. But there wasn't much more I could do. I had told them the truth at teatime and taught them doubt at dinner; no professional historian could have done more. I had done my best by this alien time. I had treated its characters like flesh-and-blood equals, as free, self-willed individuals carving out their destinies. Like me. When in reality they were cardboard figures playing bit roles in a tightly scripted play without a happy ending. In fact, Masroor right now had rather less depth than a paper cut-out. Perhaps he is in hiding, I said, tossing them a final crumb of comfort, thinking vaguely of the Mahdi figure in Islam. That was a nice little touch, it seemed to me, just the right note. It should strike a fuzzy chord in them somewhere – they were Muslims after all. That done, I wished them goodnight for ever, without a pang.

The next morning I woke up crisp and clear-eyed. No gum in my eyes, no fur in my mouth, both nostrils unclogged and smoothly breathing. The alarm in my head had gone at four, so

I brushed my teeth in near-darkness, though I hardly needed to, since my teeth felt new. But I did anyway because a few hours from now I would be starting life over again in the world I had lost and it didn't seem right to carry over the dirt of another time.

Washed and dressed, I strapped the thermos on, counted the money and set off. I peered through the grille that roofed the courtyard – the house was still. I crept down the stairs, steadying the flask against my hip. There was a light in the courtyard that I hadn't seen from above: the frosted window-panes on Ammi's bathroom door were glowing orange; did she always shit this early in the morning or was it worry? Quietly I sped across the courtyard in my canvas shoes as I had done the previous morning, though yesterday it had been brighter and I hadn't been alone.

The courtyard door frightened me with a great metallic squawk, but then I was out of the house and into the lane, the first leg of my journey home. My plan was to walk to Charbagh station and buy myself a reservation – I wasn't chancing the horror of not getting a place on the train. Nor was I going to walk up to Gomti Bridge and wait. It would have been properly symmetrical to climb on where I had dropped off, just as if the dropping-off hadn't happened, but what if the signal wasn't red this time and the train didn't stop? It was safer to board the train at Charbagh station and go directly on to Banaras to drown Dadi's ashes. There was no point stopping in Lucknow, even a Lucknow of my own time, because I had lost my camera to the Gomti. No, Banaras was the better bet. I would drown Dadi's ashes and then recover from this misadventure at home, in Delhi. In a Delhi where Kingsway and Queensway were Rajpath and Janpath, where a republican president lived in a once viceregal palace. I didn't once consider the possibility that the train might not reach me back to my own time, that my displacement in time might not be reversible . . . some things are matters of faith and for me the Mail was sacred.

The first bad sign was the soldiery. Scores of men in khaki carrying rifles were patrolling the streets and they weren't policemen. They had called out the army. But military men keeping the peace was normal where I came from, so I didn't really notice. But I was struck by the emptiness of Charbagh station. The floor was clear of people; there were no overnighters asleep on spread-out bedrolls. The ticket counters were generally deserted and that did send a premonitory chill slithering down my neck, but the counter for the Mail and other eastbound trains had a small crocodile of eight or nine travellers in front of it which gave me hope. I joined the queue and felt excitement build again as the window got closer minute by minute. When an old man came and stood behind me, I relaxed. I felt secured.

My turn came suddenly because the three in front barely bent to the level of the ticket window before they straightened up and moved to one side, looking disconsolate. Almost before I knew it, I was looking through dirty glass at a bald man with a Hitler moustache. One seat to Banaras on the Mail, I said. I didn't know how the words came out because my mouth was dry and my ears were filled with the hammering of my heart.

The ticket clerk had a long suck at the tea cooling in a saucer. He put it down and looked at me sourly.

How many times do I have to tell you (the dirty ticket window had smudged all his clients into one incorrigible ticket buyer) that the Mail from Delhi is cancelled? All Delhi trains are cancelled till further notice because of sabotage. But, he said, putting on spectacles and peering at an illegibly chalked-over slate, if you want to go to Banaras, there is a special train starting from Lucknow at eleven tonight.

I left the counter, stunned. Another train. What would I do with another train? I needed the Mail, the train I had come on – only that could haul me back again. And it was cancelled. These Quit India heroes had ruined me. Do or Die I remembered Dadi muttering. Do or Die – Gandhi's rallying cry for the August rebels. Well, they had done . . . and I wished them dead. They had done me in just as surely as they had done Dadi; worse if anything. She had been eaten up by the remembrance of things past, but these nameless patriots had buggered up my future.

I lowered myself on to a bench by the main entrance and sat there for hours, unable to think or move. Lifetimes later – from the heat overhead it must have been ten o'clock at least – I rose and walked slowly back, not to the Lalbagh house, but in the general direction of Hazrat Ganj.

By the time I passed the legislative assembly building, I had recovered enough to knit a few rags of hope together. The Mail was bound to start running once the troubles were over. Another fortnight, a month perhaps and I could try again. If I kept to myself and stayed away from lice and other trouble, there was still a chance. By the time I got to Hazrat Ganj I had even thought up a reason for Ammi and Asharfi to explain my early morning getaway: I had been scouring the streets of Aminabad for Masroor.

But virgin hope, the innocent faith of true believers – that had gone. For a week I had never once doubted that the Mail would arrive on the morning of the tenth and whisk me away to my time. I had put my faith in the impossible happening because it had happened before. I had watched and waited and schemed to be struck again by lightning, but the bolt had been deferred, my faith had wavered and doubt and common sense had scurried in. Why should it happen? Why should it happen again? Why should it happen again to me? By the time my feet walked me into Haasan's coffee house, my plan was more a mantra than a blueprint . . . not an amulet, just a prayer bead.

Between the yellow colonnade that fronted the coffee house and its green fly-mesh doors ran a broad corridor. One section of it to the right of the doors had been blocked off by a newspaperwallah sitting with his back to the wall on a low stool, surrounded by stacks of papers. I bought the *Pioneer* – it would give me something to do while I breakfasted in solitude. It would also give me a reason for ignoring Haasan.

I stepped through the doors and entered a dark world wrapped in coolness. For a moment I could see nothing but the glow of shaded bulbs suspended midway to the ceiling like grimy moons in a murky ether. Gradually as I groped and felt my way to a corner table, the deep-sea aquarium changed into an eating place. A waiter wearing a cockaded turban and a green-and-gold cummerbund appeared from somewhere. He swept the crumbs and wetness from the tabletop on to the floor with a folded rag which smelt strongly of damp, and waited without otherwise acknowledging my presence.

Timidity stopped me from asking for a menu, so out of college canteen memories I hazarded an order: coffee, mutton dosa, vada-sambar. That seemed acceptable because he turned and moved away without a word.

The *Pioneer*'s front page was dense with news of the government's crackdown on the Congress. Even the war on the Eastern Front had been moved to the right of the masthead to make room for it. Jinnah had denounced the Quit India movement in small headlines, while Rajagopalachari, ex-Premier of Madras Presidency and Congress maverick, had condemned the sabotage of railway tracks and ascribed it to a class of non-Congress villains called miscreants.

There was a letter on the editorial page about the cricket match Masroor had plotted to stop, written by a Madrasi maharaja.

Sir, Committed as I am to the defence of civilization against fascism, I pause in my strivings for the Allied cause, to pen a protest against the patronage extended by H.E. the Governor of the United Provinces to sectarian sport. I refer to the tie to be played between the cricket teams of Banaras Hindu and Aligarh Muslim universities, in aid of the Provincial War Fund. It is repugnant that India's cricket and her war effort should be tainted by communal division and that the same British government that is fighting this war to assert the resilience of democracy and the brotherhood of man should still support the arbitrary bond of religion as an organizing principle in sport. May I earnestly appeal to His Excellency Sir Maurice Hallett to cancel this fixture and arrange for some less provocative way of filling the war chest. Yours etc., Maharajakumar Masulipatanam
P.S. I do not advocate regional teams either. Parochialism is no better than sectarianism. Instead, the principle of property or education can be fruitfully applied. Thus landlords could play tenants or graduates could take on illiterates. The lower orders would inevitably have a great

number to choose an eleven from but this advantage would be balanced by our qualitative superiority. Teams constituted in this manner would have the merit of reflecting real social arrangements instead of the false and arbitrary divisions that exist only in the minds of bigots.

The food when it came was wonderful. The dosa was folded into a triangular envelope and filled with finely ground meat. In form it wasn't different from the mutton dosas I had eaten as an undergraduate but otherwise there was no comparison. The filling was squishily tender and not at all like minced and salted rubber. The coffee didn't taste of chlorine. It was authentic, like the ur-cuisine of a pre-lapsarian coffee house from which its republican descendants had strayed.

I nibbled at the corners of the dosa, saving up the middle where the meat mainly was for a couple of huge, tongue-swamping bites. Then Haasan found me – in spite of the newspaper, my not looking up and the gloomy corner I had chosen. He was wearing a white bush-shirt over a pair of dark trousers and an expression of conspiratorial anxiety.

Where have you been? he asked, not wanting to know. I've been visiting everyone this morning telling them to get to the coffee house by eleven. Bhukay and Bihari said they would come. Ammi thought it was improper for her and Asharfi to be seen in a coffee house. So I reminded her that the point of the meeting, the only item on its agenda, was Masroor's disappearance and what to do about it. Also that nobody would recognize them in their burqas. She agreed in the end.

I took a big sip of the coffee and tried to make sense of what he was saying. But why do Ammi and Asharfi have to come here? I asked. Why can't we go to the Lalbagh house?

Because I can't leave the coffee house till the evening and this Masroor business needs to be sorted out at once, answered Haasan simply. Besides, with Masroor gone, there isn't a man left in the house. It wouldn't be right for us to visit.

I thought of Moonis but servants clearly didn't count. There was also me – but perhaps guests were sexless. Then it turned out that they weren't, because Haasan looked broodingly at me and abruptly suggested that I had better move in with him till either Masroor or my memory returned.

Grateful, I said I would; Haasan nodded abstractedly and told the hovering waiter to get us four cream coffees. Sugar separate, he shouted after him. Then he pulled his chair up, hunched his shoulders, lowered his voice and said: Now listen . . .

The rest of the morning unfolded like a play slowed down by fussy stage directions. The cast had barely assembled when it was dispersed by Haasan. There were six of us: Haasan, me, Bhukay, Bihari, Ammi and Asharfi. Bihari wanted to drag more chairs up and sit around a single table but Haasan wouldn't have it . . . there was a rebellion on and even in tranquil times the government kept an eye on whisperings in the coffee house. A huddle of six with two shrouded in black burqas would just invite attention. Besides, he had heard a rumour that the government had imposed or was about to impose Section 144 in potentially restive parts of Lucknow, under which a group of more than four people together in a public place was forbidden. If quintets were seditious, sextets were a crowd and six of us whispering furtively might well be seen as riotous affray.

So to deceive the dogged, bearded man who sat at the table by the door watching people coming in and people leaving, who ordered twenty-four cups of coffee, two every hour over twelve hours, and let them grow cold, who spoke to no one and who everyone knew was a spy, Haasan decided to split the meeting into two adjacent but visibly separate groups.

Ammi and Asharfi, you go into the one on the right and the rest of you into the one next to it on the left. I'll join you in a minute.

The things on the right and left which we were meant to enter were the semi-enclosed family cubicles at the further end of the dining room. They were screened off from the other tables in the open-plan hall by green-painted wooden partitions and bat-wing doors. From the cobwebs in their corners it didn't look as though families ever visited Haasan's coffee house.

The doors of the cubicles screened our faces off from the

58

eyes of the spy by the door. If he wanted he could, by bending over, monitor our feet, but there were only three pairs each in either cubicle, well within the limit of the most stringent law. Even counting the ghost of Masroor and allowing for a waiter, we still made up two loyal, legal foursomes.

Like the doors, the plywood wall that separated Ammi and Asharfi from the rest of us ended a foot and a half from the floor, so any talk there would be clearly audible to us and vice versa. Only, there wasn't any conversation – we sat there silently waiting for Haasan to give us our cues. Till then all we heard was the steady rhubarb drone of a coffee house at peak hour.

When Haasan finally made an appearance, he was wearing a waiter's uniform and carrying a tray loaded with coffee and cutlets. More normal for me to be a waiter and for you to be eating, he whispered. He isn't looking this way but we shouldn't take chances. Then he moved on to serve Ammi and Asharfi and soon the two cubicles were full of clatter and sipping sounds as, falling into the spirit of place, the meeting began to eat and drink.

After serving Ammi and Asharfi, Haasan returned to our cubicle to light a cigarette. Masroor is gone, he opened abruptly, and we've waited twenty-four hours. What should we do? he asked rhetorically. Whom should we ask for help?

The police, I thought at once. The thing to do, if instant doing was important, was to tell the police. I was about to say this aloud but Haasan got there ahead of me. He had thought of everything. That's when I realized that not only did he have the only costume in this dining-room drama, he also had all the lines.

We can't tell the police, he said decisively. If my hunch is right, Masroor has gone into hiding and the last people he would want to find him are policemen.

Into hiding? I waited for someone else to ask the obvious question, someone like his mother or sister, but when they didn't, I did.

Why? I asked.

The better to stop the Aligarh train, said Haasan.

Eating sounds died suddenly. Haasan had our undivided attention.

It's simple if you think about it, he said. He wants to sabotage the rail track. Then, while eating jalebis with you, he notices a newspaper vendor. He buys a paper and reads that because of the Quit India resolution, the Congress has been banned and its members are being arrested. He's afraid that the police might pick him up, because he was a four-anna member of the Congress till a year ago and his name probably still figures in their membership rolls. So as soon as he reads the news, he steals a lift on that passing army truck.

But he wouldn't have gone without telling me, protested Bihari. He had been eating my jalebis till five minutes before vanishing. He would have told me if he was planning to run away.

He hadn't read the newspaper then, pointed out Haasan. He probably just assumed that you and Bhukay would meet him as arranged at the site of the sabotage early tomorrow morning.

And if his hunch was right, if Masroor had in fact gone underground only to surface at the appointed hour to derail the Mail, then that was where we had to be to find him. But first we needed to know where on the hundreds of miles of railway line from Aligarh to Lucknow was the track to be shifted.

Bhukay and Bihari looked irresolutely at each other.

We'll tell you where we planned to meet if you promise not to stop us, said Bihari finally.

To my surprise, Haasan agreed. All he wanted was to put an end to this agonizing uncertainty about Masroor's where-abouts. Masroor was a responsible adult – Haasan had no plans to tie him up and bring him home in a bag.

But – if he was going to swear not to interfere, he had a condition too. Bhukay and Bihari would have to convince him that they understood the implications of the plan they had hatched with Masroor.

Relieved that Haasan was being agreeable, the conspirators agreed. That was a big mistake. Bit players in a plot that Haasan had scripted, they never had a chance.

What do you plan to do after dismantling the track? began Haasan.

60

There was silence. Haasan started all over again.

Do you plan to actually derail the train?

They shook their heads.

You only want to stop it?

Bhukay nodded.

So you must have a scheme for alerting the engine driver to the break in the track.

There was a pause – then Bihari spoke:

The spot we have chosen is five miles down the track from Unnao station. Masroor had planned to phone the station master there ten minutes before the train reached Unnao station and tell him anonymously about the sabotage, to give him time to flag the train down at the station till they repaired the rails.

Which would be too late for the cricket match tomorrow morning, added Bhukay.

What is to stop them from starting the match the day after? inquired Haasan politely.

We'll think of something, said Bihari, uneasily defiant. Even if the match is postponed that will be something . . . at least we shall have done something.

Something more than selling coffee . . . or making up reasons for doing nothing, muttered Bhukay in support of his comrade.

Haasan ignored the gibe. All right, he said, let's forget about what will happen afterwards. Just tell me what you plan to do if you don't get through on the phone to the station. I'm not even asking you how you plan to find a telephone within reach of a rail track running through mango orchards.

Let us assume you have the receiver in your hand and your finger on the dial, but all you get is the engaged tone. How are you going to warn the station master?

Bhukay and Bihari began to look hunted. Haasan was implacable.

There are two possible arguments you can make in your favour, he continued. One, it is not your intention to derail the train or cause the death of its passengers. Now, intention in itself is no excuse. Two, you plan to back up your good intentions by ringing up the station master. But this is obviously not a cast-iron guarantee against derailment which could cause the deaths of countless innocents. So what is the answer? What is the answer where nothing is guaranteed and yet something must be done?

Do or Die, muttered Bhukay, quoting Gandhi in desperation.

It didn't work. The problem, as Haasan quickly pointed out, was that they would do but others would die. There was only one way of getting around the moral problem this posed: they had to find a practical way of taking responsibility for the terrible risk of derailment and death. And not just in some abstract, conscience-ridden way . . .

You must make this responsibility real, said Haasan.

Abruptly he left the cubicle leaving us to wonder how this might be achieved. We didn't have to wonder long because he returned quickly with another round of coffee and cutlets. The spy, he explained, would think it odd that we were sitting so long around one cup of coffee.

This time he sat in the adjacent cubicle with Ammi and Asharfi and picked up his lecture-inquisition from exactly where he had left it. We could hear him clearly but listening to an invisible person made Bhukay and Bihari look like disgruntled spiritualists at a seance: heads cocked to one side, eyes not really looking, ears tuned to the sounds of the other world.

The only way you can make responsibility real, said Haasan on resumption, is by taking the same chance that you are forcing the train's passengers to take. So the best plan is for Bhukay, Bihari and Masroor to tie themselves down to the track after disarranging it. That way, if the train isn't stopped in time to prevent derailment, they will go with it.

Two of the three saboteurs reached for their coffees and took great scalding gulps.

Haasan reprieved them. This is the ideal plan but it isn't, unfortunately, a practical one. There is one great flaw – who will tie the last man down? Who will guarantee that in the face of possible death, he will remain true to his pact with the others? Solidarity in extremis, said Haasan austerely, is rare.

Relief made Bhukay fertile.

I have a cow, he began. Or rather his father did, but Bhukay

had virtually grown up with it. It was a member of the family
. . . even now when age had dried its udders up, it was fed and
cared for. It would be a terrible loss but he was willing to make
the sacrifice: he would tether it to the track. And if the
warning about their sabotage didn't reach the engine driver,
he would be mortally responsible for the death of a cow. It
was a burden he was willing to take on.

Both cubicles were silenced by Bhukay's reckless courage.
But he wasn't finished. The cow could represent all of them
on that fateful track. It could be the sum of their collective
responsibility. Bihari could buy a share in it, so could
Masroor. It wouldn't mean the same to them, not being
Hindus, but it would still be appropriate. It could be like Id.
Yes, like Baqr Id where cattle were bought to be sacrificed.

In the context of that unreal conversation about an absurd
conspiracy, Bhukay's idea seemed plausible. Then Bihari
raised a theological objection.

If the train hits the cow, it will be killed with a single blow.
The meat will be jhatka, not halal.

Haasan had the last word.

No cows on railway tracks, he laid down. You are trying to
stop a riot, not start one.

There was silence again. Haasan dissolved it by reflecting
on an earlier suggestion. Perhaps he could tie the conspirators
to the track? Since he planned to accompany Bhukay and
Bihari, he could rope them down once their mission was
completed. And Masroor too, if he was there.

Amazingly Ammi and Asharfi had nothing to say about this
incredible idea. In my cubicle Bhukay and Bihari examined
their coffee cups and mopped the heat away. Again Haasan
rejected the idea. They might change their minds and resist
being tied down. But even if they kept their word and allowed
him to lash them to the rails, how would he feel if the train ran
them over in the end? He would go mad with guilt. Even if he
had only helped them come to terms with their responsibility,
he would relive for ever the nightmarish act of tying their
knots. No. He wouldn't do it. He wouldn't blight his life for
the sake of their scheme.

Our cubicle was now rank with the smell of sweat; where

before Bhukay and Bihari had been sweating with terror, they were now secreting rivers of relief. So when Haasan came back in with his final suggestion, they agreed without thinking. Like men reprieved from the guillotine, they were primed to say yes to anything.

Haasan suddenly pulled out from inside his uniform two sheets of yellow stamp paper with identical statements typed on them. They have been prepared by a lawyer, he said. They were confessions to this conspiracy. Once Bhukay and Bihari signed them, they would be returned to the lawyer for safe-keeping. If he learnt the next day that the train had been derailed, he would post the confessions to the Superintendent of Police, Lucknow City. After that, Bhukay and Bihari would be hunted men. Masroor too, if he reappeared – Haasan would carry the twin of the confessions that Bhukay and Bihari had signed.

They signed without reading what the closely typed sheet had to say, without wondering at the devious premeditation by which ready-to-sign confessions were magicked out of nowhere to clinch a solution that had seemingly emerged after long argument. They just signed.

Haasan pressed them for a time. After some calculations of distance, the rendezvous was fixed for 3.15 in the morning. Bihari had wanted to leave earlier because the site they had agreed with Masroor was fifty miles from Lucknow and hours away by bicycle. But Haasan informed them that he would be driving them there in the Ganjoo Stonely. They didn't argue. Nor did they stay for more coffee. They stopped long enough to confirm that they would meet Haasan outside the Lalbagh house at three – then they rushed through the bat-wing doors and were gone.

Looking satisfied, Haasan went across to join the ladies. I followed him. But when I entered the neighbouring cubicle, I couldn't see any women. There were three men there; Haasan and two little men in waiter's costumes minus the turbans. The two burqas, till recently Ammi and Asharfi, were spread like inkblots on the floor.

Changing Faces

I T WASN'T TILL we visited Lalbagh at teatime, till I actually saw them with my own eyes, that I was convinced of their uninterrupted existence. Haasan explained the sleight of hand that had puddled the burqas; he would have liked to draw the mystery out, to savour his great trick ending, but when he saw my hands begin to shake and my colour fade, he sat me down and told me how the thing was done.

Ammi and Asharfi had never been in the coffee house at all. Nor had Haasan been the only one in costume. Haasan-into-waiter and waiters-into-women . . . just a matter of putting on one turban and taking off two. The burqas helped, as did the de-cockaded littleness of the waiters (their size was why he had cast them), but these were just props. It was, he said grandly, all in the direction.

The coffee-house drama had been the means to an end. Two ends. One, to find Masroor, and two, to spike the scheme he had hatched. Once Haasan had his Masroor-in-hiding hunch, it was merely a question of pumping Bhukay and Bihari for the relevant place, the site of sabotage. That's why he had pencilled Ammi and Asharfi in, in silent roles. In the normal way, Bhukay and Bihari would never have given their rendezvous away, or agreed to let Haasan accompany them tonight. But the presence of a grieving mother and sister had forced their hand.

Unthinkable, though, to bring respectable women to a coffee house. Unnecessary too. Two burqas, two waiters, two family rooms and a little contrivance was all that it took to make the plotters sing. The rigmarole about Section 144 and government spies had helped quarantine the impostors in a separate cubicle, against the risk of conversation. The charade had been got up for an audience of two: Bhukay and Bihari.

And it had turned out to be, even if he said so himself, a considerable moment in theatre: the first entirely self-sufficient play – its audience built into its cast.

But what was the need for it? I asked. If the womenfolk couldn't come to the coffee house, the coffee house could have gone to the womenfolk. Why hadn't he just arranged for a meeting in the Lalbagh house?

Because Ammi and Asharfi were in no condition to receive visitors. When he had stopped over in the morning on the way to work, Ammi could hardly see or speak for weeping. But he wouldn't have taken Bhukay and Bihari there even if Ammi had been more composed – with Masroor gone there wasn't a man left in the house and there was such a thing as propriety. It wasn't as if Bhukay or Bihari were friends of Ammi; they were part of Masroor's acquaintance, not hers.

When we reached the Lalbagh house for tea, Ammi was her usual comfortable self. She was sitting in the middle of the drawing room, fitting tea-cosies on two fat silver tea-pots. The ground-glass windows of Ammi's bathroom, which had seen me off in the morning, were still burning orange when we crossed the courtyard.

Where's Sharfu? asked Haasan stupidly, as if it were she and not her brother who was lost. What? said Ammi absently. Oh. She's bathing.

Between Ammi's bowel movements at dawn and Asharfi's evening bath lay less than twelve hours, but epochs had ended and begun in that span. For me, the time before the ticket window now seemed like the world before time. Gandhi's rabble had made their move and punched my clock; I could almost hear my hair rustle and begin to grow.

Haasan summarized the coffee-house meeting, leaving out nothing, not even the impersonation. Ammi didn't mind. The only time she seemed concerned was when he came to the bit where he'd promised Bhukay and Bihari that he wouldn't interfere with their work of sabotage. Haasan reassured her. There would be no heroics – no track would be dismantled, no train derailed. Even without him to keep an eye on them, they were incapable of significant mischief. They didn't have the equipment and now, after his coffee-house lecture exposing the ethical vulnerability of their plan, they no longer had the will. The price they'd have to pay (by his prescription) for the armour of practical responsibility was so steep that it was demoralizing. They didn't have the stomach for sabotage any more.

Ammi wasn't convinced. What if Masroor turned up? Mightn't he talk them into it again? she asked, half hopeful at the prospect of finding her son, half fearful of the havoc he might wreak.

Haasan shook his head. If we find him, he said grimly, he won't have the chance to either talk or do. And if he won't listen to reason, we'll tie him up and bring him home.

Clearly, his promise not to interfere was one he didn't intend to keep. Only, counting Masroor, there were three of them – so if he wanted to bundle Masroor away by main force, who was there to do it; who were the 'we'?

I shouldn't have asked, especially not in the presence of our missing hero's mother and sister. Asharfi had just joined us looking damp and clean. Self-preservation should have kept me quiet – but the need to pick holes in Haasan's elaborate, misguided scheme made me rash.

Well, said Haasan thoughtfully, there will be you . . . and me. That's all the manpower necessary, he finished cheerfully, we don't need more than us.

What could I say? That I wasn't 'us' or 'we'? Just yesterday Asharfi had claimed me for the family: 'every inch a Ganjoo'. So it was natural for them to assume that I would be glad to help.

I might still have pleaded a headache or heatstroke or something, when Ammi made that impossible.

Asharfi will go with you, she said.

Wha-aat? asked Haasan unbelievingly.

Ammi nodded.

Haasan exploded into a frenzy of protest and reasons. Sabotage, mere girl, danger, dead-of-night, police arrest, the shame of it, etc.

Ammi was unmoved. Asharfi hugged her with excitement.

If he can take the risk, said Ammi, looking gratefully at me, for whom Masroor was a stranger, so can someone of his family.

67

Haasan erupted again, but she stood her ground.

Yes, Haasan bhaisahib was part of the family, more than family even, but she had the past to think of. Intezar's wife and Intezar's son had sat in the Lalbagh house and waited for him to return from his vanishment. They were still waiting. She wouldn't let history repeat itself. She would have gone herself but for the rheumatic knots in her knees. So Asharfi would stand in for the family – for Ammi and the absent Intezar. And if Masroor needed persuasion, Asharfi's presence would help – they had always been close.

Haasan gave in. He warned Asharfi that we'd pick her up in the car at three on the dot, and he expected her to be ready. Then, almost as an afterthought, he told Ammi that I would be moving in with him. Ammi said nothing; she either hadn't heard or she didn't care. Feeling a little hurt, I went up the stairs one last time to fetch my toothbrush. I didn't think it would be right for me to take the clothes Masroor had given and there was nothing else I owned. Except the thermos flask, which I had been carrying since the morning, strapped slantwise across my chest.

By the time we left the house, I was committed to Haasan's mad midnight sortie. I couldn't back out when Ammi had nominated her own daughter to the expedition. That left me just one way out – I had to talk Haasan out of his scheme between now and three o'clock. Partly, of course, because I was scared to death, but also because I was worried and guilty about the idiot premise on which Haasan had built his scheme: his hunch that Masroor hadn't vanished, but gone into hiding. Now that Asharfi was going with us I would never forgive myself if something happened to her. It was my fault. I'd planted the seed for this absurd enterprise in Haasan's head the evening before. I had flown this kite about Masroor in hiding and Haasan had tricked it out into a plan. But it had been intended as a kindness, no more. Prompted by Ammi's stricken face when the news of Masroor's disappearance had sunk in, I'd extemporized some words of comfort in the way I'd often seen my Dadi do in grieving houses. How could I have known that Haasan would take them seriously?

Given his name, I should have known. I vaguely knew that

Muslims in general and Shias in particular were liable to believe in Mahdis and Redeemers, currently in hiding, but programmed to turn up when the time was ripe. Perhaps the fact that my audience of three that evening was Muslim had subliminally prompted the Masroor-in-hiding fiction. Even so, I'd never intended things to go so far.

On that walk back to the coffee house, I tried to put matters right. I could have insisted on the truth of what I'd seen on the side of the truck that morning. But I didn't. First because I didn't want him to think me mad and second because last evening, in an effort to keep Ammi's spirits up, I had pretended that I could have been mistaken.

Instead, I stressed the improbability of the 'in-hiding' hypothesis. Why would he disappear without a word to his fellow conspirators? Even after reading the headlines about the Quit India resolution, he could have told Bihari across the road what his plans were. It wasn't as if the Amina Bazaar road was crawling with policemen looking out for him. That early in the morning there were hardly any people on it.

Haasan was not persuaded. He just kept walking in his splayed and leisurely way and turned right into the noble length of Hazrat Ganj. How do you explain it, then? he said finally.

He was kidnapped, I ventured. The British are so desperate about the Japanese now that they're abducting able-bodied men for the army. Masroor was shanghaied by that army truck and conscripted.

Haasan just shook his head. We were halfway down Hazrat Ganj now, less than five minutes from the coffee house. It would be impossible to change his mind once we reached it – the coffee house was, after all, his territory and the setting of his morning triumph.

Pressed for time, I screwed my courage up and explained to him that his belief that Masroor was in hiding owed much more to his Shia upbringing than to intuition.

That stopped him in his tracks. In fact he stopped so abruptly that the strollers behind us nearly ran him over.

How do you know that I'm a Shia? he asked wonderingly.

It wasn't hard. There was his name for one. Sunnis were less

69

likely to call themselves Hasan. And then his accent. His speech was full of double consonants and strenuous retroflex sounds: classically south Indian, especially the broad 'a' sound, by which sir became saar and Hasan became Haasan. His name and enunciation taken together pointed to Hyderabad, where the Nizam ruled over the largest urban concentration of Shias in Peninsular India. It also explained why he was in Lucknow. If a Hyderabadi Shia struck out northwards, his logical destination was Lucknow, the cultural heart of subcontinental Shi'ism. It was simple, really.

Haasan shook his head but didn't speak till we reached his quarters, which were directly above the coffee house. The room he used to sleep in had one cot, two chairs, one steel tumbler on the arm of the bigger chair, six clothes hooks in a row hung with checkered lungis, a large framed picture of a crisply clean-shaven man and a calendar.

He disappeared into the other room and returned in a lungi and kurta. Then he sat me down in a chair, fetched me a tumbler of water and said (quite sternly):

You shouldn't jump to conclusions.

Then he poured a tumbler of water down his throat from a great height and resumed his lecture.

I had to be insane, according to him, to believe that Muslims were more suggestible in the matter of hiding, concealment, I spy, vanishment, etcetera because they were subliminally acted upon by their faith in the Mahdi, the Redeemer in hiding. There was no danger of any Muslim mistaking a delinquent Masroor for the Rightly Guided One. Especially not Haasan.

Especially since he wasn't a Muslim.

The tumbler dropped out of my hand and wet the front of my trousers.

He looked at the spreading dampness with satisfaction and carried on. The only thing I had got right was the provenance of his accent. It was south Indian and so was he. He pronounced Haasan with a broad 'a' not because of a Dravidian inability to say Hasan, but for the simple reason that his name referred to a temple town in Mysore, and not Hussain's martyred brother. The broad 'a' came with the name – it wasn't optional. His full name wasn't Muhammad Ali Hasan or Ishaque Gibreel Hasan or Syed Ehteshamuddin Hasan – it was Haasan Yamanachar Narasimhamurthy. Ancestral place name, father's name and given name, in that order. His vanished friend Intezar was the first to call him Haasan; he hadn't been able to get his tongue round the other two.

I stared dumbly at him. He had to be telling the truth. His name was too elaborate to be extemporized.

H.Y. Narasimhamurthy, he ground out, remorselessly. Iyengar Hindu, not Shia Muslim.

He must have mistaken my speechlessness for scepticism because he suddenly pulled his kurta up and said: Look!

I looked . . . and quickly shut my eyes. Between his nipples and down to his navel ran raised and puckered scars in long straight lines that joined to make a swastika.

I opened my eyes and looked again – it was still there. Then Haasan of the temple town shrugged the kurta on again and the swastika vanished behind a veil of muslin.

But now I knew it was there like a title embossed on a hardback novel, hidden by a dust-jacket. I wanted the story. Why was this middle-aged Hindu from Mysore branded like a cow? Sitting in that room atop the coffee house I forgot about my schemes to get out of Lucknow, 1942. I just wanted to know how Haasan and his swastika got in.

It's a long story, he warned, but I knew he'd tell it by the way his face blurred over with nostalgia. I asked again. He hitched up his lungi, the better to cross his legs, and began.

His father moved from Haasan to Mysore, the capital of His Highness' kingdom, in 1910. Thanks to Mirza. He had been friends with Mirza in Central College, Bangalore. Then their careers forked: Mirza shinned up his tine to become Superintendent of Police, Mysore City, while Haasan Keshavamurthy Yamanachar, Haasan's father, found a clerk's job in the municipality of his native place, Haasan.

Luckily for Yamanachar, despite the responsibilities of a job, a wife and child (he had sired Haasan at age sixteen when the century was a year old), he kept in touch with his classmate.

Three years after becoming Superintendent, Mirza leapt again – this time into the heart of the palace bureaucracy; in his letter to Yamanachar he described the new position as assistant secretary to His Highness, Krishnajirao Wodiyar. Two years later, when he had consolidated his position and staked out his share of patronage, he invited his old friend to join the Public Works Department in Mysore City as one of its accountants. Yamanachar abandoned the municipality within the month: not only did the job mean four hundred rupees a year, four times his current salary, it also meant a career in the capital instead of a dead-end job in a district town.

Haasan was nine years old when the family shifted to Mysore. No one called him Haasan then. He wasn't called Narasimhamurthy either. The only name he answered to was Chikka. Little one.

I loved Mysore, said Haasan. After the mofussil tedium of Haasan, Mysore was a non-stop Ferris wheel, a blur of diversions. There were the Brindavan Gardens where the fountains danced to music. There was the new palace with enamelled pillars and gorgeous domes and elephant-sized chandeliers. There was the endless extravagance of the Dussehra procession every year, with the Maharaja bobbing in a golden howdah and the elephants tied with silken bags that caught their shit before it fell and blotched the road. And finally, there were the Turkas.

I'd never seen a Muslim before we shifted to Mysore, said Haasan, though I knew from Appa that Mirza was one. But not all Turkas were like Mirza. Some were quite poor, many wore little lace caps and none of them ever entered our house. None, that is, except Mirza, who sometimes came home with Appa. They sat in the hall and Mirza was served coffee in a silver tumbler, which, as soon as he left, Amma cleansed with burning coals before washing it in the normal way.

According to Mr T.C.A. Desikachar, Census Commissioner and Yamanachar's sponsor to the local Masonic Lodge, one in every six persons in Mysore City was a Turka. He worked this into the conversation every time he came home, which was often, and everyone he cited this figure to agreed that one in six was one too many. Once, long ago, before the reign of a demon called Tipu, there had been none.

It was during a picnic that the young Haasan learnt how there were so many Turkas now. Yamanachar had taken the family for a drive in the second-hand Lagonda he had bought that week. He drove them to the ruins of Seringapatam, Mysore's old capital when Tipu the Terrible was king. Now Seringapatam had the feel of a large village, lumbered with an inexplicably ambitious past. In the heart of the ruins, Haasan and his family came upon an old domed mosque in perfect repair, the Gol Gumbaz. The Friday prayers had just ended, so crowds of Muslims in white were streaming out of it, looking crisp and starched in their Jumma best.

I didn't know what a mosque was, said Haasan, half-defensively. I was only ten. His mother explained that the Gol Gumbaz was a Turka hatchery, that its dome was a mother egg, which went to work once a week on Fridays, and produced hundreds of freshly laid Turkas. He believed this for years.

Sometime during their second year in Mysore, Yamanachar brought home an aquatint of King George V and Queen Mary, a souvenir from Delhi, where he had gone as part of the Maharaja's retinue to attend the great Durbar. A year later Haasan stole it from its frame and gave it to Sabiha, who attended the girl's school adjacent to his, who was a Turka and whom he loved. Had he known then, he might have learnt to love another, but he had only ever seen men, and mostly bearded men, stream out of the Friday hatcheries and it had never occurred to him that Turkas could be girls. By the time he found out in 1915, he was too much in love to care.

I hardly ever spoke to her, confessed Haasan. Turka or not, she was a girl. But they met with their eyes each morning because till the end of middle school, girls and boys lined up together for morning assembly on the single playing field that both schools shared. Her row lined up next to Haasan's because they were the same age and her class was the female counterpart of his. Besides the aquatint, Haasan stole other things to give her, like the spoon from the set of silver utensils

73

he ate off at home, or the magically tensile spring from the broken mantel clock. She never refused a present, but neither did she ever say thanks or give him anything in return. But Haasan's love was true, so it needed neither word nor sign.

He later learnt that there were only two Muslim girls in that entire school. One was Sabiha and the other was her friend, Nafisa, Mirza's niece. Mirza, it turned out, was trying to set an example by sending Nafisa to school; to make it easier for her, he'd sponsored Sabiha as well, who was the daughter of his groom. Which was why the two of them were always ferried to and from school in a crested buggy. It also explained, though Haasan didn't know it then, why Sabiha disappeared.

I have a personal interest in disappearances, you see, said Haasan wryly. My first true love just vanished. In 1916, two years into the war, about which I knew little and cared less, Mirza decided he had done enough for the emancipation of women in general and Muslim women in particular. Nafisa was sixteen already; she was duly removed from the school and married off. Being a fair-minded man, he did the same by her classmate and companion, Sabiha, which is to say he married her off to a very respectable man of Shirazi descent, whose family had been horse traders in good standing with the princely courts of the Deccan for generations.

But in 1916 Haasan only knew that she had disappeared. Right through that year – or for at least two months of it – he was heartbroken. He lost his appetite, developed chronic constipation and took to spending hours in the lavatory. One day Yamanachar read him a lecture on irregular living in youth. Then he asked him if he had developed any habits, whether it was really pent-up turds that kept him in the lavatory . . . or other things.

He thought I was masturbating, running marathons with my fist, recalled Haasan, half-smiling. He began to look for girls for me before I went blind. I had just lost Sabiha to some hole in the world; the talk of marriage pushed me over the edge . . . into mutiny.

First he cut his top-knot off. He hoped his father would take the cane to him and give him reason to run away.

Yamanachar's eyes popped when he saw his son but he didn't reach for his stick. With awful reproach he reminded Haasan that his forebears had once been priests at the temple in Tirupati. That his lineage entitled the family to one three-hundredth part of the profits made on the sales of the temple's legendary laddoos. That only an immature adolescent would desecrate this great tradition. That more than ever he, Yamanachar, was certain a wife would help Haasan grow up.

That night, said Haasan, I thought of running away. But Appa hadn't hit me or threatened to lock me into my room, so running away seemed . . . too much.

He did the next best thing. The next morning he applied to join Mysore's traffic constabulary. Fortunately, the recruiting inspector didn't recognize him as his father's son or he might have referred Haasan's application to him. He gave his name as one Bindignavalle Kesavan Pavankumar, and upped his age to eighteen. The force was delighted to take on an educated youth and inside a week he had been assigned point duty at the Malleshwaram crossing, from nine in the morning till noon. I asked for the job, said Haasan, because I knew Appa passed the traffic policeman's kiosk every day on his way to work.

The first day on the job was uneventful. Appa either took another route to work or didn't recognize me in the flared shorts and regulation turban. I didn't have the time to look around. Directing traffic, even in 1916 Mysore, was a full-time job for a novice policeman. I wouldn't have noticed him the next day either, if he hadn't run the Lagonda into the kerb, trying to get a better look at me. I went on waving my arms about while he reversed and carried on to work. He was probably too embarrassed to acknowledge me. But dozens of his friends and a few of his enemies went through the Malleshwaram crossing and had no difficulty recognizing Yamanachar's son. By the evening, all Mysore knew and so did Mirza, when my father went despairingly to him for help.

Despite having achieved the dizzy eminence of Huzur Secretaryship (just one rung short of Dewan) Mirza always welcomed Yamanachar as a friend in deference to that college past where all men were equal. He summoned the Superintendent of Police and had Haasan discharged on a technicality: flat feet.

But he also gave his friend some advice. He advised him to send Haasan away from Mysore to some other town, any other town where Yamanachar had a responsible relative. Preferably a town in British India, because that was where all the jobs were now. Let him do his matric there, he urged. He has to get used to the world outside – he might have to make his living in it.

The absence of one Turka had blighted Haasan's life; now the advice of another changed it for ever.

Mirza opened out the world for me, said Haasan, his eyes far away. I'll always be grateful. I think the advice he gave Appa had something to do with his being a Turka. His ancestors had wandered from Meshed to Mysore – so travel must have been for him the tested cure for restlessness.

Whatever his views on Turkas, Yamanachar enjoyed deferring to his superiors and the Huzur Secretary was an extremely superior person. So within a week, he had arranged for Haasan to be sent to Calicut on the west coast to complete his education. Yamanachar had a poor widowed cousin there, his mother's brother's son, Ramanujam, whose poverty was compounded by daughters. Yamanachar's offer of maintenance money for his son drew an enthusiastic yes by return post and barely had the letter arrived than Haasan was bundled off on his voyage to maturity.

But unknown to his father, Haasan didn't head direct to Calicut. He had decided to make the most of his first long journey alone, and had worked out a hugely roundabout itinerary. Measured in a straight line, Calicut couldn't have been much more than a hundred and fifty miles from Mysore, but the route Haasan dreamed up involved a journey several times that length, that took him three days farther into his seventeenth year.

First the train to Bangalore, then east to Bowringpet and down to Jollarpet, where he spent the night illegally in the second-class retiring room on a third-class ticket. From there the train went west and ploughed through boring fields all day till it reached Mettupallayam in the early evening. This time he slept on the platform because the only retiring room in Mettupallayam station was tenanted by an irascible white planter.

It was still dark the next morning when Haasan climbed into a small metre-gauge express which huffed its way through flatlands that slowly tilted and rearranged themselves into hills and the hills closed in on the train. For an hour it moved through a valley so moist that it seemed to sweat, then, just as Haasan had begun to take the great green walls on either side for granted, they disappeared. The train had breached the Western Ghats and chugged into the rampant green of Malabar.

I nearly missed getting off at Palghat, said Haasan, because the main junction was in Olavakkot across the river and the train only stopped for four minutes at Palghat station. I had a friend in Palghat's Victoria College, an old schoolmate two years my senior, called Photo Chetty. Photo had lots of money because his father was the Kodak agent for Madras Presidency. I spent two days in his hostel room and got drunk for the first time in my life at his expense. Then, reluctantly, I caught the train from Olavakkot junction to Calicut.

My father had told me, with some embarrassment, that Ramanujam ran an eating place. He didn't any more. He was a cross between a cook and a motorized vendor. Right through the week his daughters helped him make non-perishable foods like murukku, chatnipudi, bottles of gojju, large tins of pickle and sacks of banana crisps. Then on Tuesdays and Fridays, he mounted one of the most ancient motorcycles in Peninsular India, a Triumph, filled its sidecar with the eatables and hawked them from house to brahmin house in Calicut. This was what he was doing when first I went to live with them. His daughters, though they were twenty-one and eighteen years old, were unmarried. There was an acute shortage of Hebbar Iyengar boys in Calicut. The eligible ones were unaffordable; besides, the girls were dark.

It had worried their father once, they told me, but by the time I came to live with them, he was too busy scratching out

77

a living to care. Also I suspected they were so valuable to him as unpaid labour for his pickle and preserve making that he didn't really want to marry them off. He used me in exactly the same way. None of the maintenance money that my father sent me went towards college fees for the very good reason that Ramanujam never made the slightest push to enrol me. He apprenticed me instead to his trade, which mainly meant that there was an extra hand helping Sujatha and Vishala in the kitchen courtyard where the cutting, the drying, the stirring and chopping was done. I didn't mind; I didn't want to study any more and there was some satisfaction in knowing that my father wasn't getting his money's worth, that he was losing the equivalent of his annual share of Tirupati's laddoo receipts. At that time I held him obscurely responsible for Sabiha's disappearance.

But more than that, Haasan was content with his lot because of the sisters. Predictably dissatisfied with their spinsterish state, they had tended their discontent into a little garden patch which they manured with longing and frustration. Vishala, the younger one, would occasionally smile or express enthusiasm but Sujatha's every waking expression and movement was improvised on the theme of martyred discontentment. It didn't bother Haasan because they were excitingly made and curious, and he was the only young male they had ever been thrown together with. But even after Haasan and Sujatha had danced the agonizingly oblique mudras of attraction and consent, even when they began regularly making savage oral love in the triangular store room beneath the courtyard stairs, she never once allowed herself unfettered fulfilment; even as she lurched in orgasm the only sound that emerged from her was a kind of sinister hissing. Vishala was easier but she drew the line at taking off her clothes or reciprocity, so she allowed his groping and feeling and tweaking through layers of cloth, she opened or forgot to close her mouth when Haasan kissed her, but beyond that she permitted herself no response, and even the rest for no more than a minute at a time.

Their only other diversion was creative adulteration of the stuff they made, especially the tamarind chutney or gojju which, besides being Ramanujam's most popular item, had a rich brown colour in which all manner of things could be safely blended. The root of this adulteration campaign was Ramanujam's brahminical obsession with purity. Haasan and the sisters were forbidden to use the left hand to stir a cooking pot on pain of starting all over again. The kitchen was washed six times a day. Sneezes, unavoidable when masalas were fried, were entirely forbidden; one achoo in his hearing meant throwing that batch away. Production slowed down each time either girl had her period because she was automatically banned from the kitchen area and confined to her room.

Everything they made tasted wonderful but the business was doomed. Most of Ramanujam's clients were Tamil brahmins who had come searching for the chimerical riches of the timber boom. As they died or drifted off, his business shrank and in the two years that Haasan lived there, it barely managed to feed the family. In a place like Palghat where migrant brahmins had lodged themselves in dense, compact settlements, he might have made a livelihood out of being a cook as Palghat Iyers had, but in Calicut it was a desperate struggle. Had he diversified into garlic and onions, had he worked a larger market, say the Mappila Muslims, he might have made ends meet, but for Ramanujam even tomatoes were taboo, so where was the hope of that?

By the cold weather of 1919, said Haasan, there were days and weeks when we didn't eat enough. The only thing that kept him in Calicut was Sujatha and the sullen, salty squeezing in the store room. Also, Haasan knew that his father's monthly postal order was the only hedge between the family and destitution. Ramanujam was deaf to any suggestion that in the interest of production, his standards of ritual hygiene be relaxed. In fact the worse things got, the more dementedly finical he became about the cooking. It was as if, having taken a beating at every step, having sold every last thing he owned to keep starvation at bay, he was now defending the last thing left to him, his brahminical essence: purity.

Hunger is a galvanizing thing. The discontent of the sisters bubbled into rage. Rage didn't mean confrontation. They said nothing to their father; their fury was expressed in more furtive, yet more appropriate ways. Even as their father tried to embalm himself in the formaldehyde of purity, the girls began to make the food more interesting with unorthodox garnishes. They began in the way common to discontented cooks: they sweated into the food and then took heart and spat into it. After that they broke loose, as each tried to outdo the other in dreaming up the grossest violations of their father's ideal of purity. Colds, coughs, periods – every emission, every secretion was pressed into the service of their rage. Afraid of what they might do next, Haasan asked him once to vary the cuisine, to compromise. Ramanujam just looked at him. He'd have rather died.

And then he did. On the ninth of April, I remember it perfectly, said Haasan, he stopped eating. For two weeks before that date he had given up loading the Triumph and hawking our food. Then he gave up food. After three days of that, he forsook water. At the age of sixty-seven, in perfectly good health, Ramanujam renounced the world and ritually starved himself to death in twenty-three days. Towards the end he was so dehydrated he couldn't urinate, so the poison ate up his empty insides and for days he sat hunched on the floor, ennobled by pain. Two children, no friends, no savings, and still he died an exalted man, convinced of his salvation.

A week from the day they burned the skin and bones, I took the Triumph out along another route.

Haasan rode east-south-east away from the coast into the interior, stopping at Manjeri, Tirurangadi and other towns in the Mappila Muslim country to find a larger market for the food. Like the route, the food was different too. Fat, naked cloves of garlic pickled in mustard oil and chillies. Clams in vinegar. And canned meat. Yes! said Haasan. I swear. We were canning meat on the Malabar coast in 1920.

The cannery in Calicut was Photo Chetty's father's brain-child. He had set it up halfway through the Great War, vaguely reasoning that armies on the move needed preserved foods. Mr Chetty was a buccaneer among businessmen and his enthusiasms always carried him away. He ordered Nicholas Appert's great treatise on canning (written to help feed men in another, older war) in a good English translation.

He studied each advance in the history of the canning process from Appert to the Englishman Durand (who replaced the former's sealed bottle with a can), down to the frontiers of contemporary canning, the open-top can invented in Europe in 1908, which in 1918, Haasan pointed out, was barely a decade ago. Having read every last word on the business, he mail-ordered the machines, built a pukka tiled and plastered factory in Calicut because it was on the coast, close to the fish and the shipping, and began canning, confident that the contracts would come.

At first he canned indiscriminately. He was so impressed by the time-retarding power of the process that he canned a batch of living prawns in an effort to prolong their lives. For a while he was possessed by a scheme to can the holy water of the Ganga so that it could be sold in its pristine state to distant Hindus. Then, in the very nick of time, the day before he was about to order a dozen tankers of Ganga water by rail, it was brought to his notice by his son, Photo Chetty, that the holy river's water was sought after precisely because it never went bad. Canning it could only be the act of an unbeliever.

After this he tempered his passion with his native business sense and concentrated on canning seafood and meat. He never got the war contracts that had been his early inspiration, but he found a steady internal demand for his sardines because it turned out that the English preferred the taste of canned sardines to fresh ones. They were also sentimental about canned beef, which in their dialect, for reasons Mr Chetty never understood, was called potted meat.

Photo Chetty put in a word for me and his father let me have the canned beef at a discount. I peeled the labels off. Not that my Mappila market would have minded but I didn't want the girls to know I was trafficking in flesh. Especially beef. The new route served us well. The canned meat sold briskly at my discounted prices, the garlic pickle was a great success. In six months our sales quadrupled and I fell into a routine of two-day marketing trips on the Triumph over weekends.

The sisters had turned pious after Ramanujam's death. In death, or in the manner of his death, he achieved spiritual celebrity. It began with the neighbours coming in to hang garlands on the sepia portrait of him that Photo Chetty had blown up and framed as a favour to Haasan. It developed into a regular pilgrimage where perfect strangers from beyond the town limits came to pay their respects. The orphaned sisters overcame their astonishment and joined in with gusto. A fog of incense filled the house; prayers and hymns and chants became so frequent that they sometimes overlapped.

Sujatha and Vishala had money to spend for the first time in many years. They bought blue-white solitaires and temple saris, even brassieres. I never saw them wear the saris or the diamonds – these were stored away in their wedding arsenals. Not that I saw the brassieres – as first votary of her father's cult, Sujatha now wrestled me in the store room with her blouse on. Ramanujam's picture, though, was with us all the time, his touched-up eyes luminous with beatitude.

But the next winter this new-found prosperity disappeared. It was the year of the great rebellion and business didn't just slacken, it disappeared. The troubles coincided with the boundaries of Haasan's new market: it was the Mappilas who bought his cans and pickles and it was the Mappilas who tried to create the Kingdom of God in Malabar in six bloody months. The army sealed south Malabar off, so Haasan backslid into vegetarian orthodoxy and banana chips. We had to live, said Haasan.

In December he heard rumours of British garrisons being put to flight by mobs of rampaging Muslims. Photo Chetty wrote from Palghat to say that his great aunt's niece's son knew a forest officer, who, with his own eyes, had seen the rebels forcibly convert a Nambudiri brahmin family to Islam. Being brahmins, the expatriates in Calicut felt this rumour more keenly than others. Being literate, they petitioned the Governor of Madras Presidency for protection. Being timid, they formed vigilante squads and falteringly patrolled the town and nothing happened. By April the rising had been ground down and in June Haasan took to the road again.

Besides the food he took with him a few precautions.

These were a beard recently grown, trimmed Muslim-fashion and a small lace cap. He also took another name along in case . . . Ali Musaliar, a label both pious and easy to remember.

I'd planned a longer trip than usual, recalled Haasan, three days instead of the usual two, in the hope that the shortages of the last six months would have enlarged the demand for choice food. It turned out to be a silly assumption. Everywhere I went I found sullen indoor people and rumpled, rubbled settlements. Somewhere along the way the British had taken to exemplary destruction, so the Mappila townships were too busy rebuilding to have the time or money for travelling vendors. At Manjeri, usually my best market, I sold two packets of banana chips. That afternoon I decided to cut short my trip and return to Calicut. The trips to the Mappila country would have to wait on better times.

I almost didn't stop at Garudapuram because its only eating place was a fanatically vegetarian enterprise where brahmins looped with sacred thread served the food and oppressed-looking lads in torn dhotis took the used plates away. Its squeaky cleanness had nothing to do with hygiene and everything to do with a driving ritual purity which offended me because it was a reminder of Ramanujam's suicidal fastidiousness, of Amma's laborious coal fire purification of Mirza's silver tumbler, of – in some oblique but pressing way – my hopeless love for his daughter's friend, the translucent Sabiha.

But the Triumph was so hot it was scorching the skin off my calves and knees where my lungi had ridden up. So I shelved my principles, parked the motorcycle by the hand pump and found an empty table in the eatery. I asked for a glass of rasam and a thali and then stepped outside to the hand pump to wash the dirt of the journey off. When I returned I sensed there was something not quite right because the food was brought to me not by a threaded brahmin but by one of the torn-lungi brigade. Also there was a cockroach swimming in my rasam. I looked up at the boy who had served me. His thin, sullen face had made room for a snarl of anticipatory relish. I looked around – no one was eating. Then, from the kitchen, connected to the eating room by a door-less entrance, emerged a square man, running to fat, wearing wavy black hair, a bristling but subtly unmilitary moustache, a dhoti rucked up to his knees and a red checkered Bleeding Madras shirt several times too small for him. He was the cook. I pointed at the cockroach silently. He ignored the question.

Where have you come from? he asked abruptly.

Manjeri, I answered, without thinking.

A knowing sibilance ran round the hall. There was silence for a long while, so I pointed out the cockroach again. The cook picked up the tumbler and inspected it at unnecessary length. He looked at the others in the room in the knowing manner of a grandstanding bully, then turned to me with his face, like a Kathakali actor's, knitted into the stylized lines of Wrath.

Manjeri, he repeated heavily. What is a cockroach for you? For your kind I should serve the rasam with a cow's udders or your father's foreskin!

Then the coffee was in my eyes. Scalded and blinded, I was hit on the side of the head and then in my stomach. Someone kicked my jaw, another my temple. I must have stayed semi-conscious because I can remember the others closing in around me and kicking me in the ribs a few times. Someone shouted cut it off, cut it off and another one laughed and someone else said no . . . and then that terrible line of fire and pain spread across my chest . . .

It was perfectly dark and deserted when Haasan woke on the road outside. The skin on his chest and stomach felt scorched and swollen but he couldn't see what they had done because it was a moonless night and Garudapuram didn't run to gas-lit streets. Bent over, he staggered to the Triumph, which was still intact. Kicking it into life set off great spasms of pain across his chest, but then it was done and as the engine idled he examined by the dim light of his head-lamp the running weal of discoloured blood and scab and skin. Two angular 'S' figures joined in the middle. They had etched him with the logo of their faith.

This swastika.

The percolator whistled and Haasan broke off to fetch us coffee. He waited till I'd tasted it for sweetness before taking up the tale again.

84

In the weeks of pain it took for the scabs to form properly, he often wished that they had lifted his lungi and looked. And seen that he was already a member of their flock, that further markings would be redundant. But it was his fault that he'd been mistaken for a Muslim. The initial markings had been his: cap, lungi and the careful beard. He had simplified himself into a cut-out Muslim. The cook had simply gone by appearances.

For months after the wounds healed, Haasan felt so depressed he wouldn't shit in days. But once every three days or so he forced it all out because it crowded out his inner man on which he wished to brood. He felt mixed up. He hadn't liked being himself because that had meant top-knot, sacred thread, vegetarianism and a fetish about purity. It hadn't been comfortable being Ali Musaliar either. In the end he brought himself around by pumping his heart, his mind and his inner self full of a love for essential humanity, unclassified, unclothed.

But he didn't know how to put this love to work. It welled and lipped and sloshed within him and made him feel pent-up. There was no one in Calicut to talk to. His dead uncle's daughters were full-time servants of his posthumous aura. The donations of a growing band of devotees meant they weren't dependent upon the Triumph and Haasan any more.

Sometimes Photo Chetty and he split a bottle of rum and once Haasan took him in the sidecar all the way to Ooty, where they bet on horses and won. Sometimes he thought of home in Mysore, of Amma and Appa, and ached with longing, though he knew he couldn't go back to that narrow town sewn up with spacious streets. Not yet.

But I needed something to do, said Haasan with remembered urgency. Hawking cans and preserves on the Triumph was no longer an option – my nerve had gone. The daughters didn't need me – from being the provider I had gone directly to being the poor relation. Then, accidentally, Photo Chetty's father gave me a vocation.

He had diversified. He bought the old theatre at the insolvency auctions, outbidding Vedagraham Bioscope and Talkies Ltd, ripped out the seats and the proscenium and laid out rows of long tables flanked by running benches on the floor. The part of the hall that had been the wings and the stage was partitioned off and made into a kitchen. It was an extraordinary eating place, the first ever of its kind. There were no proper meals served, no large metal thalis with real food like rice and rasam and papad. The kitchen only produced little foods, snacks. There were sets of small stacked dosas, idlis, vadas, but also mince cutlets, sandwiches, a curious pumpkin sauce in smeared bottles and listless omelettes made dosa-fashion. But its single greatest attraction was that a single cup of cheap grey coffee bought unlimited tenancy at a table. Which was why Mr Chetty called it a coffee house. The Queen Victoria Coffee House.

Haasan was taken on as a waiter, which meant long hours, six days a week, but the months he spent there through the monsoon and winter of 1922 added up to a wonderfully happy time. Serving those cheap, hybrid foods in the flamboyance of a coffee house waiter's uniform to thin young men who never stopped arguing brought contentment to Haasan's furrowed soul.

When Mr Chetty saw that his brainchild was an unqualified success, his enthusiasm became missionary zeal. He decided, like his Malayali predecessor, Sankara, to memorialize his genius by planting a coffee house in every corner of the subcontinent. The first of the branches was the Imperial Coffee House in Hazrat Ganj. That's how I came to Lucknow. He needed one of us in Lucknow to tend it in its early days – there was nothing left for me in Calicut, so I volunteered.

So now I knew. Having accounted for his presence in Lucknow, Haasan stopped. But he stopped in the city he knew in the early nineteen-twenties, not the one he lived in now. Which meant he had left the best bits out: his first meeting with Intezar, if he ever went back to Mysore, Sujatha's wedding – if it ever happened, the loose end about Sabiha, Mr Chetty's other coffee houses, Intezar's disappearance. . . In another time, I might have urged him on. But not in August 1942. He couldn't, not with the best will in the world, have brought the story up to date for me.

He announced that he was going to nap for a couple of

hours to cope with the scheduled exertions of the early morning. I promised to wake him up if he overslept. He began to snore almost immediately. The steady rhythms of his sleep were infectious; ten minutes of listening had me nodding off. I shook myself awake, washed my face and drank the tepid decoction in the percolator. Then I picked up the book by Haasan's bedside and settled down to read. It was Gandhi's autobiography, *My Experiments with Truth.* I chose it over the competing claims of the day's newspaper and a pamphlet explaining the economic infeasibility of Pakistan (should it come about), because like Haasan's account of his life, the Mahatma's autobiography had the great merit of ending in 1921.

We drove to Lalbagh in the Ganjoo Stonely that had been in Haasan's care ever since Intezar vanished in 1927. Masroor had been too young to drive at the time, so Ammi had given the responsibility for its upkeep to Haasan. She never once thought of selling it; it had to be kept in readiness for Intezar's return.

On the way we first picked up Bihari and Bhukay at the Lalbagh roundabout. It was a clouded night, and Haasan had doused the headlights to escape notice. Bhukay was carrying a large crowbar, two inches thick, and Bihari had slung a clanking sack across his chest. They hadn't formally abandoned their plans of sabotage but their sweaty silence smelt (it was too dark to read their faces) of nervousness. This made me hopeful.

Haasan kept the engine idling while I ran down the lane and knocked softly on the courtyard door. It opened at once. Asharfi was dressed in a burqa as Haasan had told her to be – it would keep her from being recognized in case there was trouble. Also Bhukay and Bihari were virtual strangers. She hugged her mother, who clung to her, then let her go without a word. The door closed behind us and we hurried to the car.

Haasan pointed the car westward and it wasn't long before the city was left behind. We might have gone quicker still but the Stonely was an old car and Haasan was a self-taught driver who drove slowly in the top gear. Our progress was marked by metallic clamour and terrible stalling sounds which carried for miles around and made a nonsense of his carefully doused headlights.

It was an oddly made car, with more room in the front than the back, so Bhukay and I shared the front seat with Haasan, while Asharfi and Bihari had the little pit behind us. I was sitting in the middle, which meant bracketing the stick shift with my thighs, so it was just as well that Haasan didn't believe in changing gears. Asharfi, fired by the prospect of finding Masroor, sat hunched forward, her elbows propped on the back of my seat, her chin resting on her hands, smelling wonderfully of some delicate sandalwood soap. She had flung the veil flap of her burqa over her head and the uncovered crescent of her face in profile was so lovely that I looked away.

Half an hour into the expedition my bladder was taut with tension about everything that could go wrong. Each time Haasan, still driving blind, blundered into a pot-hole or lurched off the edge of the road, I nearly pissed myself. Given controlled circumstances (and no Asharfi in the back seat) I could have pissed clean over the windscreen of the convertible Stonely and the winged griffin on the nose of the bonnet, without wetting either.

It began to rain gently but Haasan didn't stop to put the roof into place, neither did he switch on the head-lamps to improve visibility. The Stonely didn't feature parking lights, so Haasan was navigating by the smudged light of an overcast moon. Over some stretches, Bhukay and Bihari leaned over the side and shouted our bearings relative to the edges of the road. Even so Haasan went over the side of the road a couple of times and the jolting nearly undid me. With the gear-stick in between, even the comfort of crossing my legs and squeezing my thighs together wasn't available to me. I wondered how much wetter the rain would have to get to let me piss unseen.

As the drive wore on, Asharfi removed her chin from the seat and settled back. Bhukay had begun to doze on my left and when I twisted around to look at Bihari, he was grinding his teeth in a feverish coma. A thin sheet of sleep settled over the car, as fine and porous as a mosquito net; some sounds filtered through, dying night-time sounds that rose and faded like weak transmissions on the shortwaves.

On that last leg of the journey the road and the rail track ran parallel to each other, separated by perhaps half a mile of mango orchards. A few furlongs short of our destination, the car splashed through a puddle of greater than average depth and immediately began to gasp and stall. Grimly determined, Haasan nursed it through its convulsions till we had covered the distance, then he drove it off the road under the unnecessary shade of a wayside tree and cut the engine. He put up the Stonely's hood. The carburettor was waterlogged; it would take a while to dry.

No one looked concerned – there was no urgency now. Bhukay and Bihari showed none of the purposeful enthusiasm of committed saboteurs. They didn't reach for the crowbar or their sack of track-dismantling tools, they didn't even move to open their doors. The worm of scrupulous doubt set burrowing by Haasan in the coffee house had gobbled what remained of their resolve.

Their paralysis left Asharfi and Haasan free to look for Masroor. Asharfi rushed out of the car, repeatedly asking Bihari if this was the place, alertly scanning the lifting darkness for tell-tale signs of Masroor. Spurred by Asharfi's enthusiasm, Bhukay and Bihari disembarked and followed Haasan's lead in plunging into the stand of mango trees that separated us from the rail line. Haasan's plan was to climb on to the elevated embankment on which the rail track ran; from that vantage point they would stand a better chance of spotting Masroor. Sitting in the car, I watched them disappear into the murk. I should have been pleased that sabotage was no longer on our agenda, that the track on which my saviour train would one day come to take me home would stay intact. But this distant prospect of a happy ending did nothing to lift the terrible sense of anti-climax that weighed me down. Nothing was going to happen tonight: not sabotage, not the recovery of Masroor. They were wasting their time – Masroor was part of the surface area of an army truck.

I tried to frame my listlessness in a grander ennui. It was, perhaps, the jadedness of hindsight? Sated by omniscience? It was a nice idea but given the lunatic unpredictability of my own life in '42 it didn't explain much. I was just disappointed. So much had happened in the last forty-eight hours – Masroor's disappearance, the coffee-house masquerade, Haasan's odyssey, the alarums of our midnight drive – that it seemed a shame that the excursion was set to whimper out. Nothing seemed urgent or pressing any more – not even my bladder. In the end I followed them to the embankment. Not to participate in the charade of Masroor-spotting, but to be a vigilant spectator, to watch the train with its precious cargo of history chug by, on the rails and still on schedule.

It was four o'clock, so the train must have passed Unnao station – according to Bihari, it would pass by this place in less than fifteen minutes. I shivered; there was a damp, monsoonal sharpness to the wind sweeping out of the orchards and over the track. I climbed the stepped stone buttress that shored up the embankment and joined the others.

After ten useless minutes of looking about, Haasan accepted defeat and prepared to go home. But Asharfi looked so stricken that he decided to let her play at look-out a little longer while he returned to the car to see if it was functional again. Before he left he told her sternly that she was to get off the embankment the moment the train came into view. Bhukay and Bihari trailed after him. That left Asharfi and me standing pointlessly on the track, under a dark early morning sky, now marbled by streaks of pink and grey.

The track began to thrum – the train was on its way. Asharfi glanced at me for confirmation, then swept the track and orchards with a look – as if the tell-tale tremble of the coming train heralded Masroor. In the distance I dimly heard the car cough into life. There was a muffled clang as the lifted hood slammed shut and I turned to see Haasan pulling out the crank. He waved at us but I turned away to watch Asharfi moving down the track. She was looking about her as she walked, more frenzied now, more desperate as the time left for her brother's scheduled re-entry ran short.

Get off that rail line, you can look from here, called two voices in chorus; Haasan had sent Bhukay and Bihari to fetch us. The vibration was stronger now and their voices came to me in a fluctuating way. From some remote place ahead of me I thought I heard a chuffing roar.

Asharfi had gone farther in the direction of the coming train and stopped. The train swung into view, its face a black round set with a glowing eye. The cloudbanks had split and the cracks between them glowed with the radiance of the hidden sun like still, pink lightning. The clouds shaded into the smoke rising from the funnel – breath by breath the looming train was puffing out the sky.

Asharfi was still standing on the track looking expectantly over the side like a heroine in a suicide scene waiting for directions. I was slow to start, but there was no danger yet because the train was safely distant and Asharfi just twenty steps away. I began to walk towards her through the roaring sound; behind me, faintly, I heard Bhukay and Bihari shout, I heard someone hurrying up the steps of the buttress which I had left some way behind. Then she turned around and screamed and the splendour of the scene dissolved to let me know this was a nightmare. Even as I raced towards her and the blinding, searching, moving sun, my insides melted and whistled out into my trousers.

A yard away I made to grab her hand but she had turned to rush into my arms so my fingers closed upon her burqaed breast. So even as we leapt over the side, as my clutching hand went soft with shock, as my piss-wet trousers cooled against the rushing air, the world exploded with disapproval and the night was whitewashed by a flash that flew us yards across the side, into the orchard.

It was a bomb. When I could see again, the buttress and a section of the embankment had been superseded by a smoking pit of ruined things. It was all clearly lit by the head beam of the train, which was a furlong or so away and wasn't moving. I must have been unconscious for some minutes because already there was a crowd of passengers inspecting us and the damage, marvelling at their escape. Asharfi was getting up from where she had fallen, three yards away from me. She had lost her hood and veil and the rest of the burqa was in tatters. It was a bomb.

So: there had been no need of Bhukay, Bihari or the still missing Masroor. Some intrepid party of Quit India patriots had done their job for them. Only . . . where were Bhukay and Bihari? They weren't visible in the angle of the beam and anything outside it was pitch-black in contrast, impossible to see. Suddenly there were men in uniforms about, with torches, and it seemed to me that they were sizing us up. I didn't know enough about colonial uniforms to tell if they were army or police. Perhaps the authorities had begun assigning security guards to trains because of the Quit India troubles. I backed away towards Asharfi and took her hand, trying to organize my concussed wits. Scorched, bruised, clothes shredded, we were clearly not passengers and any other class of person in this situation was automatically suspect. Sooner or later, these uniformed men who were currently examining the mangled track would return to us.

I heard Haasan's voice. Haasan! I'd forgotten him. I looked in the direction of the whisper – he was three trees away, frantically miming stealth. Relieved at knowing what to do, I pulled Asharfi slowly towards the cover of the trees. Just as we turned and began to run, there was a shout and a commotion – someone had spotted us. Haasan led the way and I brought up the rear with Asharfi in between – and how we ran. Neither she nor I were certain of our balance after the blast, so we stumbled regularly. I even ran into a tree but so pressing was the instinct to flee that I nipped my bleeding nose with two fingers to stanch the flow, rose to a half-squat and resumed running.

We made the car comfortably ahead of the men in uniform, whoever they were. They had just broken clear of the trees when we slammed the doors shut. The Stonely started at a turn of the key, Haasan swung it round and like homing birds we raced towards Lucknow.

2000 A.V.

THAT EARLY MORNING when we fled the bombed-out rail track at Unnao, there were just two thoughts in my mind as the Stonely bucketed its way down the pot-holed road to Lucknow. One was unspoken but I knew the other two were thinking it as well: what had become of Bhukay and Bihari? Had they been thrown clear of the track like Asharfi and me or had the bomb gone off under their feet and broadcast them in little jigsaw bits into the flanking orchards? Or had we left them crippled to be picked up by the law?

Not being a practical thought at the time, it wasn't discussed and I tucked it into the back of my mind to make room for the second thought: Banaras. It was a thought whose time had come. The track on which my saviour train was to come one day was gone, wrecked by marauding patriots. Nor could I wait on healing time to join the track and run the train again – I was an outlaw now, my face etched on uniformed minds, wanted for the capital offence of violent sabotage, for subverting the state, for treason. There was no going back – the past had claimed me for its own.

But the thought of Banaras kept me from despair. It reminded me of first things. I had set out that evening in that distant epoch to sink my grandmother's ashes at Kashi. And that is what I would do. Once we reached Lucknow, I would recover the flask and head for Banaras as if 1942 had never happened. In that city of guaranteed salvation, in that vestibule to moksha-filled eternity, time was trivial and some mislaid decades were as specks of nothing. I would tip Dadi's ashes into the Ganga at Dasashwamedh Ghat, never mind 1942, and keep faith with my time.

Haasan had been making plans as well. We didn't go directly to the Lalbagh house. Instead he drove the car to the shed behind the coffee house where it was usually garaged, wiped the tell-tale mud off its wheels and covered it with a tarpaulin. Meanwhile I raced up to his room and retrieved my flask. From there we walked to Lalbagh. Down Hazrat Ganj we went, trying merely to stroll, sweeping the street with furtive eyes, seeing in every milkman and crack-of-dawn geriatric a plain-clothesman tipped off by wireless.

When Ammi opened the door she clapped her hand to her mouth and swayed, which is when we realized that Asharfi and I had walked down the main street of Lucknow in our singed and tattered state. Haasan sent us off to tidy up. By the time we returned, Ammi and he had worked everything out. Haasan would stay in Lucknow, managing the coffee house as if nothing had happened. He was in no danger of arrest because the police had never got a good look at him.

He didn't think that Asharfi or I were likely to be picked up either because a brief inspection by torchlight of two dishevelled faces was unlikely to result in recognition. But there was the outside possibility of identification, so Ammi and Asharfi would retire to their orchards in Malihabad for a couple of weeks as they sometimes did in summer, and when Haasan was satisfied that it was safe to return, he would send word. And as for me, I could . . .

I didn't wait to hear what Haasan had planned for me. Banaras, I said simply. I was headed for Banaras. I tapped my head. The blast, I revealed, had restored to me a small bit of my forgotten past. I was carrying my grandmother's ashes and I was off to Banaras to drown them at Dasashwamedh Ghat. It was something I should have done a week ago, I explained. This much at least was true.

How will you go? where will you stay? asked mother and daughter, transparently concerned. I had thought they might have been relieved at my going, so when they weren't, my throat choked up and my eyes prickled and I nearly told them everything, but there wasn't the time – Haasan told them to hurry with their packing and took me off with him to find a tonga that would take them to their orchard.

But first we went back to the garage. He stepped around the shrouded bulk of the Stonely and whipped off a smaller tarpaulin. It was a dark green motorcycle, glinting with chrome and brass, with a round headlight sitting on a long-stalked neck. I knew it at once from his potted account of his past: it was Ramanujam's Triumph from the old days in Palghat, complete with sidecar.

He didn't use it much any more, he said sadly. When Masroor was a schoolboy, he used to fit him into the sidecar and treat him to long drives. But now he just wheeled it out on Sunday mornings for ritual outings to keep it in working order. He wouldn't miss it for a month or two, he said, but I was to take care of it and he wanted it back when the troubles were over. I nodded, overcome. He kicked the engine into a wheezing roar, stowed my flask in the sidecar where once canned meats had ridden and stepped back to open another leaf of the garage's folding doors. It was time to go.

Ordinary leave-taking seemed out of place after last night's strange work, so I said nothing. I just chugged past him, out of the garage and into the street, leaving him to find Ammi a tonga, to tie up loose ends, to fret about Bhukay and Bihari and Masroor. I wanted to look back, only I hadn't ridden motorcycles much and the Triumph needed my whole attention. But at the end of the lane, before turning the corner into Hazrat Ganj, I remembered to wave.

Trains in my time had covered the distance between Lucknow and Banaras in roughly eight hours, but I rode eastward for twelve and found Azamgarh instead. Somewhere along the way the road had forked and I had missed the southern turn. It wasn't my fault: the rains had turned half-metalled roads into mud and for miles on end there hadn't been a person in sight to ask directions of.

When I did find the odd passer-by, he would gesture eastward down the road as if Banaras was round the next bend. Some likely-looking informants disappeared when I slowed to hail them. This puzzled me till I realised that dressed in khaki trousers and sola topi, and riding a motorcycle with a sidecar, I probably looked like a bedraggled arm of the law, unwelcome in this, the heartland of the '42 rebellion. That was another thing I couldn't understand: here I was, riding

95

through the eastern United Provinces, where, if Dadi was to be believed, the writ of the Raj had ceased to run for the first fortnight of the rebellion, but I hadn't yet seen a single revolutionary spectacle. I had no fixed expectations – anything insurrectionary would have done, but the rains seemed to have driven the rebels indoors. Then I reached Azamgarh.

Azamgarh lay in the loop of a river which had used the monsoon to colonize the whole town. The river was called the Tons, which I didn't know then. What I did know was that the streets were channels of lapping filth, ridden by buoyant turds. I removed the flask from the sidecar as a precaution: the water was wheel-high at places.

It was nearly dark but I was determined to push on that same day to Banaras; the only reason I stopped at Azamgarh was because it seemed a good place to ask directions. I could see people in its lanes despite the rain, sodden trails of pedestrians all walking in one direction. They were headed for Shibli College. I found that out when I was taken there.

It happened like this. I had braked to a stop on one side of a narrow lane as a preliminary to asking directions, and I was wondering if my topi would scare the good people of Azamgarh away as it had scared others, when suddenly, without my saying a word, I found myself surrounded by potential informants. They were all young men and the odd thing was that they didn't look like locals. Dressed in shirts and trousers and sometimes spectacles, they looked like students from a proper city, which Azamgarh, from what I had seen of it, wasn't nearly.

Anyway, I asked them the way to Banaras, which resulted in a series of rapidly exchanged frowns. One of them walked up, a thin, mean-looking boy with wild hair, straddled the front wheel of the Triumph and, holding the handlebars with an elaborate show of menace, asked me why I was going to Banaras. My heart was beating faster because the circle had closed in (one of them fitted himself into the sidecar), but when I told him why, my voice was steady.

I was half afraid that they wouldn't believe me but they did. It was reasonable that a dead grandmother's ashes should take me to Banaras; besides, I had the thermos flask to back up my story. The thin wild one actually uncapped it and shook a little of Dadi's leftovers into the palm of his hand, but when he saw the bits of bone and smelt the bottled-up incense-sweetness of the aromatics that deodorize roasting flesh, he hurriedly slid the sample back and stoppered the flask, looking sick. The man in the sidecar removed himself from it shamefacedly. Let him go, yaar, he said.

But they didn't. They took me to Shibli College instead, to which all roads in Azamgarh town seemed to lead that rainy evening. No one twisted my arm or actually issued an ultimatum – my inquisitor rode pillion and gave me directions; his comrades followed on foot.

The college, a low building with pitched roofs and thick walls, stood out by looking less temporary than the rest of Azamgarh. It was cordoned off from the shabbiness of its host town by a high whitewashed wall, free of graffiti, topped by a vicious crop of embedded glass. The grounds the wall enclosed were probably well kept – I couldn't tell as I slowed the motorcycle to a crawl while entering the campus through the open gates, because there were people growing out of the ground like grass.

They were watching a man scrambling over grey slate tiles to get to the top of the sloping roof. The going was hard because he had only one hand free to use – the other one was holding the Congress tricolour. A flag hoisting? A crowd like this for a flag hoisting? Finally, the man with the flag reached the top of the roof and sat astride it. He couldn't find a place to stick the bamboo flagstaff in, so he made sure he was stable and got down to making the flag fly manually.

This led to scattered applause which came mainly from the knot of eager people in the porch below his perch. A thin line of similarly youthful enthusiasts running along the periphery of the assembled audience took up the clapping and made it last a while. My minder clapped as well.

There was silence and from among the elect in the porch a thin, beautiful woman rose and began to speak of revolution. She was dowdily dressed in a white khadi sari and she was older than the young men who flanked her, but the line of her neck and the cut of her face marked her out and her voice was a thing of strident beauty.

It was a clear, carrying voice, too big perhaps for indoor argument, but good for speech-making in the open air. But there was nothing rhetorical about her manner except in the beginning, when she saluted her brothers and sisters although there wasn't another woman to be seen.

Her body was as inhibited as her voice was free. When she gestured to underline a phrase, her hands fluttered around her midriff in incomplete arcs. Never once was the whole arm unleashed to make a point – her elbows stayed glued to her waist while her hands and forearms made helpless little movements. I think she was afraid that the palloo of her sari would slide off her shoulder; she also stooped a little to level out her breasts.

I could tell the moment she began speaking that she was Bengali but it took me longer to work out that her audience was mainly Muslim. It was impossible to tell by looking because not many of the men assembled wore white lace skullcaps and in any case, most were completely obscured by umbrellas. It was the things she said that tipped me off.

You must have heard them say that the Congress doesn't speak for the Muslims, that our Quit India movement is a Hindu plot. She paused. Now tomorrow, we will march on the last unliberated police post in this part of Azamgarh and, inshallah, tomorrow it shall be as free as the whole of Ballia is free already. But I cannot prove to you that this freedom will mean freedom for Muslims. I cannot because freedom is not a thing that can be portioned – it is the air you breathe, it is indivisible. I cannot prove that the Congress is secular; I don't know if there is a single Muslim among my comrades. But I will not apologize for this because I know that there isn't a single Hindu either; there are only nationalists.

There was applause from her colleagues who were neither Muslim nor Hindu but only nationalists, but the people she was addressing gave no sign.

Congressmen cannot, she said, defend their party by counting Muslim heads because we are blind to labels that divide us. I speak for myself, she said, making another of her attenuated gestures, her hand patting her stomach when it should have covered her heart.

I am a Hindu but my husband is Muslim. My language is Bengali where his is Urdu. My skin is dark where his is fair. He is a moderate and I am a socialist. We have nothing in common but we're married because we are Indians first!

I couldn't see how that followed – I was Indian too and she wasn't married to me. She didn't explain; perhaps as a symptom of Indian nationalism she didn't have to. Then she moved from generalities about the Congress to her business in Azamgarh and how they had got there and it became clear to me why her comrades had brought me to the meeting.

We have come from Banaras, she said. My hunch that the young men were students from a city was right. They were probably all from the Hindu University there. They had reached Azamgarh by capturing a train outside Banaras' city limits and taking it over. She made it sound simple, but who knew better than I did that this took some doing.

They had stopped the train and thrown the passengers out and forced the driver to go west at Mau where the Banaras line met the track running to Azamgarh. Tomorrow they would set off in their captured train to conquer Madhuban, a rural police post, important only because it was the last place flying the Union Jack in this part of Azamgarh. But there was a problem – and that is why she was making this speech.

Madhuban was ten miles to the north of the rail line. Ten miles on foot would leave them with no energy for the actual siege; besides, a fortified post could hardly be stormed by foot-soldiers alone. Of course, she was confident that the post would surrender when the policemen inside saw the armies of the revolution, but even so, a show of strength needed mounts.

She spread her hands out as far as her fixed-elbows style allowed and appealed to the crowd to loan them horses, elephants, motorcycles, anything they had – even bicycles. They would be returned the next day, after the post was taken, and the provisional government of the Indian Republic of Azamgarh would be grateful to its generous citizens.

She stopped and the rain, which had slowed to a drizzle, pelted down again. The generous citizens of Azamgarh, who had begun to shift restlessly when she made the appeal, now fled the park, helped along by the storm. The rat-faced revolutionary had been joined by his friends and together they pushed the Triumph into the shelter of the porch. No one asked my leave – it had been pressed into the service of the revolution.

I said nothing; there were too many of them and I wanted no trouble. Besides, nothing was lost yet because I still had the thermos flask and she had promised to return all borrowed mounts the next day. They stood the motorcycle on its stand and went indoors. Ratface, I noted, had the Triumph's key. I hugged the flask for luck and followed them in.

That night I slept in a library along with twenty others. More than half the assault party had returned to the captured train to watch over it through the night. The vanguard, I was told, was already in the vicinity of the targeted police post, where it was mapping the terrain and carrying the insurgent message to neighbouring villages. Everything, said Ratface, had been planned.

The library was the largest room in Shibli College and the rebels turned it into a dormitory. The caretaker didn't want us there, but there was nothing he could do about it. The college had been closed when the troubles began and with its students dispersed, he lacked the numbers to make his displeasure effective.

The woman who had made the speech tried to keep order. She reminded the rebels as they sucked tea off saucers and smoked and talked till late into the night, that this was a place of learning, a Muslim place of learning, that they were unbidden guests. No provocation, no damage, she kept saying, and generally, except for the spilt tea and the dead cigarettes, she was obeyed.

Not that she was the leader of this band. On the evidence of one evening's observation, she seemed to be a kind of mascot. She was waited upon and deferred to (more and more I was convinced that she had taught some of them) but all the argument, the speculation, the fevered planning for the next day's expedition, centred on a finely muscled man, tall, dark and moustachioed, who had brown-green eyes and huge white teeth which were always smiling.

He smiled at me as well when Ratface took me to him. He was sorry, he said, to hear of my grandmother's death. After all this was over, he would personally escort me to Banaras and arrange for her last rites. He knew all the priests at the ghats by name. He was sure that my sacred grandmother wouldn't grudge me the time I spent serving the cause of Mother India. He was right – perhaps I was Dadi's proxy in 1942.

The woman disappeared around eleven o'clock to bed down alone in some other room. Ratface and his comrades began to scour the stacks, fingering the books now that she wasn't there to warn them off. They wanted something to read themselves to sleep with but all the books there were in the Persian script which no one in that library could read. They didn't feel inadequate, just annoyed. Ratface pulled out some books and let them drop as an experiment. A little cloud of dust rose upwards. He looked around and shook his head. The others looked knowing as if he had proved something. They were college boys and a room full of books in a script they couldn't read must have struck them as a monstrous affectation. Then all of us pulled out some books to make up pillows with, and there in that store of mute, unreadable things, we slept.

It was raining when I woke up. The sky in the ventilators was grey and the others were drinking tea again. Ratface and three others were playing carom. I knew this without opening my eyes because one corner of the board was a few inches from my ear and the air was full of ricocheting sounds.

Half-asleep on one elbow, I marvelled at the badness of my breath and watched them play. Ratface was very good. With practised efficiency, he struck the whites and blacks into the relevant pockets and when there was just the one black on the board, he took aim at the maroon, the queen.

After we throw the English out, he said, grinning lewdly, there'll be no kings and queens. Everyone's equal in a republic. No special treatment. If we were a republic now,

Bose Madam wouldn't have a room to herself. She would sleep here, with us. He stopped to swallow a gob of excitement and explained in the fluent phrases of rehearsed fantasy what he would do to Bose Madam in a republican country. When he finished, his pink striker deflected the queen into the further right-hand pocket. The others round the board laughed their appreciation of this subtle climax. Ratface winked.

There were exactly thirty-three of us excluding the leader and including Bose Madam, a fact I discovered by counting when all of us were arranged in three lines and drilled in the covered porch after breakfast. It was a sluggish drill because breakfast hadn't been an ad hoc, frugal meal unfussily eaten by an urgent rebel band. It had been spread over an hour and a half with the leader showing the way. According to Ratface, besides being a long-time student of the Hindu University, he was also the best young wrestler produced by Banaras in years. He drank five huge glasses of milk with two raw eggs mixed into each. The milk was supplied by a buffalo tethered in the college grounds. The eggs, twelve dozen of them, had been exchanged for a credit note made out in the name of the provisional republic of Azamgarh – like any good army, we were living off the land.

Chaubey, our leader, made a speech about now and nineteen hundred and forty-two.

Remember, he said, this is no ordinary year. It is not the nineteen-hundredth and forty-second year of the imperialist era. If we are to free ourselves of the foreigner, we must free ourselves from his way of telling time. This is the two-thousandth year of the Vikrami epoch. Fifty-eight years before the first year of their Lord, Vikramaditya founded the kingdom of the just. We are the armies of Vikramaditya and it has fallen to us to ensure that India enters the third millennium of his era, a republic of the free.

If we are true to our cause, he said, by this time tomorrow you and I will be the rulers of Azamgarh. By this time next month there won't be an Englishman left in Agra or Awadh. And by the end of this year Delhi will be ours and the tricolour will fly on the Red Fort.

But the vanguard of Vikramaditya had to wait an hour for the rain to stop. And when it did, the problem of transport remained outstanding. If Bose Madam had hoped to find the grounds of the college filled with cycles and horses, she was disappointed. When the weather cleared, Ratface and the others fanned out to remind Azamgarhis of the need to mount the revolution. The net result was a string of six unwilling mules loaned by a nervous brick-kiln owner when Ratface threatened him with consequences. Except for him, Azamgarh seemed reluctant to anticipate freedom.

In the end it fell to me to ferry Bose Madam and Chaubey to the railway station. It took us no more than ten minutes to get there but the road was bad and, unused to the curious helplessness of sidecar travel, she brought up her breakfast on the way.

It was a short train – just four bogies and a luggage van. In the interest of speed and fuel economy, the rebels had uncoupled the rest. Bose Madam was led away immediately to the comfort of a first-class compartment; I accompanied the Triumph to the luggage van and helped to load it on. Since no one objected, I settled down next to it – that way I would make certain that it reached where we were headed in one piece.

The engine, crouched on the tracks, was already gently panting gusts of steam into the humid air. Everything was ready and we left as soon as the rest of the Shibli College party caught up with us. Ratface rode up to the luggage van on mule-back – it wasn't difficult to work out how he had directed the beast: its ears were half torn off and bleeding where they joined its head. He was going to travel with me – so was his mule. Flushed with pride at his prowess as a cavalryman, he ignored both the derision of his peers and the protests of the mule and hauled it into the van. We left Azamgarh at a quarter to twelve.

It took us an hour to get to base camp. I panicked for half that time and brooded for the rest. There was reason to panic – I had been shanghaied in the name of the Nation and pressed into serving a doomed rebellion. When they wrote the histories of this time, even the most chauvinist of them would have to record that the rebellion's back was broken inside a month. I was risking my life for a movement that would fail quite nicely without any help from me. And then to learn from a toad like Ratface that the sequence or chain or (why not) train of events that had slotted me into this luggage van need never have happened . . . it was enough to make the Laughing Buddha brood.

This revelation came when, halfway into our journey, Ratface got bored of tormenting the tethered mule. He had been tickling its balls with a stick out of scientific curiosity. He was testing it to see if it could achieve an erection. He knew that mules didn't reproduce but he wasn't sure if it was because they were impotent or because they were sterile. What happened was that the mule became excited without becoming erect and began to thrash about and bray so violently that Ratface abandoned the experiment. That left me.

He decided to play catch with a cricket ball he produced from his pocket. Coming from a mule masturbator this seemed such harmless sport that I agreed quickly before he dreamed up some viler pastime. I even suggested the D-O-N-K-E-Y game: a letter each time a catch was spilled and the first one to make DONKEY the loser. I lost eight times in a row before the journey was over because I was lobbing gentle catches at him while he shot bullets back at me which sometimes hit the mule and set it squealing.

Then Ratface got bored of playing catch and pulled out a cricket bat from one of the bags in the luggage van. I hadn't attached any importance to the fact that he had a cricket ball handy, but the bat set me thinking. It was a proper bat with 'English Willow' written across its splice, the kind of bat a good club cricketer would use. What was it doing in the luggage van of a rebellion? Even more curiously it wasn't the only bat in the van. Chasing Ratface's pushes and deflections, retrieving the ball from gloomy unlit corners, I found not just more bats but whole kits of cricketing gear: pads, gloves, crotch-guards, studded shoes, even caps.

It was hard to think in the din of a moving train made worse by a mule's complaining but in the end I worked the puzzle out. Yesterday had been the date for the Governor's cricket match between the Muslim University of Aligarh and the Hindu University of Banaras. That match had been cancelled. I knew that because I'd seen and felt the blast that had wrecked the track and kept the Aligarh team from getting to Lucknow in time for the match. Now I had gone one better: I was actually riding the train which should have carried the Banaras eleven to Lucknow early yesterday morning. Only, it had been hijacked by Ratface and his patriots.

I wondered what had become of the team. Nervously, I asked him about the fate of the cricketers.

What happened to the team, he repeated absently. Nothing. It was a big match for us to miss but we decided that all-India struggle was bigger than inter-varsity cricket.

I had my answer. The rebels had done nothing to the cricket team because the cricket team was the vanguard of the rebel band. Chaubey, their leader, was also their cricket captain besides being their opening bowler. Chaubey it was who had menaced the guard and the engine driver with the business end of a stump to hijack the train.

The team had never intended to reach Lucknow for the cricket match. Everything, said Ratface complacently, had been pre-planned.

The team had never intended . . . I thought of Masroor's suicidal determination to prevent the match; of Bhukay and Bihari, who, for all I knew, had been maimed or killed by the rail-track explosion; of Ammi and Asharfi cowering like fugitives in their own city; of me flying east into the arms of this mad rebellion. And all this needlessly, to no purpose, for no reason at all, because the Banaras team wouldn't have turned up anyway.

The futility of it all was so infuriating that I forgot myself and slung the ball back as hard as I could at the unready Ratface, who was hit, not thereabouts but unambiguously on the balls, and felled. Fortunately for me, we reached the appointed place soon after, so by the time he could leave his crotch untended he had his hands full, off-loading the insurgency.

105

We had stopped at a tiny station that consisted of a water tank on stilts and a signboard. The original name had been painted out by Chaubey's advance party and foot-high black letters on orange ground now proclaimed 'Azad Hind'.

There was an elephant on the station's single platform and six horses besides. Outside, four bullocks had been yoked to a cart carrying the rebel band's siege instrument, a battering ram. Obviously the reconnoitring party had done better in the matter of mounting the rebellion. They had also succeeded in broadening the social composition of the uprising – there were real peasants to be seen in the crowd that welcomed us when we disembarked. They were wearing dhotis and shoulder cloths and turbans. It was hard to tell if they were there out of commitment or curiosity and I didn't really care. Mechanically, I strapped on the thermos flask and eased the Triumph down a makeshift ramp on to the platform.

There were turds everywhere; it was the animals, especially the elephant, who let go from such a height that besides the blob at the centre, there was a pointillist halo splashed all round. The leading wheel of the Triumph carved neat tyre-tread valleys through the firmer mounds.

Bose Madam hurried out of the station holding the palloo of her sari to her nose with one hand and hitching up the pleats and hem with the other. A few minutes later the rest of the party joined us in the little clearing outside the station gate. There were sixty or seventy of us now, not including the animals. When everyone had settled down, Chaubey stepped forward to outline the plan of action: his face was tense and unsmiling – this wasn't a picnic any more.

Our goal, he informed us, was the police post at Madhuban, some ten miles to the north. The scouting party had received information that it was thinly garrisoned: only fifty constables and chowkidars headed by a sub-inspector, with no more than ten police muskets between them. There was no immediate danger of reinforcements because the Gorakhpur Road that led to it had been washed away by the rain. Supplies by rail weren't likely either because the stations at Kidihdapur and Bilthara Road and also the one at Ghosi had been captured and were now under nationalist control.

He broke off as the leader of the scouting party came up to whisper something in his ear. He looked nonplussed, then cleared his throat and told us that as far as Ghosi, the last-named station, was concerned, we were the nationalists in control: Ghosi was what Azad Hind had been called before liberation.

The lack of reinforcements notwithstanding, the idea was to get to Madhuban quickly – three in the afternoon was the time nominated by Chaubey. It was a quarter to two already, so the crowd was reorganized into a straggly crocodile and the trek began. I led the procession by virtue of driving the leaders. My passengers were the same as those in the earlier leg from Azamgarh to the station, but the seating plan was different: the Bose woman rode pillion in deference to her unpleasant sidecar experience and Chaubey risked low-slung nausea instead.

Ratface didn't like the arrangement at all. He wanted her on the elephant next to him. In place of a howdah, they had tied around the elephant's middle a small cot upside down, with its legs sticking up in the air; for Ratface, this was the closest he would ever get to sharing a bed with her. Chaubey vetoed the suggestion because the elephant's swaying gait would probably make her sea-sick. It had nothing at all to do with me but Ratface cast me a look of shocking hate.

Fifteen minutes into the journey it became clear to everyone that we weren't going to get to Madhuban by three. This had something to do with the churned-up, half-metalled road but mainly was because, despite Chaubey's brave words, the sixty of us weren't certain that we wanted to take on fifty of them. The odds didn't seem right. So it was nearly three by the time we reached Rampur, but once we got there the expedition gathered momentum. Because at Rampur it became en-couragingly apparent that we were not alone. The siege of Madhuban, we discovered, wasn't just a plan hatched by college boys – it was currently the most popular local pastime. Rampur was alive with people determined to assault Madhuban, only they had been distracted by the temptation of burning Rampur's post office down and then its deserted police post. It was deserted because its armed guard had been recalled by the beleaguered Station Officer at Madhuban. This reinforcement didn't amount to much because while stealing away in the dark hours of the early morning, they had forgotten their weapons, taking with them nothing but their undress uniforms.

It was a thousand-strong crowd that watched Rampur's police post burn in dress rehearsal for the main performance in Madhuban. Then, without any orders, these participant observers re-formed themselves into an infantry and marched off in the direction of Fatehpur, the last major settlement before Madhuban. The university contingent now brought up the rear, happy to be relieved of its vanguard role. Chugging slowly behind them on the motorcycle, it was hard not to be awed by the spectacle. The procession was armed with lathis and spears mainly but there were also saws and spades and hammers and ploughshares: it was a bristling jungle on the move.

At a quarter to four we reached Fatehpur, where the post office was routinely prepared for burning and Chaubey managed to meet his counterpart among the peasants. When the post office's records had been piled high, a middle-sized man in a dhoti and a forage cap approached our elephant, accompanied by a few others, and invited Ratface on the elephant, mistaking him for our leader, to ceremonially light the bonfire. Chaubey intervened to correct the misunderstanding and the stranger introduced himself: he was Tojo.

Things became clearer after Chaubey had set fire to the heap with all the deliberation of a chief guest cutting a ribbon. In the little summit meeting that followed it turned out that Tojo had been a tailor in Malaya before the Japanese occupation forced him to return to the district in India where he had been raised. Ramlakhan was his real name but after the Japanese overran Malaya he had taken on Tojo as a good name to fight the British with. Ramlakhan Tojo.

Tojo had a request: he wanted to ride in the sidecar. Chaubey agreed at once. He shouted up to Ratface to lower the elephant to take Bose Madam and me on board. Tojo was ushered into the sidecar with the utmost formality and Chaubey took over the driver's seat. Chaubey was delighted:

this one reshuffle put him on level terms with an authentically plebeian leader and at the head of genuine peasants, the Indian masses made flesh.

Once the post office was burning properly, the rebel army set off on its last lap to Madhuban, which was now just over four miles away. The procession in front of us was a wonderful sight: nearly a mile of miscellaneously armed men between us and any trouble.

It was half-past four in the afternoon when we reached Madhuban and there wasn't a human being in sight. The police post was visible from miles away because it stood on perfectly level, barren ground with no trees to obscure our line of sight. There were a few houses north and north-east of it but other than those, nothing relieved the massive flatness of the scene. We moved closer till the front of our ragged column was within two hundred yards of the perimeter walls. Then it stopped and redeployed: the reassuring depth of the column melted as everyone pushed to get to that invisible frontier.

At the end of fifteen minutes the rebels were strung untidily parallel to the police post's northern wall. We were still well at the back, but much closer now to the likely scene of action. Ratface offhandedly let drop that the range of a police musket was less than a hundred and fifty yards, but his hand on the upturned cot wasn't quite steady and his knuckles showed white with fright.

Seen from this distance, the police station consisted of low, yellow buildings set in a large compound which was defended by high walls to the west, south and east and a lower one to the north, the side facing us, in the centre of which was set a splintering wooden gate. The gate hadn't been designed with a siege in mind: neither the door nor the walls were loopholed and, given the low north wall and my elephant-back elevation, I could see that most of the defenders had to do without cover of any sort. There were fifty of them in all – we outnumbered them twenty to one.

The siege and the storming went like nothing I had expected. I had vaguely imagined a continuous assault, an unbroken din of battle sounds, a bloody milling about till the battle was won. In fact the action unfolded in a curiously formal, intermittent fashion, like the old plays where there was silence during a change of scene.

It began with a parley. Tojo climbed out of the sidecar and, using an improvised loud-hailer, called upon the garrison to surrender. They had not come, he boomed, to fight their Indian brothers. Swaraj had been attained, independence was imminent, so they merely wished to fly the tricolour from the thana's roof and burn the Union Jack.

There was silence from the other side. So with remarkable or reckless confidence, Tojo and Chaubey walked towards the gate holding their hands up, palms outward: they had come as peace-makers. They stopped five yards short of the gate and Tojo shouted something I couldn't hear. A minute later, the doors of the main entrance opened a little and a man in jodhpurs and a loose white shirt emerged, accompanied by a uniformed policeman, probably the Station House Officer. The negotiations barely lasted half a minute: the Englishman and the S.H.O. returned to the compound and the doors were shut smartly behind them. From where we were sitting I heard the distant slam.

Someone came with the news: the assault was on. Tojo had half-expected a surrender but it hadn't happened because of the unexpected presence of Niblick. Niblick was the District Magistrate of Azamgarh, its administrative chief, its all-in-all, its king. He had been touring the district because of the troubles and last night he had got wind of the siege and hurried from Dohrighat to Madhuban. He wouldn't listen to reason. It was war.

But not right off. Tojo and Chaubey returned to the ranks. Tojo held up his hands for silence and there was a hush. Then from my perch on top of the elephant, I saw him fist the air and my ears resonated to a wave of chorused sound: I-N-Q-I-L-A-B Z-I-N-D-A-B-A-D! And then again. And again till even our elephant tossed its head and trumpeted. There was a lull; then the fight began. But no direct assault yet: first the besieged were to be softened up by bombardment. We watched a group of men close in another fifty yards, carrying fist-sized stones in their dhotis. They laid them on the ground and then, in concert, began to volley them in. Some had proper slings, others removed their dhotis and improvised slingshots, but however they did it, the stones travelled incredible distances.

In the first two minutes, nearly six of them hit Niblick; sitting on the elephant, I could see him rallying his men and being hit. But he wasn't seriously injured. It was a piece of bad luck for him that he was hit at all because the men who were slinging the stones in were on foot and couldn't see over the police post's compound wall, as I could, to aim at him. The sentries in exposed positions had a much harder time. The man on the ladder by the well had his head and shoulders over the wall as he aimed his musket, when he was hit in the eye. He clapped one hand to his eye and, unbalanced by the blow, fell sideways off the ladder into the well. There were other similar casualties and the sight of injured sentries disappearing from view did great things for rebel morale. The defenders hadn't yet fired a single shot; the rumour was that they barely had two rounds for every gun. The brickbatting went on for fifteen minutes and stopped. That was the end of the siege's first episode.

The next move was Chaubey's brainchild and it was born of over-confidence. After a conference with Tojo he called for the battering ram to be unloaded. So the bullock cart was summoned and the battering ram, which was basically a smallish tree-trunk with the branches trimmed off, was moved into action. Besides the eight people needed to carry it, a column of some twenty men lined up behind and Tojo signalled the resumption of the brickbat barrage. The idea, obviously, was to provide covering fire while the battering brigade breached the door, allowing the others behind them to rush in and overwhelm the defenders in close combat by the weight of numbers.

It turned out differently. All went well till the ram was some hundred feet from the door. The stones kept the defending heads below the wall, so there was no answering fire. Then suddenly the leaves of the targeted door parted, Niblick appeared in the opening and, standing side-on, firing-range-fashion, shot the first two ram-bearers at point-blank range. Then the doors closed again. Robbed of its four leading hands, the ram ploughed into the ground whereupon it was abandoned at once by all except the dead men and one unfortunate in the middle whose legs were pinned by the tree-trunk as it dropped. Not everyone got away, though: three men dropped in mid-flight, whether struck by fright, self-preservation or bullets it was impossible to say.

Frontal assault was abandoned for the time being. Tojo feinted; a contingent of some hundred men, led by Tojo himself to make its offensive intentions credible, headed towards the eastern flank of the police station at a distance that kept them beyond the range of police muskets. Meanwhile the main body began lobbing stones again as a supplementary diversion. Masked by these competing distractions, a small band sprinted towards the north-western corner of the station, guarded by a constable posted on the sloping tin roof of one of the quarters there. But he was looking eastward at Tojo and his men, so it was a simple matter for the leader of the raiding party to scale an angle in that fifteen-foot wall and spear him. There was a great roar from our ranks as the constable doubled up and toppled off the roof into the compound below, but this was a disservice to the rebel cause because the sound alerted the Station House Officer to the present danger. He took careful aim and shot the assailant in the face, lifting him off his feet and knocking him over the compound wall. Then the S.H.O. raced up to the vacated tin roof to hold off the rest. There wasn't any need: the spectacular death of their leader had scared the others off.

Thwarted, Tojo returned with his diversionary force to the north side again and nothing happened for a while. Meanwhile, on the elephant, Ratface had completed a successful manoeuvre. When Bose Madam and I had first mounted the elephant, we'd found ourselves seats right up in front on the inverted cot, where we sat side by side. Now Ratface, in his lust for her, had managed to squeeze in between the two of us. This meant that I was forced sideways so that my right shoulder was pointing towards the station; the only reason I didn't fall off the edge was that I'd wrapped my thighs around the nearest leg of the upturned cot. It was an uncomfortable perch with my legs dangling over the elephant's flank and the wooden leg pressed rigidly against me from crotch to sternum like an ambitious erection. Ratface had wedged himself in so that his back was flush against mine and his front was pressed up against Bose Madam's side even as she sat hunched forward, drinking in the battle with hungry eyes.

The elephant never stopped its restless swaying from one foot to another and Ratface was soon breathing hard in an ecstasy of friction. I said nothing – it was no business of mine. Actually I don't think she even noticed that there was a frotteur by her side. She was so consumed by the spectacle in front of her that she probably thought it natural that others would push their way up for a ringside view of the revolution. She cheered and clapped her hands and shouted and exclaimed to us in reverent asides what an honour it was to be in the middle of it. But of course we weren't in the middle of it; we were spectators, dangerously close to the action perhaps, but still not participants – for which I was grateful. Like all academics, Bose Madam couldn't tell watching from doing.

In the larger arena, skirmishing continued. One burst of brickbatting and firing so demoralized a chowkidar stationed on look-out duty on a roof to the north that he leapt off the fifteen-foot wall to get away. But not being in uniform he was mistaken for a rebel and shot dead by his own side. Immediately after, Chaubey led his students in an assault upon the northern wall, which was pierced by windows at regular intervals. It was a good plan because the garrison couldn't possibly defend them all and since that flank was interrupted at several points by abutments, no single rifleman could command any length of wall. They successfully broke some windows open but they couldn't get past the iron bars that guarded them. The effort wasn't a complete waste: they managed to reach in and fish several things out of a room that was obviously some kind of store. One of the items was a greatcoat but the luckiest find was a musket.

Clutching their prizes, they returned to the parent body in time for the crowning event of the afternoon, the final storming. Chaubey would later argue that it should never have happened, that the grand front assault had been un-necessary at the time. Given the rebel advantage in numbers, another five skirmishes, another ten casualties would have broken the garrison's will to hold out. Perhaps Chaubey was right but hindsight forgets the frenzy of the moment, it sifts out the sense of urgency. Gnawing at everyone's mind had been the fear of military reinforcements, the bowel-shifting thought that khaki trucks in convoy were heading towards the station through the undefended flatness all round us.

Which is not to say that Tojo, who led the assault, had planned it. After two hours of indecisive manoeuvring he was at his wits' end when Chaubey's raiding party returned with its trophies. Apart from the greatcoat and the musket, there was a torch, a swagger stick, an enamel mug with a cut-throat razor and a shaving brush, and a standard-issue, framed portrait of King George VI in full colour. With some ceremony Chaubey showed off the first spoils of this war to the distracted Tojo, who absently tried on the greatcoat, stropped the razor, felt the brush, thwacked the cane, shouldered the musket, flashed the torch but wanted only the portrait of King George.

We watched bewilderedly as he held the picture up high above his head and began walking rapidly towards the main door of the thana. He stopped when he was less than fifty yards from it. It was a miracle that he got that far without being shot: perhaps they thought he was carrying the portrait as a token of repentant fealty. He wasn't.

Bastards, he shouted at the hidden defenders by way of getting their attention. Bastards, jackals, hiding like women . . . come out bastards, come out and fight, eunuchs . . . come save your king!

Then he smashed the picture on the ground. He put his back properly into it so the frame bounced and glass flew like shrapnel. Eunuchs, he bellowed as he stomped rhythmically on King George's upturned face, eunuchs . . . eunuchs . . . eunuchs . . . eunuchs.

None of us knew what he expected the garrison to do; neither, perhaps, did he. It was one of those rare moments of transparent suspense, uncoloured by expectation: his provocation was so absurd that just anything could have happened. But nothing did. The silence from beyond the wall wafted up like smoke to join the pop-eyed hush in the rebel ranks and suddenly the arena was still.

When, in that blanketed silence, Tojo hitched up his dhoti and pissed upon the picture, I could have sworn I heard the tinkle of urine upon broken glass. This time he didn't call out a challenge; he just stood there with his legs splayed and emptied himself upon the King-Emperor. Involuntarily I glanced at Bose Madam: her face was pink and her visible ear quite scarlet but her gaze never wavered and not once did she turn her face away from the sobering nakedness of struggle.

And still nothing happened. Then Tojo dropped to his haunches in a squat. My neighbour's nerve broke: she gasped and shut her eyes; Ratface groaned for one of two reasons, Chaubey swore and looked away while the rest of us stared with hypnotized horror at this spare, stripped-down rendering of the nationalist project: a man in a dhoti shitting upon King George. But he didn't, quite, because something gave on the other side as well. For the second time that afternoon, the main gate opened and Niblick appeared, squinting down the barrel of a rifle, the Empire's avenging angel. Tojo had gone too far.

I closed my eyes and waited for the end. There was an explosion. When I opened my eyes I saw the tail end of Niblick's collapse: he was holding his face and the rifle was a smoking ruin on the ground – its breech had burst.

As his men dragged him in and bolted the doors, the unhurt Tojo rose to his feet and walked back to his cheering people. He walked like a prophet – deliberately, as if there wasn't a camp full of enemies behind him. Looking back, I'm certain that it was on that walk that the grand assault was born.

He held up his arms and the cheering subsided. They are lost, he began, in the appropriate prophetic idiom. They have walls and guns but we have God and Gandhi. You saw how close I went. Why did I go so close? Why did I tear down their pride within pistol-shot? Because Gandhi Baba came to me and said: Their walls will turn to sand and their weapons will turn upon them. And you saw! You saw that the red-faced monkey tried to shoot me but the rifle shot his face instead.

All fire by a miracle had been rendered harmless. Now there

was no need for feints, flanking attacks or manoeuvring. With faith and courage the walls and the door could be stormed unhurt, the thana could be taken!

A hundred believers followed him in the first headlong charge. Fifty yards into the storming, the defenders fired their first volley and the miracle was borne out. As the shots rang out, the vanguard flinched and stopped but no one fell. Perhaps they missed or aimed wide just to scare them off. But for the watching rebels, it was a sign. This time, when Tojo waved them on, they went.

Not all of them. Except for one or two, the students didn't go, though they cheered the others on and lent their voices to the swelling frenzy. And then fell silent when they saw them die. For of course they died. Sitting on elephant back, I watched Niblick, holding a pad to his right eye, direct the killing. This time the garrison held its fire till Tojo's whooping men were less than a hundred feet away before they fired, once, twice, thrice. The battle for Madhuban was lost in those minutes. I don't know how many died. More than a hundred fell but of those some were injured and some others just tripped. Tojo died clutching his groin: someone avenged his king by shooting low.

But the shot that made me part of the bloody play that I had been watching, that reached Bose Madam into the thick of things, was fired by our side, not theirs. It came from the captured musket; I don't know who was at the trigger, because it was fired from behind us, or why he pulled it because from where we were standing, the walls weren't inside musket range. Perhaps it was a last flourish of defiance, of long-distance solidarity with that mad assault they had so prudently avoided; whatever the reason, the result was that some portion of the ball and shot that left its primitive muzzle buried itself in our elephant's bum.

The mahout could do nothing: prodded by this magic goad, the elephant surged towards the police post's northern wall with maddened, blinkered purpose. Bose Madam screamed as she was flung back by the standing start, Ratface grunted with surprise and I said nothing because the cot's leg digging deep into my stomach had left me short of breath. Winded or not, I remembered to check if my thermos flask was still strapped on. It was. By now the elephant was almost upon the fleeing rebel infantry. Some dodged, some stopped, some others turned and watched – wondering perhaps if their side had rallied. They saw an anguished elephant gallop past and smash head first into the wall just right of the bolted doors. The perimeter wall was almost breached at the point of impact; almost, because the brick-and-mortar gave and the beast's momentum carried more than half its body in, but with its hindquarters still outside the wall it collapsed, stunned by the crunching force of the collision. Ratface and Bose Madam, though, kept travelling. They shot off the elephant's back and followed the mahout into the thana's gravelled forecourt.

I was still on the elephant only because the wooden leg had me hooked there. Crying with the pain, I drew up my legs and struggled up on the back of the unmoving elephant. I had barely got upright when I was shot. Something hot and cold grazed my temple and knocked me backwards off the elephant, beyond the boundary wall.

I was lying there helplessly, belly up, as stunned as the elephant, when two fleeing rebels gathered me up and carried me back to safety. There were no shots fired after us; the garrison was content with seeing off the siege. I remembered being handed over to Chaubey, who eased me into the Triumph's sidecar and that's the last thing I remembered of our flight to Banaras. Not that I fainted; I was conscious through the journey but all I remembered was the pain; that and the oddly cheering thought . . . that Bose Madam was now properly in the middle of it all.

Rehearsing Sita

IT WAS A week before my nose got used to the heavy incense smell of Hindu bodies burning. In the end it became as normal as the air I breathed; it was the air I breathed. I inhaled several times my body weight in etherized flesh each day. For the week that it took my wound to heal and my sense of smell to die, I woke up every morning to a world-blotting headache, a sickly, perfumed smell and the likeness of a hugely muscled primate on the opposite wall.

It was actually a picture of Hanuman from a dead calendar, but the bullet had left me concussed and I couldn't focus on it properly till the day after my stitches came out. My scalp had been grazed two inches off-centre; the stitches ran in a straight line exactly where my parting used to be before I had my hair shaved off. When it grew back, it would divide without combing into two unequal parts, separated by a streak of dead tissue in between. Like a wig. Light-headed from sleep and huge doses of sulpha, I giggled at the thought – never would my hair look real again, now that the stitched-in parting of a hairpiece had been sewn into my scalp.

The blurred room of my convalescence was furnished with disuse: broken Indian clubs, a lame barbell, torn loincloths, single dumbbells . . . Each time I got off my bed, it cocked one leg into the air like a dog about to make its mark. It needed jumping on to become four-legged again. But my thermos flask was still in one piece; someone – Chaubey? – had placed it in a little niche in the wall below the window. It was a small room, mostly taken up with ruined things, so the pillow end of my bed was less than two feet from the permanently open window. The window was about three and a half feet square, its frame speckled with defeated blue paint. The shutters that had once hung on its orange hinges, stiff with rust, now lay on the floor under my bed.

The world outside poured in through this hole in the wall of my attic sickroom. Rain bounced off the window-ledge and sprayed my face; great gobbling pigeons blundered in and rocketed out, leaving feathers and droppings behind them. Countless times each hour the walls echoed to the unvarying chant of pall-bearers – Ram naam satya hai – as they hurried one more corpse to Manikarnika Ghat, more fuel for the smell that filled the room.

In that first week, after the worst of the weakness had passed, I spent hours at the window watching the bodies go by. From where I stood it was like watching a succession of one-man rafts floating and wobbling on a river of human heads. It was a crowded lane, full of shops and bustle, but the little rafts flowed past unchecked: here the dead had right of way. Less than twelve feet separated the buildings that rose like canyon walls on either side of the lane. This distance decreased with altitude because the structures of this ancient thoroughfare were gently sagging towards each other. The window opposite mine, for example, couldn't have been much more than a couple of yards away. To keep them from actually meeting, thick bamboo poles had been jammed between the facing walls at irregular intervals. Two such buttressing bamboos, six inches apart, began six feet below my window-ledge and ended just below the corresponding window across the lane. I couldn't see the sky from where I was, not even by hanging out of the window and craning my neck; it was obscured by the spreading branches of a tree growing out of the roof of the window opposite. Filtered through its leaves, all the sunlight in my room was green. It was like living under water.

Not counting the thermos flask, my only human link with the past was Chaubey and he was virtually a stranger. I didn't even recognize him when I became lucid after a fever that had left me incoherent and muttering for nearly two days. My eyes just registered a clean-shaven man with cropped hair and a knotted tuft growing out of the back of his head. His forehead was streaked with ash – no one could have identified him as the rebel chief of Madhuban. True to his word, Chaubey had brought me to Banaras. To start with, he had doctored my wound himself by cauterizing it with a hot knife-blade. That didn't work, so on the third day when my fever dropped, he brought the only medical man he could trust: the vet who tended the barren cows in the Maharaja's cattle sheds. He was the one who cleaned out the wound and stitched me up. I never saw him after that; Chaubey removed the stitches.

The other person who visited me during my convalescence was Guruji. He looked like a retired wrestler gone to fat, which is what he was. He was also my host. I had worked out for myself from the barbells, clubs and other such apparatus that my room was part of some larger establishment devoted to physical culture. Then Chaubey told me I was living in the oldest and most distinguished wrestling academy in Banaras, the legendary Pant Ram ka Akhara. Guruji was twelfth in the line of direct descent from the Pant Ram who had founded the establishment in 1642, three hundred years ago. I think he told me all this to underline how privileged I was to be visited by the latest in the line every evening. At the stroke of five o'clock he appeared holding a large silver tumbler full of buttermilk which he expected me to drink. We never spoke to each other because this was the time he said his end-of-day prayers. He just sat there counting his beads and moving his lips till I emptied the glass. Then, still moving his lips, he would smile and go away.

Inside ten days, though, when I was strong enough to walk about steadily and when the scar on my stubbled scalp had become less livid, my life became less solitary. Subtly, without any orders, or any suggestion that I had convalesced long enough, I was nudged into a new routine. At five in the morning, when even the thoroughfare of the dead beneath my window was still and there was barely enough light to suggest the dawn, I found myself sitting in the lotus pose with a dozen others. We sat in two rows of six or seven, along the outer edge of the courtyard, beyond the sand pits, where the ground dropped away and last night's bodies smoked forlornly on Manikarnika's pyres below. But we didn't look down; we were meant to keep our eyes on the horizon across the river and preferably not blink till the first rays of the sun touched our eyes.

The rest of the day was filled with little jobs that Guruji gave me to do. My first job was airing his paan leaves. Guruji rolled his own paans. The leaves were kept in a silver box, tied up in bunches, and my task was to untie them, examine every leaf and snip off decomposing edges. I must have done this efficiently and well because within two days of starting I was allowed to cut the betel nuts stored in the same silver box. By the fourth week of August I had been given entire charge of the silver box and sometimes, when he was busy, he even asked me to roll paan for him. I had begun to feel something of the job-satisfaction of a responsible houri.

Like the others, who, while I manned the paan box, swung clubs, did metronomic push-ups or squirmed in muscular clinches in the sand pits, I too got used to spending my waking hours in a loincloth. I ate when they did, slept when they slept the hottest hours of the afternoon away, joined them in their prayers and at dusk sat cross-legged in two rows again to hear Guruji's daily sermon on the importance of celibacy and that sapping evil, masturbation.

But from the main business of the akhara, the cultivation of muscles, I was excluded. I didn't much want to wrestle but the monotonous routine of body-building appealed to me. I asked his permission to join in; he shook his head and looked so stern that I never dared to ask again. He didn't give me a reason then and I didn't press him. But I found out.

Though I wasn't to build my own body, I was given a hand in building the bodies of others. I was given bodies to oil and, after a few lessons, bodies to massage. I was given sand pits to rake which were then pounded solid again by the bodies I had oiled and massaged. Then I raked the pits again and aired the leaves and chopped the betel nuts and watched their bodies being narcissistically, repetitively and soothingly built. The ghats filled and emptied, the novice wrestlers came and went, the corpses made their one-way trip to terminus. It was a time of dateless peace.

Actually the days were full of dateless peace but the nights were harder. The excitement began one evening – it was just around the time my wound had healed – after I had doused the kerosene lamp in my room and gone to bed. Sometime after I had fallen asleep (it could have been hours) I woke up thirsty and noticed that the window opposite had flickered into life. That wasn't remarkable because I knew that window was tenanted. I had occasionally seen a middle-aged gourd-faced man push open the mostly closed shutters and keep them open while he smoked a cigarette. I even knew him in a sense because he sometimes visited the akhara. He seemed to be a sort of religious professional because he wore only saffron clothes; also Guruji, who set great store by classical learning, often called on him to provide Sanskrit sanction for his daily warnings against sex and masturbation. One day Gyanendra rounded off Guruji's sermon with a long Sanskrit verse from a post-Vedic text which provided exact nutritional equivalents of a spoonful of spilt semen: ten seers of ghee, fifty seers of shelled almonds or two maunds of unhusked rice. From the guilt on the listening faces round me, whole granaries had been spent that day.

But it wasn't Gyanendra at the window that night; it was a woman. She was reading a book by the light of a lamp, not in the picture. The details were secondary; what was important was that she wasn't wearing all her clothes. She was sitting at an angle to the window, facing away, and except for one end of a sari thrown over her left shoulder her back was bare. This seemed like such an incredible piece of luck that I wondered if she was a woman at all. Certainly the hair was unconventionally short, given this was 1942 – almost a crop – but then she shifted, the better to catch the wavering light, and the delicate lines of her face and neck in profile confirmed my first impression. It was hard to tell in the yellowdark of the kerosene lamp but I could definitely see one naked shoulder. I used the uncertain light to try and fill in imaginatively the delicate thrust of breast beneath the flimsy sari, but that was entirely obscured by the naked arm slightly extended to support the book.

She looked like the ancient Indian women in Hindi films,

like Shobhana Samarth playing Sita, where ancient Indian detail was filled in by leaving blouses out. But I knew this wasn't a film; it was the window opposite and framed in it was a woman in the flesh. I stared without blinking in the prescribed yogic manner from the safety of my darkened room while my pulse hammered and my head whirled with one magic thought: it wasn't a film and anything could happen.

Nothing did. Ten minutes later she put the book away and then most of her disappeared below the window as she squatted to attend to something on the floor. It was the lamp because suddenly the picture vanished and the square of light in front of me went black.

After this I never managed a whole night's sleep. Every day, as soon as it was dark, I began my vigil. Sometimes she never appeared. Other nights the window stayed shuttered. But one night in three the preliminary sound of an oil lamp being pumped and primed would jerk me to electric wakefulness. The lamp came on slowly. Some nights she would be centred in the window-frame as she pumped the lantern on the window-ledge, becoming slowly more real in its deepening glow. There were nights when the lamp stayed out of the frame, as happened the first night I saw her. Those were the best times. Sound. Light. And then she came on . . . from the right or the left or under the ledge, depending on where she had been pumping the lamp. The worst nights were the ones when the light came on but she didn't, when she stayed off-stage, reading perhaps, or otherwise invisible.

Since there was no pattern to her appearances there was no approximate hour of the night that I could set my body clock by. Often I'd stay up all night then report to the exercise yard at five, to stare unblinkingly again, this time at the sun. Some things, though, were predictable. When she did show up she was either reading or writing away in a small copybook. She was always dressed in the same or similar white sari, with nothing underneath it. At least her arms and shoulders and back (when I could see it) showed no sign of sleeve or strap or any stitched cloth. And she was always beautiful. In the voluptuously shadowed lamplight and framed by the window, she never looked less than a picture.

At the end of a week I knew she had scars and discolorations on her back that were stained with what seemed like blood but was probably Mercurochrome. That she didn't look more than twenty. That no one shared the room with her. Of this I was almost sure; almost because I couldn't see all of the room through the window. But I'd never heard her speak to anyone or anyone speak to her, so I assumed she had the place to herself. This was comforting but there was no forgetting the times I had seen Gyanendra smoking at her window during the day. For myself, I hoped he lived in an adjacent room. He certainly had something to do with her.

But what? If she was his mistress why wasn't he there at night? If he was her pimp, where were her customers? And the relevant sounds? The creaking and grunting, the huffing and puffing, the sighing? Was he family? He looked too old to be her brother, and he couldn't be her father and remain credible as a sage holding forth on continence and celibacy.

Then one morning, while waiting for the sun, cross-legged, eyes straying to the smoking pyres, it came to me. She was a widow. Her cropped hair. Her white sari. Her seclusion. Banaras. Taken altogether they added up to a dead man's wife. And Gyanendra? Perhaps he had been asked by her family to keep an eye on her, to help her, to ease her way into the mendicant life. That would explain why she hadn't yet been herded into a dharmashala dormitory with other widows. It would also account for her lack of underclothes. Widows didn't wear any.

I spoke of her to no one, except Chaubey, and that only later, when I was forced to by Guruji's idiot scheme. In the beginning, the girl in the window was my secret.

About the things I did want to talk over with Chaubey, he had little to say. He would tell me nothing about our retreat from Madhuban or how we got to Banaras despite my asking him more than once. What has happened has happened, he said curtly. The past was obsolete . . . and there had been no retreat. Would he have returned to Banaras, to the lion's den, nursing a wounded man if escape had been the first thing on his mind? No, he would have scurried north and lost himself in the unpoliced hills, as so many of the others had done. He was in Banaras not as a fugitive but as an honourable man who had pledged his word. He had promised to get me safely to Banaras and he had. Even more important was the promise he had made to Guruji.

For Guruji 1942 was a big year for reasons other than rebellion. It was the tercentenary of the akhara and he planned to celebrate it in a way that would make his name as much of a household word in Banaras as Pant Ram's was. In the history of wrestling in Banaras, 1642 marked the beginning of an epoch. From the year of the akhara's foundation, no Hun, Greek or Muslim had won the Banaras Kesari title at the annual championship sponsored by the Maharaja and attended by every important akhara in the city. An unbroken line of Hindu strongmen all forged and tempered in the fire of Pant Ram's academy had been draped in the victor's shawl by a succession of kings. Singlehandedly Pant Ram's akhara had laid the sapping canard that the Banarasi Hindu had paan in his mouth, ghee in his veins and bhang in his brains. By its heroic example it had restored the manhood of the men of Aryavarta.

Of course this stirred envy, said Chaubey sadly. Vicious rumours had tried to diminish the akhara's achievement. One of them, for example, tried to make something of the fact that the akhara was situated directly above the burning ghat. It was true that the wrestling pits and the exercise yard overlooked the pyres of Manikarnika, but to build on this fact the theory that its wrestlers came by their strength because they ritually breathed in the substance of dead men burning . . . that was vileness, slander. If that were true, the pyre priests would be the strongest men in the world. And I would be King Kong, I thought to myself, nodding sympathetically at everything Chaubey said.

Despite the whisperings of jealous men, the akhara's achievement stood like a monument to its founder. Guruji wanted to be remembered in the same way . . . only his ambition was larger. Pant Ram's legend had a limited, specialist constituency: wrestlers, body builders and the like. Guruji conceived of posterity as a grander audience – every man, woman and child in Banaras for all time to come. Not that he disliked wrestling; he loved his ancestral art, but like every artist, he was stalking the popular market.

Chaubey had come back to Banaras to help Guruji make his name immortal and because he had brought me with him, Guruji worked me into his scheme. I was now a cog in his machine, a little flourish in his grand design.

Looking back, it seems clear that Guruji cast me as Sita soon after Chaubey carried me into the akhara, wounded. It explained his concern for a stranger's well-being, his daily round with the buttermilk and, later, his insistence that I grow my nails and grease my skin, especially my chest and shoulders with cream skimmed off the morning's milk. At the time I only thought that he was homosexual, which made me nervous when he came to visit, but there was never an inkling that he had slated me for stardom in an epic play.

Then one morning towards the end of August or the first week of September – I had lost track – he came to my room holding a yard of hair which he asked me to wear. It was a wig. I should have said no or asked for an explanation but I was a refugee in the akhara and I lived there at his pleasure. So I put it on and let him lead me to a mirror. It was an old mirror, chipped and speckled, but it worked well enough to show me the image of a passable woman. Guruji thought so too. He nodded and made the tiptop sign without saying anything. Then with his lips still counting silent beads, he went away, leaving the wig behind.

What was he up to? If he expected me to do the day's work at the akhara with it on, he could think again. I wasn't going to massage muscular boys brimming with sap, wearing tresses. It might give them the wrong ideas . . . and they were creatures of sinew and instinct, capable of anything.

Luckily it was Tuesday, a day of rest at the akhara, so I shut myself up in the room and prayed for Chaubey to come. He had been a pupil of Guruji's for five years, right from the time he had arrived in Banaras to study history. He would know. Maybe he would have some simple explanation for it.

Chaubey came to the akhara at seven when it was dark. That was luck again, because he didn't come every evening. He could have stayed permanently at the akhara – there was another room – but after the siege at Madhuban, Chaubey was a wanted man and Guruji's establishment was a very public place. So he lived with an old wrestler friend who had given up wrestling to become a cook at a big house on Tulsi Ghat. But he generally looked in three times a week to talk to Guruji and that evening happened to be one of those days.

Guruji was at his evening prayers, so I managed to talk to Chaubey alone for almost half an hour. I told him how his guru was trying to turn me into a transvestite. I waved the wig about as evidence of his depravity. But Chaubey seemed entirely unshocked.

I know, I know, he said. He had known any time these past two weeks, from the second or third day of our arrival in Banaras.

Known what?

That Guruji had marked me down to play Sita.

Sita?

Sita. The wife of Ram in the akhara's production of the Ramlila scheduled for next year's Dussehra festival. Guruji had planned to start rehearsals earlier, said Chaubey casually, but he postponed them to give you time to recover.

Stunned, I just sat there, wondering hysterically if I should be grateful for his consideration. One question about the wig had brought me answers to everything: why Chaubey had returned to Banaras after the rout at Madhuban, why I, a bystander, was at the centre of this story instead of at its margins, how Guruji planned to become immortal . . .

From the time he had succeeded to the running of the akhara, Guruji had been looking for a way to make the tercentenary memorable and his tenure as Guru, his steward-ship, unforgettable. But what? There was nothing more to be achieved in the field of wrestling, just more of the same. Or there was if Guruji had chosen to look at the world beyond Banaras but he couldn't be bothered with that. He wanted to be remembered by people who mattered.

Then, three years ago, the year the war began, it had suddenly come to him one morning, as he sat in a shallow tub, rinsing his bowels with milk. He would stage the greatest Ramlila Banaras had ever seen! He should have thought of it before! It was the straightest route to the heart of every Banarasi, the perfect vehicle for popular, enduring fame.

Every child knew the story of Ram, God Incarnate, King Dashrath's son and Sita's husband, who had first conquered Lanka by way of a land bridge no longer extant; whose chief lieutenant in this campaign, Hanuman, the Son of Wind, hung framed on every akhara's walls in his subsidiary capacity as patron of all celibate strongmen. He really should have thought of it before.

Not only was it the best-known story ever told – in the world that counted – it was also the greatest theatrical event in Banaras' calendar. For ten days every year, the epic unfolded on both banks of the Ganga as it flowed between Ramnagar and Banaras. For ten days the whole city watched till the heaven-assisted Ram felled that ten-headed trier, Ravana, who was then, along with his brothers, burnt in effigy. Forty feet of figured evil stuffed with fire-crackers.

At first, when he aired the idea, people were sceptical. Even Chaubey was unconvinced. Banaras already had a Ramlila sponsored by His Highness himself, the Maharaja of Banaras. Most cities had more than one Ramlila but in Banaras the Maharaja's version was accepted as definitive, so no one else had bothered for at least a hundred years. There was no point trying now, said Guruji's friends – no one would watch it.

But Guruji just knew they would. They would because this wouldn't be just another Ramlila; his production would re-write the rules for its staging. It would do for the Ramlila what the talkies had done for the pictures.

Banarasis watched the Maharaja's Ramlila out of habit, he argued. They watched because there wasn't an alternative. Why else would people watch a play in which warrior kings were played by girlish men in top-knots? Where Hanuman, who had lifted a mountain with one arm, was impersonated by degenerates who couldn't shoulder a mace. In our Ramlila, said Guruji to Chaubey, the audience won't need a monkey's mask to spot Hanuman – they'll know him by his muscles. He convinced Chaubey that the akhara was a ready-made repertory company for an authentic, virile Ramlila.

Besides, who had the time, in the modern bustle of 1942, to follow a play for more than a week? The Maharaja's Ramlila was spread over ten days. The akhara, instead of stretching one performance through ten days, would stage ten, one every day. He would compress the *Ramayan* into a six-hour show, starting at noon and ending at dinnertime, with all the slow bits cut out. His production of the Ramlila would play to the strengths of the akhara, namely, strength. Proper fight scenes, single combat between Hanuman and Sugreev complete with throws and hammer-locks, and a final battle with no holds barred. Also, the characters would talk sensibly. No verse. Fighting men didn't speak in couplets.

He wanted to stage it on Tulsi Ghat, in the open air where political rallies were sometimes held. By the time Dussehra ends next year, he predicted, Banarasis will be climbing trees to get a look at our Ramlila, because there won't be room on the ground.

I believe him, said Chaubey, sitting with his back to the window in my little room. That's why I came back to Banaras. I had promised him in January, long before this Quit India business, that I would play Hanumanji. That's why when the movement failed, I couldn't head for the hills with the others.

What about the police? I asked.

Chaubey shrugged. There isn't really any risk. In a year from now the police will have forgotten me. Besides, I'll be wearing a snout during the performances – nobody will recognize me. I'm lucky Guruji didn't cast me as Ram, he said. And grinned.

I came back to the original question – the matter of the yard of hair. Why had I been cast as Sita?

Because I was slim, soft and nearly beardless, Chaubey informed me. And because I had smooth shoulders, not tufted with hair. Shoulders were critical since women of the epic age didn't wear blouses.

I still didn't understand. Why me? Slim, soft or not, I was still a man. There was a world full of women with softer bodies, smoother shoulders and less stubbled chins than mine. If wrestlers were playing Ram and Hanuman so that men could be men, didn't it follow that Sita ought to be a woman? And wasn't the tradition of Sita being played by male impersonators the main reason for the low credibility of the old-style Ramlila?

For the spur of the moment it was a good argument and I made it well. Chaubey agreed with me. Apparently Guruji agreed with me as well. He too had wanted a woman complete with bosom and hips and dulcet voice to play Sita, but no respectable woman of a reasonable age would agree.

That's why it has to be you, said Chaubey.

Being told, in that room littered with the apparatus of man-making, that I was to be the woman in the piece made me shiver. It was August and warm and my situation was more absurd than dangerous. But I shivered – and all of me not covered with the loincloth pimpled like a ping-pong bat.

Since getting to Banaras I hadn't thought beyond bedtime. I'd fled Lucknow knowing that Banaras was my goal. Immersing Dadi's ashes seemed then a kind of dénouement, an ending, a way of keeping faith with my own time . . . I had, after all, set out that long-ago evening to take Dadi's ashes to Kashi. Now I had been in Banaras for more than two weeks and her ashes still lived in a flask in a niche below my window. Endings were for people who had other things to go on with. All I had by way of a purpose were the ashes and I wasn't going to sink them till I found out what came afterwards.

It was only after being billed as Sita that I thought seriously about afterwards. Till then I had been occupied with injury, convalescence and the window opposite, with no thought for the world beyond the akhara. There wasn't much to think about – the only people I knew in this world had been left behind in Lucknow. After the fiasco at Madhuban I was a fugitive from justice twice over and the akhara represented safety, shelter, food, and nightly entertainment. It was my oasis and I saw no reason to brood on the desert outside.

But this Sita business set me thinking. It wasn't the future that I thought about; the schemes I hatched were limited to salvaging the present. That is, how to protect my comfortable routines, or, how not to be an epic heroine. Having been dislocated in time and place, I wanted no uncertainty about gender. Not wanting to be a transvestite on the amateur stage was part of it; the more important objection to Sita was the spit-drying fear at the thought of being part of a public spectacle. Everything I had been through in 1942 had taught me the importance of being offstage. Cast as a mere spectator in the productions at Unnao and Madhuban I had almost lost both life and liberty – and now they wanted me in the play. And not as an extra; as a star.

Of course I could have run away, but that wasn't practical. The akhara represented perfect security and besides . . . where would I go? There was just one other way of not being Sita and I took it. I swapped excitement for safety . . . and told Chaubey about the girl in the window.

I did better than that; I invited him to one of the nightly screenings so he could see for himself that she was perfect for the role. As usual she was in a state of chaste undress, but even in broad outline it was easy to see that she fitted the part a lot better than I did. It was a brief appearance; she wrote for less than half an hour before turning down the lamp. Chaubey didn't say a word during that time but each time he breathed in, the air in my room became thinner. He sounded like a randy bicycle pump; I worried that she might hear him rasping and snorting.

He went home that night without saying a word, but when we met again after lunch the next day, he was as enthusiastic as I was about the window-girl replacing me as Sita. We must tell Guruji immediately, he said. Before rehearsals begin. He wrung my hand. What a top idea! At last a Sita worth abducting! Worth bridging the sea with stones for, worth fighting a war about!

I calmed him down. There was no point going to Guruji without finding out if the girl was available. I told him about the Gyanendra connection. She is his ward, I said confidently. Gyanendra was often at the akhara for the evening prayers, so Chaubey could catch him outside for a private word about the girl.

Chaubey saw the wisdom of this at once. Good to be cautious, he said, nodding. Though once her guardian agreed, there would be no problem. He was certain Guruji would see at once that she was indispensable to a virile Ramlila.

It was a good plan. She was perfect for the role, Guruji would have loved her, I would have been left alone . . . it was a good plan and it might have worked . . . if the terrible magic of the movies hadn't ambushed epic theatre. It wasn't my fault: what happened to us was a local instance of a global phenomenon.

But at the time the signs were good. Gyanendra came to the akhara in the evening and after the prayers were over, I saw Chaubey following him out of the door. My plan was in motion.

I didn't see Chaubey again till the same time the next evening. Meanwhile, in the morning, Guruji had launched his path-breaking production. He had us all assemble by the wrestling pits and made a speech which for once was not a sermon on self-abuse. It was as much about himself as his revisionist Ramlila. I, me, mine occurred frequently. The only other person he mentioned in his speech was Mother India. He was staging the Ramlila on her behalf, he said. He didn't explain and he didn't have to: in 1942 the Nation was another word for reason.

So. My life as Sita was upon me. But no sickness started in my stomach, because I believed in my scheme and the signs, as I said, were good. I even lived through the first rehearsal with reasonable composure. It wasn't easy though, especially after Guruji personally began turning me into a woman. It was a complicated business and the wig was only one part of it. I was dressed in an orange sari which, like the girl in the window, I wore without a blouse. Little circlets of white flowers were tied around my arms and wrists; my wig was drawn up into a little bun on top of my head and that was ringed with flowers too. My lips were painted fiercely red and a large black mole was fixed just east of my mouth. All this happened in the wrestling yard with Guruji's students watching. I didn't look at them in the beginning, afraid that they would snigger. When I did meet their eyes, what I saw frightened me even more; they weren't laughing – they were staring at me with a blank raptness that made me hurriedly look away.

My host and director was dissatisfied. How could the image of the Hindu wife be in character without red sindoor in the parting of her hair – in this case, her wig. The wrestler in charge of props made a note of sindoor. There was also the matter of my figure. Guruji gestured approximately in the region of his chest and the wrestler entered another requisition.

Guruji had his own ideas about how a play was made and he started with a dress rehearsal. I wasn't the only character fitted out that first day; every individual in the akhara was given a role and the costume that Guruji thought went with it. After casting the main characters, he divided the rest into the two opposing armies: the hairy ones made up Ram's monkey brigade and the others, by default, became the ten-headed Ravana's terrible horde.

In an inspired move, he decided that both sides would be dressed only in loincloths – this would show their muscles off besides saving the expense of clothing them. To help the audience tell them apart, he issued papier-mâché monkey masks to one lot and fanged demon faces to the other.

Hanuman, along with the other main characters, was exempted from the loincloth norm. For him there was a dhoti in yellow silk and a gilt crown that looked a lot like the onion dome on the Taj Mahal. Guruji wanted Chaubey to try it on but he wasn't there. He hadn't turned up that morning. Guruji was furious: I have to know if the crown will stay on in the fight scenes, he said to me, his brows knitted with displeasure. Besides, he had planned to get the costumes out of the way in the morning and rehearse the climactic battle right away. It was a matter of getting the bloodier set-pieces and the action sequences right; the speeches, the good and evil, dharma, drama and love-shove would fall into place once the fighting and the killing seemed real. Lots of hand-to-hand fighting . . . and throws. But where was Chaubey?

Chaubey arrived at one but I didn't get to talk to him till four when Guruji, delighted with the authentic violence of the battle scenes, let his cast off an hour earlier than scheduled. The credit for this belonged to Chaubey entirely. He came in looking preoccupied and apologized to Guruji for the delay. Then he undressed and put on his character. The crown fitted snugly, the yellow of the dhoti gleamed and winked. Guruji wanted Hanuman to look as nearly human as possible, so he didn't make Chaubey wear a mask. His make-up consisted of a false nose with flared nostrils, and, instead of a mask, two pads which he tucked between his lips and teeth just to hint at the simian. In common with the other monkeys, he didn't wear a tail. That was another of Guruji's improvements on conventional Ramlilas. Tails are ridiculous, he snorted. They come off if you step on them and they get in the way of the action.

How will he burn Lanka without one? asked Ram, who had been given the part because he was so intensely black he was nearly blue. Isn't it written that he set his tail on fire and used it to set fire to the city?

It's a lie, snapped Guruji. So what if it is written. The *Ramayan* wasn't written down for thousands of years. Just because some lying clerk made up that Lanka-burning story, people have been acting it out like parrots. In my Ramlila, Hanuman will hold a flaming torch in his right hand to set Lanka on fire. Remember three things, said Guruji sternly. Hanuman is a god, not a monkey; Hinduism is a manly religion and the *Ramayan* is a tale of heroes. Do heroes wear tails?

After that there were no more questions and no further talk. Chaubey demonstrated, by personal example, the dramatic possibilities of hand-to-hand fighting. Still looking abstracted, he executed perfect aeroplane spins, hip-throws, arm-locks and other manoeuvres which made his partners who were spun, thrown and locked scream, bleed and faint in a very realistic way. Chaubey gave no sign that he noticed these reactions and sometimes Guruji had to intervene to ask him to be less lifelike.

When Guruji called it a day after all the available actors had been used up, I led the unusually subdued Chaubey to the edge of the yard that overlooked the pyres and asked him the critical question: will she play Sita?

He almost gave me a straight answer. She doesn't have a — he began and then stopped and reached inside his mouth to remove the Hanuman padding. Guruji will be here soon, he said in thinner, mortal tones. We'll talk outside. Outside? only there wasn't time to chat because Chaubey was out of the akhara already. I followed him; already this was a landmark afternoon: I had never stepped out of the akhara before.

I found myself on a broad flight of flagged steps that led down to the burning ghat. Chaubey was already halfway down, very visible in his yellow silk dhoti. I set off in measured pursuit, kicking the folds of the sari outward to make sure that its hem didn't curl under my feet and trip me up. Also, I wasn't wearing a blouse; since no one outside the akhara knew that I wasn't a woman I had to walk slowly to make sure that the sari's palloo didn't slide off my shoulder. Specially since I was going to be on view a year from now as Sita.

From the steps, looking down, the ghat looked like a blistered palm with the morning's pyres still smouldering redly. Chaubey threaded his way through the heaps of smoking ash till he reached the edge of the bank, where steps led down to the river. Where the steps met the water, a rowing-boat was leashed with a short chain to a metal ring embedded in the stone. Chaubey waited for me to catch up with him and then we went down a few steps and sat down, keeping our feet just clear of the water. I kept looking over my shoulder but no angry priest or cremation ground caretaker appeared.

Don't worry, said Chaubey, pointing at the pyres. They probably think that one of those is ours.

Reassured, I settled down, reflecting that in another time and another place, one of those had in fact been mine. It wasn't so long since I had sifted Dadi's still-warm pyre for her leftovers.

Chaubey's meeting with Gyanendra the previous evening had begun well.

He was so friendly, said Chaubey, his voice still coloured with yesterday's surprise. I went up to him to ask if he had five minutes – and he put his arm around my shoulders and took me home.

Home for Gyanendra wasn't the room attached to the window opposite; it was the one right next to it. Gyanendra and the girl lived in a dharmashala. Chaubey knew as soon as he walked into the building that it was some kind of boarding house, because the courtyard around which it was built was hung with crisscrossed washing lines, sagging with clothes.

No single family, however extended, could have generated so much washing. As they climbed the steps to the second floor where Gyanendra lived, he told Chaubey that the dharmashala had been built by a Maratha nobleman at the end of the eighteenth century, thirty years too late for a site on the ghats with a view of the river. But it suited Gyanendra. The manager's ancestors had come from Baroda, as had Gyanendra, which made for a bond. So in that pilgrim hostel meant for transients, Gyanendra had found semi-permanent lodgings.

His room was large and windowless; light came in only through the ground-glass panes set in the door. It had a bed, an umbrella hanging on a clothes peg, a tattered Gita Press edition of the *Ramcharitmanas* and a large book covered in newspaper. One corner of the room was home to a heap of machine-like things; in the gloom of the room it was hard to tell what they were.

Then I asked him, said Chaubey. I said that we were looking for a good girl to play Sita and would he allow his ward to play the role?

How do you know that I have a ward? asked Gyanendra sharply. Chaubey hadn't thought up an answer for that one, so he told him the truth about the window. Not the whole truth; he left out our voyeur's vigil and made it out to be a glimpse by accident.

Did you speak to her about this?

No, said Chaubey truthfully. I wanted to ask you first.

I'm glad you didn't speak to her directly, said Gyanendra, benevolent again. She had suffered so much so recently that he was trying to insulate her from the world outside. About her playing Sita . . . it was impossible.

Why? I asked Chaubey dully.

Because it wouldn't be right. Not because he thought acting was disreputable; Gyanendra was quick to assure Chaubey that with Guruji at the helm he was certain that everything would be respectable. It was just that she was entirely unsuitable.

Why? asked Chaubey.

She's a widow, said Gyanendra simply.

He had first met her on her husband's pyre from which he had rescued her because he was a progressive in these matters and didn't believe in burning widows. Now he was trying to nurse her back into the world by instilling in her a sense of her own worth. For himself he would be delighted to have her play Sita – it would lift her morale wonderfully. But there were limits to reformism. Sita was the perfect Hindu wife incarnate; she just couldn't be played by a widow. What would people think? Gyanendra shook his head. When it came to the Ramlila, you had to allow for the people.

Also, the girl was mute. The burning pyre had singed her back before he managed to snatch her off and the shock and pain had struck her dumb. The doctor he showed her to said that there was no telling when she'd be able to speak again. He himself had never heard her say a word. Casting a speechless widow as Sita would be worse than risky. It would be a scandal.

He has a point, said Chaubey defensively, turning to me. I thought he had a point too. Even as an interested party I could see that Sita was better played by a bachelor who could speak than by a widow who couldn't. Never mind, I said more to myself than Chaubey, it's only a play and in less than a year it'll all be over.

I got to my feet and made to leave, but Chaubey wasn't finished yet.

You know what he did after that? he asked, looking pent-up and righteous.

No, what? I asked automatically, though I didn't want to go on talking to him. He was the bearer of bad news and I couldn't love him for it. I wanted to nurse my disappointment in private.

He offered me a role, huffed Chaubey. Two minutes after saying we couldn't have the girl for Sita, he said he had the perfect part for me!

He said he was making a film. A film! That fakir offered me a role in a film as if he owned Bombay Talkies!

I shrugged. Chaubey was silly to get so worked up. Given Gyanendra's age, it was obviously some senile fantasy about being a film maker. Or a joke.

137

But it wasn't a joke. Smiling at Chaubey's angry in-credulity, Gyanendra walked to a dark corner of the room with a lantern. He lifted the lantern high and abruptly unnameable shapes were resolved into a large camera standing on a tripod.

A movie camera? I asked, despite myself.

No, said Chaubey. A camera for photographs. Gyanendra said that he would hire a movie camera when the shooting began. This one he was going to use for framing scenes and taking publicity stills. But even this was a big one, the sort professionals used.

So then, said Chaubey quietly, looking at his knuckles, I asked him what kind of film it was.

A classic, said Gyanendra grandly. A classic. Guruji isn't the only one who can breathe life into ancient Indian epics. So can I. That's why I want you: your epic body for my epic film.

Stunned into submission by the ratifying presence of the camera, Chaubey heard him out.

It was an epic on a budget – but without any stinting on authenticity or art. The film would be faithful to the classical text. It just so happened that the original (and therefore the script) didn't call for extras, props, costumes or other budget-bloating paraphernalia. No location shooting either . . . just the one indoor set. The biggest saving was on the soundtrack . . . there wasn't any. Twenty years after the talkies had overrun cinema, he was about to produce a silent epic. No sound. This classic's theme demanded a purely visual treatment. In this country of a hundred languages, speech was no way to communicate. To reach its target audience, it would have to be the greatest story ever shown . . . not told. Racier than the *Ramayan*, more climacteric than the *Mahabharat*, as arduous as the *Odyssey* . . . there was no reason why it couldn't become an international hit.

What is it? I asked Chaubey, hypnotized.

What is it? asked Chaubey in the lamplit gloom.

Gyanendra didn't answer at once. He stroked the underside of his chin with his knuckles and looked keenly at Chaubey.

Vatsyayana's *Kama Sutra*, he said matter-of-factly.

Vatsyayana's *Kama Sutra*, mimicked Chaubey for my

138

benefit with remembered indignation. Like Valmiki's *Ramayan* or Vyasji's *Mahabharat* – all respectable. Author's name first makes it a classic.

Curiously agitated, he let his rage run on. What did Gyanendra think? That he, Chaubey, was a fool? That he didn't know that the *Kama Sutra* was a filthy sex manual written by an ancient Indian pervert?

He wanted me, he said, his voice trembling, he wanted me to actually act out all those positions with the girl in the window! I said I couldn't act. Then he said that I didn't have to . . . because I would actually do all these things with her while he filmed us.

Chaubey took a deep breath. I told him that I was a brahmachari, celibate and pure. So was the film, he said. Pure form and pure pleasure in perfect harmony. Celibacy was but one of the four stages in life. Sooner or later Chaubey would become a householder, and before he did it would be useful to get in some practice.

But she's a widow, protested Chaubey.

Gyanendra had an answer for everything, even that. I don't believe that widows should be condemned to barren chastity, he said solemnly, just as I don't believe they should be burnt.

Besides, if she was to make her way in life instead of shaving her head and waiting for death as the other widows in Banaras did, she needed a livelihood. And if this, her début feature, was a hit, she'd have a career. In any case, it wasn't really sex – it was art.

But Chaubey wasn't taken in . . . or so he said. No, he knew a pimp when he saw one and that was all Gyanendra was under the Sanskrit. He had seen through the lecherous scoundrel at once.

Not quite at once, I thought, trudging up the steps to the cremation ground, as we made our way back to the akhara. For someone so outraged by Gyanendra's proposition, the debate on acting, art, celibacy and widowhood had gone on too long. He should have stormed out of the dharmashala the moment the film was named. His warmed-over indignation didn't ring true.

But it wasn't my business. The news relevant to me had

come early in his story: the girl wasn't available, so I would have to go through with Sita. That's all that mattered. I wasn't even worried that the girl wouldn't turn up in my window again, now that Chaubey had told Gyanendra where he had first seen her. It wouldn't be the same now, not after hearing what she had been through. Whether the film would actually get made, whether the poor girl would have to act out the *Kama Sutra*, whether Chaubey was secretly excited by Gyanendra's offer – about all this I felt no curiosity, just indifference.

What I did feel by the time I had picked my way through the pyres and reached the akhara's threshold, was a sense of relief. Already, by the river, listening to Chaubey, I had resigned myself to being Sita; now I felt almost reconciled. Things could have been worse. Guruji could have been Gyanendra. I pulled the sari round my shoulders with a shiver. Better Sita in the Ramlila than a lesser woman in a blue film.

A Girl in the Window

THE FIRST TIME Chaubey made me nervous was on the second of March. It was a Tuesday, the day we first ran through the Lanka scene under the peepul tree.

We had been rehearsing for more than four months by then and Guruji was worried. He had rewritten the *Ramayan* to showcase Chaubey, because in an all-action Ramlila, Hanuman was the hero's role. But Chaubey didn't seem committed to the part. He never learnt his lines, which slowed down rehearsals; nor could he be trusted in the run-throughs for the fight scenes because he often forgot Guruji's cautions and maimed his partners with terrible, absent-minded violence.

Guruji didn't know it, but the hero of his sacred epic was dreaming of secular stardom. Two weeks ago, Gyanendra had repeated his offer, and since then Chaubey had spent his evenings rehearsing new arguments against a proposal he had already denounced months ago by the riverside.

Sometimes it was his concern for the poor girl in the window, at others it was the need to dam his nectar up to give it the chance to congeal into muscles. And besides, if a widow couldn't play Sita, a carnal man couldn't play Hanuman. If she was the model of Indian womanhood, he was the prototype of celibate strength. How could he freelance as a sexual gymnast while rehearsing to be Hanuman? Moreover the girl was a defenceless young widow. It would be different if she was a used woman, used to that kind of thing. Different, that is, for someone else. He couldn't do it, no, there was no question of that.

Till that watershed Tuesday, my policy was to listen. It wasn't hard to tell that Chaubey was dying to get his hands on the window-girl. At least once a day, he would climb the stairs to my room, knotted with lust, to stare longingly at the window opposite, which stayed shuttered. Chaubey wanted me to tell him that his elaborate arguments against the *Kama Sutra* were trivial, that her honour, his semen and Guruji's Ramlila didn't matter, that he ought to go ahead and say yes to Gyanendra. But I said nothing. It was no business of mine. Still, there was a noncommittal pleasure in watching him burn.

Then he looked at me in a certain way under the peepul tree and everything changed. The tree was critical for the Lanka scene because the kidnapped Sita had to sit forlorn beneath one. The clearing near Tulsi Ghat where our Ramlila would eventually be staged had a majestic, spreading neem tree, custom-made for this purpose; luckily for Guruji, the akhara had an approximate substitute in the peepul which grew by the east wall of the courtyard.

The rehearsal had begun and I was sitting under its branches, wrapped in a sari, my wig and arms fragrant with flowers, my rosebud mouth wilting with melancholy, longing for my blue-black Ram, when suddenly, there was the thud-like sound of a large fruit dropping. I looked up and there was Hanuman. It was a spectacular descent and Chaubey did it very well. He knelt before me and gave me news of my husband, the monkey army, the bridging of the straits, the last dreadful battle and my imminent liberation. This part was harder for Chaubey, because it was a long speech and he had no head for words.

That Tuesday morning, though, the words tripped off his tongue with startling fluency. He threw himself into the speech and got it in one go, gazing intensely into my eyes all the while. So intensely that I dropped my eyelids and looked away shyly, whereupon Guruji cried out in joy and declared the scene a success.

I knew better than to make a noise about that burning look. Guruji wasn't likely to believe that his favourite pupil was so wound-up with wanting to do it that he had begun eyeing the nearest thing to a woman at hand – namely me. Even if he did, he would probably get rid of me rather than risk losing the best-muscled Hanuman in history. No, carrying tales would make me homeless and friendless all at once. So when it happened again the next day, I applied myself to the delicate task of retaining Chaubey's friendship and redirecting his love.

I had to move quickly. Being eyed in public was one thing – there was only so far he could go. But in my room the possibilities were limitless. It was an isolated attic room, so there would be no witnesses, not even the girl in the window opposite, now that it was permanently shuttered.

Chaubey confirmed my fears the next day. He visited me in the evening and spent the first half hour, to my great relief, in the usual way: staring at the window opposite, willing it to open. But when this didn't happen, he departed from the set routine. Instead of listing his many good reasons for not embodying the formulae of the *Kama Sutra* on film, he offered to give me a massage. Offered is probably the wrong word. Basically he let me know that he wanted to knead my body into desirable shapes.

That's when I realized that he was far gone because I wasn't looking like a woman at the time. I wasn't wearing my costume: no wig, no flowers, no lipstick, no sari sans blouse. So Chaubey was either using his imagination to fill in my missing bits (as I had once done with the shadowed parts of the girl in the window) or he was past caring. Either explanation spelt rape. Wild thoughts of valour and never surrendering lit my mind as I reached for the dumb-bell under my bed. It wasn't needed – the door opened and Guruji entered with my glass of milk.

Chaubey left soon after but tomorrow was another day. I didn't sleep that night. The safe cocoon of darkness unravelled minute by minute, thread by thread, and the sinister light of dawn found me still wrestling with that same, stark choice: be buggered or be gone.

I didn't want to run away. It would solve nothing because the world elsewhere was an uncomfortable place. I had been on the run since that terrible night by the rail track in Unnao – Lucknow, Azamgarh, Madhuban – each panicked flight more shattering than the last. I just wanted the here and now to go on for ever. Faces I recognized and a familiar place to feed and sleep in – that was enough for me.

Gripped by an intense nostalgia for the present, I crept down the stairs to join the novice wrestlers in their pop-eyed salutation of the early morning sun. Fifty deep and even breaths flushed the brain clean of the night's stale dreams, according to Guruji. That morning I breathed with a will. I inhaled at such measured length that by the fortieth breath my head was filled with a giddy calm and into that void, briefly freed of the buzz and static of the world outside, dropped the perfect solution to Chaubey – like a free-fall artist landing on a handkerchief. Like a shortwave signal finding a Third World radio. Like a miracle!

So instead of hiding when Chaubey reported for work, I sought him out. Guruji was rehearsing the confrontation between Ravana and Angad, so neither of us had anything to do till lunch. Greatly daring, I took him by the arm and led him down to the ghat again to implement my plan. We could have talked in my room but I wasn't ready yet to risk a private conversation.

Once again we sat on the top step of the staircase that ran into the river. The river seemed higher this time – most of the steps were under water, but the boat was still there, bobbing about on its metal leash. Even the things we spoke about were the same as the time before: Gyanendra, the girl in the window, the *Kama Sutra* and the morality of saying yes. Or no. Only this time the roles were reversed. This time I did the talking.

In less than half an hour I set out every argument he had ever wanted to hear but hadn't had the wit to invent. With terrible fluency, pausing only to push the girl's face from my mind, I showed him why he ought to accept the offer without pang or reservation.

Luckily I had been Chaubey's confidant for so long that I had his reasons for saying no in serial order. One. Rape. That was easy. It wasn't. We knew she was a widow. It followed that she had been a wife; so she was used to sex. She could have been anything before she nearly became a sati, even an actress – in which case it certainly wouldn't be rape. Besides, for all we knew, perhaps she was doing it of her own free will. Having once been snatched from the jaws of death, any experience was probably a bonus for her: fates-worse-than-death lived only in the minds of those who had never tried dying.

In any case, where was his self-esteem? Surely he would be an improvement on any man that she had ever known? Better him than someone else. And there would be someone else because Gyanendra was clearly set on making the film. Did Chaubey want some degenerate getting his hands on her because good men said no?

This brought me to manhood and its frittering away. Guruji's warnings, I explained to him, weren't relevant in this case because they applied to masturbation, which doing it with the window-girl was not. One was unnatural, the other was not. One was self-indulgent, the other was classically pre-scribed. One was solitary and barren; the other was salutary and fruitful because it would illustrate for a mass audience the *Kama Sutra*, this glorious text from the golden age of the Guptas, since when there had mostly been darkness. Didn't he see?

Chaubey wavered. He wanted to be convinced but he was still worried by the thought of squandering his substance on sex. I tore out that doubt by the roots.

It was only a film, I told him. Not real life. The whole art of film-making was simulation. Here death wasn't death, fire didn't burn and love didn't lead to lessening. Here the act was an act: fornication without ejaculation, sex without spending, free!

He would squander nothing because conservation was the need of the hour. There were so many positions to be fitted into a reasonable shooting schedule that he would have to exercise rigid self-control. If he let himself go each time, the wait for the sap to rise again would prolong the filming impossibly.

But once he learnt restraint, sex with the window-girl, far from being a violation of the celibate life, would become its supreme test, its ordeal by fire. A beautiful girl and the time-tested routines of antiquity on the one hand; Chaubey and the iron discipline of Pant Ram's akhara on the other. He could do it; it was no different from looking at the sun for a long time without blinking – and we did that every morning. If he did it, if the austerities of pious bachelorhood – sun-staring, deep breathing, bench-pressing – withstood Vatsyayana and the wiles of the girl in the window, he, Chaubey, would be revered beyond the dreams of nationalists or film stars. For then he would have extended the scope of celibacy right into the vixen's lair; he would have made sex vegetarian.

Here Chaubey and I had to move to one side to allow a group of people through. It looked like a bereaved family with a priest in attendance. One of them, a young man, was carrying an urn, but neither he nor the others looked particularly sad. Perhaps it was a grandparent who had died in the fullness of age. They got into the boat with the priest muttering formulae in a preoccupied way, and cast off. When they reached the middle of the river, the young man held the urn suspended over the water for a while and then let it sink into the river.

You're worrying about nothing, I told him gently. If you hold back and don't blink, you'll carry it off and still stay chaste and pure.

A shy smile smoothed out Chaubey's knitted face. My shoulders sagged with relief. I had done it . . . everything for nothing, the world at no cost – better men than Chaubey had fallen for that bait.

We walked back slowly, skirting the fierce heat of the livelier pyres. Halfway up the steps, he thumped my back in gratitude – man to man again – and said: I'll do it this evening as soon as rehearsal ends. I'll walk him back to the dharmashala and say yes on the way.

I didn't care how he did it. It wasn't my business. It was enough to know that after three unnerving days, Chaubey was on my side again.

After my talk with Chaubey, I set time and worry aside and began to live in things that were the same. Every morning I confirmed the world by ticking off the sand pits, the wrestlers in their loincloths, the figure standing on his head by the full-length mirror, the evenness of fifty breaths cross-legged, the sweet, permanent smell of Hindu bodies burning. I memorized the riverfront bit by bit and sorted out its bustle into patterns and routines.

The sameness of rehearsals was a balm. When the fight scenes had been choreographed, Guruji ordered run-throughs of the entire play. The others complained, but I liked the slogging repetition. To say the same lines and do the same things, to become a little better every day, to strain for that perfect state where lines came pat and cues fell right – this for me was the ground plan of the good life.

If Guruji's Ramlila was a success later this year, it could become a fixture in Banaras' cultural calendar. It would be something to anchor my life with. At the very least, an annual Ramlila would keep me supplied with a set of people that I knew. Even if the actors changed, the characters they played would stay the same: that much was enough. Familiarity was enough – I didn't ask for friendship. Masroor had been a friend . . . now he was a recruitment poster on an army truck. Haasan, Ammi, Asharfi – in less than a week they had become family: but here I was, cowering in Banaras, while they lay low in Lucknow. Guruji and Chaubey and the others in the akhara weren't friends but at least I knew them and that was precious to me. It was money in the bank, a bird in the hand, half a loaf. Changes now would mean strangers again.

To tend my little life, I pruned out the world. I never asked Chaubey what happened that evening, but I couldn't help noticing that from the day after my say yes speech, he and Gyanendra always left the akhara together. Nor did I think about the window opposite except to wish that mine had shutters too. I simplified my life till it was peopled only by the Ramlila's cast . . . the trouble was that one of the actors had a double role.

But for a week at least, Chaubey kept his other life to himself. Everyone in the cast noticed how clean he suddenly was and how closely shaven. And Guruji told him off sharply the day he arrived without his body hair. Chaubey offered no explanations.

Then one evening, after rehearsal, he came to my room, holding two glasses of brick-red tea. Premonitory shivers tickled my arms but what could I say? Since the odds were that

147

he didn't have designs on my body now, I let him in. The tea was so sweet my teeth ached. I made a production out of drinking it, blowing and slurping in turn to keep him from telling me things I didn't want to know. Then I ran out of tea and he began.

He had taken off his nose and his gum-pads. Now with great deliberation he swivelled his eyes towards the shuttered window opposite and turned them back in my direction, looking coy and vaguely knowing. He began to speak but I couldn't hear a word, not a word, though he was speaking so emphatically that I could read his lips. You Were Right The Girl Is Nothing But A . . . Slut!

The sound came on with the last word, and so loudly that it startled Chaubey into silence.

I'm sorry, he said, collecting himself. Sometimes it's difficult keeping things apart. It was a continuity problem. There was the film where he couldn't speak and the play where he had to be louder than life. Then there was normal life in the middle.

So you've begun shooting? I asked, feeling vaguely left out.

No, no, he said, shaking his head. First I have to learn about acting without words. It's much slower. There are more actions. More faces to be made. He repeated the business of looking at the girl's window and then back at me as an example of such mime.

They hadn't begun shooting but he had met the girl. He had been taken to her room three days after he had agreed to do the film.

You were right, he said again. She isn't a respectable woman. Doing it to her won't be the same as the thing I've been afraid of.

By which I understood that raping her wouldn't be the same as rape.

Her sluttishness had been evident in several ways. The room that she lived in was small and dark and it stank of unventilated sweat. It was lit by a single kerosene lamp which showed her lying on a mattress, dressed in a blouse and petticoat, the working dress of a city prostitute. The red-light district of every town had balconies hung with whores in petticoats.

148

Besides, she made no move to cover herself when Gyanendra and Chaubey entered; she barely acknowledged their presence in the room. She was lying half-propped up on high bolsters, facing the shuttered window. Her fixed and passive eyes looked sightless.

I knew that look at once, said Chaubey proudly. Every other sadhu in Kashi has just that expression. It's the opium.

He was relieved that the girl wasn't respectable. Instead of ruining a girl of good family, he was helping Gyanendra raise a fallen woman. But he was honest enough to admit that bloused, petticoated and drugged, she still had a film star's body. I'm looking forward to doing it to her, he confessed to me in a manly way. Not doing it all the way, of course, not so that he lost control and squandered himself, but doing it as an education, as a test of will and discipline.

After that one rash question early on when I had asked if shooting had begun, I listened to him in silence. The matter fell outside the tightly drawn circumference of my world. It needed no response from me. Certainly Chaubey didn't wait for one – he just told his tale and left. He had wanted to unload a fraction of the uncontainable excitement that the film had stirred in him and I was the only one in the akhara whom he could safely tell. In the interest of discretion, I had supplied him my ear. It was just a story, not true or false. And it wasn't my story, so there were no sides to be taken, no judgements to be made. I had taken a hand in making Chaubey a major character in it but that had been forced upon me. I wasn't an accomplice because it had been self-defence. Imminent buggery was my extenuating circumstance.

Two days later Chaubey was back with a folio copy of the *Kama Sutra*. I asked him for a script so I could study the role, said Chaubey, but he gave me this instead.

One look at the illustrations persuaded him that large parts of him needed reconditioning. He could do more with his body than most men but some of the positions worried him. Gyanendra told him not to take the pictures seriously because most of them were just examples of that ancient Indian sport, the permutation puzzle. One point of junction and eight limbs: how many positions, given some suspension of disbelief, did that allow? Fortunately cinema could fake the real thing. He needed some junction frames and penetration shots for the literal minded, but the rest of it would be sleight of hand at the editing table. But Chaubey wasn't reassured. He was a strongman-athlete – he did nothing without going into training.

Which brought him to the reason for his visit; he wanted to leave the *Kama Sutra* in my room.

Why? I asked discouragingly.

He blushed and got to his feet. Standing by the window with his back to me, he cleared his throat.

I need your help with my training, he said. Then he told me why.

He had lost control of his body. From the day he had said yes to Gyanendra, he had been plagued by dreams . . . wet dreams. Only he had them during the day as well. As soon as he thought of the girl or looked at a picture in the book . . . Now he had the dhobi launder his dhotis twice a week. He couldn't wear loincloths anymore; his condition required something more obscuring. Another month of this and he'd be a husk, a pith-less hollow man. Freed of celibate scruple, his mind extemporized images of such wanton lewdness that they frightened him.

He turned round and looked pleadingly at me.

You have to help me tame these pictures in my head, he begged.

Warily I said nothing. I thought of Gandhi sleeping naked with his niece to monitor his carnality. He had failed that test, that much I remembered, and Chaubey was no Mohandas.

But it was nothing like that. He didn't want to sleep with me. He just wanted me to read out parts of the *Kama Sutra* aloud to him. Daily readings might build up his immunity to the erotic charge of the book. If he could learn to think of the *Kama Sutra* as a sort of textbook filled with theorems and formulae, he might last longer. The key, he thought, was to think of the book in words, not pictures. That's why he needed someone else to read it out: when he looked at the illustrated text himself, it set off a multi-media floor show in his head, a sexy son-et-lumière.

This seemed harmless enough, so I agreed. After that, for an hour most evenings, Chaubey would lie face down on my bed while I read out yards of Vatsyayana's pedantry. It was less arousing than an anatomy lesson. How anyone could find excitement in this crammer's guide to sex (Biting – Placement, Kinds of and Severity) was a mystery. But Chaubey did; every few minutes he would toss and groan and sigh and sometimes cry out to me to stop so that he could keep from boiling over. Occasionally his cry for respite came too late; times like that he'd cut the reading session short and go home to change.

As the days passed there were fewer and fewer mishaps. I learnt to read the text in the manner of nationalist orators: deliberately, with momentous pauses in between. This way Chaubey heard every word of a sentence without quite registering its cumulative meaning. By the end of the first week he could weather an hour of reading without spillage. I even began to feel a stirring of pride in his endurance. That should have warned me. No involvement is without consequences, not even reading. Especially not reading. Words haunt all beginnings.

But nothing happened for another week. Then, in the middle of March, around the time that the Ramlila rehearsals had achieved a clockwork frenzy, one thing finally led to the other.

Chaubey asked me if I would help with the photographs.

Photographs?

Photographs, confirmed Chaubey. Gyanendra wanted photographs, still pictures. He wanted several dozen for several purposes: as production stills, publicity material, to make little albums to persuade distributors with, for posters and advertisements – no film could do without photographs.

And what would I have to do? I asked.

Chaubey was reassuring. Nothing out of the way; just what I had been doing for the past fortnight – speaking the *Kama Sutra* out while Gyanendra took the pictures. He had been practising self-control for a while now, and quite successfully, but this was the first time he would actually share a frame with her. He didn't want his glands to let him down.

151

No, I said immediately. I want nothing to do with the film.

You don't actually have to do anything, said Chaubey earnestly. Just read the book aloud, the way you normally do. That's all. It will help me be calm when I pose with her. Your voice makes what I'm doing sound like print. It slows me down. I need that – I don't want to make a mess all over her.

I thought of myself not looking at the window opposite but sitting in it, declaiming the *Kama Sutra* while Chaubey and the girl posed for dirty pictures. It wasn't a scene that I wanted in any footage of my life. So the answer was easy.

No, I said again.

But Chaubey was reading my mind now.

You don't even have to be in the room with us, he said. You can sit right here and read the book aloud. That window's less than eight feet from yours, so your voice will carry. You don't even have to watch if you don't want to. Read with your back to the window.

He didn't let up. Every other minute he found a new way of telling me that I was indispensable. He needed my voice because it made the whole thing seem less like pornography and more like an instruction manual. And I would only have to do it once – just for his camera début with the window-girl. Even maestros needed the tanpura's drone to get their pitch right . . . and he was just a novice.

That was so absurd that I laughed. I shouldn't have, because while I didn't precisely say yes, I forgot to say no again. Which meant that two days later, I was at my window with the book in my hands. The window opposite was alive already; I was a little late.

I would have been on time but Guruji had decided that morning to shift rehearsals to Tulsi Ghat where the play was to be eventually performed. He wanted us to get a feel of the actual arena. At four-thirty (the photo-session was scheduled for six o'clock) Chaubey pretended to twist an ankle and disappeared with Guruji's permission. An hour later – so as not to arouse Guruji's suspicion – I shammed diarrhoea and raced back to the akhara. I was still wearing a sari and flowers in my hair; along the way lounging men made wet, sucking sounds as they watched me run. By the time I got to my room and dived under the bed to pull out the book of the film, the show had already begun.

The girl was standing in the middle of the scene, framed by the window, dressed in ancient Indian female costume in a sari with white flowers in her hair (exactly as I was), but there was something wrong. Her eyes were streaming and her mouth was open in a scream which I couldn't hear. Gyanendra entered the frame and the girl retreated. I noticed Chaubey in the background watching.

Suddenly the girl dipped and straightened. Now she was holding a lit kerosene lamp with both hands and swinging it in flaming, menacing arcs. It was Gyanendra's turn to retreat. This didn't look like the *Kama Sutra* and she didn't look as if she was in character. The room was hung with lamps and lit with a yellow radiance in which her red silk sari gleamed and winked. Gyanendra was speaking to her in a deep, velvet voice which sometimes cracked with nervousness, telling her to put the lamp down. But she kept swinging. I didn't think that she could keep it up because she looked drugged and unsteady. Already the sweeping lamp swings had begun to waver as the semi-circular movement made her dizzy. The end came quickly. As Gyanendra, sensing opportunity, moved in to wrest the lamp from her, she flung it at him. It missed him, glanced the upper edge of the window-frame and smashed down into the street below. I didn't see it land because I had ducked the moment I saw it in flight. When I got to my feet and looked over the sill, all I saw was a shuttered window. The matinée was over.

Fifteen minutes later Chaubey was sitting in my room. She wants more money, he said. At least that's what Gyanendra had told him. He had pushed Chaubey out of the room after the lamp-swinging incident and had a little talk with her. Chaubey hadn't seen her afterwards, but Gyanendra had come out of the room and told him all was well. He had threatened to drop her from the film and she had come around at once. Apparently it was always like this with starlets; they would sell their bodies for a part but the second they were asked to take their blouses off before the camera, the sluts wanted money. And they hadn't even tried to take her clothes off this time. Gyanendra had planned to start off gently, with a kiss in full costume.

You saw the way she cried and shook and swung the lantern, said Chaubey, shaking his head. What an actress. You'd think she was a virgin and not a used-up widow.

Anyway, the important thing was that they were going through with the photo-session tomorrow and they needed me again.

No, I said quickly. The scene in the window that evening had changed my mind for me. What Gyanendra and Chaubey did with the girl was between them and their consciences – they were the actors in that drama. But if I spoke the text out loud for Chaubey I'd be an accomplice. It was always possible that Gyanendra's story was true, that the scene I had watched had been scripted by a wage dispute, but I wouldn't have bet on it. So saying no was easy.

But I don't want you to speak the text out any more, said Chaubey triumphantly. We began before you arrived and I managed very well without you. I was in control – a little excited but not about to dirty my dhoti. He grinned. Boyishly.

Now they wanted me for another reason. Gyanendra couldn't take the pictures because he needed his hands free in case she acted up again. They wanted me to man the camera.

No, I said immediately. This time I didn't even have to think. I wasn't going to set foot in that room. Nothing would make me feature in any scene framed by that window.

Don't worry, said Chaubey soothingly. You won't have to do anything. He'll adjust the camera. All you will have to do is click when he tells you to.

Look, I said patiently, I don't think you understand. I am not going to set foot in that wind . . . in that room.

But you don't have to, said Chaubey, trumping my ace. We'll put the camera in your room.

I was so taken aback that I didn't know what to say. Chaubey pressed on. Gyanendra was happy for the pictures to be taken from my room. In fact he liked the thought of the window-frame figuring in the pictures: whoever saw the photos would feel the special excitement of the outsider looking in. It would be good publicity material.

In the end it was the camera that swung it. If it hadn't been for the lovely prospect of taking pictures again, I would have gone on saying no. But the thought of handling a camera again . . . watching through a viewfinder didn't really mean involvement. It wouldn't make me responsible for the contents of the window-frame the way speaking the *Kama Sutra* aloud would have done. Playgoers weren't responsible for the play, but prompters were – and taking pictures was just another way of looking. I don't know if I actually said yes, but by the time Chaubey left my room that night, we had an understanding.

That night I dreamt I heard the mute girl scream.

For the second day in succession the alleged looseness in my bowels got me off earlier than the rest of the cast. Chaubey sent word that he was nursing his sprained ankle and didn't turn up at all. When I got back to my room, I found the camera in place; it was standing on a tripod, looking out of my window.

Gyanendra and Chaubey were visible in the opposite window but the girl was missing. Chaubey was wearing earrings and a wig which supplied him with shoulder-length hair as worn by personable men of the Golden Age. His neck was looped by a double string of pearl-like beads and enormous biceps were set off by a gilded armlet.

Gyanendra was wearing his customary saffron but today he was wearing dark glasses as well. When he saw me he began shouting instructions about the use of the camera. To be taught my craft by this saffron lecher who, I suspected, was more interested in taking dirty pictures than making a film was intolerable. I told him curtly that I was a professional photographer; there was nothing he could tell me about any camera that I didn't know already.

That shut him up but it was entirely untrue. I might have been a professional photographer once, but I had never used a classical view camera, complete with black focusing cloth, bellows and eight-by-six-inch glass plates for each exposure. That was what I had in the room. But I wasn't going to own up to ignorance; in any case I knew from books how it was meant to work. The rest would come.

I stuck my head under the black cloth and located the viewfinder. Then I worked the bellows till Chaubey's earrings were in glinting sharp focus. There was too much brick wall under the window in my frame and here book-learning helped. I had read somewhere that tilting the lens board up would set that right and it did.

So by the time the girl came into the picture, I had composed a fairly tight frame: just the window and an unavoidable red border of brick. I didn't notice which side of the frame she entered from – she was suddenly there, just off centre to the left, wearing the same red sari she had worn yesterday. Her face looked a little puffy and the right side of her jaw looked swollen but that could have been a trick of the light or perhaps her lower face was naturally asymmetrical. It didn't show once I had softened the focus a notch.

Both Chaubey and the girl managed to hold their poses long enough for me to expose four plates. The pictures had them arm in arm, her leaning on his chest, him biting her ear lobe and them kissing – in that order. The girl didn't resist this time, though sometimes she shook so much that I had to wait till she stopped or her outlines would have blurred.

After those four exposures there was a pause. In my viewfinder Chaubey walked off the right-hand edge of the frame and disappeared. Gyanendra went up to the girl, who shrank against the window sill as he approached. He said something to her which I didn't catch because under the black cloth hood all outside sound was muffled. As soon as he finished speaking, she vanished to the left of the viewfinder. Two minutes later, Chaubey reappeared. He had been bare-chested to start with, so it took me a minute to realize that he was entirely naked now. Not only was he not wearing his dhoti, he wasn't even wearing his loincloth, and as he walked into the centre of my frame, he was preceded by his feelings. He seemed worried about how long the excitement would last because he never took his eyes off himself, not even to see how the girl was doing.

He embarrassed me, so I moved the camera a little to the left to cut him out of the frame. Just then Gyanendra dragged the girl into view again. She still had all her clothes on, which seemed to upset him because he shook her hard. I didn't want to see this, so I turned the camera back on Chaubey but he was still intensely self-absorbed. I reverted to the original frame. This now had Chaubey on the right monitoring himself and the girl on the left. She had her back to the camera as she struggled with Gyanendra, who was trying to take her clothes off. She was so busy trying to keep them on that for a while she didn't seem to have registered Chaubey's nakedness. Then Chaubey, still gazing raptly at his loins, took another step forward and she saw.

She wrenched herself from Gyanendra's grip and spun around, clutching the window sill and breathing raggedly. Her face was ugly with fright: eyes staring, nostrils flared, mouth spread in an unending scream which I couldn't hear but suddenly the dogs in the lane below were barking.

Gyanendra took a step towards her, my eyes closed in self-defence and, quite unmeant, my shaking index finger pushed the trigger. The flash exploded and when I opened my eyes only Chaubey and Gyanendra were in the frame – the girl had disappeared. First I thought that she had retreated to some part of the room not visible in the viewfinder. Then I saw that the two men were looking out of the window. Dear God! I thought of the lamp she had flung out of the window the day before, the hideous way it had crunched on the lane below. I shut my eyes again.

When nothing happened I opened them again and tilted the camera downwards. The window sill disappeared and the viewfinder filled up with brick and then more brick till the camera couldn't swivel any more. I gathered courage, flung the black hood off and leaned over my window. There she was – not smashed and dead in the lane below but suspended in mid-air, or so it seemed, till I saw that she was lying on the two parallel bamboo stakes driven into the walls under her window and mine to keep the buildings from falling towards each other.

Chaubey and Gyanendra were hanging out of their window, which ended some four feet over the bamboo stakes. They were waving their arms and calling to the girl. I couldn't catch what they were saying.

This was rape, I allowed myself to think. No one walked out of a window because of a wage dispute. What was she going to do next? Her choices were limited. She could either let go and fall to a certain death or return to the window and a fate worse than the first. Being mute she couldn't even call for help.

Then, as I watched, she gathered herself up till she was balanced on her hands and knees and opened up another possibility. It was one I should have anticipated but didn't – these things often depend on one's point of view. She steadied herself on the bamboos and began to crawl towards the window. Not the one she had left – but the one I was watching from!

I battled the urge to dive under the black cloth hood to check if it was really happening in the viewfinder. By the time the moment passed she was crouched directly below me. Now I could see her shoulders shake as she scrabbled for finger holds in the brick wall, to give her the purchase she needed to straighten up. Inch by inch, fingernail by fingernail, palms glued to the brick, her hands moved upwards, pulling her body up along with them. Then her fingers found the window sill. Her hands reached in and gripped. She was standing now, more firmly anchored than she had been since leaving the other window. But now there was a difficulty. My window was a little higher than hers, so there were six feet between the bamboos she was standing on and the window sill that she was holding. She had managed the four-foot drop on to the bamboos at the other end on her own, but at this end she needed a helping hand up.

It was still no business of mine but this time I didn't have a choice, now that she had walked out of the viewfinder into my life. I probably would have hauled her up in any case but what made me hurry were the cracking sounds the bamboos made when Gyanendra lowered himself on them. He looked insane with rage and he must have been, because he was standing upright on the stakes. Not for him the girl's caution in crawling the length of the chasm. No, he clearly intended to walk across. How he planned to drag her back, balanced on two bamboos some forty feet above the ground, I didn't know, nor did I care. He would have to catch her first. I lifted her hands and linked them round my neck. Then, bracing my knees against the wall to keep from toppling over, I gripped her under the armpits and began to lift. When her feet left the poles, my arms nearly left their sockets but I set my teeth and held my breath and heaved and suddenly I was falling backwards with a body in my arms and I knew I had beaten Gyanendra to the girl.

Actually Gyanendra wasn't in the race any longer. When I got to my feet and looked out, the bamboo stakes were free of traffic. Then I looked more closely and saw bloodless fingers wrapped around one of them. Gyanendra had lost his footing and was now dangling over the street, looking silly in his dark glasses. The girl was on her hands and knees by my bed, vomiting breathlessly.

Up to that moment I had no intention of running away with the girl. I had kept her from falling but there had been no plans for a grander rescue in my mind. It was Chaubey who decided me. I had forgotten him in all this excitement but, after tearing off a bit of my sari so she would have something with which to wipe the vomit off, I remembered that he was the un-accounted-for actor in this four-cornered drama. I looked across at the window but it was empty. Then I heard steps below and looked down to see him run across the lane, unmindful of his director, who was still hanging on, scissoring his legs uselessly. Gyanendra wasn't shouting for help. He was either too frightened to scream or he had confused real life with his silent film.

A minute later I heard Chaubey's unmistakable step on the staircase that led up to my attic room. He was coming for her. She heard him too and struggled to her feet, looking wildly about her. I put a finger to my lips asking for her silence. Picking up an Indian club from the many that littered my room, I retreated to the hinged side of the door that opened into my room. I was shaking with fear but in the end it was simple. He flung the door open and rushed in – then stopped dead when he saw the girl standing vomit-stained by the window. He had his back to me, an utterly motionless target, when I swung the club from right to left and connected firmly with his temple. He fell to a half-crouch, so I hit him again and he was still.

It wasn't out of chivalry that I did it. It was something simpler than that. It was the fact that we were both wearing saris. When I heard him climb the steps to my room I remembered the times I had been terror-stricken by that very sound in the days when he had taken to ogling me. So when I saw her start in terror, I picked up the club out of a sense of solidarity, of sisterhood. I put a stop to Chaubey because she was a woman too.

She had doubled up to vomit again but there was no time for the luxury of a second spasm. The moment the club crunched home my lien on the attic room stood cancelled. We had to get away before Guruji returned or Chaubey recovered, whichever was sooner. I briefly mourned my leisured days as Sita – then pushed the thought away. Sita could afford to mope about a bit – her rescue was written into the script. Mine wasn't. Not being Sita any more, I didn't have a script to go by, no lines to say. But in the context of the scene that had just given over, I knew that I had to extemporize a rapid getaway.

So I pulled her up in mid-retch, paused; remembered Dadi just in time; scooped her up and hurtled down the steps with the flask in one hand and the girl in the other. The yard was blessedly empty – Guruji and the others hadn't yet returned from Tulsi Ghat. As we stepped over the akhara's threshold on to the steps that led down to the cremation ground, I had no plans beyond losing ourselves in the city. So we turned right and raced up the steps towards the sanctuary of Banaras' dark and twisting lanes. We might have made it but at the head of the steps I ran headlong, literally, into Guruji's stomach and knocked him off his feet. He hadn't lingered at Tulsi Ghat long enough.

We didn't stop to help him up; reversing course, we now sped down the steps, towards the burning ghat. The blood-curdling thought that some other members of the cast, Ram perhaps, or Lakshman, might have walked Guruji back and could be now in grim pursuit urged me on and towards the end we were taking the steps three at a time. Trauma or not, the girl was game.

We didn't waste time weaving round the pyres – some we

hurdled, the longer ones we ran across. Luckily none of them was actually flaming; they were smouldering at worst, and fear lent our soles the indifference of asbestos. I wasn't sure what we were going to do when we reached the river but that didn't matter. The girl had jumped out of her window with fewer prospects – something would turn up.

And something did. When we got to the steps that led to the river, I didn't even have to stop and think. Because there on the water, bobbing gently, was the boat, tethered to the bottom step just as it had been on that afternoon when I had sold the role to Chaubey. I pulled the boat to the bank and looked inside – the oars were there. Shaking with relief, I tumbled into it and dragged the girl aboard. The chain was just hooked on to the prow and came off easily – all I had to do was to push off the steps.

With my back to the river, facing the bank, I began rowing. There was no one chasing after us. The pyres smoked unconcernedly as the boat pitched and yawed and slewed in little arcs. The last time I had rowed was on the lake in Naini Tal, where the senior year had gone on a school picnic. There hadn't been a current then to cope with.

I finally found the knack of it. The trick was not to row at right angles to the current, but diagonally across it. Where we were headed was simple. It was the other side, the other bank, where the Maharaja of Banaras lived in his palace at Ramnagar; the home of another, earlier Ramlila, in which, God be thanked, there wasn't a part for me. That was reason enough for going there.

But there was something I had to do before we reached the other bank. In the middle of the river, I shipped the oars and reached for Dadi's flask. It was, after all, the reason why I had set off from Delhi, so impossibly long ago. She had wanted her ashes drowned at Banaras and now the time had come. It didn't matter that at this moment she was alive and well and probably carding cotton in her house in Delhi – this was the timeless Ganga. I tilted the flask into the water, watched it bubble a little and then let it go. Perhaps I'd go to Delhi and call on my grandmother. She would be less than forty years old – and alive. I was done with the dead.

Waiting on Jinnah

My GRANDMOTHER AND I became neighbours in early April when winter had dwindled into warm days and pleasant nights and the full heat of summer was still a month away. I was lucky the weather was mild because my first month in Delhi was spent sleeping in the open – on the floor of the running verandah that fronted the shops in Kashmiri Gate. My only covering was the sari in which I had fled Banaras.

The first night I had bedded down in front of Student's Stores, twenty arches east of a row of unconscious waiters who worked in the Carlton Restaurant by day and slept by its shuttered façade at night. So I wasn't the only one sleeping rough, but the waiters were better off – they at least had their bedrolls and their uniforms. I was still wearing (for the fourth day in a row) the costume I had made up in Banaras by tearing Sita's sari into two unequal pieces. The longer piece I had wrapped round my waist like a dhoti while the strip left over was shawl and towel as the need arose.

Dadi lived behind the shops in a small house that her husband had rented from Major Multan Singh, who owned everything in that part of Kashmiri Gate, including the arcade of shops outside. The way to the house was through a great arched entrance in the centre of the arcade, which had MULTAN SINGH BUILDINGS blocked around the arch.

The morning after that first night in the open air I must have walked through that arch and the dark passage that followed (which was as long as the shops on either side were deep) at least a dozen times. Twice I even turned left into the lane that turned past the Carlton's kitchens and led to Dadi's house. But both times my feet grew roots by the rear end of the restaurant. It wasn't just my clothes that stopped me or even the strangeness of visiting a cremated grandparent. It was simpler than that. Since I couldn't call on her claiming to be her grandson not-yet-born, I needed an excuse to ring her doorbell, and nothing remotely plausible occurred to me.

I was standing, irresolute, by the Carlton's kitchens, wondering what to do next, when the quality of my life improved unexpectedly. A man in an apron by the kitchen door was beheading chickens. Preoccupied with Dadi, I hadn't noticed him, despite the spouts of blood and the headless birds running around. He must have thought that I was a beggar angling for the restaurant's leavings because he snapped his fingers in an oye boy! way and set me plucking the nearly dead chickens. It was messy, slippery work and I lived in fear that the still-warm birds might move in my hands. But after two hours of this, I was allowed to join the waiters for lunch. It was the first time I had worked for a living in 1942.

Plucking chickens was my lucky break. From cleaning poultry I rose to serving sahibs, the moment Mr Rosario, the manager, learnt that I was fluent in English. He had one question, though. He wanted to know why I was wearing a dhoti.

You're not a Congressman, are you? Old chap? he asked suspiciously. People either wore dhotis or spoke English. Only Congressmen and Bengalis did both and Rosario didn't want either.

No, no, I said, reassuring him on both counts. The dhoti, I told him, was an accident. I didn't even know why I was wearing one because I had lost my memory.

Rosario nodded his approval and had me measured for a waiter's uniform. People generally left me alone when I told them that I had forgotten my past. Amnesia disarmed them.

Once the uniform was sanctioned, the bedroll followed and in a day or two I was on level terms with the other waiters. They were kind; they made room for my bedroll at night and showed me where to store it during the day. It was strung on to a branch of the old neem tree that shaded the road in front of the restaurant. The neem was hung with a dozen such bundles. No one ever stole them – they just dangled there, swaying like great baggy fruit.

At the end of a month at the Carlton, my life improved

again: I found a better job and started sleeping indoors. In the last week of April, Rosario gave me an afternoon off. I had worked thirty twelve-hour days without a break but he still made it seem a favour.

Once I got the half-day off, I had to decide where to spend it. That wasn't easy, because my entire life till I was twenty had happened inside a half-hour walk of the Carlton. Apart from Dadi's house, which, in some extended family sense, was home, I had gone to school in this neighbourhood and college, too, had been in the hinterland of Kashmiri Gate.

Since Dadi's house was out of bounds for the moment, the choice was between the old college and the old school. The old school won: twelve years of a daily past lay buried inside its walls when college had accounted for only three. Besides, school had come before and it seemed proper to rediscover the past in sequence.

School was a mile and a half away in the sahib quarter, the Civil Lines. The road to it passed under Kashmiri Gate, the northern opening in the city wall, which had given its name to the whole neighbourhood. It was good to walk through the great stone arch again because by the time I'd finished middle school, the municipality had closed it to traffic.

The road was narrower than I remembered it and there was no motor traffic, so walking was an easy, unharassed business. On my left the double row of date palms in Nicholson Park stood stiff and still just as they had done in my time, like honour guards who never stood at ease. On my right the Interstate Bus Terminus in dark, sinister concrete was beautiful by its absence. In its place were playing fields in mottled green and brown, set off by sightscreens and men in white. It was a sunny day.

I wasn't surprised by the playing field, which had survived into my middle school years, and I remembered the declamatory ugliness of the bus station growing before my eyes. But further up the road, the shop called Nancy just before the petrol pump was gone. It lay on the route of my school bus and every morning I had watched out for the eyeless heads wearing steepled bouffants in its shop window. My older female cousins, who had yearned to bob and perm their boring single plaits, always pointed it out to me whenever we walked down to Ludlow Castle for an ice-cream. That's where Mrs Gandhi goes to dye her hair, they would tell me, dropping their voices to whispers. It had been a landmark as permanent and timeless as the Old Fort . . . and now it was gone.

But I was relying upon the old school buildings to be there. I wanted to walk round the dining hall that smelt of bananas and milk, the rose garden with its wrought-iron frames and its flowering climbers, the formal lotus pools filled with pouting goldfish, the padre wing where the Fathers (it was confidently rumoured) seeded sons, the fifteen-metre swimming pool that was fifty per cent piddle, old Knockwood's room where he caned little boys – all the landmarks on that little map that had been my world away from home. The Old School was old, I told myself as I rounded the bend which led to the main gate. Those double-storeyed, high-ceilinged, whitewashed buildings pre-dated the 'forties. They were bound to be there.

And they were. The Old School was just as I remembered it. Better than I remembered it – the whitewash was whiter, the gardens were greener, the goldfish were sleeker than they had been in my time. As I looked around in a haze of proud affection, it seemed to me that this was school in its golden age; no dirt, no wear . . . cellophane-skinned, pristine.

Half an hour into my tour of the campus I started to notice the differences. They hadn't built Our Lady's grotto yet and the long shed inside the gates on the right where I had been taught woodcraft was being used as a garage. School seemed to be running a lot of cars: there were nine parked inside the shed, all shiny black, their faces set in glittering chromium snarls. I had only ever seen two in all my twelve years in school – an old Mercedes with little fins and a Volkswagen Beetle.

And oddly, there weren't many children about. The campus was full of smartly dressed adults: adults in livery, adults in dresses, adults in formal summer suits. The pillared verandah that fronted the dining hall was crowded with men in planters' chairs, drinking frosted gin-and-tonics, instead of boys in grey drill shorts playing table-tennis. On my left the red clay tennis courts were just the same, down to the bougainvillaea creepers on the wire fencing, but the place seemed alien. It didn't feel like a school at all . . . more like a hotel.

Cecil.

A name fading on the school's back gate, that the padres had forgotten to paint over. I must have passed by it ten thousand times without giving it a thought, but now it slid inside my head like a coin in a slot, each serifed letter clearly blocked in black.

The Cecil.

Of course.

The old school buildings were older than the Old School . . . which explained everything. The campus had been custom built not for a missionary school but for a colonial hotel. The Cecil had outlived its host, the Raj, by ten whole years; it was only then that the Jesuits had moved in. I had always known these facts, but in a disconnected way. The gin-and-tonics joined them all together.

The Cecil Hotel.

I had come looking for a piece of 'forty-two to call my own, only to find that the Old School wasn't old enough. I had no claim upon this place: it wasn't yet the school I knew and hotels weren't suitable alma maters. I wasn't an Old Boy, I was a trespasser – a uniformed menial from a lesser place.

I nearly left at once but tiredness stopped me. I was fed up of travelling, so between the covered verandah and the gravel courts I made my stand. School or not, this was an old, familiar place, a place to settle down in, a fixed address. On impulse I walked through the verandah and turned right, through the large swing doors into the dining hall where I had eaten countless midday meals. It was now a restaurant for the hotel's guests and in less than half an hour I'd signed on as one of its waiters. English-speaking waiter material had been used up by the war, so they were glad to have me. I had walked in through the gates an Old Boy, a shareholder in my school's past; I walked out of them a waiter, an extra in its pre-history.

I left the Carlton without regret because my new position was better paid and, more important, it meant a room of my own. They didn't house waiters within the hotel grounds but Captain Nazar, the Estate Manager, found me a room in Kashmiri Gate. It was on the upper floor of a double-storeyed building right next to the arcaded line of shops that housed the Carlton.

The ground floor was occupied by the Imperial Leather Tannery, which had its frontage painted over with rows of crests and coats of arms. These told passers-by that the tannery was by appointment to every Viceroy in the recent history of the Raj. After Linlithgow's name and style, there was barely enough space for two more names. Luckily for the Imperial Tannery, the end of Empire was due.

The upper floor was occupied by the East India Something – the weathered signboard hooked on to one of its balconies was unclear about the last word. The paint had rubbed off – only the first letter was visible, a 'C', which could have meant anything, from Club to Company. It had been a disputed property for some twenty years and, legally, no one lived there, but the caretaker, a man called Ghosh, made a little on the side by letting out rooms.

My room had a ceiling twenty feet high, a tallboy filled with two near-complete dinner services, a dining table of the old-fashioned sort, with leaves to stretch and shrink it, and a cheap string cot. It let out into a narrow balcony which looked directly on to the only cinema near the Civil Lines, the Ritz.

I never got round to visiting St Stephen's College, where, in another time, I had been an undergraduate, neither the day I visited school and found the Cecil in its place, nor any time later, even though the college was right next door, in my neighbourhood. It was on the other side of the park from the Carlton, the oblong green that sat in the middle of Kashmiri Gate. I passed by the college gates several times, without once going in, because this wasn't the campus I had slept through lectures in. That lay miles away beyond Kashmiri Gate, past the Cecil Hotel, over the Ridge, in the new university campus to which St Stephen's had shifted in 1945, immediately after the Second World War, which was still being fought. I never entered its Kashmiri Gate premises because I didn't know what I had the right to feel in the circumstances. It was the same with school. One building with two histories. One history with two buildings. A place had changed names and a name had changed places, creating practical difficulties for memory and nostalgia.

It was the Ritz that helped me settle in. I worked the seven-to-seven shift through my first three weeks at the Cecil, which left me a comfortable hour to wash and eat before the night show. I saw a dozen films in those twenty days. Such films! *Argentine Nights. Congo Maisie. Twenty Mule Team. Hawaiian Nights. Mein Kampf.* So glitteringly strange that the unreliable world of the 'forties began to feel ordinary and routine. Even *Edison, the Man*, made life outside seem dull and somehow normal.

Banaras became a bad movie. I hardly ever thought of Gyanendra or Chaubey and when I did, it was as fading cameo villains. Even the girl in the window figured less often in my dreams, but here the credit was mine. She could have developed into a real nuisance if I hadn't edited her out at Allahabad.

I knew that she would have to go before our rowing-boat touched Ramnagar's bank. I wasn't about to take her with me to Delhi. She was a complete liability – neither wife nor mother nor sister nor any recognized sort of kin. Who would give an unmarried couple a place to stay?

That night we slept on a slope of grass by the walls of the Ramnagar Fort, more than a mile from the rowing-boat we had abandoned. The bulge of a bastion hid us from the view of possible pursuers. The girl seemed to have no objections to my sleeping arrangements though she did walk a hundred paces away before settling down for the night. Since I had decided to desert her early the next morning, this suited me very well.

When I opened my eyes the next morning, the first thing I saw was a white paddle-steamer sitting on the river in front of me. Three black elephants in single file came out of it and walked down a metal ramp on to the bank, escorted by brightly liveried men. They were the Maharaja's elephant grooms, though I didn't know this then. Nor did I care. The steamer was pointed in the right direction – west. That's all I wanted to know. It was a way of getting out of Banaras. It was my ticket to Delhi. It wasn't a steamer, it was an act of God.

I would have left the girl behind – she was still asleep – but I had no money for the fare. I would have to beg a passage, so I needed her for pathos. When I shook her she woke with a little shudder but then looked composed and unafraid. I explained my plan to her, slowly and loudly, till I remembered she wasn't deaf, only mute. When I had finished she nodded and we walked up to the boat together.

The steamer seemed to have a crew of two. There was a Gurkha dogsbody in khaki shorts, and his master in a stiff peaked cap trimmed with dirty braid, a greying vest with little sleeves and a blue lungi. The captain didn't wait for us to get there; once he was certain that we were headed towards the ship, he ran down the ramp to greet us. The moment I timidly asked him for a passage on his ship, he virtually herded us aboard.

I'm Captain Mitter, he said eagerly, holding out his hand. Where d'you want to go?

Delhi, I said, looking at his hand, wondering if it was in order to shake it, bewildered by his enthusiasm.

Captain Mitter's round face fell. He spun the wheel sadly. She can't get you to Delhi, he said. Fifty years ago there was enough water in this river to get to Garhmukteshwar without running aground. But now the best I can do for you is Allahabad. He looked at us hopefully. But why don't you come with us to Allahabad? Trains run to Delhi every day from there.

I nodded a yes, not trusting myself to speak in the presence of this guardian angel in a lungi. What luck! I felt a tiny pang that I had brought the girl along; there had been no need to produce her or to recite the pathetic circumstances that drove her westward. But now it couldn't be helped.

But . . . said Captain Mitter. There was a string attached. A condition. Payment in kind. He had another cargo to collect thirty miles downstream from Chunar, a medieval fort built on a strategic bend in the Ganga. There had been a saying once, before the railways came: He who holds Chunar . . .

but now it was just another obsolete citadel. It had once shaped the fortunes of empire – now it housed its casualties. Captain Mitter ticked them off on his fingers: British soldiers who had lost their minds for the Raj; juvenile delinquents, white; adolescent bastards, white; and military orphans of European extraction. The August Rebellion had scared the fort's commandant, explained Mitter. He wanted his charges moved to some less isolated place. Normally they would have been transferred by rail but trains were still being sabotaged, so the authorities decided that a steamship was the safer option.

They want me to carry them to Allahabad, to the cantonment there, he said. Fifteen rupees a head – it's the best business that I've been offered in years. But what am I going to do about the dung?

I followed his gaze as it swept the steamer's deck despairingly. The better part of the deck was just a swamp of elephant shit.

It's three days, you know, from the elephant fair at Sonepur to Banaras, said Mitter gloomily. The Maharaja of Banaras had asked for the elephants, because there was a wedding in the royal family, and the elephants he normally used for ceremonial were all constipated.

So I was told to make sure that their replacements never stopped shitting, said Mitter. Gurung and I mixed two maunds of fleaseed husk in their feed . . . and you can see how well that worked. How am I going to collect the Chunar passengers with this on board. Gurung won't do it, he said, looking balefully at his first and only mate. He has suddenly become a warrior from a martial race. Gurkhas don't sweep elephant dung, apparently. Warrior race! He used to clean the monkey cages at the Alipore zoo when I found him and now he's too good for elephant dung!

Gurung looked peaceably at his captain and said nothing. I can't do it either, said Mitter. I've a bad back.

He certainly had a problem on his hands. The inmates of Chunar fort were delinquents, orphans and madmen, but they were also wards of the British Empire – they couldn't be installed in a sea of dung. The commandant wouldn't like it

170

and Captain Mitter would lose his commission: fifteen rupees a head times fifty heads . . . seven hundred and fifty rupees!

The girl and I earned every paisa of our passage to Allahabad. Luckily for us the boat hadn't been refitted with a diesel engine, it was still a proper steamer fired by coal, so there were shovels aboard. We used them to scoop the dung overboard as the boat chugged westward. We worked steadily for three hours in a half-crouch, moving to the rhythm of the paddle-wheel slapping the water, till our backs forgot to ache, till the monstrous smell of days-old elephant shit became unremarkable. By the time the modest ramparts of the fort at Chunar became visible, the girl and I had washed and swabbed the main deck clean.

It paid off. When we disembarked at Allahabad he clapped me on my shoulder and pressed money into my hand. It was two third-class fares to Delhi. For you and your wife, he said, looking fatherly.

There was no point setting him right, so I just thanked him and headed straight for the railway station. The girl tagged along. I considered abandoning her and making off with the money but that seemed unacceptably swine-like. She had shovelled her share of the shit, after all. But I couldn't take her to Delhi with me since a new start meant travelling light.

I chose the middle way. I bought her a ticket to Lucknow and wrote on it the address of Ammi's Lalbagh house. Now it was up to them . . . if she ever managed to find her way there. Tell them that the bald man sent you, I said, just before leaving her. The bald man on the three-wheeled motorcycle. And that he is well.

Often, through those first weeks in Delhi, I wondered if she had found the house, if Ammi had taken her in. Most of all, I wondered if they had asked after me, if they had missed me. I had certainly missed them: my memories of Lucknow were more vivid than the movies I saw at the Ritz.

For nearly a month and a half after getting to Delhi I didn't write them a letter, though I wanted to. A dim fear that the intelligence bureau would intercept it stopped me each time. With rail sabotage and armed rebellion a part of my recent past, there was no doubt in my mind that I was a wanted man.

Then one evening in the middle of May loneliness got the better of caution. I was careful. I addressed the letter simply to the Manager, Imperial Coffee House, Hazrat Ganj, Lucknow. Haasan's name figured nowhere on it. It began Dear Sir. Formally I asked after Begum Ganjoo and her daughter, then I asked for news of my old friend, Masroor. I mentioned in passing the wanton destruction of an old Triumph motorcycle with a sidecar by rebellious vandals and how sorry I was to lose it. Nowhere did I mention the window-girl. I signed off with a yours faithfully and an illegible squiggle. I sealed the envelope and wrote on its back in small letters, my name and address: Cecil Waiter, c/o Manager, East India C——, Kashmiri Gate, Delhi.

Haasan's reply reached me by return post. I had been on duty right through the night and I found the envelope slipped under the door when I got home. For a moment I thought it was for someone else because it was addressed to A. Ganjoo, Esq. Then I understood. A. Ganjoo. A Ganjoo! If my eyes hadn't filled with tears I might have laughed. Dear Haasan! Concerned about the loneliness of my amnesia, he had found me a name and a family.

Ammi was well. As was Asharfi. There was no news of Masroor, but the girl's arrival had taken the edge off that loss. They had bought her a slate and she talked to them with that. Her name was Parwana (imagine being called a moth!) – that was the second thing she had written out for them. The first thing (on a piece of paper since this was before the slate was bought) had been her references. The bald man and the motorcycle – they had known it was me at once! Which was just as well because otherwise they wouldn't have taken her in. With Masroor gone and rail tracks exploding, these weren't reliable times. But now the Lalbagh house was unthinkable without her. She was a sister to Asharfi and they were inseparable. And Ammi! She had been inspired by Parwana's scars to start up *Khatoon* again. She hadn't written a line since Masroor's disappearance but what Parwana had said

172

about being burnt had fired her up again. Burnt. Imagine! But the good thing was that she didn't need to imagine. Parwana was there to tell the tale. She wasn't ready to tell it yet, but when she was, Ammi planned to write it up in a special number of *Khatoon*. Sati in the nineteen-forties . . . unbelievable! As if Ram Mohun Roy had never lived.

It wasn't a long letter but it was irritatingly full of the window-girl. Right at the end, Haasan asked after me. They were pleased I had a job, he wrote, and perhaps when it was pukka I could visit them . . . perhaps in the winter. I wasn't to worry about the motorcycle. These things happened – the important thing was that I was well. Had any memories come back? Did I remember my family? Asharfi had asked him to send me her salaams, Ammi wanted me to know that I had a family in Lucknow. He would write at once if there was any news of Masroor. He was sending me on behalf of Ammi, Asharfi and himself, their best wishes.

The window-girl, I noted unkindly, sent me nothing.

That one bad thought apart, the letter was a tonic. Winter, I decided, was too long to wait. In another two months if I worked hard and kept on Kilmartin's right side, perhaps I could get a week off. Even three days would do because Lucknow was just one night away.

For a week I was quite perfectly happy, but it didn't last because every morning the date on the masthead of the *Hindustan Times* ticked off another day in the countdown to Partition. At the end of those seven days there were one thousand five hundred and thirty-six days left for the 14th of August 1947. For Partition.

I wasn't worried for myself. I had been born a Hindu and in Delhi from all accounts it was mainly Muslims who died. Nor was I concerned about India because it was difficult to feel for a subcontinent. I was just worried for my friends in Lucknow. Not for Haasan, since he was a Hindu too, but for Ammi and Asharfi, and Masroor if they ever found him. Four years from now I could lose them in one of two ways: they could get killed in the Partition riots, or they could choose to leave for Pakistan. How many Muslims had died or migrated from this side of the border in '47? One in a hundred? One in fifty? One in five? Endlessly, uselessly, I attempted statistical reckonings with nothing to go on.

Sometimes I wished that I had asked them. But asked them what? Will you go to Pakistan? when it wasn't carved out yet, when no one knew if Partition would actually happen? Even if I did ask and they said: Pakistan? Rubbish! No, never! – what comfort would I find in that? Because thousands trekked in '47 who wouldn't have moved in '43.

But still, I wanted to know how they felt about the Muslim League's call for a separate Muslim state, just as I had wanted to know, the very first time I went to the lavatory in the Lalbagh house, why they used a kettle with a curving spout to wash their bottoms with instead of a mug or a lota like everyone else. I hadn't asked then, partly because it was a strange thing to talk about but mainly because, like other secular people in independent India, I had been brought up to believe that religion was a private matter confined to the inner space between brains and bowels, so it couldn't possibly make a difference to arse-washing techniques, which fell outside its scope in the secular realm. I was also taught that differences were unimportant since we were all identical in our essential humanity. So I never asked and I still didn't know what the kettle was for.

But things were different now. In Lucknow I hadn't felt the need for curiosity because I had thought of myself as an accidental tourist in another time. But now that I was permanently resident here and Partition was a part of my future, I needed information to cope with it when it arrived. That's why I was itching to visit Lucknow – I wanted to ask them questions. But until some leave came through, I was stuck in Delhi.

The days passed.

Then, one day, Jinnah came to stay at the Cecil. So I asked him instead.

The night I waited on him, he was already the Qaid-i-Azam, the meaning of which I did not know, though I assumed that it roughly meant Father of the Nation. Captain Patrick Kilmartin picked me out to serve him dinner because I spoke

English well and, as he put it, the Caddyazzum might ask for something fancy, like. In real life Patrick had probably been a non-combatant ranker in the Great War and the only food he really understood was beef and mash, but the Cecil kept him on as maître because, even in the penguin idiocy of dress clothes, he looked like a viceroy: lean, clean-shaven face, tired eyes, middle-parted greying hair.

Got in this afternoon, he said to me as we checked our appearance in the pantry mirror. What's he here for? I asked. To Confer, said Patrick importantly, tucking a hair back into his nose. Then he pushed the pantry door open and we walked the length of the dining hall to the Qaid's table. He was set apart from his neighbours by three Chinese silk screens framed in wood – at first sight he looked like someone dying in an expensive nursing home. As he looked at the menu, I noticed that his teeth were discoloured and his skin, though stretched tight over his bird-like skull, had the crinkled texture of purse leather. When he made his order, his voice reminded me of Kobad Sir, who had taught me geometry in a room not fifty yards from Jinnah's table in precisely these tones: the Empire accent nicely earthed by the Gujarati stresses of western India, where both Jinnah and the Parsis had their roots.

When I returned with the soup, I dropped a fork to peer at his shoes under the table – in the photographs I had seen of him he was always shod in two-coloured brogues. So was he this time. I liked them – they were like the shoes American gangsters wore in the films I had seen at the Ritz. Besides, they were so bizarre that they saved him from the merely wog. Pouring water into his glass, I wondered if he too used the kettle thing. The shoes, the suit, the Windsor knot suggested paper. No, I decided. Not paper. He was the Qaid-i-Azam after all, an anti-imperialist. He wouldn't ape such grossness.

He wasn't fussy about his meal and even took the trouble to look up and thank me each time I filled his glass. In between, other diners came in their ones and twos to say hullo or pay their respects. With them he was neither Father of the Nation in the making nor a sahib: he was the distinguished public man – avuncular, grave, aloof and kind in turn. When he ordered chicken I felt disappointed for a moment because years after Partition I had heard my aunt gloat over the unnaturalness of Pakistan: an Islamic state founded by a pork-eating barrister. For her, this made the land of the pure a state defiled on its own terms by its founder's private sins. In this my aunt found some obscure solace. But in the course of serving that solitary figure in his absurdly natty clothes and extravagant shoes, I felt glad that he hadn't eaten pig or ordered wine. It had been a long road for him, from the Parsi Bombay and the Hindu-Muslim advocacy of his early years, to the Qaid-ship and the demand for Pakistan, and he must have had his reasons. If he observed the taboos of Islam as a public man, it was only proper.

He asked for coffee afterwards. It was the ordinariness of the request that made the incredible truth sink in: Jinnah and I were contemporaries. This was such a bewildering thought that I confused contemporary with peer. I must have done or else I would never have had the nerve to ask him the question. When he was about to sign the bill, I took leave of my senses and asked: Mr Jinnah, sir, do you really want the country partitioned? He stopped in mid-signature and looked up, startled, but also, I was relieved to see, amused. He signed the bill, then flipped the paper over and scribbled a few words. Without looking my way again, he rose and walked out slowly, as thin as a shadow in that food-filled room.

In a clear, spiky hand he had written: Leading question. Barristers do not have opinions – they have briefs. Unlike the bill, it wasn't signed.

I read it more than once, to no purpose. There was nothing to read between the lines, no truth to be distilled. It served me right; what else could he have said? That he had been misquoted? And what difference would that make? Partition had once been part of my past, so now it was an unchangeable part of my future. Nothing could change that, not even an assurance from the Qaid.

There was a letter waiting for me when I got home. From Lucknow, addressed in Haasan's handwriting. I let myself into the room and stepped out on to the balcony to read it.

Across the road the Ritz was silent and deserted. A little boy was changing the names on the marquee. From away on the right, I could hear concerted yogic laughter rising out of the early morning regulars in the tear-drop park.

It took me a while to read the letter. Then I read it again. And a third time. When I had finished, the view from the balcony was unchanged: a desolate cinema hall, a little boy pulling off big letters, unnatural laughter. Everything was the same. The letter was long, four pages and a little, but after three readings all I remembered was this:

> Parwana was kissing Asharfi in
> the zenana by the hand press when Haasan
> caught them – properly kissing, on
> the lips, no cheek or anything.
> On the lips. She was pregnant
> too, he didn't know who, Parwana
> that is, not Asharfi. Ammi only
> knew about the pregnancy he
> hadn't told her the other
> thing it was too
> shocking but obviously she
> couldn't stay and I had
> sent her. So would I please now
> Take Her Back.

It was what Father Montfort, S.J., who had taught us the art of précis in Class IX, used to call the *gist*.

The Day's Happenings

I COULD HAVE KILLED Parwana. Scotched her like a snake.
But she wasn't to hand, so I balled the letter up and
squeezed it till the ink ran.

What they must think of me in Lucknow . . . sending
them that girl! And poor Ammi! First a missing husband,
then a vanished son and now a daughter seduced by a
pregnant widow. It was like a bad dream, only worse, since
it had actually happened. The only silver lining I could see
was that they didn't think I was responsible for her
pregnancy. I read it twenty times inside an hour of opening
it, but nothing changed. It always ended in underlined
capitals: <u>PLEASE TAKE THIS GIRL AWAY</u>.

But I couldn't. It was impossible. She couldn't stay with
me and there was nowhere else for her to go in Delhi. She
couldn't be a maid and live elsewhere because nobody would
take on a pregnant single woman without references and I
didn't think that Haasan and Ammi were about to vouch for
her. If only Haasan had simply turned her out of the house. It
was what he had intended to do when he found out, but
Asharfi had closed that option. She had been shamelessly
adamant about it – if Parwana was dismissed without other
arrangements being made for her care, she, Asharfi, would
stop eating, which would bring the affair to the attention of
Ammi, who would then have to be told the whole truth. This
was the last thing Haasan wanted to happen. He knew that
Ammi, even without being told, suspected something unnatural had passed between Asharfi and Parwana, but he
wasn't about to confirm her suspicions. He thought the
whole, explicit truth would drive her mad.

So he had written to me demanding help because it was
my fault that she was there in the first place. And this was

true, but accepting responsibility wasn't the same as finding a solution. There was nothing I could do to make her disappear. Really, there was nothing I could do.

I should have written back to Haasan immediately, pleading helplessness, but I didn't want to fall in his estimation, so I kept putting it off. I even stopped checking to see if any of the letters pushed under the East India C—— door were for me. If Haasan had written a sequel to his letter I didn't want to know. At the hotel I waited on twice as many tables as before, filling so many orders that I didn't have time to think. For twelve hours of the day, my mind was wholly given to gimlets, shandies, lemon twists, cocktail sausages, boiled duck, roast pork, Melba toast and the enigmatic kerosene freezer that was good only for runny ice.

I stopped sleeping. Earlier I had always napped till noon after coming home from the night shift. After work I would return to my room to wash fatigue away with a bucket of water and then make straight for Mitthan Halvai's for a cup of tea and breakfast. Then I usually shifted to the park to read the newspaper that I filched every morning from the Cecil's reading room. I had a favourite spot, a green bench donated by Lala Bishambernath Goyal in memory of his mother, Lalita Devi, shaded by a small gulmohur tree. Sitting there, with my back to the distracting bulk of St James' Church, I'd read the paper line by line and page by page. I made newspaper reading a vocation because once Parwana had done me out of a family, I had to get acquainted with this history-book world.

The papers were full of people I knew. There was a boxed report on the front page of the *Bombay Chronicle* which said that Nehru had been prevented by his jailers from writing to Indira. I felt for Jawaharlal. I too wanted to write letters. To Ammi and Asharfi and Haasan. And couldn't . . . thanks to Parwana. Some days I sat in the park for hours, till the sun became intolerable. Not always reading; often I'd doze on the bench and the paper would slip from my fingers and scatter. Invariably, one of the young boys in khaki shorts who were for ever drilling along the broad end of the park would gather it up and return it to me. Watching their simple, ragged rhythms was restful – sometimes that was why I nodded off.

The newspapers did more than fill the time I would have spent sleeping; they gave me a sense of proportion. The headlined casualties on the Eastern Front kept me grateful for being alive. More than that, the papers were a place where I could walk my feelings at a time when I couldn't exercise them on family or friends.

So I responded to each column-inch of disaster with conscious feeling. Some things, though, were harder to feel for than others. One day the paper had a story on the three heart attacks that Kasturba Gandhi had suffered in jail. The government surgeon in attendance was guarded: unfortunately, he said, a recurrence of the condition cannot be ruled out. The tragic prospect of her death dropped through my heart, without a ripple. It was hard to think of her as a person; for me she had always been a part of the Mahatma, like his spectacles or his walking stick.

I read the paper whole, except for the leader page. The editorials were always about the inevitability or impossibility of Partition and their opinions didn't much interest me. But I read everything else, from Mutt 'n Jeff to the Day's Happenings. Especially the Day's Happenings because after a week of monastic paper reading, when a second-hand life in small-print became boring, the Day's Happenings became my window into the world of people.

The day I decided to rejoin the real world (it was a Sunday) the Day's Happenings didn't suit me. There was a pageant in honour of the Patriarch of the East Indies (St Theresa's school, 6.30 p.m.) and a meeting of the Maharashtra Lingayat Sabha (Above Madras Café, 8.00 p.m.), but I was still on the night-shift so they were both at the wrong time of the day for me. Nearly everything was scheduled for the evening and I had just two options: a special Sabbath sermon at St James' to be delivered by a visiting pastor, Rev. A.J. Carrick of Sylhet, and a lecture at the Blavatsky Lodge, where Mr Kulkarni would talk about What Incarnates? I wanted to go to the lecture because I liked its title and perhaps there would be seances but

I didn't know how to get to Blavatsky Lodge, while St James', in all its whitewashed massiveness, was twenty yards from the bench where I was browsing through the Day's Happenings. So that morning I packed the paper away an hour earlier than usual, changed into the starched grey trousers and the even stiffer white shirt which the dhobi had just returned, fastened the collar button to compensate for no tie, and left the East India C—— at 10.20 a.m. to attend a church service for the first time since that wonderful winter day in 1965 when Father Noel broke his neck and the school gathered to remember him.

There were just three cars parked by the church's compound wall but scores of bicycles and two huge powerful-looking army motorcycles with BSA painted on the menacing bulge of their petrol tanks. The two leaves of the compound gate hung from their hinges at irregular angles, their lower corners wedged fast into the gravel path which led to the church's main entrance. The garden was withering as summer dried out the grass but the flowering borders by the path were still holding out and the bougainvillaea bushes strung along the compound wall had burst into pink.

Inside, there were fans at the altar end but halfway down the nave, where I took my place, the air was still and I could feel sweat break out on my forearms. The glare outside could have been another country. Uncertain light from high green windows made the nave glow darkly.

The benches were more than half full by the time I entered and the service had just begun. A man not dressed like a priest read a long passage from Matthew and there were hymns. Another man, also in mufti, read a shorter bit from the Epistle and there were hymns again. In between we stood and sat and knelt, all more than once. Then a third man, properly turned out in collar and cassock, took the stand and declared that we were honoured to have the Reverend A.J. Carrick with us today who would deliver the sermon. Another man in padre costume replaced him in the pulpit.

He was tall and very thin and his face was blotched with overlapping freckles. In profile it looked like the crescent moon of comic books: nose and chin curving extravagantly till they nearly met. He began without preliminaries, without greeting the congregation or thanking the incumbent reverend for the honour done him. He didn't even look at the book lying open in his hands.

And the Passover, he said, a feast of the Jews, was nigh.

He paused.

Then without once referring to the book in front of him, he recited his chosen text from memory.

And the Passover, he said again, a feast of the Jews, was nigh. When Jesus then lifted up his eyes, and saw a great company come unto him, he saith unto Philip, Whence shall we buy bread, that these may eat?

John 6, he said quietly, almost inaudibly, closing the unread book.

Twelve years in a Jesuit school helped me spot the miracle of the loaves and fishes at once. After twelve straight days of newspaper reading, it was nice to know that I had something in my head besides the news. But Carrick took no chances – he spent five minutes paraphrasing the story, down to the names and numbers. There were Philip and Andrew (the brother of Simon Peter); there were five loaves and two fishes; these did for five thousand people and there were twelve baskets full of crumbs left over after they had fed.

Then he stopped again, for what seemed to me a longish while. I settled into the pew and closed my eyes. Fairy tales in a dark, submarine place . . . sleep oozed into my head like a soothing oil.

It didn't last.

I come from Bengal, where the poor have only just begun to starve, he said, resuming.

I came awake, betrayed. John 6 was only a shortcut to the present time. It was the news again.

A thousand times five thousand must have food, he said, sub-biblically. Not for feasting . . . simply to live out the summer. If we do nothing there will be millions dead before the year is out. Six months will bring more corpses to Bengal than the Western Front has seen in three long years. The Saviour does not walk with us today, but we must show that we can still work miracles in His name Who died that we may live.

If we are Christians, our minds must every moment be consumed by a single question:

Whence shall we buy bread, that these may eat?

He finished and stepped down, having ruined my morning. The worst famine in the recorded history of India, the largest proof of the wickedness of the Raj, the calamity every schoolboy knew by name and date . . . and, living in '43, it had taken a sermon by an English padre to make me remember.

But on the other hand, serving five-course meals six days a week made hunger a distant notion. In all the gossip that I overheard while serving dinner, no one had yet mentioned famine in the east. Nor had the front pages carried any reports of hunger, much less death. This Carrick had anticipated the headlines; his was inside information – he had probably seen Bengali peasants die at first hand.

So there was some excuse for me. Still, the cool, dark peace of the church now suddenly seemed like self-indulgence. What was I doing at a Sunday service? I wasn't even Christian. I crept away before the Creed was said, communion taken, collection tray sent round – these were for believers. Outside, the hard white glare slapped my eyelids shut.

The outdoors brought a sense of proportion. Guilt was presumptuous. When I hadn't been able to take one troublesome girl off Haasan's hands, it was silly of me to fret about the five million famine dead of history books. They were written. I stood in the porch, waiting for my pupils to shrink. It was hot, even for June.

I went back to scanning the Day's Happenings, looking for an entry into normal life, a life uninfected by the unnatural eventfulness of newspapers. Even in 1943, there had to be an everyday sort of world made up of schoolboys, postmen, general stores, astrologers, Freemasons' Clubs, etcetera that jogged on, undisturbed by war, famine or the prospect of Partition. Between an eternity of filling orders and the tyranny of history there had to be a middling kind of life for me.

I passed up the chance to attend Mr Kulkarni's second lecture to the Theosophical Society (all are welcome) at the Blavatsky Lodge on the subject of incarnation. From 'What

Incarnates?' he had moved on to 'Incarnation and the Creatures of Limbo – Ghosts, Poltergeists and Churails'. Nor did I attend the Eighth Annual Ansari Memorial Lecture (16 Ratendon Road. 11 a.m.). Dr Raghavachar was the speaker and he had taken as his theme 'Indivisible India'.

My luck turned on a Monday, exactly a month from the day I had received Haasan's S.O.S. That day I was forced to steal the *Hindustan Times* from the Cecil's lounge because all the readable papers were taken. Strictly speaking, therefore, it wasn't the Day's Happenings that changed my life: in the *Hindustan Times* the listings column was called What's On Today.

It wasn't the first notice in the column or even the last but it was the first one I read. It fairly leapt off the page into my eyes:

Smt Kaushalya Devi, Secretary-Treasurer, Nari Niketan, will speak on 'The Role of Handicrafts in the Uplift of Fallen Women', under the auspices of the Delhi Chapter of the Indian University Women's Association. Venue: Indraprastha College Auditorium. Time: 6.30 p.m.

The time was wrong for me; 6.30 was right in the middle of the busiest hour in my day, when late teas overlapped with early dinners. But it wasn't the time that grabbed my attention; it was the name. Kaushalya Devi was my grand-mother. There could be other Kaushalya Devis but none that lectured on fallen women. The Secretary-Treasurership of Nari Niketan clinched it. Nari Niketan was a reformatory for repentant prostitutes where they were taught alternative crafts like embroidery, crochet, knitting and simple methods of candle manufacture. Dadi had visited it every Friday down to the last year of her life.

I had forgotten Nari Niketan just as I had the Bengal famine, but thanks to What's On Today, I had found my mislaid memories. My world had suddenly fallen into place. Parwana, unmarried and pregnant, was a fallen woman; Dadi specialized in them. I just had to bring them together. In one stroke I would redeem myself in the eyes of my foster family in Lucknow and get to know my grandmother here. From the day I had arrived in Delhi I had been looking for an excuse to meet Dadi and all this time it had been staring me in the face. Stunned by the simple perfection of God's design, I hurried to Mitthan Halvai's, where I ordered two cups of tea and composed a telegram. Clipped bravado – send her I'll mend her – was modified by ordinary humility into a page-long letter but the gist remained the same: Dear Haasan Mamoo, if you can put Parwana into a Delhi train at Charbagh station, I will arrange a new life for her at this end. Yours sincerely.

I took the envelope down to the G.P.O. where I sent it Registered Post (Acknowledgement Due), making the man behind the counter cancel the stamps in my presence. Walking back home, I had to stop my feet from dancing with excitement. I reminded myself that Parwana would be a while coming. First there would be a letter from Haasan telling me when she was due; then some days, perhaps a week later, she would arrive. There was no point getting stirred up into a state of asthmatic excitement. Long deep breaths.

It didn't help. I wanted her in Delhi immediately. Couriered. Wired. Faxed. I could roll anticipation on my tongue, taste it in my spit. I remembered that taste from a long time ago when, flush with the takings from my ninth birthday, I had ordered a balsa wood glider kit pictured in the *Illustrated Weekly*, seduced by the dizzy promise of its advertisement: By Return Post, We Guarantee, No Money Now, It's V.P.P.!

Parwana

ARWANA ARRIVED ON the fifteenth of June.

Haasan's telegram reached me on the seventh, three days after I posted the letter. School holiday rush stop soonest confirmed berth fifteenth Oudh Express sixoclock evening new delhi please receive letter follows grateful Haasan.

But grateful Haasan's letter didn't find me and the week-long wait for her was unrelieved by information. Was she reconciled or resentful, tame or jungly, biddable or wild? By the fifteenth I had worked out a dozen ways in which my plans for her could fail. The only thing in my favour was her muteness. When I summarized her squalid life for Dadi, she wouldn't be for ever butting in.

I was on the morning shift the day her train was due, which meant less than an hour to recover in before setting out for the station. Biscuits and tea, a wash, then a long time squatting because the first one wouldn't drop and I was too tense to let it be for a while and then take it by surprise. Long drags on a Capstan helped, but nothing's the same after prompting. Unformed and pale, it filled the loo with the sourness of curdled excitement.

The tongawallah refused to take the shorter route through Darya Ganj because his horse was too old for the steep climb just before the Red Fort stretch. I didn't argue, so he turned the tonga around and tooled us into Nicholson Road. I remembered it as a narrow crowded lane, but we managed to travel at speed. On the right, for half the way, the old city wall kept us company.

My only memory of the ride was that the roads seemed empty, even the twisting ones. The station building was small and new and nearly all the parking space was taken up by army lorries, which puzzled me till I remembered that there was a war on. I didn't go near them, not within fifty feet. Less than a year ago a lorry like one of these had swallowed up Masroor before my eyes. Ten months and one week ago to be exact and the thought of it still left me breathless in a nasty, strangled way.

I stopped by a khaki motorcycle with a sidecar, glanced around and stroked its headlight. Then I snatched my hand away and I marched off to buy a platform ticket. I wasn't here to raise old ghosts; the past was past and about to arrive any minute on platform three was the key to my future – Parwana.

I climbed up to the over-bridge from which, at regular intervals, metal stairways led down to the platforms. In less than five minutes my teeth were gritty with the coal smoke puffed up by the steam engines shunting about below me. The first stairway on the right led down to platform three where the Oudh Express was expected, but I stayed on the over-bridge because according to the station clock it was only half-past five, and assuming the train was on time, I still had half an hour.

The over-bridge cleared the tracks by more than thirty feet, but even at this height the world became noise when two trains crossed each other, panting and whistling like dirty old men. In the rare lulls between trains, ordinary sounds became unnaturally loud: I could hear the coolies breathe as they hurried past, weighed down by baskets, bedrolls, cabin trunks. It was during one of these silences that I heard the call to prayer. I was lucky. A train would have drowned out those skirling Arabic sounds and I might never have noticed the mosque between the railway tracks.

It sat precisely between platforms one and two, so conspicuously out of place that it was almost invisible. It was, in fact, in plain sight of the over-bridge – three lumpy, whitewashed domes, a little flattened by my point of view, and a tiny courtyard. From my elevation, I could see the bearded maulana and his congregation, bending and straightening in prayer. By the time they finished I had discovered that the Oudh Express was late by half an hour, so I stayed where I was, idly mosque-watching for no reason other than the pleasure of spying unobserved.

187

The congregation didn't leave and the maulana, facing them now, began to speak. I lost his opening words because a shunting locomotive thundered past platform four, but after it had gone, his sentences floated up to me with faraway clarity, just the odd word missing.

. . . face today. Last week Janaab Yusuf Qureishi, secretary of the North-Western Railways Muslim Employees Association, showed us how injustice was done to Muslim workers by this government. Before him, Maulana Nomani explained the League's demand for Pakistan. Your speaker today is not a leader or a scholar but he is a Muslim who feels for his community. So please pay . . . to my young friend . . .

The young friend's name was drowned out by a whistling train. A tall, bearded man took the maulana's place and began. It was harder to catch what he was saying because his voice was heavier than the maulana's and didn't rise so well. I leaned over the railing and cupped an ear but for nearly a minute all I heard was a bass rumble. Then he got warmed up and his words began to travel better.

Nineteen forty-one.

These were the first words of his that I understood.

. . . nineteen forty-one we were counted. Thousands of census officers counted millions of Muslims, then they added us up, checked their totals and announced that there were eight crores of you and me. Eighty . . . million . . . Muslims. This is the truth, the government's own truth – printed, bound and published.

But for us, for Muslims, this is not the whole truth. The whole truth is that there are eighty million Mussalmans in this country, who are invisible!

He paused to let this sink in.

Not invisible to every one, he said, rocking a little on the balls of his feet. Not to the British who count us. Not to those Hindus who hate us, who see us everywhere – circumcised monsters who bathe once a year and breed all the time. It is the Congress which can't see us. It is the party of the Nation that is blind.

It first bleaches us with its secularism till we are transparent and then walks through us, as you and I would walk through jinns and ghosts. For Nehru's Congress, we are permanently invisible. When we're for it we aren't Muslims, we're human beings, transparent in our humanity. When we're against it, we still aren't Muslims, because then we are feudal or bourgeois, some abstract sort of anti-social villain.

Till a year ago, I was a Congressman. I had been a four-anna member since the Faizpur Congress. And like other Congress Muslims I had been called a token Mussalman, a show-boy, but that had never worried me because I had friends in the party who happened to be Hindu, Sikh or Christian, but in the end we were basically human beings together. Basically human beings.

But when the Congress met in Bombay last August I discovered that basic human beings came in two varieties: those who wanted the Quit India movement immediately and those who didn't. The first sort just happened to have names like Jawaharlal, Shyamaprasad, Mohandas, Purshottamdas, Narendra Deo, while the second sort coincidentally answered to Khalid, Ibrahim, Shaukat, Mansoor, Ahmad . . . When Khalid, Ibrahim, Shaukat, Mansoor and Ahmad got up and opposed the launching of the Quit India campaign because they felt the Hindu–Muslim situation was too tense, they instantly became invisible. They were hidden by the lengthy shadow of the masses. They were told by the Congress Working Committee that the masses favoured the campaign. Perhaps the committee was right; if the masses simply meant more than half the people counted by the census, you could subtract eighty million Muslims from the total and still have the masses left over. And so the Congress looked through us again in the name of the Masses and History and Freedom.

How shall we help it see us? he asked rhetorically, and then set about answering his own question. Since the Congress loves simple ideas like Freedom and the Masses, Muslims must simplify themselves. Since our problem is transparency, we must become opaque in the name of Islam. Even here, in a mosque, I can see Muslims dressed like civilians – but remember, they can't see you in those clothes. So burn your shirts and trousers and grow your beards. Put your mothers, sisters and wives in big, black burqas. Don't save your skullcaps for these prayers, wear them everywhere. Wear them like soldiers wear uniforms. Force the Congress to look at you in your beards and burqas . . . because only then will they know we are here. Only then will they see.

He hadn't finished when I tore myself away and hurried down the steps to platform three because the Oudh Express had made up time and was shortly arriving. I could still see the mosque from the platform but the speaker and his audience were hidden by the walls around the courtyard. Nor could I hear him – perhaps his voice didn't carry across as well as it floated upwards. I wondered if Masroor, wherever he was, felt the same way because he had been against the Quit India decision too. But there wasn't the time to wonder, because just then, in a haze of smoke, the Oudh Express drew in.

She was sitting on the lower bunk of a ladies' compartment, holding what looked like a bread knife in her hands, and looking young, calm and more or less the same. She considered me silently for a while, matching my face, perhaps, with her memory of it. Then, with a little nod, she stowed the knife away between a bottle of water and thermos flask in a wicker basket by the window. On the floor between the bunks sat a large tin trunk, labelled in Asharfi's name, a green hold-all straining at its straps, a fat surahi with its waterspout worked like a lion's head, a basket of mangoes, a tiffin carrier and a large black umbrella.

She was wearing Asharfi's hooped earrings and I thought I recognized her salwar kameez from my time at the Lalbagh house. It worried me that nothing about her suggested vice, not even her stomach, which seemed quite perfectly flat. Would Dadi accept her as a genuinely fallen woman when she looked like a sheltered young girl? I put the thought away; it was pointless worrying about it now. Luckily she couldn't speak for herself, so Dadi wouldn't be able to question her directly. I was the go-between and that was good. More immediately, her muteness was convenient because it eliminated the need for ice-breaking preliminaries. The sight of her had driven all small talk out of my head.

After a small silence I decided to take command of the situation by counting the pieces of her luggage aloud. One, two, three, four, five, plus the tin trunk and the umbrella, and that made se——

You'll need a coolie, said Parwana.

I was speechless for the length of the journey home. I concentrated very hard on the tasks at hand: engaging a coolie, showing the man at the gate our tickets, hiring a tonga, loading the luggage on, paying the coolie, climbing on. I gave each one of these jobs my whole attention because in a world where the dumb spoke unannounced, nothing could be taken for granted, and there was no such thing as a journey home. It was just a notion which depended on discrete events occurring in sequence and since no event implied the other – hiring a coolie didn't mean that a tonga would follow – a journey home was an idea to be realized by will alone.

I had no eyes for anything else. I noticed the bearded orator from the railside mosque standing near the tonga as I loaded the luggage on to it, looking at Parwana, but I didn't give him a second thought. Then I saw him again at the end of our ride, at Kashmiri Gate, as we were getting off in front of the East India C——, leaning over the side of his tonga as it passed us, staring at Parwana. He seemed to be following us but I didn't allow his persistence to distract me from the present task of off-loading Parwana's belongings. Once we were safely inside the East India C—— there would be time to think of other things. But not before. In this world I was trapped in, there was no guarantee that an unwatched tonga wouldn't turn into a wayside mosque. Eternal vigilance was the price of sanity.

But the shock of hearing her speak wore off over the four days that she spent with me before Dadi took her in, during which she explained how she had got her voice back and why she had lost it in the first place. Having nearly died once, she was quite emancipated from history, from the habit of seeing time as a series of events, tending to an ending. As far as I could tell she wasn't against the plans I had for her. I told her what I knew about Nari Niketan and she listened comfortably. I had the uneasy sense that if I had told her she was going to die the day after, she would have reacted in the same way. Parwana didn't believe in the future.

I decided to present her to Dadi the coming Saturday because my waiter friends at the Carlton had told me that Kaushalya Devi gave audience to the disadvantaged over the weekend. In the time we had till then, I tried to get her to remember that she was my sister, at least while she was staying with me at the East India C——, because that was what I had told the caretaker. I spent hours coaching her, helping her memorize a plausible history of her fallen state – one that she could recite and Dadi could believe. Every evening, for diversion and relief we would see a film at the Ritz. By the time Saturday came round, Parwana was fluent in her story. It helped that she didn't have to memorize a made-up tale – she had merely to forget a part of the truth.

Saturday morning. Dadi's audience hours were from nine to one, so we left the East India C—— at a quarter to nine. Parwana looked scrubbed and young; she had twisted her hair into a single plait and I had made her take Asharfi's gold hoops off because naked, pierced ears made girls look curiously vulnerable.

We reached the lane behind the Carlton in plenty of time and dawdled there. Then just before nine, we started up the lane again, hurrying past the Carlton's kitchen entrance where they were preparing to murder the first of their lunchtime chickens.

We hardly hesitated when we reached the four steps which led to the raised porch. I stopped only to pluck a leaf off the tulsi plant in its large green vat, which I ate for luck and old times' sake. For a moment or two I stood there silently, watching pigeons flap across the porch's ceiling, not saying anything. In front of us were the closed double-doors which in my time had opened into the European sitting room.

High on the right of the door, a wooden name board gave my grandfather his name. At about the same level as his name was a new-looking electric bell-push, a black button set in a white porcelain round. It stared down at us with pop-eyed contempt. I took a deep breath and jabbed it.

There was a muffled bong somewhere inside and a voice shouted Jumna! A moment later, one of the double doors was

192

unbolted and opened by a large middle-aged maid. She stood aside and motioned us in. We were obviously expected, or at least someone interchangeably like us was. It was dark inside and cool but it wasn't the drawing room I remembered from my childhood. It looked more like a film producer's notion of a rich lawyer's office. Escritoire was one of the words that came to mind; chaise longue, ormolu clock, damask and mahogany were others – not because I knew what they meant but they seemed to match the poshness of the room.

In the middle of a lot of Burma teak and leather, Dadi was sitting cross-legged on a large white mattress looking plump, blackhaired, unlined and not at all like herself. Her head and the rest of her was dressed in handspun cloth; set in front of her was a spinning wheel quite like the one on the Congress flag.

Sit down, she said, never taking her eyes from the thread she was drawing out, so we pushed our slippers away and settled down on the edge of the mattress. Jumna shut the door and bolted it. Dadi didn't talk to us for an impressive length of time, about two minutes, but the effect was spoilt by her spinning because the thread broke twice in that span. When she judged it was time, she set the wheel to one side with a vicious little push though her face remained calm. Ignoring me, she fixed her eyes on Parwana. Yes, my child, she said with nun-like seniority (though she couldn't have been above forty), tell me how it happened.

I cleared my throat, hoping to put Parwana's difficulties to her in précis, but she hushed me into silence with an imperious little wave of the hand. Let her speak for herself, she said severely. You can explain your role in this later. She returned to Parwana. Come dear, she said briskly, begin. Her senior-citizen manner grafted on to the authority of that room was enough to command obedience. So Parwana began.

She began with the Bombay orphanage where she had lived from infancy to adulthood. I was named on my fifth birthday, she said. I didn't have a name when they left me there and then the office lost my file, so they kept putting it off because they didn't know what I was. What religion, that is. Then, when I was five, the orphanage's golden jubilee happened. Our Visitor was the Governor of Bombay, so they whitewashed the building and gave me a name. The superintendent named me Chandrakanta.

But she had had the name only six months when it was changed. There had been a rash of riots across the country and feelings were running high in Bombay when *Noor*, a local paper, accused the municipal orphanage of giving its children Hindu names. So Chandrakanta had to be renamed. The superintendent scribbled Ruth, Shireen, Shama and Parwana on separate chits and allowed Chandrakanta to pick one out of his sola topi.

I asked if I could see the other chits after I picked Ruth, said Parwana, just to make sure that I was getting a proper name at last. The superintendent was kind; when I asked for Parwana instead, he gave it to me. He was a Madrasi and I was little, so we both didn't know that Parwana wasn't a suitable name for a girl.

Dadi wasn't interested. Yes, yes, she said with steely patience, but how did you come to be homeless and destitute?

These were large assumptions because with her dark green kameez and her dead-white skin, Parwana was looking particularly well-born. But it wasn't Dadi's fault. Most people who came to see her on Saturdays were probably both homeless and destitute, and certainly Parwana had no permanent home.

That didn't happen till after I left the orphanage, said Parwana, unoffended. We learnt shorthand in our last year there. This was to give us a skill because we were meant to leave the orphanage at eighteen and make our own way. We were taught by Miss Furdoonji, who was old and single and lived near by. She charged the orphanage nothing for the lessons because she loved us. Actually she spent more time on English conversation than shorthand. You'll all become ayahs, she would scold, when we got sick of repeating phrases after her. Then she would read us poems – lovely poems about ships and battles, England and America . . . Whitman not Pitman, she used to say, and she was right. The English helped. At least to start with.

Some of us did become ayahs but I did better – I joined the airways. There was a wonderful picture in the papers: five laughing girls in caps and uniforms with a pilot in the middle and a propeller in the background. It was part of an advertisement which said that I could fly. That I could fly and be paid for it if I was pretty, healthy and spoke some English. Nothing else. It was a fairy tale. I applied, they interviewed me and I had the job. Actually it wasn't that surprising that they gave it to me. You see, all the girls in the newspaper picture had names like Sally, Pamela and Doreen. They were quite pleased to have a Parwana on their rolls. I think they would have liked a Parvati even better, but for the first ever Indian airline, I was a start.

So I left the orphanage six months before I was eighteen and moved into a chummery in Bandra. The airline had rented a large second-floor flat in a broken-down building called Dhotiwala Mansions, where all us trainee hostesses had to stay. That's where I spent eight months with Maureen, Patsy, Sarah and Pam.

For a moment Parwana was silent, her lips curving in happy memory. It was the happiest time in my life. I learnt to polka and to waltz; every evening Maureen wound up her gramophone and we all danced, with each other or cushions as partners. I usually danced with Sarah because I wasn't very good and she led strongly. She always smelt of Afghan Snow. Patsy had a boyfriend; she was the only one of us who did. He was in the merchant navy, I think, and mostly around because he had just been given months of shore leave. He took us all driving every Sunday in his open Morris. He even drove us to Khandala once . . .

Parwana, interrupted Dadi firmly, but with a gentleness which surprised me; perhaps, but for duty, she would have liked to hear about the Khandala excursion too. Parwana, she said, you must tell me what actually happened.

Like an audience in a horror film, she was waiting for the bad parts. It wasn't her fault – she was a social worker, her province was hardship, not joy.

Parwana was silent for a long while. Then she looked up and said: more than one thing happened. Let me tell you what happened, one thing at a time – then you can add them up.

Perhaps it all happened because I didn't have a boyfriend

like Sidney with a car and prospects. And perhaps I didn't because I was brought up in an orphanage. But that couldn't have been the only reason because Maureen, Sarah and Pam didn't have boyfriends either and all of them had families. But the fact was that Patsy, the only one who actually went on to become a hostess, was the only one with a boyfriend, so there might have been a connection. The rest of us never flew. We trained for the whole eight months – deportment, balance, proper make-up, emergency exits, vomit detail, natural smiling – but in the end we all dropped out. And we all went into the movies.

The movies were Sarah's fault. Nothing would have happened if she hadn't been a distant cousin of Nelson Deane, who choreographed the waltzes for birthday-party scenes in all the films. Three months before their training ended, he turned up at the chummery – he needed a partner for a quickstep in a strapless silver dress. Sarah, who loved dancing as much as she loved the movies, didn't think twice. We managed to keep it from the airline initially, said Parwana. For the first week Sarah rehearsed her steps with me each night, wearing her slip in place of the costume she couldn't take home. Close up, she smelt of greasepaint, frenzy and sweat, she smelt of excitement. But in the end the management found out and she had to leave. Maureen cooked her a huge roast dinner the evening before she moved in with Cousin Nelson.

Even so, the rest of them might have been stewardesses today if they hadn't skipped class to be at the sets the day Sarah's dance was shot. They went in their uniforms because they were the smartest clothes they had: tapered skirts, short jackets, cravats and cheeky little caps. They stood out, even in the shabby glitter of the studio. They stood out in their uniforms and got drafted. Pamela got a bit role in Sarah's film as the junior vamp and Maureen was absorbed in the big dance scene when the producer decided it wasn't big enough. Parwana got the attention of the stubbled assistant director who suffered every minute of the shooting because his heart was in tragic realism.

His name was Satyakaam. He pestered Parwana till she

agreed to be cast in his first film. Perhaps it was her name that made him want her: Parwana, the moth which flutters to the flame, the champion metaphor of filmi song. Satyakaam's realism sought its melancholy truth in the language of dust, blood, vines, doves, drunkenness and ashes, so Parwana's name was a bond. Things might have been different for Ruth or Chandrakanta.

He managed to raise money for the film over the next two months, by which time there were only Patsy and Parwana left in the chummery. But between Sidney and Satyakaam, they hardly ever met after classes. For seven evenings in a row before shooting began, he explained the plot which thickened with every passing day. In its bare bones it was the tale of a widow forced on to her husband's pyre by a cruel, hidebound world, from which she was rescued by an oppressed idealist in the nick of time. She was, though, singed into shock and the rest of the film was about the idealist (Satyakaam himself) nursing her into the world of the living. The widow was social reality; Parwana was to be the widow.

The shooting began with the pyre scene to get it off to an authentic start, and Satyakaam staged it with unlimited realism. Realism. From Parwana's story it was clear that it all happened because of Satyakaam's obsession with reality. Wary of imagination, he believed that art was the sum of authentic detail. Before shooting, he had made an inventory of the realities he needed and then gone shopping. One of the items he bought was Parwana.

He couldn't find a convenient riverbank to shoot the burning, so he settled for the studio, where he bathed the scene in moonless black to obscure any unreality lurking around the edges of the frame. There was genuine sandalwood and pure ghee for the pyre, a real pandit to recite traditional slokas and a proper cadaver from the hospital morgue to act as the dead husband, even though he would be mostly hidden by the sandalwood with only his forehead showing. Wearing the red sari prescribed for self-immolating widows, Parwana would be laid upon the pyre, her arms bound to her sides and her feet roped together, though this was artfully concealed by the sari. But not so completely that the audience couldn't see the bonds. Being a disciple of real life, Satya wished to make it clear that sati was a coerced act. Then to cries of Jai Sati Mata! the camera would close in on the torch being touched to the ghee-stained logs. Parwana would begin writhing and screaming amid flames which, in a grudging concession to the contrivance of art, would be superimposed later.

Parwana's voice, which had faded to a whisper, now tailed off altogether and the room was filled with an eerie tinkling as the glass bangles on her wrists shook with her body's shaking. She recovered quickly and took up her story again, but by then both Dadi and I could have supplied the climax. And yet we listened with that possessive thrill that comes of knowing the end.

When the shot was set up and the cameras rolled, the priest, who had thumbed her breasts twice in the course of arranging her on the pyre, brushed them with his knuckles one last time while putting the rudraksha beads around her neck. The chant of Jai Sati Mata! rose gradually, the high camera trolley did a slow circle of the pyre in a bizarre parody of ritual circum-ambulation and Parwana felt a gentle glow of warmth and smelt the nutty smell of roasting meat.

Perhaps the extra holding the torch exceeded his brief, perhaps it was an accident that the logs caught, but from Parwana's description of Satyakaam, it seemed more likely that gritty realism was the culprit. In the end, I think, he couldn't bear the thought of synthetic flames because he was an honest film maker, not an illusionist, and real life was lived without sleight of hand.

I screamed very hard, said Parwana, because I wasn't sure if it was the dead man burning or me.

She found out later that her buttocks had been badly singed. But Satyakaam was intent on his footage and the camera kept circling – it was a professional crew. Left to them she might have died because the hem of her sari caught fire and even then they didn't stop. She was screaming silently by then, though she didn't know that her voice had gone. It was the priest who saved her life by jerking her off the pyre when the sari flamed and yanking out the pleats tucked into her petticoat. She was free in seconds of its folds, which burnt like shavings on the studio's floor.

The priest was Gyanendra, Gyanendra of Banaras and the window opposite. Afterwards he told her that her underclothes, by some miracle, didn't catch fire, though the petticoat was scorched into the stiffness of papad.

That didn't stop the skin on my bottom from peeling off in brown strips for months, said Parwana.

All her memories of the week that followed were secondhand, given to her by Gyanendra after they had fled Bombay. Only one sensation survived the shock and the subsequent sedation: the intense cold in the region of her bottom as she lay on her stomach, half-comatose. For four days small blocks of ice lay balanced on her buttocks. When she had healed, Gyanendra explained that the ice was meant to soothe the skin and prevent scarring. But it wasn't solicitude that moved him to save her buttocks from blemish. He had plans for her. Poor Parwana! Ravaged in the name of realism, then ravished for the sake of fantasy.

His footage in the can, Satyakaam wanted her off the sets and out of Bombay before some troublemaker told the press or the police. Gyanendra was the only volunteer for the job, so he named his price and got it: three hundred rupees, a flash gun, a hundred bulbs and a camera mounted on a tripod. Then he took her to Banaras, to that room opposite mine, across the lane from Pant Ram's akhara.

He could have taken her anywhere but he took her to Banaras and not Quilon or Quetta or Nagercoil because for three hundred years, his gourdfaced ancestors had taught Sanskrit in the classical academies of Kashi. But the slow death of sinecure, wanderlust and lust of a simpler kind had prompted the young Gyanendra's feet westward, to Bombay, where over six miserable months he learnt that classical learning couldn't be traded and didn't appreciate, that priestcraft was an economy fare to starvation.

But he didn't starve in the end because harsh facts like hunger applied only to the real world where housewives whored in the afternoons and lawyers slept on the streets. In the more freely imagined world of the Bombay film, there was a living to be made for everyone, because everyone, no matter how obscure or bizarre, was already cast in some script-writer's fevered story. It was a matter of being in the right place.

So one mild winter afternoon, Gyanendra, along with a thousand other gawpers, had gathered to watch a scene being shot on the steps of the Taj Mahal Hotel, when the director, who had a temple scene in mind, cast him on the spot as the officiating priest. His face, already brahminical from centuries of inbreeding, had become nobler as his hairline receded, more ascetic with malnutrition. Gyanendra filled a need and soon became compulsory for any film that needed a holy man. He eked out this income by conducting film muhurats, the ritual essential for all good beginnings.

It was a living, but after some years he became homesick. He yearned for Banaras, for the perfect cadences of those early morning chants, which, for their duration at least, imposed metrical order upon an anarchic world. What kept him from returning was his loathing of the shabby-genteel poverty in which his father had ground out his life and in which he too had crawled to manhood. To return to the city of guaranteed salvation, he needed an income which would allow him to commit himself to the oral tradition as an artist – not as a hereditary professional.

It was in the course of finding a solution to the difficult problem of enough money that he had imagined Parwana . . . long before he met her on Satyakaam's sets. For years he had dreamed of publishing an illustrated edition of the *Kama Sutra*, annotated with all the erudition of his ancestors. But he had never had the money or the courage to persuade a starlet to pose for the project. So when it happened that a lovely girl, only slightly damaged, fell – no – was thrust into his hands, he was unsurprised because he knew her to be preordained. He knew that his dream had been father to this woman.

He made up the story about the silent film to lure Chaubey into the photographs. He couldn't say he was making a talkie because I had lost my voice, said Parwana, half-smiling. Dadi frowned – it was unnatural to smile while recalling such misfortune.

It wasn't so bad at first, said Parwana, trying to explain. I trusted him – he had saved my life. I missed the girls, of course, especially Sarah and her wonderful smell; I missed the gramophone too, and the dancing most of all. But I didn't want to go back right away. Not till I found my voice again, not till I was normal. I had so much to tell them, so much to explain, and I wasn't going to act it out, like a monkey.

For three months, said Parwana, I never left that room. Not because of him, though he did like to keep my window shut and sometimes, I think, mixed opium in my food. He offered more than once to take me for a walk. I didn't go. I didn't want to walk into the world I could see from my window.

It was the litters that stopped her. The litters and the corpses moving down the street and turning left into the steps that led to the pyres of Manikarnika. She had had enough of that. She never left the room because her window on the world kept showing her trailers of her début film. It had nothing to do with Gyanendra.

Dadi looked disappointed. After all this, would Gyanendra turn out to be an eccentric social worker, merely? There was a long silence. Then Parwana took up the story again – and this time she gave Dadi her villain.

I wasn't there to hear it told. When she began describing the time that Chaubey raped her, Dadi told me to wait outside till she called me in again. Once more I stood in the covered porch, warily watching the pigeons flap past. But I was missing nothing that I didn't know – Parwana had described the rape to me not once but several times while rehearsing the story that she was telling my grandmother. Besides, there was everything I had heard and seen at first hand.

But I knew that I wouldn't figure in her tale as the voyeur opposite – she had given me her word. She would leave me out of the Chaubey episode. We had agreed that halfway through the rape she would be overcome by the trauma of remembering. Then she would retreat into silence, which Dadi would understand. I didn't want Dadi to know that I had known Parwana in Banaras – she would jump to the conclusion that I was responsible for her pregnant state. We needed a story to explain her escape from Gyanendra which didn't feature me. A traumatized silence would buy her the time to invent one.

She also needed time for another explanation – how she had found her voice again. Perhaps she could put it down to some later accident, as awful as the singeing. Shocked into normalcy could be her story. Or perhaps she would make up a better one. Because what she couldn't tell Dadi was the truth: that her voice came back to her in the dust of a disused zenana, when, after three weeks of tenderness, she had wanted to declare her love.

Company Again

Technically the meeting was a success. I introduced myself to Dadi in her prime and she accepted Parwana for Nari Niketan. In fact Dadi insisted on keeping her in the house till a place was found for her in the reformatory across the river. The trouble was, I didn't gain a grandmother – I simply lost a brand-new friend. Before I left the house, Dadi took me aside and told me plainly that I was not to visit Parwana. She was about to begin a new life and I was a living reminder of the old one that she was meant to forget. She wrote my address down perfunctorily . . . then reached into her string bag and tipped me. I was so stunned that I took the coin and went away without saying goodbye to Parwana. Life didn't look up. Blood didn't tell.

Nothing changed for me except the weather, which, as June yielded to July, went from hot to hottest. Summer had seen the Cecil emptying out as the sahibs followed the government and the cold weather to the hills. As the Season in Simla got properly underway, more and more waiters were transferred to staff the Cecil there. Patrick himself left at the end of June to raise the tone of the dining room with his proconsular profile. He had put me down for a transfer as early as end-May but then I hadn't wanted to go and he had let me stay on in Delhi as part of the summer skeleton staff. But waiting on empty tables, with no news of Dadi or Parwana, I began to wonder if I shouldn't have gone.

When my letter to Haasan reporting the successful rehabilitation of Parwana didn't find a reply in more than three weeks, I wrote to Patrick asking for a transfer to Simla. He wrote back asking me to wait because all the places were taken. There would be vacancies only towards the end of the Season when extra hands were needed to cope with the last burst of sahib festivity. So it looked as if I was stuck in Delhi for most of the summer, with no one, not even Patrick, for company.

It was just loneliness that pushed me into learning Urdu. I was going through the classified advertisements in the *Hindustan Times*, idly looking for another job, when I saw a notice in bold print which announced that the Anjuman-i-Taraqqi-e-Urdu was offering free correspondence courses in the language.

It had been weeks since I had communicated properly with anyone except to suggest good things on the menu or to ask if they would like something to drink, so I wrote off to the Anjuman-i-Taraqqi-e-Urdu at once. A correspondence course wasn't the same as a friend but it was the next best thing. I'd get letters.

For the early lessons the letters I wrote to the Anjuman were so cryptic that the war censors probably thought they were coded in some knotted cipher. Lala tala la; la tala lala; la lala tala; tala la lala. Bleached by translation, drained of their vernacular sap, these phrases meant: lala lock get; get lock lala; get lala lock and lock get lala. My teacher-correspondent at the Anjuman liked my letters: he said in one of his replies that I had mastered the basics of Urdu prose.

Lessons three and four coincided with the fasts of Ramazan. I thought I saw my pen-friend's flourishing script waver with hunger. I didn't know his name (I addressed my letters directly to the Anjuman) but I could tell from reading in-between the lines that he was a kindly, bearded maulana with grey-green eyes, known to everyone as Inayatsahib.

It was the first time in my life that I had even noticed the month of Ramazan, and that because solitude had made me critically dependent on the written and printed word. According to the *Hindustan Times*, the Imam of the Jama Masjid in Delhi and his counterpart in the Nakhuda mosque in Calcutta had fallen out – they couldn't agree on the date on which the fasts of Ramazan would end, each having seen the risen moon on different nights. They finally settled their differences and Muslims around the country went back to normal eating, but for many Bengalis, Muslim and otherwise, the fasting continued. Member, Food, on the Viceroy's Council felt that unfounded rumours were creating unnecessary mortality and cautioned Bengalis against panic starvation.

The visiting pastor from Sylhet had read the signs by the end of May. The daily press, obliged to see the world in perspective, took a little longer. In early July a small boxed item about gruel kitchens in the famine areas of rural Bengal made the front page. It wasn't until the twenty-sixth of August, not till starvation deaths on the streets of Calcutta stabilized at fifty a day, that the famine was promoted to the headlines.

Long before this, in the third week of July, around the time that I began turning the pages of my Urdu primer from left to right without thinking, the famine reached the frontier outpost of Bengal in which I lived, the East India C——. The caretaker was from Chittagong in East Bengal, from where his elder brother had sent him a postcard. On one side he had written that the ancestral lands were yielding as well as could be expected in a bad year; on the other he urged his brother to return to the village with as much cash as he could raise. The hungry were trading land for nearly nothing in ready money . . . it was a good time to buy. The caretaker took me aside and gave me the keys to the premises. He wouldn't be more than a fortnight, he said wheedlingly. All I would have to do was to lock up securely when I left for the hotel. I agreed immediately, thinking of my friends at the Carlton, who would enjoy the brief luxury of beds and a roof. Besides, I would have company. The next day the caretaker loaded four sacks of rice into the tonga in lieu of luggage, and set off for the railway station.

But the Carlton's waiters never sampled the C——'s hospitality because the famine that pulled the caretaker east drove Lucknow westward to my doorstep. The morning after the caretaker left, I woke to persistent knocking on the front door. Sticky-eyed, furry-mouthed and nearly choking on my own bad breath, I opened the door to find the landing stacked with tins, trunks, baskets and bedrolls. I could hear panting sounds from the bottom of the stairwell; whoever had been knocking had gone down again to haul more luggage up. A minute later, a huge, rusted, boiler-type thing came into view. The man underneath it was Haasan.

He couldn't talk for a while after he put the thing on the floor, so we watched in silence as Ammi and a drawn-looking Asharfi followed him up the stairs. Ammi, fat and breathless, was the first to greet me. Salamaleikum, she gasped, as she cleared the last step and lowered herself on to the nearest trunk to get her breath back. She looked at the subdued Asharfi and the silent Haasan with disapproval.

Why so longfaced? she asked in a bullying way. Climbing steps is good training for a hill station.

So. They were en route. Till she spoke of hill stations their unexpected appearance outside my door had filled my mind with visions of a family reunion. But I should have known better; they were only in transit. Still, after those long weeks when Urdu lessons and newspapers had filled in for people, even en route was enough. Leaving their baggage on the landing for later, I led them through the spacious emptiness of the C——, letting them choose their rooms, feeling like a made-good migrant who had brought his family over.

By the time they washed and I brought the luggage in all by myself, in deference to Haasan's years, it was a quarter to eight, so I made us all tea. I couldn't find any table mats, so I used antimacassars instead and laid four places. It was the first time I had used the china from the tallboy and the service was thick with curly dust. The business of rinsing and wiping, the delicate clinking of teaspoons on china and the convivial sound of chairs being drawn up as Ammi, Asharfi and Haasan settled down to tea made me feel like a homemaker.

For a time there was a comfortable silence broken by sipping sounds, but when it threatened to go on beyond the first cup, I asked Haasan what the rusted boiler thing was meant to be.

It's a room heater, said Ammi, before Haasan, who was looking unhappy, could answer. Don't ask him. He doesn't even want to go to Simla. Her tone suggested that this was on a par with being impotent or vegetarian. It's been in my husband's family ever since they migrated from Kashmir. But Lucknow was never cold enough. Now in Simla it will have work to do again.

I waited but when no one explained, I asked why they were

going to Simla. It was an innocent question, but it touched off a quarrel which made my room echo for the next half hour. Asharfi didn't take part in the argument – she just carried on looking pinched and taut. I wondered if she was pining for Parwana.

Ammi and Haasan did all the quarrelling. It was hard to tell what the larger argument was, but it had something to do with corpses in Lucknow.

The first one was found in a friend's car. It was standing in Charbagh station's car park at the time. The friend had gone to buy a ticket to Ajmer Sharif to visit the shrine of Shaikh Moin-ud-din Chishti. When he came back to the car, exclaimed Ammi, there was a dead woman sitting in the driver's seat, stark naked, with a baby at her breast and her head on the steering wheel.

That's not true, interrupted Haasan angrily. Rifaqat said that the woman was lying next to the car on the shaded side, with her head on the running board. And the child wasn't being suckled. The station doctor told Rifaqat that it had been dead nearly two days. The mother had been carrying its body around. And she wasn't naked; she had just torn off a part of her palloo to swaddle her child. You shouldn't make up things about dead people!

Taken aback by the strength of Haasan's feeling, Ammi abandoned the Charbagh corpse in favour of her next example.

The day after Rifaqat bhai told us about the car, there was a dead body in the lane in front of our house. And this one, she said, looking challengingly at Haasan's disapproving face, I saw with my own eyes.

It was obviously a quarrel they had had before, but I still didn't know what the point of it was, because Ammi believed in setting out her examples before making the argument that they were meant to prove.

Then the week after that, she continued, a dozen bodies appeared all over Lucknow. There were two found in the porch of the legislative assembly building. The watch-and-ward staff found them lying there early in the morning. And there was a whole pile of them right outside Haasan's coffee house, she said triumphantly, as if the nearness of the corpses to Haasan's work place clinched her case. Then there were the six they found in the Residency ruins. Twenty deaths in less than a week – what else can it mean? You tell me!

I looked at her, alarmed. What could I tell her? I didn't even know what they were talking about. Haasan must have noticed because he began explaining with clenched restraint.

According to him, Ammi believed that Lucknow was being wasted by an epidemic. There had been rumours for the past two months that the war in the east was spreading disease before it. The favoured disease was smallpox, but Haasan had heard rumours which named cholera, typhoid, 'flu – even the plague. Ammi believed it was all of them. She was certain that those corpses in Lucknow had died of some spreading sickness.

That's why we are here, said Haasan resignedly. Ammi thinks that epidemics can't climb hills, so Simla is safe, but Lucknow and Delhi aren't. And of course it's nonsense. There was no need to leave Lucknow. Those corpses died of hunger, not disease.

He retreated into his tea cup and emptied it with loud, angry sips. Ammi was unimpressed. Twenty in a week, she repeated. Moths and earthworms die overnight, not people. It takes time to die of hunger.

Ammi, said Asharfi softly, speaking for the first time, that woman outside our door . . . in the lane – her face was so thin it was like a skull.

Because she was thin already when the plague got her, said her mother confidently, reaching for the sugar bowl. She must have been a beggar. Unless Haasan sahib who knows everything can also guarantee that there are no thin beggars in Lucknow.

Ammi rested her case.

They were not beggars, said Haasan tiredly. They died over many weeks and hundreds of miles. The corpses in Lucknow were starving Bengalis who had caught westbound trains to run away from famine. But their hunger caught up with them and they died. That's all. They died of hunger. We were in no danger in Lucknow – starvation isn't an infectious disease. He

208

watched with austere distaste as Ammi poured out another cup of tea and ladled sugar into it. Even if it were, he said cuttingly, you would be immune.

You're just guessing, said Ammi with insulting casualness. She wiped her face and looked up at the fan. Sharfu, just make it go faster. Uff! I'm dying.

All theory, she said, returning to the battle. There was nothing Bengali about the body in the lane outside. She didn't have those sly, chinky eyes that Bengalis have and she wasn't wearing one of those red-bordered saris either. And those bangles that Bengali women wear, one red, one white? she wasn't wearing those either.

Even before we reacted, Ammi must have realized that this evidence was less than conclusive. I can only tell you what I saw, she said defensively. What do you expect me to say? That she spoke Urdu? She didn't. She was dead. I still think she was a local beggar woman. The plague – or cholera or typhoid or whatever it is – it gets them first because they drink dirty water and never clean their hovels. And they would have given it to us if I hadn't thought of Khala's cottage in Simla. It's been empty since she moved to Lucknow. Anyway, even if you are right, she said, looking at Haasan with the magnanimity of the victorious, why don't you think of it as a holiday – now that we are going there.

The argument stayed unresolved and it was a relief to leave for work, though not before promising to book them into the Kalka Mail as soon as I finished my shift at the hotel. I spent most of the morning turning napkins into peacocks then wedging the birds into glasses where they sat waiting for the Cecil's lunchtime clientele to turn them into napkins again. Today was a Saturday and by one o'clock the dining room was full, which never happened on weekdays in the hot weather.

It was a long lunch for me; I got a table ringed by uniformed men in no hurry to eat. A young lot, mainly subalterns, so it was gin-and-tonic and beer for an hour, though an American voice asked for a Martini and some comedian called for port. The talk around the table was, for some odd reason, entirely about three men called Archie, Percy and Claude. These three were actually two men – this I gathered from one of the soldiers who wondered aloud if Archibald's friends called him Percy.

When I served the prawn cocktails after an hour of steady drinking, they were still on about Archie and Claude. I began to think they were heatstruck. Surely no one, not even the victims of military academies, could keep this up through an afternoon?

I returned to the pantry and overheard one of the Beverley twins say to the other: Dad'll love this – Archie's the first one from the army. I went directly to the sink and splashed my face. Why were British subalterns and Anglo-Indian waiters concurrently discussing Archie and Claude? I went up to Ronald, the older Beverley, and asked him. The mystery cleared. They were all discussing the morning's headlines which, because of my visitors and their quarrel, I had forgotten to read.

Incredibly, these names out of vaudeville had been promoted to the two most important jobs in the country. Field Marshal Sir Archibald Percival Wavell had succeeded Lord Linlithgow as Viceroy, while General Sir Claude Auchinleck had been raised to occupy the Commander-in-Chiefship vacated by the knight Archibald. I knew Wavell from the history books but not in a first-name way. According to Ronald's father and the newspaper that he took, these appointments meant that the war in the east was expected to last till 1950. Walking through the swing doors of the pantry, holding the veal cutlets aloft, I found myself envying this freedom to speculate. I was stuck with the certainties of hindsight.

But since historical hindsight was an unreliable guide to individual destiny, I tried to take charge of my life by asking the Kitchen-in-Charge if the transfer to Simla was likely to come through. Now that Ammi and the others were going there, that was where I wanted to be. The Kitchen-in-Charge, who doubled as the Estate Officer, was Captain Nazar. When I first knew him, he had been the genial soldier type, fond of the bottle and very good about matters like leave and transfers. But then Jinnah came to stay and Nazar wasn't the same again. He took to natty cream suits, to brushing his hair back, to sitting in his office with his cheeks sucked in. When I pumped him about Simla, he at once steepled his fingers and arched his eyebrows. After a long, silent, considering pause, he measured out two words: Can't Commit. I wasn't too discouraged because underneath the Jinnah act, he was a kind man. I knew that after a span of being non-committal, he would do his best for me.

When I got back to Kashmiri Gate I noticed that Archibald's appointment had already altered my environment – the Imperial Tannery's painted gallery of viceregal patrons was being updated. Watching the man on the lean-to ladder paint Percy in, I wondered uneasily about the speed of his muralization. From headlines to history in less than a day – it was unnerving. I remembered those early days in school when I had passed this shop-front every morning, silently mouthing the unfamiliar names. After Wavell's there had been just one other name: Mountbatten.

Upstairs, Ammi was heating a potion to lift Asharfi's spirits. Haasan was smoking a cigarette called Caravan which featured a palm tree, a camel, two Arabs and a mosque on the packet. Asharfi was bent over an embroidery frame. My foster family didn't think that the end of Empire was at hand. I changed out of my uniform and set off to book those bunks on the Kalka Mail.

This time I didn't need a tonga because the Kalka Mail left from Delhi Main, which was less than fifteen minutes away on foot. I stood in the queue for an hour and then the clerk told me that the train was full for the next four runs. The best he could do was the waiting list for Wednesday. I bought the tickets. Walking back in the half-light, I thought of Archibald again and shivered. Time was revving up. It wouldn't take long to use up the four years before August 1947. I had to start working on Ammi and Asharfi so that when Partition came, they stayed on. But how? What was the master argument? And where was Masroor? I needed the answers quickly – because between Archie and the edge, there was just one more space on the wall.

Sunday Outings

A T SIX ON a Sunday morning, the road below the balconies of the East India C—— was asleep. But further down this road, Asharfi, Ammi, Haasan and I, bathed, breakfasted and laden, were shifting about on the pavement which skirted the park where barbells rose and fell. For nearly twenty minutes, we had been trying to wave down a phut-phut that would take us to the Old Fort. We hadn't found one, largely because there weren't many about at that time of the morning, and those that were wanted to go to the Jama Masjid or further to Darya Ganj, but not to the Old Fort because it wasn't on the way to anywhere and they wouldn't find a fare back to civilization. Finally, the fifth one took us, on the promise of an extra eight annas. We climbed on and wedged the wicker basket between the seats, but Asharfi, for whose benefit the whole excursion had been organized, looked as long-faced as before.

The idea for the picnic had been germinated and nurtured in the rich, dark loam of Asharfi's gloom of the night before. By looking stricken in the run-up to dinner, then staying stricken unwaveringly right through the meal, Asharfi had convinced her mother that an outing was in order. Ammi chose a picnic as a diversion over the powerful claims of the shops or the sights, even though picnics meant a lot more work. For her, picnics were a learnt enjoyment and she knew that they had to be earned. As we resentfully cut sandwiches late into the night, Ammi reminded us at intervals that the proper attitude was joy – it was in the nature of picnics that they consisted mainly of the work that went before.

But cutting sandwiches was only one part of the architec-ture of picnics as built by Ammi. From inside one of the many Simla-bound trunks, she produced a small square case. Inside it were unbreakable cups and plates made of green bakelite, held in place by cracked leather straps. There were spoons and forks held fast in cunning slots, even an unbreakable vacuum bottle in a dull metal finish. Rolled tightly into two clamps on the inside of the case's lid was a large waxed sheet of cloth, printed with the yellow-brown-orange leaves of some American autumn. This was to slide between the surface of the picnic spot and the picnic things.

The place was as carefully picked as the paraphernalia. It had to be distant and greenly wooded over, deserted and not quite of this world. Ammi had chosen well. City sounds dropped abruptly as we left Delhi Gate and the old city behind. The great newspaper buildings of my time between the old city's walls and Hardinge Bridge weren't yet built and when we turned left after the bridge on to Mathura Road, there was silence. No Supreme Court building on the right and on the left a scrubby forest where the pyramids of Pragati Maidan should have been. Just a road with nothing on it except the 750 c.c. Indian Chief hauling our passenger box, and the drumbeat of its engine daring the silence. Then the Fort came into view, more battered than I remembered it.

The Old Fort came by its name partly because it was older than the Red Fort, but mainly because it was a ruin. Its ramparts were crumbling and overgrown and despite the medieval style in which it was built, everyone except pedants believed that it was incalculably ancient, at least as old as that epic war, the Mahabharata. It was a good place for picnics: green, remote, lonely and timeless.

The picnic began well. The ramp of earth that sloped up to the main gate was rough underfoot but gently inclined so that even Ammi managed it without difficulty. Inside, the ground was level and the mosque with the shallow dome seemed a good place to spread our hamper. The Fort was mostly scrub within, except for the mosque and a few stubby buildings. One of these was meant to be the Emperor Humayun's library only it didn't seem large enough. The life that had made sense of these structures was long gone and they looked more like the carelessly quartered parts of a sandstone giant than ruined buildings. We shuffled up the spiral stair of the runtish library and viewed the Fort's interior from an elevation. It really was the perfect setting for a picnic: ruffled but not wild, ruined splendour in the nominal care of the Archaeological Survey.

Ammi was vindicated but she wasn't happy. The purpose of the Fort was to bring joy to the sad heart of Asharfi but her daughter, though obediently atop the library with the rest of us, looked as pinched as she had done when we started. For Ammi picnics were occasions when time was stilled and the world shut out. She had hoped that in the absence of event and memory, a dose of innocent pleasure would pump the sullens out of Asharfi. Like an enema. Haasan, who knew things Ammi didn't, was likewise hoping that Asharfi's yearning for Parwana would be dissolved in the sexless bliss of this weekend Eden. That, at least, was the plan. It didn't work.

It failed partly because the sandwiches suffered the time-sickness. The waxed autumn sheet kept the earth from the eatables but in the hours before eating, the heat crept in. The bread curled, the butter ran and the cucumbers began to taste of original sin. The bitterness had more to do with place than time. India was a poor place for Edens. Asharfi spat the half-chewed mouthful out and retched upon the flagstones. The sandwiches were bitter for the rest of us too, but we did our spitting more decorously into napkins. In a country where a vegetable couldn't be given the benefit of the doubt, what hope was there of innocence?

But fundamentally, our Sunday outing was destroyed by hindsight. Mine, naturally, because I had more to look back on than everyone in 1943 put together. Once upon a time in 1947, four years from now and years before I was born, this ruined Fort had been jerked awake and made a home for thousands, for more people than it had ever hosted, even in its pomp. The pillars of the mosque had been hung with washing lines and each night the scrubby plain had changed into an inverted sky of winking campfires. Each day the smell of shit had risen higher but the neighbours hadn't complained because there weren't any then: the localities that I remembered clustered near the Fort were still twinkles in a town planner's eye. Nor had the zoo been built yet along the Fort's outworks, so no zealous warden protested that his exotic charges were threatened by faecal infections. Or there *was* a zoo, but within the Fort, where a single species, Homo Islamicus, had been corralled for its own safety and well-being. A superior zoo, progressive and opposed to cages, because its charges were being held only till they could be released into their natural habitat, which was then being fenced a few hundred miles away.

Later, the Fort went back to being a timeless ruin again and the Mahabharata theory became general once more. The makeshift zoo within the walls was superseded by a permanent one outside them. Parents, lovers, peasants and convoys of schoolchildren found simple joy inside its campus, some even learnt a little natural history on the side. The first zoo was slowly forgotten.

But not completely, or else there would be no hindsight. There are always the survivors, who live to tittle-tattle. My survivor was Siddiqi Sir who taught us civics in middle school though his heart was given to history. His sister had entered the land of the pure via the refugee camp in the Old Fort. He had visited her twice a day with food till she gathered her children and left for Karachi. He had told me all about the Old Fort camp after school was over, not once but several times. Absurdly, I now wished I had asked him if he had seen Ammi and Asharfi inside.

For me the picnic had been a bad dream from the time Ammi settled on the venue. As we approached the Fort down Mathura Road, I had a vision of Ammi, Asharfi and Masroor, piled into an army truck, one of an endless convoy, carrying their baggage, currently Simla-bound, to the refugee camp in the Fort. The phut-phut journey, the open-air meal, the Old Fort setting – the whole business felt like a casual rehearsal minus props and extras for that epic flight four years from now. And it wasn't impossible that Ammi and her children had bit parts in this play – they were, after all, Muslims. By the time we unpacked the sandwiches, I was sick with premonition, with the fear of losing my world again, and I may have infected the sandwiches.

By unspoken consensus we packed the picnic things and left the Fort, less than an hour from the time we got there. The phut-phut was still waiting – it hadn't found another fare. Haasan and I had taken bits of carved rubble for souvenirs, chips, perhaps, from a fallen buttress which might have once held up a roof.

As we rode home in a silence deepened by the engine's din, Ammi didn't know that her plans for Asharfi would unravel by dinnertime. Unsuspecting, she had cast off her disappointment by the time we reached the stretch between the Jama Masjid and the other Fort. As we ducked under the railway bridge and passed the General Post Office, she was happily canvassing suggestions for a jolly evening. Luckily for her, when we drew up in front of the East India C——, the site of our second Sunday outing suggested itself. Stuck on the one blank space left on the Imperial Tannery's wall of patrons, that same space which Mountbatten's name and style would one day fill, was a handbill (white ground with borders in saffron and green):

EXHIBITION!
Everything Made-in-India
SWADESHI!!
Attend and support
Sunday Evening 6 to 10

Then in smaller letters at the bottom, under a large asterisk was written: Ferris Wheel! Merry-Go-Round! Ice-Cream! Kulfi and Chaat!

Ammi left us to pay the phut-phut man and collect the hamper, while she inspected the poster more closely. As I passed her on my way to the stairs, lugging the wicker basket, she was drinking the poster in, looking fertile.

Ammi made the mistake of taking Asharfi's past for granted. Parwana was history, she thought, a stain on the family's virtue which was dry-cleanable, a snapshot that would yellow and fade in time. This was a miscalculation, because her daughter's past was in the neighbourhood as pasts are prone to be. Asharfi's past, in fact, was literally round the corner, about to walk into view. Ammi didn't know it then and neither did

216

we, but her second essay in excursion therapy was responsible for setting her daughter on a collision course with her sundered lover. If she had just left well alone, Parwana might in time have turned into a painless, sepia memory. But she meddled. And so Parwana guest-starred in Asharfi's life again – in full colour and, more dangerously, in the flesh.

Parwana's trajectory in this fated encounter was set by a crisis in my grandparental home. It wasn't a major crisis, only a little one . . . or it would have been a little one if it hadn't been for Gandhi's charkha and Dadi's guilt. In any case, all this took time to brew. In the beginning, in those first weeks after my grandmother took her in, Parwana's days were drowned in sensuous domesticity. She was given a room set apart from the rest of the house because she was neither servant nor family nor friend. The stairs that led from the backyard next to the kitchen to the upper floor turned right to meet a landing and Parwana's room opened on to it. It was actually a trunk-filled store, where space had been cleared for a bed. Here she slept after looking through a cache of brittle family albums that she had unearthed, by the dusty light of an ancient bulb. In time she came to take the smell of naphthalene balls for granted.

In the mornings she harassed Dadi by asking for things to do. The first week, she quartered four hundred hard green mangoes on the cleaver board. Then she rolled the chunks in salt, dyed them yellow with turmeric and spread them out on a sheet to soak up the sun. She begged to be allowed to make chapatis. Dadi was hesitant about letting an orphan of uncertain origins cook their food, but the Judge reminded her that Ram himself had accepted fruit from an untouchable woman during his forest exile. Yes, said Dadi, only that was fruit and this is cereal. But the Judge was principled and firm – which was why he had been nominated for the C.I.E.

But principled acceptance changed to heartfelt delight when Parwana produced soft, perfectly round chapatis in pancake stacks, rolled in the Gujarati style with a little ghee kneaded into the dough. In fact the ghee made the cooking arrange-ment more acceptably orthodox because it allowed Dadi to think of Parwana's chapatis as fried – and fried food was acceptable, even from strangers.

None of this meant that Dadi turned Parwana into a drudge. Dadi was a moral woman and the thought of using her ward as cheap labour never occurred to her. She didn't want Parwana to do these menial jobs. She had plans for her. Two facts from Parwana's potted biography of herself had made a great impression on Dadi: she spoke English fluently, and she had, under the influence of Anglo-Indian flatmates, once worn dresses. From these bits of information, she had arrived at Parwana's natural vocation: she would learn typing and shorthand and become a secretary. She decided not to send Parwana to the reformatory across the river. She would stay with them and if she didn't want to give her child away (having been an orphan herself), it could stay with her. There was plenty of room.

Dadi kept meaning to bring up the matter of a secretarial education (imparted at home with the aid of Pitman's primers) but her plan was deflected by a superior will – Parwana's ferocious and inexplicable determination to wash, swab, dust, chop, cook, sew, even spin. It was her talent for spinning, along with her fluency in English (and therefore her obvious if anonymous breeding), that made Dadi decide to virtually adopt her. Parwana took to the wheel and spindle quickly, and by her second week there, could spin with fewer breaks than Dadi – though this wasn't difficult.

The snake in this Eden was the C.I.E. In the third week of Parwana's stay, a franked manila envelope, sealed, embossed and stamped with On India Government Service, brought formal confirmation that His Imperial Majesty etc. was pleased to make the Rai Bahadur a Companion of the Indian Empire. It destroyed Dadi's peace of mind. She was happy for her husband, happy that his integrity and consuming competence had been recognized. But the honour made her uneasy too, because she had, once upon a time, picketed shops selling foreign liquor and even gone to jail with Gandhi. Different jails, of course, but the same cause of liberty.

And now her husband was a companion of this empire. In her mind's eye, she saw him brushing the lion and walking the unicorn. She knew that he was a just and upright man, not a toady, never mind what the demagogues said about Rai

Bahadurs. And still she felt inadequate and guilty, which was intolerable because Dadi's life until that time had been as cut and dried as a ledger. Now suddenly, reconciling her husband's professional achievement with patriotism was proving impossible. So she abandoned book-keeping and embraced magic. She decided to exorcize her guilt and the mantra that she chose was khadi.

The exorcism began with the Judge's professional wardrobe. His black linen coat, his striped twill trousers, his shirts and lawyer's ribbons of finest Egyptian long-staple – all these were replaced in a week by homespun equivalents. Parwana was delighted by the avalanche of work: she scissored swathes of cloth and ran up shirts, handkerchiefs, ribbons, even socks, which, in place of garters, the Judge wore with rubber bands. The coat was farmed out to Masterji, the tailor with hennaed hair, who had the thickest khadi available dyed black and made up. When it was over my patient grandfather looked oddly rural for a metropolitan judge, but he had always respected conviction in public life, and never once did he complain.

None of this would have prompted Parwana's re-entry into our lives if Dadi had stopped with her husband. The Judge had made his sartorial statement, his patriotic bona fides were now patent to all except the fanatical and short of returning the C.I.E. there was nothing more to be done. But like vegetarians and nationalists, Dadi was driven by the need for consistency. Everything in the Kashmiri Gate house, she decided, was to be dressed in khadi – this homespun armour of the nation-in-the-making. After Dadaji's potential had been exhausted, the mattress and the bolsters of the takht in the living room were re-upholstered in khadi. Then the chintzy curtains in the European drawing room were replaced with coarse, dirty-white drapes. But in her next sortie Dadi suffered a check. She was set to assault Grandfather's leather-bound law reports when he drew the line. His person was mutable but precedent was not. There was no precedent in the history of these sacred compendiums of precedent that permitted their preservation in anything but leather the colour of pomegranates. Dadi protested that it was the principle of the thing. With austere finality the Judge ruled that principle untempered by precedent amounted to zealotry, not idealism.

It was this reverse, coupled with Parwana's developing waistline, that fathered that fateful Sunday meeting. Now well into her fourth month, Parwana had begun to outgrow the salwar-kameez outfits which Asharfi had pressed on her before she left Lucknow. Parwana kept letting out the seams to keep them on, but finally, that is approximately the week that Dadi lost out on the law reports, it was clear that time and tummy could no longer be denied.

Two Sundays before our picnic, Parwana's kameez, made of super-fine muslin, tore with an audible rip as she reached for the clothes-line and the sound was picked up by Dadi's crusading ears. Parwana, she decided on the spot, was to be remade in khadi. Parwana didn't mind, not even when it was decided that no salwar-kameez outfits would be made for her – she was to wear only saris now. Dadi was eloquent about a sari's advantages: it was more modest, more authentically Indian than the foreign salwar, more respectable than a dress. It was indispensable if Parwana was to be developed into the prototype of the nationalist stenographer – draped and demure, not skirt-clad and wanton. The greatest advantage of all was left unmentioned – saris would use up so much more khadi. Six yards for the sari, a yard and a half for the blouse, three yards for the petticoat, and then there were the under-clothes to be added to the yardage.

To start with (before she actually tried them on) Parwana was quite taken with the six new saris that Dadi had bought her. She liked to think that she would carry them off like Dadi, who wore saris with regimental smartness: crisply starched and stiffly pleated. Her excitement grew as Dadi ran up blouses for her on the sewing machine. These had raised round necks and pretty puff sleeves which rose above the shoulders like little wings. When Dadi sewed a thin, six-yard length of tatted lace on to two of the saris to relieve their beige sobriety, Parwana began to dream of herself in one. Then, on a Sunday, so that the Judge could witness the transformation, Dadi taught her how to wear a sari. With great simplicity, slowly, step by step, she demonstrated to Parwana the petticoat tuck, the wraparound, the finger pleats and finally the option of taking the end round the back or across her chest.

But Parwana heard none of it. She was on fire. It had begun as a prickle when she pulled on the huge extemporized brassiere which looked like a corset and the khadi drawers that reached halfway down her legs, rather like the striped kacchas carpenters wore. By the time Dadi got to the pleats, Parwana needed eight hands to scratch the itching. Dadi led her out into the Judge's presence and they settled back to watch her walk about in the new costume. It was the walking that settled it: each time she took a step, the petticoats chafed her shins and calves and knees and thighs; after one length of the living room, her legs were pillars propping up a rash.

Suddenly she dropped the charade and ran into Dadi's dressing room, moaning. When Dadi followed her in, bewildered, she found her with the sari yanked off, one hand shaking talcum indiscriminately on bared skin, the other tearing at the clothes that remained. Her bra-harness had rubbed her nipples raw, her waist was ridged with a running weal of fire where the drawstring of the petticoat had bitten. Her back had flushed an angry red and she thought that she would faint with the terrible pleasure that scratching her bottom was giving her. Dadi took all this in silently. She powdered the bits Parwana couldn't reach and folded the sari away. Then she walked out into the takht room to let Parwana get back into the too-tight kameez. As she struggled to pull the skirt over the slight hump of her belly, she heard Dadi tell the Judge: It must be the starch; it will be better once it's washed.

But it wasn't. Three washes later, the khadi ensemble, aided by the sticky heat of July, could still turn Parwana into a walking weal. On Wednesday, three days before our Sunday picnic, she dug her heels in and refused to wear the sari again. This spelt crisis because in a fortnight at best, Parwana would completely outgrow her much-taxed clothes. But Dadi refused to acknowledge defeat. She would make no concession to mill-made cloth. That would be backsliding from principle in the face of mere reality; she had done a lifetime's worth of that in August 1942. No more. The household was plunged into panic as nakedness or at least dishabille stared Parwana in the face. She grew depressed because the river of domesticity in which she had swum each morning was barred to one strait-jacketed by bursting seams.

Fortunately, hope appeared before they burst. On Friday, in the evening, the Judge got a letter from the Committee of Unarrested Nationalists (a euphemism for Congressmen who hadn't been jailed after the Quit India campaign) inviting him to patronize an exhibition dedicated to self-reliance and swadeshi enterprise. From Spinning Wheel to Bicycle, the might of indigenous industry, the letter promised, would be displayed. Punctiliously the Judge wrote back, thanking them but regretting his inability to attend. He nearly thwarted fate. Luckily for Parwana and Asharfi, Dadi vetted her husband's letters before throwing them away, and thanks to her, the exhibition mounted by the Committee of Unarrested Nationalists found another patron.

The moment she read it, Dadi was convinced that the invitation was a sign. A sign that her unwavering commitment to the livery of freedom was about to be vindicated. In her single-minded zeal she saw a display not of spinning wheels and bicycles but one of looms and their produce: bolts and bolts of khadi of every conceivable texture and quality, out of which she would pick one so fine and soft that it wouldn't mortify Parwana's flesh. At once the tension in the house eased. When Dadi told Parwana about the exhibition, her ward was delighted – not because she believed in super-fine khadi but at the prospect of going out again. Indoor nationalism had made her so claustrophobic that patriotism in the open air seemed like a treat.

Fate rolls on humble castors.

We got to the exhibition half an hour before it began, which was Ammi's fault. She began making tea too early, at a quarter past four, a whole hour before the time to rise from Sunday afternoon sleep. She wasn't used to making tea either: she left out the large-leaf Darjeeling and brewed four spoons of tea dust. We drank a deep brown detergent which stripped our tongues and raised us to electric wakefulness.

Ammi watched the clock and changed her rings about – turquoise, opal, amethyst, coral; little finger, ring, middle, index and back. Asharfi used a fork to dig her fingernails clean, until Haasan took it from her. He began pinching its tines and grounding the other end on the table to produce metallic resonances. I leaned back in my chair and listened to my stomach, which had worked on nothing all day except tea and poisoned sandwiches. Haasan moved offstage to the balcony with his cigarettes and began using up time in five-minute fuses which ended quietly in stubs. The air was thick with worked-up expectation though none of us knew what we were waiting for. Asharfi pushed her chair back and turned on the radio. Sounds from Sehgal's sinuses filled the room. Haasan stubbed a half-smoked cigarette (three minutes) and lit another.

By a quarter to six Haasan was out of cigarettes and when he went downstairs to get some more, the whole company rose in relief to join him. He bought a tin of Players from the paanwallah outside the Carlton. Opposite the restaurant, the park had been transformed by a striped marquee, sections of which were still being hauled up. The road between the shopping arcade and the park was choked with carts being unloaded. We were early because the exhibition was running late – gangs of men in homespun white, wearing rosettes as large as their faces, were rushing about in purposeful frenzy, but it was clear that it was going to be a while. So I asked a waiter I knew to unlock the restaurant and let us into the cool darkness of its interior. We sat there in silence, nursing free glasses of iced water.

Half an hour later, Haasan and I emerged to check if the fête had begun. The street was free of carts, though from the noise and dust around the main marquee, stalls were still being erected. As we watched, a tonga carrying a man and a machine drew up. The man got off and helped his co-passenger down. Sitting on the road, the machine was as tall as a dwarf and the colour of gunmetal. It had a horizontal lever attachment where its head should have been. The man was wearing a beard and a lace cap. That's a hand press, said Haasan, who knew a great deal about miscellaneous things. There were signs that the fairground was coming to life. The giant wheel was spinning and we could hear the breathless shrieking of the whirled-about from where we were standing. Haasan went back into the restaurant to fetch the ladies. It was time.

We walked along the park till we found the main entrance. As we entered, the giant wheel was to our right, set apart from the exhibition tent. The dust of summer had been damped down by liberal hosing and there was even a red gravel path which crunched its way up to the opening in the main tent from which rosetted Congressmen appeared and into which they vanished. Around the marquee ran an outer fence made up of stretched cloth staked out with bamboos which created a circular corridor fifteen feet wide in which the food and entertainment stalls had been set up. There were chaat-wallahs, paanwallahs, kulfi vendors, puppeteers, snake charmers, instant photographers, a magician making marbles disappear from under chipped tea cups, a man spinning pink candy-floss by pedalling a stationary bicycle, two weighing machines that also told fortunes and a strength machine which read off the power of its customers' grips in pounds.

In order to raise Asharfi's spirits, we did this merry outer circuit first. Ammi ate a kulfi, Asharfi was pressed into eating two balls of candy-floss so she could relive the careless joy of childhood, I squeezed the grip-machine's needle past the sixty-pound mark, the magician plucked a sparrow's egg from Ammi's hair and yet, with the circuit nearly completed, on Asharfi's face no happiness was seen.

For the first time that day I saw Ammi's head go down. She had taken the disappointment of the morning in her stride, but now she looked close to despair. Perhaps she was wondering what the next few months in Simla would be like if Asharfi's mood held. She might have given up but just then, at that critical moment, she saw the whirling giant wheel.

We'll take a ride on that, she said to no one in particular, her face alight with hope. Asharfi used to love them as a child.

Asharfi, now grown up, seemed indifferent to this treat, but Ammi's last-ditch optimism was unshakeable. Looking neither left nor right, we surged towards the snake of people waiting for a ride.

I wanted to stop and take a better look at the man in the beard and his dwarfish machine. He had set up his stall at the end of the fun-fair circuit. We had passed him standing between the press and a tripod easel, wearing dark glasses at dusk. Displayed on the easel was a printed map of undivided India. I wasn't interested in the map or his machine – just his face, which was familiar. Just as Ammi sighted the giant wheel, I placed him. He was the rabble rouser at the railway-station mosque who had ogled Parwana and followed our tonga home. Ammi didn't notice him because she had eyes only for the giant wheel. Nor did Asharfi, which wasn't surprising since she was looking sadly at the ground.

When we reached the tail end of the giant-wheel queue, I realized that Haasan wasn't with us. I looked back in the direction that we had come from . . . and nearly fell over. Haasan had just embraced the bearded, rabble-rousing, hand-press man!

I wanted to rush back and find out what was going on but I couldn't. Since Ammi and Asharfi were gentlewomen and couldn't stand in a queue, our place in the ticket line depended on me. There were already a dozen people behind me and Ammi was so keen to get on the giant wheel that she would be furious if I lost my place. With agonizing slowness, the line inched forward. When I turned round to look for the embracing twosome, they had disappeared. My turn came after ten long minutes. I bought four tickets. There was still no sign of Haasan or the bearded man. Inconsequentially I wondered if one of the tickets would be wasted; we were among the next batch of joyriders and already the wheel was slowing to a stop. Even Ammi noticed that we weren't a foursome any more. Where's Haasan? she asked.

I didn't have to answer because Haasan did. Here I am, he said, appearing from behind me as if he had been there all along. I opened my mouth to ask him a hundred questions but he cut me off with a little shake of the head. The wheel had stopped and Ammi was urging Asharfi towards the spot where two attendants were helping the passengers on. Wait till we get on, hissed Haasan from the side of his mouth.

Each bench on the giant wheel sat two and the women were

put on first, so Ammi and Asharfi were vertically above us when it was our turn to get on. It was only a small giant wheel and it didn't need a motor to power it. Two men shinned up its spokes to the fulcrum and began to work it like a treadmill, pushing the spokes down with their feet as the wheel turned slowly round. Seen side on, they must have looked like gracefully walking men who never made any ground. At another time I might have wondered why they didn't fall off but just then I could only think of what Haasan was about to tell me. The ground was forty feet below us and the wheel was fully loaded when he leaned across and whispered in my ear. He was brief. Four short words which made no sense but had me clutching at the safety bar.

I have found Masroor, he said.

Masroor.

For one revolution of the wheel I couldn't think of anything to say. Haasan said nothing either. He just sat there, savouring my dumbfoundedness.

That man in the beard . . . ?

Yes.

It can't be, I whispered, as my last memory of him spooled through my head in unhinging slow motion: Masroor flattened to fit the two dimensions of a recruitment poster, speeding away on the side of an army lorry.

Arrey! What do you mean can't be, said Haasan impatiently. I've watched him grow up. I'd know him in a burqa.

Mother and daughter were below us now as we plunged earthward. Asharfi was sitting still and upright, looking straight ahead, showing no sign of being airborne. Ammi was more animated. She was being sick over the side.

Why haven't you told them? I asked.

He told me not to, said Haasan unhappily, looking worried and puzzled. He said he would come home in January and tell us everything.

Didn't you ask him where he has been for so long? I demanded, nearly stamping my feet with curiosity.

Haasan gave me a look. Of course I did, he said. But he wouldn't tell me.

I stared at him incredulously. How could he have taken that for an answer? I would have shaken the truth out of Masroor.

What does he plan to do? I asked, trying to be patient. Why can't he tell us till January?

Haasan shrugged. I just told you, he said defensively, he wouldn't say a word.

Haasan sahib, I began calmly, trying not to bite him, you were talking to Masroor for more than ten minutes. He must have told you something. Even if he didn't tell you where he's been for the past ten months or what he's going to do in the next six, he must have said what he was doing here now, with that machine.

Yes yes, said Haasan eagerly, nodding his head and looking relieved. That much I know. He said the machine was for planting doubt.

Masroor had a machine for planting doubt.

It consisted of maps and a modified press and it made jigsaws which cost an anna apiece because money gets people to attend. His maps were drawn to scale and they showed the political boundaries of India as they were – before Partition, the death of the princely states and the birth of linguistic provinces changed the shape of the country. Before, that is, Pakistan, Bangladesh, Tamil Nadu, Andhra Pradesh, Meghalaya, Mizoram, Gujarat and Orissa had happened. Before Karnataka and Uttar Pradesh meant anything. This was a map where a letter to Hyderabad could be delivered in Sind. It showed each one of the innumerable political units that made up India then: the kingdoms large and small, the huge presidencies and provinces of British India, the tiny remains of miscarried empires: Goa, Pondicherry, Chander-nagore. . . After buying the map, Masroor's customers could either take it away intact or have it cut into a jigsaw. This was where the press came in: in the manner of a printing block for cloth, Masroor had commissioned a sharp-edged India map exactly as large as the one displayed on his easel. This block was fitted into the lower jaw of the press. When the customer pulled at the lever and the jaws of the press closed, the map was neatly cut into its constituent political units and the jigsaw was born.

He also gives them an instruction sheet, said Haasan. The two men at the hub of the giant wheel were walking much faster now: with their singlets soaked in sweat and their shoulders darkly gleaming, they looked like a logo for a guild of labouring men. As the wheel whirled more dizzily each descent meant leaving my stomach behind. It was hard taking in instructions for putting a jigsaw together. But Haasan shouted them patiently into my ear till I learnt them. They went like this. (1) This is a difficult jigsaw so do not hurry or you might mislay a piece and never complete it. (2) The projections on each piece that slot into the corresponding cut-outs on others are liable to tear because the paper is stiff and brittle. So handle with care or parts of the map will stay detached. (3) The game can be played by more than one player. You can ask another person to help you put the map together.

By the time Haasan finished the men had stopped pedalling and it was time to get off. Ammi and Asharfi were the first to disembark. Asharfi looked wind-blown but unmoved. Ammi had her kerchief pressed to her mouth. We thought she was still being sick but in fact she was discreetly pushing her dentures back which had come unstuck on a downward plunge. She looked at her daughter's stolid face and shook her head. I turned in the direction of the hand press and Masroor but Haasan pulled me back. You'll draw their attention to him, he said sternly. Go later.

Somehow I stopped myself from racing off to find him, the most important character in this, my second life. Midwife, brother, friend . . . Masroor. He had vanished ten months ago and I had felt like a missing person – he was, after all, the only one who had seen me fall into this time. When Haasan told me he was back, I felt vouched for . . . like a hearsay history whose footnotes had been found. He had seen me fall into his world and I had seen him flattened into limbo. Now that he was back among the living I wanted to run up to him, to wring his hand and find my friend beneath the beard and cap. Instead, obediently, I followed the others into the main marquee.

While the fun-fair and the stalls outside were exploding

with people, the marquee which housed the centre-piece of the fête, the indigenous industry exhibit, was vastly empty. Mainly because there was nothing to eat inside and rosetted busybodies were stopping eatables at the entrance. As we walked in, the exhibition began from the left with a single wheel, as a Films Division documentary on technology might have done. It was a bullock-cart wheel. But not just any bullock-cart wheel because that would have been a symbol for timeless India and this was an exhibition about progress. This was a revolutionary bullock-cart wheel because its rim was fitted with a rubber tyre which would ease the cart's passage over ruts and generally speed things up.

We looked at it respectfully before passing on to the next display which was a portable spinning wheel fitted into a wooden box with a suitcase handle. Three little boys were squatting near it and we were impressed by this precocious curiosity till we saw that they were actually trying to put Masroor's jigsaw together. Watching them fumble diligently, I suddenly felt embarrassed for Masroor. It was all too elaborately meaningful, his jigsaw. First cut your country into pieces with your own hands. Then put it together piece by piece to understand how complex Indian unity is, how hard to build. Those significant instructions! The jigsaw was to teach Congressmen that they were dropping their Muslim pieces. Masroor wanted to raise consciousness through puzzles, like some progressive kindergartenist . . . but this was a grown-up world. Suddenly I felt decades older than my hero. Haasan took my arm and urged me towards Ammi and Asharfi, who were inspecting a bicycle-shaped machine.

The volunteer guide sitting on the bicycle explained that the machine he was about to operate was not a finished product of Indian ingenuity but an experimental prototype, a machine-in-the-making. It was a tentative answer to the problem of rural electrification: the quest for an appropriate generating unit. The principle behind their machine was borrowed from the back-wheel dynamo used to power bicycle lamps. But since villagers needed more power than cycle lights, a bigger gearwheel had been installed and the Hind Cycle Company had built a double-seater or tandem cycle for the project. At this point our guide-demonstrator summoned another volunteer who climbed into the seat behind him, and with the shy deliberation of inexperienced public performers, they began to pedal.

For a while none of us knew what to make of this till we noticed that an unshaded lamp sitting on the ground by the front wheel had begun to glow. First the filaments reddened, then as the duo gathered momentum, the glow became more generally diffused. At its brightest the bulb shone mutedly like a dying dwarf star, then the cyclists braked and the glow faded away.

The volunteers were flushed with effort and embarrassment: the effort of pedalling and the embarrassment of the fifteen-candle-power result. This was, they repeated, just a working model – it was the principle that mattered. There was a possibility that the cycle format would be scrapped and the principle incarnated in some other device, such as a waterwheel or . . . or a Ferris wheel, suggested Haasan . . . or a Ferris wheel, they agreed eagerly, and before they had time to review his offering, we moved on.

The next exhibit was a semi-circle of six pedal-operated sewing machines with handles fixed on their flywheels, so that they could be worked by hand as well. The display was intended to encourage spectator participation so there were stools in front of the sewing machines, all of which were occupied. Two of them were filled by the ladies in our party: Ammi and Asharfi had taken the opportunity to sit down.

Haasan nudged me. Everything has gone in circles this evening, he said with perfect obscurity.

I just looked at him, uncomprehendingly.

Can't you see, he whispered, this exhibition is made up entirely of wheels.

Now that he mentioned it. Ferris wheel, cart wheel, spinning wheel, bicycle wheels, flywheels.

It can't be a coincidence, muttered Haasan, looking uneasily around him. We thought of possible explanations. The Nation is on the Move occurred to me, because this was a Congress exhibition. Haasan was more fertile. Were the wheels symbolic of the unstoppable march of Congress nationalism? Did they refer to the implacable wheels of Jagannath? And if they did, was the idiom of Congress politics borrowed from the Hindu carriage procession? Did it follow that Indian nationalism was a giant rath yatra with Gandhi in the main float and the Congress strapped to the ropes?

Fifty years from '43, Haasan would have been a social historian because questions like this occurred to him unbidden. But in that marquee, in the press of indiscriminate events, there wasn't time for classy speculation to ripen into insight. Here crises threatened, derailing trains of thought. To start with, Dadi and Parwana suddenly appeared at the marquee's entrance.

Shocked into stillness for a moment, Haasan recovered quickly. He moved two paces to his left to block off Asharfi's line of sight, hoping that her absorption with the sewing machine would give him time for the manoeuvre. Till then Asharfi had been working the pedal desultorily, watching the shuttle snicker up and down; but like a magnet needle finding north, her gaze fastened on Parwana the instant she appeared. Haasan moved in vain.

She made to rise but Ammi, obsessively sensitive to her melancholy daughter's every twitch, had seen Parwana too and she held out a hand. Not to hold Asharfi down – she didn't touch her – but merely as a mute caution. Without taking her eyes off Parwana, who was bent over the portable spinning wheel, Asharfi sank back on her stool, her lower lip caught between her teeth, looking stricken.

On cue, Parwana turned and their eyes met. Unhampered by an ancestry and thus untrained in Indian womanhood, Parwana had no sense of shame. So she surged towards Asharfi, mouth open to shout her name. But used to the ways of fallen women, Dadi proved a vigilant chaperone. She had followed Parwana's incredulous, delighted stare and seen me. Jumping to the wrong conclusion, she took steps. Reaching out, she yanked Parwana's plait, stopping her excited ward in mid-surge, turning her shout of welcome into agonized yelping. Just then a knot of gawpers walked between us. By the time they passed the moment had passed as well. Where before Parwana had only seen Asharfi, this time she took us in as well. Silently she went back to inspecting the spinning wheel and Dadi let go of her hair.

The marquee became stifling as it filled up with people who, having fed, wandered in to be modestly entertained. There was a fair-sized crowd inside when suddenly the tent began to heave with homespun activity. Men in khadi and rosettes began rushing around again. There were loud crashing sounds as collapsible chairs were moved about and attention shifted from the exhibits to the source of the noise. I wiped the sweat off my face with a sleeve and looked around.

People weren't walking about as much; most of them were standing on tiptoe or craning their necks, waiting for something to happen. Parwana had found herself a perch on the front seat of the generator bicycle. Luckily it was a lady's bicycle otherwise she wouldn't have been able to sit astride it. Ammi and Asharfi had sensibly kept to their stools because at the rate at which the tent was filling up, there wouldn't be standing room. Haasan, a few feet away, was looking eager in the way he usually did when first-hand experience was in the offing. It looked as though there would be a speech.

I slipped away to find Masroor. He was still standing by his press, gathering his maps and papers by the light of a kerosene lantern. There were no customers round him and I had his attention by clearing my throat. Masroor, I said baldly, not wanting to be there all of a sudden, abruptly aware of the slenderness of my claim on him. He came around the makeshift table and looked at me more closely in the yellow twilight. Then, without warning, his hands came down on my shoulders and I was swept into an off-centre hug, which given his height meant that my face was pressed against his armpit. I could feel his ribs through the sherwani – he was frighteningly thin.

What's all this about maps? I said feebly, when we disengaged. Masroor made a wry face. So Haasan Mamoo told you. He was silent for a moment. It isn't about very much, he said dismissively. Just something to do. Anything is better than just waiting.

He didn't say what he was waiting for and I didn't ask. There would be plenty of time for questions now that he was back. I pointed at the marquee. They're in there, I said. Sharfu and Ammi? I nodded. Masroor swept his maps into a cardboard box and stowed it behind the press. He called to a neighbouring stall-keeper, a balloon man, to keep an eye on his things and then walked with me to the tent's entrance. Just to look, he said to me as we entered. I don't want them to see me.

A speech was in progress. A tall, thin man in a dhoti was standing on a table moving his right arm back and forth in an ever-onwards way. No other part of him moved – just that arm and his mouth, pouring out words in rhythm, like a figure in a meagrely animated cartoon. It was hard spotting Ammi and Asharfi because the standing kerosene lamps that lit the tent had dimmed and in the bustle of the speech the organizers had forgotten to pump them up again. But the flywheels of the sewing machines glinted even in that light and with some pointing I found them for Masroor.

We pushed our way into the crowd to get Masroor a better look, but not so close that they would notice him. Asharfi was sitting in a curious way, with her feet working the pedal of the sewing machine and her head turned sharply to the right. She was staring at Parwana on the bicycle but Masroor, for a moment, thought she was looking at him.

Look, I said, there's Ammi sitting next to her. That diverted him from the object of Asharfi's gaze, to my great relief – I didn't feel up to explaining the additional complication of Parwana in the heat and frenzy of the tent.

Parwana for her part was staring back at Asharfi while her feet moved in sympathy with hers, working the pedals of that stationary bicycle. Above the saddle she was stillness incarnate: back erect, hands holding the steering grips like a heroine miming a cycle ride on an indoor set. There was nothing to indicate the passionate effort of her blurring feet, except the little runnels of sweat streaking her face. Below her, to her right, the bulb attached to the dynamo had begun to glow.

We were less than fifteen feet away from the raptly pedalling girls but we could hear neither the clatter of the sewing machine nor the whirring of the cycle wheel over the

233

hubbub in the tent. The speaker had now begun to vary his ever-onwards routine by lightly thumping his chest at intervals. His speech, fiercely nationalist in tone, was collage-like in actual substance. He took his role as a proxy for imprisoned Congress leaders so seriously that he sounded like an album of nationalist quotations. There are only two forces in India today, he said, the British Raj representing imperialism and the Congress symbolizing nationalism (ever onwards). If the Congress can humble the imperialist eagle why can't it deal with the Muslim League crow (fist and chest)? The Congress is the party of all sections, of all classes, of all sections of all classes. Those who do not support the Congress will rot in the dustbins of history (applause). They are falsely conscious, in fact, unconscious (laughter).

Encouraged by the response, the speaker soared above the authorized texts. In Karachi, he shouted, fisting the air more jerkily now, the Congress resolved that it would never accept self-determination if it meant secession. I warn them (he didn't have to say who) that they will have to build their separate state six feet underground (sustained applause).

Masroor's breath was hissing through his nostrils in disapproval. I looked towards the sewing machines: Ammi was leaning forward attentively, but Asharfi and Parwana were unaware of the world around them as they pedalled away in their places, eyes fixed on each other, like straining flightless birds. The bulb attached to Parwana's bicycle was glowing more strongly now, or perhaps it was the waning of the lamps.

The British think that by jailing Congressmen they have strangled the Nation. He paused. The British are wrong. Freedom doesn't live only in rebellion. It doesn't die when the rebellion is crushed. It lives on in the bodies of patriots, in the hands that made these machines in this tent, in the swadeshi minds that designed them. So let the Raj and its friends remember . . .

Masroor looked around worriedly. This place must be full of informers, he said. If he goes on this way, the police will be here soon. Get Ammi and Sharfu out of here . . . I'll go and find Haasan.

I pushed my way to within six feet of Ammi and called as loudly as I dared. She turned in my direction and cupped her ear. Get up, I shrieked in a whisper which she didn't hear because the tall thin one had started up again.

They have seen the calm of Brahma and the peace of Vishnu, he announced. Let them fear the wrath of Mahesh. I warn them – let the sleeping eye lie, let Jin . . .

The loud-hailer sliced his speech off clean on the Jin . . . and the tent suddenly became a cave of silence except for the whir of the bicycle wheel and the sewing machine's clatter.

This is an illegal public meeting, boomed the hollow voice. You will disperse immediately. Under Section 144 you are ordered to disperse.

For a second the tent and its contents were as still as a snapshot. Then there was a sharp popping sound near Parwana and an incandescent flare as the bulb burst and she slumped over the handlebars, moaning, spent. The orator took fright and leapt off his table. Seconds later the clattering stopped as Asharfi cried out hoarsely and held on to the sewing machine for support.

Then there was chaos.

By the time I got to Ammi, the police had entered the tent and were laying about them with lathis to encourage peaceful dispersal. Hauling Asharfi to her feet, I saw Dadi drag Parwana off the bicycle. There was no sign of Haasan or Masroor.

A few feet short of the door we heard a terrible cracking sound: the marquee had begun to collapse in sections behind us. A policeman loomed with lathi raised; I shrank, farting with fright, drawing Ammi and Asharfi closer. He made allowances for the women and didn't hit me. Then we were out of the tent, stumbling over fallen people, trying to outrun the panic at our heels. As we ran for the road in the general direction of St James', I glimpsed Masroor's press fallen on its side, looking like a disused robot. We weren't actually running because top gear for Ammi was a rolling stumble. We surged towards the rim of the park in flailing slow motion. When we reached the perimeter railing, by what seemed like dawn, Ammi couldn't step over it because of her weight and her sari. Without asking her leave I slung her on to my back in an untutored fireman's lift and leapt the two-foot fence with the ease born of perfect fright.

Ammi collapsed on the pavement but that didn't matter because the railing we had cleared now seemed a cordon around chaos. We waited till she could breathe through her nose again, then set off unhurriedly towards our refuge, the East India C———. No one spoke till we were inside, or turned to look at the shambles behind us.

I hurried to the kitchen to make some tea. Haasan arrived ten minutes later. He had lost Masroor in the madness. When I took the tray into my room, mother and daughter were sitting at the table. Asharfi took the pot from me and poured. She poured till Ammi's cup and Haasan's were full and brimming over. It was then, I think, that Ammi saw her daughter smiling: a faraway, sated smile which made the day-long sullens seem a dream. There was a heavy-lidded happiness in that smile. And a kind of triumph.

The Truth According to Masroor

AFTER THEY LEFT for Simla, I filled my life with mangoes – thanks to my grandmother. Towards the end of her life, Dadi had tended to go on about the betterness of then; in time her scorn for now congealed into a speech which always ended with the price of mangoes in the reign of George V. A rupee for a whole basket, she would say, shaking her head in sorrow and in pride. Alone again, I bought two basketfuls for company. They cost me two rupees, so she hadn't lied. These were the days . . .

I put two slabs of ice in the enamel bathtub that I never used and stored the mangoes there. Long summer afternoons in a bathroom's shade, eating mangoes . . . not one or two but ten and twelve as Dadi would have done in that epic age when Indians were contemporary with King George. Time passed in an ooze of pulp.

By the fourth morning of the mangothon I had a boil on the rim of one nostril and another growing in the right corner of my mouth; breathing in was painful and each time my lips came together, the sandwiched pustule stabbed my heart. I examined the little bulbs of goo in the mirror over the wash basin, wondering if it was safe to burst them with a fingernail. Thank God for Captain Nazar. He had dropped in at the pantry after dinner to say that he had put my Simla transfer through. I'd be there inside a week. No boils to agonize over in a cold climate. No solitude either. There would be Ammi and Asharfi to visit – Haasan had settled them in and returned to Lucknow. Parwana was safe in Dadi's care. But where on earth was Masroor?

I hadn't seen him since the evening of the fête. He hadn't come by once – this was a son who hadn't seen his mother and sister in nearly a year. Even if, for some unknown reason, he wanted to avoid his family, he should have tried to get in touch with Haasan or me. Having sworn us to silence, the least he owed us was an explanation. In a compromise I decide to burst the riper boil on my mouth and leave the one in my nose alone. Perhaps it was the police that were keeping him away. Or tuberculosis. If he was tubercular he was better off in Simla with the rest of us; there were sanatoriums there for people like him. My nails were dirty, so I prodded the pimple with the blunt end of a pencil. It collapsed at once and something warm trickled down my chin. Now the boil was just a pink bump the same colour as my lips. I pushed the bump experimentally. The doorbell rang.

Dabbing the raw spot with Mercurochrome, I went to answer the door, knowing even before I opened it that my visitor was Masroor. Call it premonition. But he looked a lot shorter and I knew at once that he had changed faces with Parwana. Nothing surprised me any more. Come in, I said, with iron poise.

Is she here? asked Parwana, coming to the point at once.

I shook my head.

She seemed prepared for that because her expression didn't change, but her shoulders dropped and she closed her eyes for a moment. Then she made to leave. After three days of loneliness, someone I knew was at my door and she was about to go away without asking after me, without a civil word.

I can send her a message if you like, I heard myself say. Come in. I'll . . . make some tea.

I wasn't proud.

She looked uncertain, then stepped over the threshold.

No tea, she said, not sitting down. At home they might start wondering where I've gone.

She produced an old envelope and a pencil stub and scribbled something. Then she gave me the envelope.

The Judge rents a house in the hills for the summer, she said. That's the address. Could you, she began timidly, then stopped. She began again, matter-of-factly this time. I want you to post it to her, wherever she is. But tell her not to write to me at this address. Tell her to write care of the G.P.O. I'll collect the letters from there. Her gaze never wavered and her

238

eyes held mine for a while after she finished, daring me to comment or pry. I didn't. But when I looked at the address on the envelope I began grinning uncontrollably. 'Holcombe' it began . . .

'Holcombe'
Lower Mall Road
Near Cecil Hotel
Simla.
Simla!

She sat down in the end and I made us tea. She was thrilled at the prospect of Simla and she wanted to talk to someone about it. She told me about her problem with clothes and how the imminence of Simla had solved it. Dadi had had a nightmare about Parwana walking down the Mall in clothes bursting at the seams with all British India watching. Judge Rameshwar Prasad, a Companion of the Indian Empire, promenading his ward in rags! Dadi decided to make an exception to her homespun rule for Parwana's Simla wardrobe.

It wasn't an exception that was hard to justify. In the first place Simla was cold and since there wasn't such a thing as hand-spun woollen yarn, she would have had to buy Parwana mill-made woollies in any case. Once the khadi rule was breached for reasons beyond her control, it didn't matter if, just this exceptional once, Parwana's other clothes – salwar-kameez suits, a sari or two, and undies of course – were run up in machine-made cloth. Besides, Simla wasn't a real place. Dadi had been there every summer for close on a decade and each time she went it was like living in a fairy tale. A foreigner's fairy tale, filled with schlosses, gables and tall white ladies. Broken pledges only counted in the real world . . . and Simla was a kind of dream.

Masterji will finish making the clothes today, said Parwana, pouring herself a second cup, her eyes glowing at the thought of things she could fit into.

I wanted to ask if the baby was coming along well, but I didn't know whether she wanted it mentioned, so we talked about Simla instead. Brought up in a Bombay orphanage, she had never seen snow fall or been on holiday – so Simla promised unprecedented pleasures.

239

I don't know if we'll stay there long enough to see the snow, said Parwana cautiously, not wanting to tempt fate. Judge Sahib has to get back to Delhi when the courts open but Madam said that we – she and I – might stay longer. It depends on what the doctor says; if he allows me to travel.

She drained her cup and stared into it like someone trying to read the tea-leaves. Perhaps she wanted to know if it would be a boy. She could look as long as she wanted, it would keep her from going away. Clothes, snow, babies, I was interested in anything she said. I made to pour her another cup but the pot was empty. I'll make some more, I said quickly, but it wasn't any use. I had made her conscious of the time.

I have to go, she said with a touch of panic, or they'll set the servants looking for me. I offered to walk her home but she turned me down. She went down the stairs unescorted and I returned to my room to savour the news: Parwana and I would be neighbours in Simla. I wondered if I had done the right thing in not telling her that Asharfi was in Simla too.

Even as I was wondering, the doorbell rang again. It was Parwana again.

Come down! she gasped, breathlessly angry. There's a man following me about! Then she was off again, running down the steps as fast as her too-tight clothes would allow her. Still gorgeous in my epauletted waiter's costume, I ran downstairs after her.

What does he look like? I asked when we were both standing in front of the shuttered façade of the Imperial Tannery, looking up and down the early morning emptiness of the road.

Parwana bit her lip in frustration. He's run away again, she said, her voice crisp with scorn. Pig! It's the fourth time I've caught him this week.

Has he . . . has he done anything? I asked diffidently.

He's tall with a really thin moustache, said Parwana helpfully, her answers lagging one question behind. She paused. No, he hasn't. Nothing like that. He just turns up, then vanishes when I spot him.

A minute or two passed and when no one appeared, I insisted on walking her up to the rear entrance of the Carlton.

From there she walked alone. I don't want Madam or one of the servants to see you with me, she said candidly. Then she smiled her thanks and hurried off.

Walking back, I felt vaguely resentful that she didn't want to be seen in my company. I tried to build this up into a sense of injury but in a half-hearted way because I knew that she didn't mean it personally. There was nothing to do in my room, so I dawdled into Nicholson Road for a cup of tea from the chai-wallah who had set up shop in one of the arched recesses in the city wall. Midway through my tea I remembered that the doors to the East India C—— were open; I had forgotten to shut them in the excitement about the pencil-moustached villain. I emptied the cup in one scalding gulp and ran back home. When I got there I bolted the doors behind me and raced up the stairs. Then I froze – from inside my room I could hear the rustle of pages turning.

I crept up to the door and flung it open without warning. A long, wheat-coloured man with a pencil moustache was lying on my bed, reading my newspaper. He was exactly as Parwana had described him, but he was more than that. He was also Masroor.

This was the third face I had seen him in. He had been clean-shaven in Lucknow and bearded at the fête; now he had Brylcreemed hair and a knife-edge moustache. With no embarrassment he put the newspaper away and sat up.

Why did you take so long? he asked, in a mildly accusing way.

Why did she come here? he asked, again without preliminaries. No names or reasons given – just the bald question. He rose jerkily from the bed and moved offstage on to the balcony, from where it was harder to hear him.

Did she tell you where she is going? I know she's leaving Delhi. That woman she lives with has hung three empty hold-alls on her washing line to air.

He came back into the room.

So did she tell you?

It was my turn now to leave for the balcony and stand by the railing. I did it for no reason except an obscure instinct that this was what the scene required. Masroor followed, taking up position beside me and staring moodily at the Ritz. After a longish silence, which made me wonder what I ought to say, he spoke again.

Did she tell you where she was going? he asked for the third time.

This time I was ready with an answer.

Why would she? I countered, letting a bitter smile play about my lips. Did you?

He told me then . . . the whole story. But first his eyes seemed to turn their backs on me and peer into his inner self, where the memories of his disappearance lay warehoused. His face rippled like a screen-dissolve before a flashback; his skin paled and his colour drained away, till he looked like a faded transparency through which I could almost see the cinema hoardings by the Ritz.

I didn't stop to check if the fault lay in my eyes or in his molecules. I reached out and grabbed his collar. Perhaps he wasn't about to vanish, perhaps it was routine for him to flicker like a guttering candle, but I wasn't about to take the chance. I wasn't going to let him vanish for a second time. Not with me as the audience, anyway. He could flicker all he wanted to in his own time, in private, at home . . . wherever that was.

So I pulled him close, half-expecting my hands to close on nothing, but his shirt was real enough even if the shoulders underneath felt skeletal. I braced my feet and leaned backwards as I pulled, allowing for the heft and weight of a grown man. But, lighter than a ninety-six pound-weakling, he was in my arms even before I had properly begun to pull. I overbalanced and we fell to the ground together, in a clinch, like hectic lovers.

TB, I thought numbly, getting to my feet. His pallor, his weightlessness . . . he had been hollowed out. I helped him up, ignoring his attempts to push me away. I had to get him to Simla – his mother was there, and his sister. And the sanatoriums. But first his forehead needed help; he had cut himself while falling. It was almost good to watch him bleed – after his terrible pallor, the red on his face was a reassurance; at least he wasn't flickering.

I helped him into the room and on to my bed. When I returned from the bathroom with cotton wool and a bottle of tincture of iodine, he was sitting up with one hand clutching his injured forehead. A thin trickle of blood had seeped through his fingers. When I dabbed the iodine on his cut he jerked and twitched like someone being electrocuted at low voltage.

The iodine stopped stinging after a minute and he stopped shaking. I lit a cigarette and gave it to him. I'd seen it done in a Second World War film. He must have seen it too because he took it, though I'd never seen him smoke. One long, fumbling pull, his lips carefully pursed, was all he needed. Looking at the glowing ash, he began to tell me his story. Four days later, when the Simla-bound rail-car stopped at Barog to let us breakfast, he was still telling it. It was a long story because it wasn't his alone.

I wasn't the only one who disappeared, said Masroor at the very beginning. He personally knew of thirteen people who had gone the same way. There could have been thousands, maybe millions of others. The ones he had met or heard about had disappeared on the same day that he had – the ninth of August. That was the second thing they had in common. The first? Everyone who disappeared on the ninth of August was Muslim.

Except for Masroor, the only time I had seen living things vanish before my eyes was when I was in primary school, when the Great Gogia Pasha came to St Xaviers. It was some time in the early 'seventies – there had been a famine or a riot and the padres had cancelled the annual class picnics as a measure of austerity. The Greatest Magician in the World had been hired to console us. School didn't have an auditorium in those days, so we were ranged in rows on the giant steps that bordered two sides of the cricket field.

The Pasha with his assistants and his paraphernalia stood on a makeshift wooden platform below us. A sullen, cheated Junior School, six hundred strong, stared down at him, but the Pasha was equal to his audience. He whipped the lid off a flat wicker basket to the sound of a snake charmer's drone. The cobra's hood came upright and it began to sway. The Pasha

243

accepted a pigeon from a caftaned helper, stuffed it into the basket and slapped the lid over the swaying hood and the flapping feathers. Gillie gillie gillie gillie, he went, gillie gillie gillie, his hands making passes over the basket where the snake was feeding, his Turkish face alight with wickedness. He whipped the lid off again and again the snake unwound itself and dutifully swayed. No pigeon.

He repeated this seven times with seven pigeons till we thought the cobra would burst. The seventh time when he lifted the lid to show us the vanished bird, he also reached in and pulled the cobra out. Replacing the lid, he held the snake by its tail and cracked it like a whip – and presto! the snake was gone . . . or else it had been turned into a stiff malacca cane. Gillie gillie gillie, burbled the Pasha, preening, gillie gillie gillie gillie. Then he tossed the cane into the air like a drum major's baton and caught it deftly. Junior School dissolved in frenzied applause.

But there was more to come. Standing over the snake basket, he twirled the cane about, looking like Zubin Mehta crossed with Haroun al Rashid. The drone reached a climax and ceased. The Pasha froze, his baton stilled in mid-movement; then the tableau broke as he swooped on the basket and flung it high into the air. Six hundred heads tilted upwards and saw the lid fly off and seven reconstituted pigeons flutter out. Twelve hundred hands clapped till the playground echoed. There was one last twist. When the pigeons had been retrieved, the Pasha brought the cane down hard over his knee. There was a snapping sound – but instead of two pieces of wood in his hands, there was a familiar length of maroon draped over his knee: the cane that was once a snake was now a new school tie.

He picked me out of the audience because I had forgotten mine at home, and tied it on while the others watched enviously. They could have had it with my blessings. It ruined the rest of the magic show for me; it was hard to concentrate with a cobra knotted round my throat. That night at home, when Pran Mausaji, my police uncle and therefore the family's authority on riots, spoke darkly of Muslim mischief, I thought of the Pasha's sinister face and shivered. For years afterwards, the Great Gogia Pasha was my private vision of the plotting Muslim.

Then I grew up and learnt not to believe in menacing Turks and magic tricks . . . and now Masroor was talking of a trick that wasn't sleight of hand; a trick which had wafted thousands into limbo – but not just any thousands, no; this was a one-time trick that worked on Muslims Only.

I couldn't choose not to believe, not when I remembered the other time so well. Here is that military lorry again with the recruiting poster painted right across one side. Take the King's Commission, reads the caption, The Noblest Life on Earth. Where the caption ends, two whiskered men in khaki gaze sternly into my eyes. Next to them, not front-on but in profile, is a figure in loose khaki trousers and a white short-sleeved shirt. His feet, shod in mud-brown Home Guard shoes, are in the air – or raised above the lower edge of the poster – in a painterly study of motion, and one half-raised hand is either sketching a salute or tipping back a topi . . . No, I couldn't laugh; I had personally seen one Muslim disappear – that much, at least, was true.

The same Muslim was now sitting across two plates of railway omelettes steaming in the cold, telling me tales of limbo. And he had been there, so I cast off doubt and listened.

Why they had vanished was simple. On the eighth of August the Congress Working Committee met in Bombay and passed the resolution asking the British to Quit India or else. On the ninth of August, said Masroor, we disappeared. One thing followed the other. Like night and day.

I had prayed so hard that the Congress wouldn't pass the resolution, said Masroor through egg and toast. For the first half of the year, he wasn't worried because each time some radical asked for mass civil disobedience, Gandhi said no. There was to be no direct action to push the British out till the Muslims had agreed.

Then suddenly, he changed his mind. Suddenly the Muslim Mind became closed to him, suddenly the masses became irresistibly urgent. Inspired by him, the members of the Congress Working Committee met in Bombay and passed the Quit India resolution, which side-stepped Muslims in favour of the masses. Like a bunch of yogis fired by the power of the mind, they concentrated on the Hindu-Muslim problem and made it vanish. Along with the problem, said Masroor, we vanished as well.

Not every Muslim – just those who believed in the Congress and in its dream of India, free and united, for whom it was critical that the Congress continued to believe in them. They had risked ostracism within the community by opposing the League's demand for a Muslim homeland because they were committed to one secular nation. But they also knew that millions of Muslims distrusted the Congress, that they would have to be brought round, that rhetorical ultimatums to quit India without addressing their insecurities would alienate them for ever. So Muslim Congressmen opposed the August resolution, praying that the party would listen, hoping that the party they believed in would show some belief in them. Because nobody else believed in us, you see, said Masroor wryly. For the Muslim League we weren't Muslims – we were Congress lap-dogs. For the British we weren't politically important enough to notice. That left the Congress; so when it went ahead on the eighth of August as if we weren't there . . . well, we suddenly weren't there.

In a manner of speaking. No one vanished without a trace; the degree of disappearance was in inverse proportion to the victim's commitment to the Congress. Some just became lighter skinned, which they didn't mind. Others, more involved with the party, sometimes became translucent. With Inayat Sahib, a veteran of the great Khilafat campaign, who had grown away from the Congress after the Kanpur riot, the most that happened was that during a meeting of the Municipal Board which fell on the ninth, he found himself completely naked in the middle of an argument. Except for the silver buttons threaded through his kurta and the draw-string of his pajamas, his clothes became entirely transparent. He had to be confined to his bedroom for nearly a month because no clothes would remain opaque on him. His sole amusement in that lonely time was examining the bones of his right forearm which showed up as clearly as in an X-ray when he held up his arm against the sun.

Some became thinner. A very few became impotent. The more committed they were, the less they left behind. One just left his name in the novel he had been reading when he heard the news. He had been reading Forster and when they found the book by the empty armchair, Aziz had become Salman on every page.

His brother Saleem had been subbing the late city edition of the *Hindustan Times* when the news came down the wire. He was translated into the left-hand corner of the day's cartoon, just under the last fold of the Mahatma's loincloth. He was turned into so many copies that when he re-materialized he was a shadow of his former self. Even now, according to Masroor, he crept around the city, living in constant dread of being confronted by his doubles.

Rizwan was standing in the sunlit courtyard of his Rowse Avenue house when he unwrapped the morning's paper. He vanished without a sound, leaving his shadow printed on the warm brick floor. The shadow stayed there through the day, a sloping shadow cast on the ninth day of August by a low early morning sun. Every evening it disappeared at sunset. His wife, Farheen, became a sun-worshipper. The nights that she managed to sleep, she was up at three, peering through the foliage of the massive peepul that shaded the eastern corner of the courtyard for signs of first light. The sun re-drew her husband's shadow on the courtyard floor and the shadow was her guarantee that there was hope. She chalked its outline in green and red so that she wouldn't step on it at night. She came to hate overcast days that rubbed out light and shade and the first time it rained after his disappearance she nearly died. She built dykes, unfurled umbrellas and swabbed like a mad woman to keep the water from the chalked shape, but nothing worked. The rain swept across the courtyard, sweeping the chalk away into the storm-water drains. Farheen cried herself into a stupor. The sun came out in the afternoon and dried the yard and when she rose from her swoon the first thing she saw was Rizwan's shadow as clearly etched as it had been the day before. Then, one early morning, some four weeks from the day Rizwan had disappeared, she got out of bed and found her husband fast asleep where the shadow used to be.

It happened to the rich and famous too. Yousuf bin Aansoo, Jubilee Star and King of Tragedy (under another name), was in the Bombay Talkies studio on the ninth of August, being made up for the morning shoot. As always the newspapers arrived stacked neatly on a silver tray. They had been ironed flat without Yousuf having to ask. The producer knew that Yousuf Bhai liked his *Times of India* crisp and uncreased and he aimed to please. The make-up man removed himself from the dressing room as always: Yousuf Sahib, who read the paper very seriously, liked complete solitude.

Yousuf bin Aansoo used the morning's paper to limber up for work. He smiled along with Mutt 'n Jeff, sobered up with the Eastern Front, allowed his eyes to fill when he ran them over the rosters of the dead. In between he used the looking glass to check if his face was keeping up. Half an hour of this and he was ready for work, idling like a well-tuned Silver Ghost.

His crooked smile was working well that morning, which pleased him. That lopsided leftward curl, that smile that never wholly happened, was a critical part of his tragic manner. Still almost-smiling, he read the comic strip again and only then did he turn to the front page. He never got past the headlines.

Do Or Die, Says Gandhi, he read. Congress Passes Quit India Resolution.

Like the others who hadn't believed that the Congress would actually go through with it, he was shocked. But he was also Yousuf bin Aansoo, so he turned to the mirror to check how shocked he was looking. That's how they found him. Fifteen minutes later when his make-up man knocked and entered the first thing he saw was Yousuf in the mirror, looking shocked. Then a moment later he started screaming – because he could see Yousuf in the mirror, but he couldn't see Yousuf in the room.

The producer, who followed the make-up man into the room, couldn't afford the luxury of hysterics. He had made improbable films for too many years to waste time on the why of it. He just moved the mirror around a little to see if the scene in it would change. But once he realized that the mirror had, in effect, become a giant still photograph, he turned to practical things. He didn't want it getting out that the hero of his film, the most bankable star in the industry, on the strength of whose name the loan sharks had loosened their purse strings, had disappeared leaving a mirror image behind – even a rumour would ruin him. So he turned the mirror to the wall, locked the dressing room and swore the make-up man to silence. Then he put it about that Yousuf, the scriptwriter and the director were locked in a mountain retreat, rewriting the second half of the film. Shooting would be resumed the moment they finished.

For six weeks he bluffed and stalled in the hope of a miracle and then, just as his creditors' patience ran out, it happened. On the morning of the twenty-third of September, he unlocked the dressing room routinely, with no real hope . . . and there was Yousuf, sitting with his face to the wall, a two-month-old paper in his hands and the slivers and shards of a shattered mirror winking all round him.

The producer suspended disbelief and carried on with his shooting schedule as if nothing had happened. It helped that Yousuf had no memory of his looking-glass limbo. Time had stood still for him. By rights he ought to have had a two-month beard but he returned as freshly shaved as the day he had disappeared. He looked just the same . . . and yet there was something about his face that wasn't quite right. It bothered the producer that he couldn't put his finger on it. It was only when the first rough-cut was screened that he saw what the matter was. In all the footage shot after Yousuf's return, his trademark smile sloped the wrong way. It was the right corner of his mouth that curled up now; in the Yousuf of yesterday it had been the left! Others in the unit noticed this too but they just assumed that the laboratory had used the negative wrong side down while printing. Some put it down to a change in style; but they didn't know about the mirror. Neither did Yousuf; Yousuf only knew that mirrors were useless for him now, because when he looked into one, no one looked back.

But his troubles were trivial. He had to learn to part his hair without a mirror image and get used to suddenly becoming left-handed – and that was all. All Yousuf really lost was his

249

reflection. Prof. Chishti was more fundamentally changed. He had just finished the first of his morning's lectures: Syncretism in Medieval Indian Islam. It was only the sixth time in as many years that he had shown his M.A.(Final) class how the more heterodox sufi orders shared with Vedantic monism the spiritual ideal of self-annihilation, but already he didn't believe a single word of his lecture notes. Wiping the blackboard clean of his idiot scribbling gave him a certain satisfaction. He was gathering his papers when, outside the class, in the corridor, a band of students who had just heard the news, spontaneously and in ragged chorus, shouted, Quit India! Prof. Chishti vanished in a puff of chalk. What remained of him was a white silhouette on the same blackboard that he had just wiped clean. Sometime during the next lecture in that classroom, a mathematician rubbed it out to make room for his numbers. It was just simple bad luck; bad luck that the professor's limbo had been rendered in something as impermanent as chalk; bad luck because he was one of the vanished who didn't return.

I was luckier, said Masroor. His surface had been the side of a truck and, like the rest of that recruitment poster, he had been done in oil paint which didn't run in the rain, though it faded a little and blistered in places in the heat of the summer sun. For six weeks he travelled the Ganga's plain because the truck he was part of had been pressed into the urgent business of destroying the Congress rebellion of 1942. Six weeks because that was how long it took to break the back of the uprising. His truck must have been recalled to Delhi to guard the railhead there because, when Masroor was sprung from limbo, he woke up in the compound of the New Delhi railway station. It happened around noon on the twentieth of September 1942.

That was approximately the date, give or take a week, when all of them returned. Inayat, Salman, Saleem, Rizwan, Yousuf and the thousands Masroor didn't know and couldn't put a name to. Masroor was convinced that their return was tied up with the life of the rebellion. They disappeared with its beginning and returned when it ended. By the middle of September, it was the turn of Congressmen to sample suspended animation – in jail. Smashed, outlawed and imprisoned, the party lost its knack of making people disappear. It had used its Quit India mantra to conjure up the masses, the faceless, faithless, rampant masses . . . and lost. And now there was room for Masroor and his kind once more.

For an hour after I was born again, said Masroor, cutting his second omelette into bite-sized squares, I sat on the steps that led up to the ticket counters, shaking. I shook till my joints ached and my neck felt tired. I was sitting there watching the coolies work, when I heard the azaan.

It was the call for the afternoon prayers and it came from the mosque between the tracks. He listened to that nasal ribbon of sound for a minute or two, then pushed himself off the steps and began walking in its direction. Tiny as it was, the mosque was less than full. A bearded maulana led the prayer and the remembered routines of childhood led him through the motions.

The Maulana's name was Muin-ud-din Dehlavi. The men of his line had been calling the faithful to prayer at this mosque for more than two hundred years before the first train had whistled its way through New Delhi railway station. The land that the Mughal had given them to maintain themselves and the mosque had been parcelled out in railway tracks and shunting yards; now the family and the mosque owed their in-between existence to the benevolence of an English emperor. Five generations of the mosque's imams had been pensioners of a Christian Raj.

Pensioner or not, Maulana Muin-ud-din ran the mosque with the heart of a millionaire. His own life was as frugal as that of the poorest coolie in his congregation; thin as a rake himself, he spent his money feeding others. Every evening, the faithful came to pray and the hungry stayed to eat; most nights the mosque's courtyard doubled as a hostel for the homeless . . . like Masroor. He went there following a remembered sound and stayed the winter.

At first he stayed because he didn't have the fare for Lucknow. Then, when he had the money, he didn't want to go, because by that time he had met Saleem: the one who disappeared into the day's cartoon and got multiplied a hundred thousand times. When he re-materialized (two days after Masroor), he was lying under the lower berth of a first-class compartment in a train heading westward to Delhi. Some passenger had wrapped his bathroom slippers in pages taken from the newspaper of that terrible morning and left the crumpled pages under his seat. Like Masroor, Saleem found refuge in Maulana Muin-ud-din's mosque.

Before he met Saleem, Masroor could have docketed his disappearance as a bad dream, or filed it under nightmare. But once he had heard Saleem's story, once he knew that his nightmare had been shared by others, he couldn't resume his Lucknow life as if nothing had happened . . . if only because it could happen again.

Through that winter, as they timidly emerged from the sheltering cocoon of the mosque, Masroor and Saleem learnt of others who had visited limbo. Some they met, others they heard about at second hand. It became as obvious as the bump on Maulana Muin-ud-din's forehead that what all the disappearees had in common (apart from being Muslims) was that they weren't supporters of the Muslim League or committed to its goal, a separate Muslim state called Pakistan. Some were properly against it, others were doubtful, the rest were simply undecided. But whether they knew it or not, in the completely polarized politics of 1942, this made them Congress Muslims.

Saleem decided that life as a Congress Muslim was inherently unstable. So, not out of great conviction but with the modest aim of consolidating his grip on reality, he went over to the Muslim League. When he got over his terror of meeting a clone risen from some other copy of that day's cartoon, he went looking for a job. He didn't go back to the *Hindustan Times* – this time he tried *Dawn*, which had just been set up by Jinnah because the Muslim League needed a paper to air its views.

The editor took him on at once. Saleem was a bargain: he was an experienced journalist, he was Muslim, and since he didn't want to live off the Maulana's charity for ever, he was willing to work for next to nothing. The editor even took on the completely raw Masroor as an irregular sports reporter. Irregular, because he was paid per story. On Saleem's advice, he started with a series of profiles: Great Pakistani Cricketers: Past and Present.

Masroor did his best to follow Saleem's example. He learnt the case for Pakistan as he had once learnt the case against. He studied the maps that plotted its hypothetical borders and tried not to notice that none of them included Lucknow. He grew a beard and bought a sherwani; he even spoke in public – not so much for the Muslim League as against the Congress. Not that anyone noted the distinction: there was no room for feeble nuance in 1942.

But his heart wasn't in it. He hadn't rejected the Congress' masses to replace them with the League's Muslims. If the idea of his country purged by struggle and glued by nationalism didn't make his heart leap, the thought of a separate Muslim state distilled into two-hundred-proof purity didn't set his pulse racing. He sometimes wondered what kind of India he wanted when the British left, as they had to sooner or later. Inevitably, having taught history for seven years to the senior class in La Martinière, he looked to the past for a prototype. What he really wanted was a sporadically republican, inconsistently democratic version of the Austro-Hungarian Empire; a jerry-built coalition of statelets, joined by local self-interest and trade, deaf to large ideas and blind to crusading visions. That's what he wanted.

But it wasn't on offer. He had tried to peddle the idea himself with the cut-out jigsaw I had seen him selling at the fête, but there was no future in being a quixotic crank. So he shelved the subcontinent's destiny for the time being and concentrated on his own. And since his first priority was to become real on a durable basis, he decided to join the army.

Masroor insisted that the decision followed logically from his circumstances. From his experience in limbo he had learnt that he needed an identity that was consistently immune to the political fluctuations of the subcontinent. The army supplied this requirement: it was fighting the fascists (which was a good thing) and it was likely to go on fighting the fascists regardless of what the Congress and the League said or did. So he would be safe for the duration of the war. Saleem and I between us, said Masroor, never heard of any Muslim soldiers vanishing. After the war, there would be decisions to be made – but those would keep.

And though he refused to admit it, the fact that he had spent six weeks on a recruitment poster painted on the side of an army truck must have had something to do with his determination to get into uniform. I knew that if I had been Masroor, I might have read that as a Sign.

The train stopped at Summerhill. It was the last stop before Simla, but I got off to use the station's urinal. Just the thought of Masroor in the army made me want to go.

He had set about his task with frightening thoroughness. The easiest way of getting in at the officer level, he told me, was the Short Service Commission; so he applied for that. He might have been in uniform by now if he hadn't failed the medical.

He was undone, ironically, by his stint on the recruitment poster. Like Saleem and many of the others, he had lost weight during those weeks in limbo – two stone in his case. For his height he was underweight. So the doctors failed him.

But the recruiting officer had been encouragingly hearty. All Masroor had to do was fatten up. If he came round again in six months' time, that is, January 1944, he could try again. His other tests would still be valid. He would just have to weigh in again. Just tip the scales at ten stone ten, said the bottle-brushed adjutant, and Bob's your uncle.

Which was why Masroor was avoiding his family till January next year. He would get in touch with Ammi and Asharfi once he was in khaki, not before. He knew his mother would have hysterics if she got to know that he wanted to become a soldier. That's why he had lurked in the shadows during the fête and sworn Haasan and me to silence – he knew that being resolute would be easier once he got his commission.

But he wasn't about to get it. Bob would be no kin of Masroor's if I had any say in the matter. I knew the war was nearly over and that the forces of light would win without

Masroor's help. No matter how many times the politics of the subcontinent consigned him to limbo, it was entirely unnecessary for him to risk a wartime death. At least limbo held out the promise of return.

Besides, I needed him. He was a third of all the family that I had and if he went and died, I would lose the rest as well. If Partition came without Masroor, they would have to move to Pakistan, to Gujranwala town, where Ammi's cousin was an engineer on the canals. To stay this side of the border they would need the insurance of a man. So the moment he told me about joining up, I began plotting to de-militarize Masroor.

Step one consisted of getting him to Simla, where I could keep an eye on him. This wasn't difficult; his skeletal thinness was a handy argument. It had been two months since the medical exam when he came round to my room at the East India C——, and for that time he had organized his life around the search for those extra pounds. Now and then, when doubt or boredom gnawed at him, he half-heartedly essayed the old routines: making speeches at the mosque, selling his jigsaws or working on his half-done profile of the proto-Pakistani bowler, Jehangir Khan, but mainly he ate and slept. At the end of those two months he had put on just four pounds. At this rate it would be a year before he made the required weight – and his deadline was January.

I offered him hope. I mentioned my transfer to Simla and showed him how a few months there would help him storm the army. Mountain walks, hotel food and the fabled appetite of a cold climate. A place to stay wouldn't be a problem; winter was the off-season and there would be several spare bunks in the Cecil's servants' quarters. He could even earn his keep by helping out. That would probably have been enough to get him on the Kalka Mail with me, but just to wrap things up, I used my trump suit queen: I played Parwana.

She was the reason that he had come to my room. It was for her that he had shaved his beard and carved his sharp moustache. He had seen her for the first time at the railway station, the day I had gone to fetch her. She was moving down the over-bridge (accompanied by the baggage-bowed coolie and me – but he didn't see us) and he was talking to Maulana Muin-ud-din in the courtyard of the mosque after having made his speech, when a passing loco drowned their voices out. Masroor raised his eyes in mimed annoyance heavenward . . . and saw Parwana perched on the billowing smoke of the passing engine, like a houri floating on the puffball clouds of Paradise.

He never completed his conversation with the Maulana. The moment the last carriage of the interminable goods train rolled past, he skipped across the rail lines, hurdling small heaps of turds en route, and hauled himself up on the platform. Taking the steps three at a time, he sped across the over-bridge and caught up with his houri at the exit gate from where he shadowed her to the tonga yard. Then he followed us all the way to Kashmiri Gate, right up to the door of the East India C——.

He committed the place to memory and rode away, determined to return. But then he caught the 'flu and it took him a week to recover, by which time Parwana was immured in Dadi's house. For two weeks he kept vigil at the bend in the road where Nicholson Road met C. Lal, Chemist, losing sleep and precious pounds without once laying eyes on her. He gave up at the end of a fortnight and returned, distraught, to purposeful feeding. But between pining for love and eating for the army, there wasn't much progress visible on the little cardboard tickets dispensed by the station's weighing scales. Nine stone nothing is what they had registered three times running, each time with the same prediction: Your Luck Will Change.

Then he heard of the fête at Kashmiri Gate and hope flared again; perhaps she would be there. So for the last time, he set up shop with the jigsaw maps and the press – and found her. It was just a glimpse in the dim marquee before the police and chaos intervened but it was enough. He tracked her down to the house of a Hindu Judge.

A modern Hindu girl! His heart thrilled at the self-evident hopelessness of his love. He shaved his face and visited a tailor – what modern girl would look twice at a bearded Muslim dressed for the turn of the last century. By the time he followed Parwana to my room, she had become an obsession. Lovely to look at, and properly unattainable, she had become for poor Masroor the perfect object of desire. I stoked this hopeless passion; I told him everything I knew about her, leaving out only Asharfi and Lucknow. Every fact that barred her from respectability – the orphanage, her brush with films, the singeing, the rape, the growing pregnancy – fired his love to dizzier temperatures, till by the end of the telling, his slitted eyes were burning filaments.

Then I told him that she was in Simla.

I won that trick with the queen of hearts and here we were approaching Simla station. Step one was done; the trouble was, I didn't have a clue about step two. Would Masroor stay once he knew his mother and sister were in Simla too? I prayed that Parwana's pregnancy would keep her indoors, hidden from Asharfi and her mother. I didn't want to think about what would happen if Masroor found out that the woman he loved had loved his sister first.

The coolies strapped the trunks and hold-alls to their backs and we emerged from the gloom of the station's awnings into crisp, cold daylight. Suddenly my worries seemed absurd. Everyone I knew and cared about (with the exception of Haasan) was safe in this hill-station capital of the Raj, removed by six thousand feet of altitude from the troubles below. What else could I want? As for Masroor and the army, something would turn up. Anything was possible. Hadn't Masroor disappeared? Hadn't I gone backwards in time? Hadn't Gogia Pasha turned a snake into a stick into a tie? Putting my faith in miracles, I breathed in the cold, pine-scented air and followed the laden coolies up the Cart Road to the Cecil.

Simla

A SHARFI AND PARWANA hadn't discovered each other by the time we reached Simla. If luck had something to do with this, so did Simla's geography. The hill station was laid out on a winding ridge that straddled several hillsides. Along the ridge ran the Mall where every evening, gentle Simla shopped and promenaded, and the middle of the Mall was Scandal Point where something awful had or hadn't happened, once. This was Simla's heart. It offered a view of the highest peaks in the loftiest ranges of the Himalaya. Lloyds Bank stood proudly double-storeyed on the left, while on the right a narrow road climbed upwards to a plaza with a bandstand; a little higher still rose a Gothic tower clad in stone – this was Christchurch, where gentle Simla prayed. To the west and east of Scandal Point dipped the Mall, which strung the great gabled houses, the Swiss chalets, the story-book cottages along the ridge and its neighbouring slopes, into the brightest necklet of gaiety in the British Empire. Parwana lived at one end of the Mall and Asharfi and Ammi at the other. The Judge had rented Holcombe, a desirable property, not ten minutes from the Viceregal Lodge and round the corner from us at the Cecil. The Gujranwala cousin's cottage that Ammi was using, on the other hand, was nearly an hour's walk from the hotel (if you walked briskly) in the obscurity of Chota or Little Simla, where commissioned officers and covenanted civilians were never seen.

Ammi's house was one of a set of three, built the year before the war by Sir Toba Singh, who had earned his knighthood by helping build great chunks of Lutyens' Delhi. The houses were small but solidly made; a kitchen and a large room below, two smaller rooms and a bathroom above, the whole wrapped in a little skirt of garden. Ammi's Gujranwala cousin, who knew Sir Toba's son from their time together at F.C. College, had got the middle one cheap. The cottage on the left had been bought by Miss Heloise Kaufman, who, for fifteen years, had run the best confectionery on the Mall. For the last four, since the war began, she had taken to telling everyone she met (including Asharfi) that she was Swiss. Forty-ish and fair, she had a thin body and a full-cheeked, china doll face which was beginning to blur at the jawline. She had a friendly way about her and trilled sociable hullos each time she saw Asharfi or her mother, but Ammi didn't like her. She thought of her as that painted woman and ignored her by affecting deafness.

Their other neighbour was the sports master at Bishop Cotton School. He was a stocky, ginger man called Tristram Greyly – even his eyelashes were a shade of orange. He was in his garden most afternoons, weeding and watering, but in the month that they had been there he had never once acknowledged them. This and a certain sallowness convinced Ammi that Greyly was Eurasian. Lucknow is full of these Anglos, she told her daughter. I can always tell.

Ammi's plan was to winter in Simla and to return to Lucknow in March. By then the epidemic she had saved Asharfi from would have spent itself, leaving the plains safe to live in again. She dug herself in, against the coming cold. The coal-fired room heater which she had hauled up from Lucknow was installed in the middle of the living room from where it radiated oppressive warmth in all directions. The rooms upstairs had no fireplaces, so she bought hot water bottles to warm their beds with and unpacked the fat, new quilts she had ordered before leaving for the hills.

At first, Asharfi didn't catch the meaning of these goings on. Ammi had put off telling her daughter how long they were staying until some imaginary date when she wouldn't mind. So Asharfi, secure in her mother's loathing of the cold, assumed that they would leave Simla at the end of the Season. By October they would be back in sunny Lucknow, where the roads were flat, where she had friends, where she could sit by a window in Benbow's over a cup of tea and watch Lucknow stroll by.

259

Then four weeks from the day of their arrival in Simla, when Asharfi was sitting by the blazing heater embroidering, out of terminal boredom, a tea-cosy cover, there was a knocking on the door. Puzzled, she put her frame down and went to answer it. Ammi was upstairs and no one ever visited them. She opened the door and found . . . Moonis, their cook from Lucknow. He was wearing a cap, a scarf and a shapeless overcoat, all in khaki; he looked like a fat deserter from the Burma front.

I had to take a coolie, he said proudly, stamping his feet. The staggering local lowered a vast hold-all and trunk. Moonis gave him a coin with the air of a twenty-one-gun Nawab and walked through the door that an astonished Asharfi was holding open. That was when she realized their quarantine in Simla was going to be much longer than she had thought. Why else would Ammi import Moonis?

Ammi denied nothing.

Till March . . . Asharfi mouthed the words in blank despair. What will I do here? There's no one I know. I can't go anywhere – you don't even let me walk to the Mall by myself!

Well, now you can go with Moonis, said Ammi cleverly.

Asharfi ignored her. She stood at the bedroom window, staring at the garden below, imagining it the way it would be two months from now – the trees naked, the grass hidden by drifts of snow.

I won't be able to take a walk once the snow starts, she said, half talking to herself. And the tea-cosy will be done by tomorrow evening. Ammi, what will I do, she wailed. It's different for Moonis and you; you're old . . . she broke off, aghast at her own impertinence.

Go on, said Ammi mildly, putting the pillowcases that she had been sorting to one side. How is it different for us?

Nothing, muttered Asharfi. I only meant that it's easier for you . . .

To sit indoors and wait, said Ammi, supplying the words.

Asharfi nodded.

Then I'm glad we're staying, said her mother slowly. Because waiting is something a woman should know. She paused when Moonis came in with tea to make his presence felt, and waited till he had set the tray down and gone noisily downstairs.

I wasn't that many years older than you are today when your father left, she said, and I've waited every hour of twelve years now; for the last year, I've waited for your brother too. And you can't wait six months? I wake up every night because I have a nightmare in which your father comes home to the Lalbagh house and finds it locked. Do you think I want to be here when I could be at home waiting for Intezar and Masroor? But I know that if we go home now and catch the sickness and die like those others did, then your father will certainly return to an empty house. For twelve years I've lived on hope. But I also know that you have to live to hope. Dead men don't hope. Nor do dead women, added the editor of *Khatoon*.

There were no complaints from Asharfi after that. She decided to treat her exile like a home science course. She cooked, knitted, sewed, embroidered for allotted times each day, using her marriage market skills to amuse herself. Moonis took over the domestic routines and left his mistress free to return to her solitary task: waiting. Sometimes Ammi wondered who would do the job when she was gone. She thought of the future, which she hadn't done for years. With Masroor gone, what would happen to the name? She didn't like to think that nothing would survive her – Masroor lost, Asharfi unmarried, *Khatoon* defunct.

Perhaps she could use the empty months ahead to groom her daughter to take over the running of *Khatoon*. She needed help in any case; she was two issues behind thanks to the troubles of the previous year. She could have her favourite proxy, Shakila Rahman – the same Shakila who had movingly narrated her pilgrimage to Mecca in the last issue but one – describe her Adventures on Horseback over the Foothills of the Himalaya. In fact she could make Asharfi write it. It would do her good to inhabit a life other than the one she lived.

In this way, mother, daughter and family retainer prepared for the winter, seldom stirring out and never meeting anyone. Shut away in Chota Simla, there was no chance of them running into Parwana.

Then, on the first Sunday in September, the Vicereine made her Famine Appeal.

I'll be Mary, offered Delia Mulholland, and suddenly there was silence round that table in the Cecil's tea room.

Patrick, who had settled nicely into his head waiter's duties after being summoned from Delhi, signalled for the pastries to be served.

The pastor sitting at the head fingered his dog-collar and glanced round the table at the rest of the committee. There was trouble in the offing. Lady Armitage had her eyebrows raised. She was miming incredulity at fat Sister Magdalena – in slow motion in case Delia missed it. Byatt had removed the cigarette holder from between his teeth.

That *is* brave, he said admiringly.

Delia set down her cup and glared at him.

It would be nice, thought the Reverend yearningly, to give them all an enema with the tea they were drinking, just this once, to flush the rubbish out and cleanse their souls. His large, tanned hands had curled into throttling talons on the table-cloth, so he took a deep breath and flexed his fingers into peacefulness. Reminding himself that he was the Reverend A.J. Carrick, he tilted his chin up and let his face go slack. It was a trick he had learnt from watching his bishop in Calcutta, this look of mitred calm.

He couldn't afford to lose his temper now. The committee had been his idea and however contemptible he found the instruments of His Will, it was still God's work that they were doing. The thought of the lives they might save was the one thing that kept him sane in this high-altitude asylum.

Nothing could have been worse than his first month in Simla – he had never been so close to leaving the ministry. From running a dispensary and gruel kitchen in Sylhet in the middle of the worst famine this century, he had suddenly found himself, less than three weeks later, shepherding the best-fed flock in the Raj. There had, of course, been no explanations for his abrupt transfer: the Church was a bureaucracy like any other – only worse, because it also had the clinching sanction of God's will.

Things would get worse in winter. Most of his parishioners would descend to the plains, leaving a marooned rump huddled in their snowbound bungalows, like plums suspended in jam. There would be even less to do . . . if that was possible in a place inhabited by the stuffed and walking dead.

Then that Sunday in September, the Vicereine's voice whispered over the ether and there was light. Her Imperial Highness didn't speak about motherhood or the festive season or nursing as the perfect expression of the feminine essence; she spoke instead of the need for the consort of every civilian and soldier to do her bit and give her mite to save the starving Bengalee. And because she made her appeal on the radio, Simla listened – the wireless in 1943 was still an urgent, mysterious thing, and during the war the English had got used to taking it seriously.

But Carrick knew that by itself the Vicereine's appeal would come to nothing. There had been four years of fundraising for the war effort and people were tired of obligatory generosity. Besides the war wasn't over yet and if it came to a choice between a provincial famine and the world war, Carrick knew which cause his flock would choose. So he decided to make sure that his parishioners wouldn't have to choose; he used the pulpit to fuse the war and the famine into a single cause.

It is our Christian duty, he declared in Church the Sunday after the Vicereine's appeal, to dedicate the Christmas season to our brothers in war and want. He stole a quick look at the text . . . 'and though I have all faith, so that I could remove mountains, and have not charity, I am nothing'. He paused. Corinthians I, Chapter 13. He paused again. Think of those one hundred and one tunnels, cut out of the living rock of the Himalayas to bring the railway to Simla. Truly we have moved mountains. But this great work of Christian civil engineering will seem mere hubris if all of us gathered here do not give generously to the starving man and the serving one. Remember the miracle of Our Lord and the loaves and fishes, he said, returning to his favourite text, the one he had used some weeks before at St James' in Delhi. 'This is the bread which cometh down from heaven, that a man may eat thereof, and not die.' So follow Him in giving generously and you shall have the soul-felt gratitude of those in need. For a starving child, all food is a miracle.

And since he had the measure of his congregation, he made it clear that in keeping with the spirit of the season, the funds would be raised festively. There would be a charity ball on Christmas Eve and a Nativity tableau; tickets would be sold for both.

He caught the attention of the flock, especially that part of it which planned to winter in Simla. Against the arid prospect of a snowbound siege, he had dangled the prospect of gaiety and supplied a worthy reason for collective merriment well after the Season was dead. Suddenly the cold-weather rump became the winter vanguard and Simla was charged with charity.

He had his steering committee by lunchtime that Sunday. It was naturally picked from those who were staying on in the station, which limited his options, and for the most part the committee selected itself. Lady Armitage was an automatic choice being the Major-General's wife. Captain Eugene Byatt of the pince-nez and the cigarette was also inevitable because he was the honorary manager of the Gaiety Theatre. If the Nativity tableau idea went through, he would be a useful man to have around for props and costumes and things. Sister Magdalena was Kitchen Sister in the convent by the Sanjauli Road and Carrick had picked her for ecumenical reasons. He didn't want the Catholics feeling left out and it wasn't going to be a Church of England affair if he could help it. Delia . . . there was no particular advantage in having her but he had asked for help and she had volunteered enthusiastically. He hadn't wanted her, originally, because Byatt had warned him, in his oblique, malicious way, that Elinor Armitage had her claws out for Delia, and Carrick knew what squabbling could do to small church committees. But in the end he ignored the warning as gossip and played fair. He also felt a little sorry for her; she was probably lonely, stuck in Simla while her husband, Major Mulholland, latterly Quartermaster, Corps of Signals, Simla, fought the Jap on the Burma front. In her favour was the fact that she had all the time in the world without the distraction of children. She was also a striking woman, not yet forty, with red hair and dark green eyes, and Carrick, like virtually everyone else he knew, preferred good-looking women to any other kind. So he had made her welcome in the steering committee.

And here she was, one of Simla's gazetted flirts (according to Byatt's latest bulletin) staking her claim to the Mother of God in the Nativity tableau. He should have listened to Byatt. He made his mouth smile at Delia indulgently by stretching his lips a little without letting any teeth show.

Conventionally, Mrs Mulholland, he said apologetically, the Virgin Mother . . . he paused to let the words sink in, is played by women of darker colouring. Your Celtic beauty, he went on hurriedly when he saw her open her mouth to object, was quite unknown in Bethlehem.

Unconvinced but flattered, Delia didn't press her candidature. She took another tack:

Whom are you planning to cast as Baby Jesus? she asked.

The rest of the committee looked at Carrick.

Yes, Reverend, do tell us, said Byatt slyly, enjoying Carrick's discomfiture. It will have to be of the proper colouring as you said, and the right age. Where shall we find this image of Our Infant Lord in the station in winter?

Capitan Byatt, said Sister Magdalena reprovingly, you should know, I think, that in my country every little one, he is the image of God. He made them so.

There was silence.

Patrick had fresh pots of tea brought on.

If any baby can be Jesus, said Delia thoughtfully, then anyone can be . . .

No, no! exclaimed the nun, holding her palms up in a stop sign. I say only for babies because they are sinless like Jesu and pure.

Delia looked affronted but Byatt got in before her.

I have a doll, he said helpfully, wrinkling his forehead, that's about the right size in one of the green-room trunks . . .

No! said Lady Armitage forcefully. This is a Nativity play to mark the birth of Our Lord – not a farce for subalterns.

Captain Byatt persevered. But Elinor, you can't have thought how comfortable it will be – it won't cry at the wrong moment or pucker up in the cold and look ugly. Besides, it's so literal-minded to have a real baby . . .

No, Eugene, and that's my final word. Then, remembering that she was part of a committee, she addressed the others. It's right to have a proper baby, isn't it?

Carrick and Sister Magdalena nodded. Delia looked offensively knowing at the use of first names.

Good, said Lady Armitage, looking at Delia steadily with only slightly heightened colour. Now that we are agreed, we have to find one that's due before Christmas.

Easier said than done, said Byatt happily. Cerise Summers is going to her parents in Sialkot; Venetia's off to her brother in Mhow; Arabella Dauntry's joining her husband in Ajmer and Sophie Tallant will have hers in the Cantonment hospital in Delhi. The McGuire girl, Jane, would have stayed, but she has miscarried.

Sister Magdalena crossed herself.

So you see, said Byatt, screwing another cigarette into his holder, it will have to be the doll. All the layers are leaving.

The pastor chewed his lip. Something will turn up, he offered feebly.

The something will have to be a baby, Reverend, said the unrelenting Byatt, looking down his nose at the smoke curling out of his nostrils.

Capitan Byatt, you are sure that these four are the only women in Simla who will give birth by Christmas? asked Sister Magdalena suddenly.

You can rely on me, Sister, said Byatt, inclining his head with practised grace. No notable development in our little society escapes me.

The nun looked unimpressed. Then who was that girl so big with child whom I saw in the Station Library last Wednesday? She wasn't one of the four that you have named.

Byatt looked taken aback. How can you be certain that she wasn't? You haven't even met all four of them socially. Why, Sophie Tallant only just got here . . .

Of course I am certain, said the Kitchen Sister briskly. The girl I saw was Indian.

Indian? repeated Byatt with polite incredulity. Well, in

which case I'm sure you're right. I'm not really interested in how the natives teem. I was under the impression that we were looking for a stand-in for Our Infant Lord – I hadn't considered the coolies of the Lower Bazaar.

We are all God's children, Capitan Byatt, snapped Sister Magdalena, pink with anger.

So we are, agreed Byatt equably. So are the monkeys on Jakoo Hill. Would you cast one as Baby Jesus?

Please, said Carrick, deciding that it was time for him to keep the peace. Does anyone know this girl's name?

If Sister Magdalena saw her at the Station Library, said Lady Armitage, she's Judge Prasad's ward. He asked me to sponsor her application for temporary membership. So I did. She shrugged. He's perfectly respectable; he was on the Honours List last year. Not in the least like a Lower Bazaar coolie.

Will she be here till Christmas? asked Carrick, absently fingering his collar.

Lady Armitage shrugged her eyebrows. I could ask if you're interested, she said.

Wait a minute, said Delia, spacing the words out menacingly. I can't play Mary because of my colouring . . . and we are considering a black woman's baby for Jesus?

She isn't black and Jesus wasn't pink – he was the Mediterranean type, asserted Sister Magdalena confidently. She has the olive complexion which is what we need.

She isn't even Christian, for heaven's sake! exclaimed Delia, waving her hands about.

Neither was Mary, Carrick pointed out gently, making sure that he smiled. Or Jesus, if it comes to that. Anyway, we don't even know if her guardian will allow her or her child to take part.

We could call on the Judge this evening and find out, said Lady Armitage practically.

Are we agreed? asked Carrick, trying to sound casual, and held his breath for a slow count of five. No one objected.

Perhaps we could go together, suggested Carrick, as Patrick had the tea things cleared away and the committee prepared to disperse.

I wasn't about to go alone, said Lady Armitage tartly,

sliding her arms into the coat Patrick was holding up for her. Of course you'll come along. They'll need the reassurance of a churchman.

Carrick watched timidly as she pulled her gloves on. We can meet here at four-thirty and walk down. Holcombe's less than a furlong away. She looked disapprovingly at his worn jacket. Make sure you wear a nice black cassock, she said, and walked briskly out of the Cecil's tea room.

Parwana's pregnancy was coming to term. Dadi was of the old school: pregnancy meant confinement, so Parwana was allowed to do nothing more strenuous than practise her shorthand. She spent the long summer days in the garden, playing at Pitman, but mainly eating sugared strawberries in cream, reclining on a deck chair, with her feet propped up on a stool to keep them from swelling. In the beginning there had been the suspense of watching her toes setting day by day beyond the rising horizon of her belly, but after that climax was past, there was nothing to look forward to.

The high-point of her Simla life had been her single visit to the Station Library, where she found a romance called *The Black Moth* which she read seven times in a fortnight. She hadn't visited the library since because as soon as she entered her seventh month Dadi decided that the twenty-minute walk to the Mall was too much for her. Dadi visited the library once after that on Parwana's behalf, but she didn't believe in fiction and returned with Gregg's *Curvilinear Shorthand* and a primer for Emma Dearborn's revolutionary shorthand technique, Speedwriting.

Parwana was bored. Her life might have been more lively if Masroor had entered it, but he contented himself with gazing from afar; literally. Every free moment he had was spent standing on the edge of the road where it overlooked Holcombe before curling round the hill, watching Parwana in the spade-shaped garden watching her toes disappear. He had come to Simla to find Parwana and now he wouldn't meet her. Seeing her pregnant had affected him seriously; he wanted to be responsible for them, for Parwana and the baby she was about to produce. He watched over her like an anxious husband, but as a father in the making, he didn't feel he could meet her, not until he had a proper job.

He was there at his look-out the evening the pastor and Lady Armitage came to call. It was a brief visit; no longer than it took to drink a cup of tea. The Judge made a point of introducing his visitors to his wife and her ward; he couldn't have them thinking that he secluded his womenfolk. Carrick didn't have to use any of the arguments he had rehearsed; his rumpled cassock and her title carried the day. Barely had they mooted Parwana's and her forthcoming baby's participation in the Christmas tableau than the Judge began saying of course, smiling indulgently at the excited mother-to-be, and taking the opportunity to say broad-minded things about Christmas, the Festive Season for All.

There was a small silence after that which the Judge quickly filled. Did you know, sir, he said in the same resonant, slightly amplified tone that he used to pronounce death sentences, that many scholars believe that Jesus Christ is buried in Kashmir? It had seemed to him a harmless, vaguely appropriate thing to say, but Carrick choked on his tea and nearly coughed himself to death, so Lady Armitage had to effect the leave-taking and guide the wheezing pastor out.

Masroor watched the mismatched couple leave the house. They turned left after the wicket gate and headed towards the Cecil. Fifteen minutes later when it became clear that Parwana was going to stay indoors, Masroor abandoned his vigil and set off for the Mall. He had discovered the roller skating rink beyond the bandstand a week after we arrived in Simla, and now he went there every day, with obsessive regularity. It was brand new, built for the American soldiers stationed in Simla for the duration of the war. He loved the parquet floor, the gleaming handrails running along the walls that propped up beginners, the smell and taste of popcorn, which he'd never met before, but most of all he loved the swooping, weightless, gliding runs which made him godlike. He had learnt by watching the soldiers, some of whom could do amazing things, like scissor backwards at appalling speeds or do the splits and come upright without rupturing themselves. He had got to the stage where he could go very fast in a straight line without losing his balance, but he couldn't change directions yet, and he hadn't learnt how to stop. Which was lucky – otherwise he might never have met Cyrus Tehmurasp Dastoor.

Or found a job.

When he reached the rink that evening he tried to purge his disappointment at not having glimpsed Parwana by hurtling across the floor from end to end at ferocious speeds. His braking technique was basic: he stopped by slapping his palms against the handrail and sliding his feet to the left at the moment of impact. In this way he had completed twelve laps and was launched on the thirteenth, when a thin someone pushed off the side rail, wobbled across the floor and became stationary at a point on Masroor's flight path. The collision was spectacular – the thin person cannoned across the polished floor on his side, flailing his arms and legs gracefully, like a dying swan on wheels, while Masroor hit the rail on schedule but off balance and somersaulted unwillingly over it.

Unhurt but embarrassed, Masroor lay slumped against the wall pretending to be winded till he was certain no one was watching. Then he got to his feet and walked across to the other party to the collision, who was still on all fours, looking about alertly. Masroor found him his spectacles. When he got to his feet, Masroor realized that he was even slighter than that first high-velocity glimpse had led him to believe. Thinner even than him. Thin face, thin nose, pomaded hair parted down the middle, long even teeth that protruded a little, and the whole wrapped in a skin so pale that Masroor first thought he was concussed. But he seemed lucid enough as they murmured apologies at each other, each insisting that the fault was his alone. Then they ran out of words together.

Cyrus Dastoor, said the one in spectacles, his eyes straining to focus through ruined lenses, spider-webbed with cracks. Guiltily Masroor grabbed the extended hand and forgot to introduce himself. They stood there for a while, in one corner of a crowded rink, shaking hands in silence.

It wasn't a great start but they were friends inside a week. Some of the credit for this belonged to the rink – they met there every evening and Masroor taught Cyrus the rudi-

270

mentary skills he had recently learnt. But the more important reason behind their friendship was the fact that they were young, educated and Indian in Simla, where polite society was invulnerably white. Cyrus was heir to a furniture empire based in Bombay, second only to Lazarus and Co. His father had sent him to Simla to win a contract for renovating the staterooms at the Viceregal Lodge. The decision was pending; so was Cyrus' social life.

He had nearly breached the bastions of the Simla set on account of his extreme pallor, his Cambridge degree, his mastery of the oboe and his money. When he first arrived in April, things had gone very well. Captain Byatt had met him in a billiards saloon and roped him into the Gaiety Theatre's first production for the '43 season, *The School for Scandal*. Not to act in, of course, but as assistant stage manager. Cyrus had been thrilled . . . until he discovered that Byatt expected him to supply the stage props at his own expense, because he was his father's son. Thrift and pride made him refuse – and so the Gaiety went out of his life. The assistant stage managership went to a débutante of the English rose variety, Miss Waters. People called her Esther.

Shaken, Cyrus grimly set about becoming self-sufficient. Never gregarious, he now became a solitary. From the day he was replaced by Esther to the moment he collided with Masroor, Cyrus' only human contact – not counting the Establishment Officer responsible for awarding the furniture tender at the Viceregal Lodge – was his host, Mr Jacob. Mr Jacob ran an antiquarian shop on the Mall where he sold old books and period furniture. Mowbray Brothers, 76 The Mall. Mr Jacob, naturally, was no kin of the founding Mowbrays, having merely bought the shop some years ago. The gossip Cyrus heard during his time with the Gaiety set tagged him as a Jew of foreign but unspecified extraction. Russia, Poland, Palestine . . . from somewhere there. Whoever he was, he was a great friend of Cyrus' father, who, over the years, had custom-built for him whole suites of plausibly weathered Queen Anne chairs.

When Cyrus learnt that Masroor needed a job, he arranged an interview for him with Mr Jacob.

I don't really know him very well, said Cyrus, apologetic- ally, as the two of them left the rink and headed for Mowbrays. I mean, he's very kind and the rest of it – won't let me pay for my keep, keeps telling me to help myself to the drink – but we don't get to talk much except over dinner when he isn't eating out, and then he goes on about first editions and the Levant, so I never know what to say. But he's a nice man and I know he definitely wants someone to catalogue his books. I heard him say so to the Reverend Carrick yesterday, when he couldn't find him the kind of Bible he wanted.

Masroor swallowed and wiped his palms on the cloth of his trousers. Then he told himself not to be ridiculous. He had known Cyrus for less than a week and here he was behaving as if the world would end if he didn't get a shop assistant's job. They were within sight of the shop now. He could see Mowbray Brothers picked out in large serifed capitals over the double-door entrance, flanked by shop windows in which globes, tables, maps and leather spines were casually displayed. It would be the end of the world if he didn't get the job – it was no use pretending otherwise. Parwana was due any day now; she had looked so large in the morning that it wouldn't surprise him if she was in labour that very minute. He had to have a job when the baby came; he had no right to be in love if he couldn't even support himself, let alone Parwana and the baby. He had begun feeling like a voyeur at his look- out above Holcombe.

They were there. Cyrus was holding the door open. Masroor swallowed another gob of spit, stretched his lips out to let them relax into a good firm line, and then walked in.

I was sitting on my favourite bench in the Cecil's private garden when Masroor returned from the interview. Cyrus – whom I only knew at second hand – was with him. I knew from their grins that it had gone well; Masroor's teeth were all set to roll back the dusk.

He didn't ask my age, or what I read, why I wanted to work in a bookshop, what degree I'd done . . . nothing, said Masroor, shaking his head in wonder. He had been expecting something along the lines of the army interview. Mr Jacob just gave me a pen and a sheet of paper and asked me to write out a sentence: the quick brown fox jumps over the lazy dog.

All Mr Jacob wanted to test was the quality of Masroor's handwriting, because the job basically meant entering the title, author, place and date of publication of every book in the shop into long black registers. He took one look at Masroor's unfaltering cursive, forged on the blackboards of La Martinière, and gave him the job. Sixty rupees a month and you can start tomorrow. With Religion, he added, pointing at the gloom at the back of the shop.

So Masroor started on Religion the next day and I, for the first time since arriving in Simla, allowed a little hope to grow. The job was only temporary (Mr Jacob wanted it done by the New Year) but it was the first sign he had shown of settling into the hill station. Also, over the next fortnight, the army figured less and less in his conversation. I was delighted; now all I wanted was for him to be reunited with Ammi and Asharfi and we could go back to being a happy family once again. It didn't seem impossible; if he had grown out of his infatuation with the army, there was no reason for him to avoid his mother and sister. I said nothing of this to him. It was early days.

But, in what I hoped were subtle ways, I tried to help him settle down into Mr Jacob's shop. I took to dropping into Mowbray Brothers when I had the mornings off. It was a welcoming place, piled high with furniture and books, and Mr Jacob didn't mind me browsing, especially since I gave Masroor a hand with the sorting and arranging, or stood on ladders reading out names, dates and places, while he wrote them down neatly into his registers. When Patrick put me on night shifts for a month, visiting Mowbrays became a habit. Most days I took sandwiches along for lunch. Punctually at half-past one, Mr Jacob hung the closed sign out, bolted the doors and went upstairs to his flat where Gama, his Goan cook, set out his lunch. And unless he had to be at the Viceregal Lodge to help his tender bid along, Cyrus made a point of eating with his host.

Masroor and I normally made our way to the back of the shop and unpacked our sandwiches in the cool, green glow of the Eden window. That's what Cyrus called it. Mowbrays was a very deep shop – as long as a tunnel, it straddled the Mall ridge: its front opened on to the Mall while its rear overlooked the dipping slopes of the foothills that built up to Simla. The scene in the window was always filled with the unploughed green of the hillsides; nobody lived in it and nothing ever happened. For an hour every afternoon, we ate our sandwiches and let our eyes drink Paradise in.

Cyrus said that it looked like a postcard view of England. Never having been there I couldn't say, but it didn't look like any part of India that I knew. I thought of the view from my attic-room window in Banaras, where the only tree in sight grew unasked out of a roof, where in the lane below the endless stream of the living paused only for the litters of the dead. Sitting by the Eden window, it was hard to believe that this scene was made in India.

The shop had the same feeling about it. A fortnight into the Mowbrays routine, I realized that among all the thousands of books in the shop I hadn't come upon a single one published in India or written by an Indian. In fact, except for a forty-seven-volume series called *Sacred Books of the East*, there was nothing about India at all . . . unless *Thus Spake Zarathustra* counted as a book on the Parsees. Cyrus, who had noticed the same thing, asked Mr Jacob about it one day, over lunch. His host looked a little affronted.

Mowbrays is a traditional antiquarian bookshop, Cyrus, he said crisply. Exactly like those in Berlin or Vienna or Prague. We do not trade in provincial exotica.

Simla being what it was, Mr Jacob's explanation was appropriate; it seemed reasonable to me at the time, and not at all absurd. Simla was an elaborately invented world – not in the sense of being freely imagined like the settings of good novels, but in the mechanical manner of fantasy, where the make-believe world was a simple inversion of everyday life. Like all hill stations Simla had one central function: it existed as not-India. The India to which the sahib gave his life in heroic service was flat, hot, dusty, brown, diseased and overcrowded. Simla was not-this.

It was undulating and cool; its landscapes were green and

the faces in sight were white; it was India's summer capital because it didn't have India's summer; it was sedate, pretty and English in the basic way of gabled roofs, half-timbered shops, Gothic churches and dateless castle spires – all built at once. Time was kept in its proper place, in regimental records and honour rolls. Newspapers with their changing dates came to Simla from the plains decorously late, bleached of their vulgar urgency. No local newspaper existed to mirror its own existence. Nostalgia was the ruling passion; not because anything had changed, but to make sure nothing ever did. Things had never been the same in Simla from the second day of its existence. It was the tree-house of a tropical empire which was proceeding directly from adolescence to senility.

This little white world spent its evenings browsing up and down the shops on the Mall, and Mowbrays was a regular stopping place. The regulars headed straight for the cabin where Mr Jacob sat, hair slicked back from a high-domed forehead, jowls so closely shaved that they glistened. With grave courtesy he offered them tea or coffee and suggested things that might interest them. If it was a book they wanted, he showed them to the relevant shelf or summoned Masroor for a consultation. He generally knew what they were on the look-out for. Tristram Greyly was mad about heraldry and genealogy and books with titles like *Tartans of the Western Highlands*, but he rarely bought anything. Captain Byatt, on the other hand, had a private income and bought nearly everything Mowbrays stocked on Freemasonry and Satanism. The Reverend Carrick, predictably enough, collected Bibles and his colleague on the committee, Lady Armitage, was always on the look-out for cunningly wrought swordsticks which she regularly presented to her husband. Even Delia Mulholland was a collector: first editions of Somerset Maugham. Lust in the tropics was Cyrus' explanation for this curious hobby.

The shop swirled with gossip about Carrick's Christmas. Lady Armitage explained to Mr Jacob that there would be a costume ball followed by a Nativity tableau. Everyone at the ball will have to be dressed out of the Bible, she said, and paused.

Mr Jacob waited in his well-bred way.

Either Testament of course, she clarified graciously.

Mr Jacob raised his eyebrows in profound something or the other – agreement? admiration? doubt? – while Masroor helped Gama clear the tea things away.

Carrick, who came in afterwards, explained the whole thing all over again to a glazed-looking Mr Jacob, and then, in his ecumenical zeal, invited him to participate in the Nativity tableau as Joseph. A shrug of the shoulders, an inaudible murmur, a graceful and meaningless gesture at his receding hairline and Carrick was persuaded to drop the subject.

Not everyone wished Carrick's Christmas well. One afternoon in November, the day dissolved into an unseasonal thunderstorm and Delia Mulholland rushed in to shelter from the rain. Mr Jacob sent her off with Masroor to inspect a slightly damaged first edition of *The Painted Veil*. Masroor couldn't find it at once; he had been distracted all day because Parwana was due any moment now; he hadn't seen her in the garden for days. Besides, Delia made him nervous; she stood too close and breathed too hard.

As Delia was making her way back to Mr Jacob's cabin, Elinor Armitage walked in, furling an umbrella.

Won't it be amusing, drawled Delia apropos of nothing, addressing herself to Mr Jacob, if that Indian woman whom the Reverend has cast as Mary should produce a girl?

There was one beat of silence.

Most amusing, said Lady Armitage crisply. But not likely. The Reverend Carrick and I went to Holcombe at noon to congratulate the Judge. His ward has had two sons. Twins, by Caesarean section.

A White Christmas

I T WAS GOING to be a white Christmas. The gravel path that
led up to the main porch of the Viceregal Lodge was buried
under last night's snowfall; the path couldn't be told
apart from the blotted-out lawns except for a running
depression where flowerbeds bordered it. Tiredly, I made a
mental note to tell the Lodge's Estate Officer that the path
would have to be shovelled clean by seven, at least an hour
before the first guests for the ball arrived.

The snow had stopped less than three hours ago, so it was
warmer outside than it had been for a fortnight, but inside the
Lodge it was still numbingly cold. With no enthusiasm I
returned indoors and began pulling the dust covers off the
sofas in the reception area; this was hard to do with gloves on.
My fingers were stiff, my nose was running, my lips were
cracked, even my nipples were chapped and sore under the
woollen vest I had to wear to keep from freezing. The
preparations for the ball had been spread over the last three
days (and nights); I needed sleep.

When all the sofas were stripped, I huddled by the reception
area's single fireplace, which had been lit early in the morning
in the absurd hope that it would warm this darkly panelled
morgue up to temperatures fit for the living. The Lodge
wasn't easy to heat at the best of times, but in December, with
its fireplaces cold for two months since the departure of the
Viceroy and his capital for the plains, it was nearly impossible.
The height of the interior didn't help – the gallery was
atrium-like, capped by a ceiling three storeys high. Railed off
corridors on every floor looked down into this central space,
and, in a nice touch, a life-sized Lord Curzon stood suspended
over the fireplace looking chilly and disapproving.

In the beginning, when Carrick was still in charge of

Christmas, the Cecil had been the venue for the ball. Then Elinor Armitage decided that the hotel's Main Dining Room was nowhere near grand enough to host Simla's response to the Vicereine's Appeal. Carrick suggested the name of the only other large wooden floor that he knew about – the skating rink – and was snorted down. Elinor Armitage and Delia Mulholland, in an unprecedented display of unity, coerced Carrick into accepting the Viceregal Lodge as the logical venue for a ball inspired by the Vicereine's Appeal. Carrick had been reluctant about housing the Nativity tableau in the Viceroy's summer residence; it seemed too much like giving unto Caesar what was God's. But he had been outnumbered and when Sister Magdalena seemed to go along with the scheme, he gave way. Patrick got the whole story directly from Carrick's mouth when the embarrassed clergyman came to the hotel to cancel the Christmas Eve booking.

But the Cecil was still catering the whole event – which was why I hadn't slept in nearly seventy hours. Major-General Armitage had got permission to use the Lodge's ballroom from the highest reaches in government; rumour had it that the Vicereine herself had intervened. The Estate Officer's interpretation of this permission, which allowed the Church Committee the use of the Lodge, was nitpickingly narrow. He turned keys in the appropriate locks and retired to his office, regretting with great relish his inability to spare his staff for a private event. This meant that the hotel's skeletal winter staff – which included me – had to do everything from waxing the floor to decorating the Christmas tree, quite apart from the main job of supplying food and drink. Somehow it had all been done: the floor was glowing, the long buffet table was spread with white linen, the six fireplaces roaring in the ballroom were doing a better job of raising the temperature than the solitary one in the lobby, which barely warmed me up and I was virtually sitting on its grate.

Carrick arrived with sacks of straw and wood shavings, looking like a fugitive early Christian in his cassock and a face-obscuring Balaclava. Reluctantly I left the fireplace and followed him into the Morning Room where the manger was being built to Captain Byatt's specifications. Byatt had volunteered and the Committee had delegated the responsibility willingly – he was, after all, in charge of props and costumes at the Gaiety and the manger was a kind of set.

At the moment the set consisted of an untidy bed of straw and a crude work-table with a carpenter's plane on it – the table was now strewn with Carrick's wood shavings under Byatt's direction.

Well? he asked. What do you think?

There was no reply. Carrick and I had just spotted the calf tethered to one leg of the table.

Well?

Carrick pointed at the animal, which was sitting placidly under the table, nosing the straw.

Oh that! Byatt grinned. Nice, isn't it? It's my gardener's – just two weeks old. I had a devilish time smuggling him past that killjoy caretaker. But we did it – you can't have a manger without a cow, even if it's only a little one.

How will you keep it from . . . umm . . . ? asked Carrick uneasily.

Byatt picked up the startled calf and showed us its bottom. An oilcloth bag had been tied under its tail. I've thought of everything, he said simply. Some real dung would be a nice detail, though. I've asked the gardener to bring some cow-pats if he has them. How do you like the caddy?

Caddy? echoed Carrick, uncertainly.

Byatt pointed.

Khadi was what he meant. I noticed then that the bed of straw was partly spread with dirty-white homespun and the same cloth had been used to drape the farther wall as a kind of backdrop. It looked appropriately shabby.

Carrick stared wonderingly at Byatt – pats of cow dung and bolts of khadi; this, from a man who not so long ago had been talking about the coolies of the Lower Bazaar.

It's the kind of homespun cloth they would've used then, isn't it? said Byatt defensively. Besides, Reverend, he drawled, reverting to his languid manner, you're the one who wanted a native Nativity.

Carrick wouldn't be baited; he just smiled and shook his head.

I'll have this done by six, said Byatt. When does your cast arrive?

Carrick looked puzzled.

Byatt sighed. Your heathen, Reverend, he explained patiently.

Oh, you mean Parwana and her child! Much later. Not till ten at the very earliest. The Judge's wife doesn't want her out of the house for more than three hours. I think that's sensible – it's so cold that the baby could catch something.

Byatt shrugged. Wouldn't really matter if it did, he said indifferently.

Despite his best intentions, Carrick glared at him.

Byatt raised his hands placatingly. All I meant, Reverend, was that the show'll still go on. You chose your Mary well. Twins, weren't they? Our infant Lord has an understudy.

The Estate Officer relented and deputed two watchmen to help us shovel the snow off the path. By the time we finished at four-thirty, my feet were frozen and my hands, despite the gloves, blistered. Patrick and I walked back together in the dusk, to wash and change into the hotel's livery before the ball began.

We passed Masroor near the hotel, on his way to his Holcombe look-out. I waved, but he didn't wave back . . . I don't think he even saw us. Later, sitting in a tin washtub in the waiters' quarters, I watched my knees goose-pimple where they stuck out of the hot water, and brooded on the way Masroor had ignored me. There wasn't even the off-chance that Parwana and her babies would be outdoors during a day as miserable as this, and yet he was so fired with the hope of getting a glimpse of them that he had looked through me. I scrunched lower into the tub, trying to get my shoulders under water while keeping my cigarette and my cup of rum out of it. The rum and tobacco in combination tasted evil, so I swallowed a mouthful of scummy water to rinse the bitterness out, but it lingered . . . like the sting of Masroor's indifference and the tiredness that had set like cement along my bones.

So often in recent months, just the thought that all of us, the people I cared for, were together in Simla had given me hope.

Parwana, Ammi, Asharfi, Masroor . . . all gathered through luck and a little scheming in the safest, the most shockproof, place in this dying Raj. Whenever I thought of the horrors in store, there had always been enough comfort in knowing that if, God willing, we stayed together I wouldn't have to face them alone.

Now, as the water in the tub cooled, this solace in togetherness seemed deluded. Togetherness for whom? Ammi didn't know that her son was in Simla. Asharfi, likewise, had no idea that she was sharing the hill station with her brother and the girl that she had loved. I had never told Parwana the whereabouts of Ammi and Asharfi and, confined as she was to Holcombe, she was in no position to find out. Masroor didn't know that his mother and sister were in the neighbourhood. He knew everything about Parwana's present – but she didn't know he existed. If she did remember him, her memory was of a sharp-moustached pest who had followed her about in Kashmiri Gate. And none of them knew that I was in Simla – with the exception of Masroor and he was so caught up in his passion for Parwana that he didn't seem to care. The only place where these separate people were together was inside my head.

I relaxed in the water and drank some more of the rum. The chill in the water had stopped bothering me now and even the rum wasn't tasting so bad. Perhaps there was a silver lining to this: if we weren't together to begin with, I didn't have to hold my breath any more or look out for calamities which might scatter us. I drank to that. I had imagined that by nudging Masroor up to Simla, I was improving our chances of staying united when Partition came; I had been trying to play matador to a fury that had split a million families down the middle. I laughed out loud. It sounded better than I expected, sort of deep, and the acoustics of the bathroom gave it a nice resonance. For the last time I let the water cover me till just under my eyes and squinted interestedly at my buoyant privates. If wishes were horses, I thought, giggling bubbles under water, that would count as an erection.

At half-past six, when we started back for the Lodge, it was dark. Both of us were carrying large metal torches to light the way – together, we must have looked like the lurching headlights of a tipsy car. I was still tired but the rum had helped the sun set into my stomach, from where it was belching radiance through to my toes and fingertips. I felt like an old limousine: metal fatigue on the body-work and neighing horsepower within.

When we reached the Lodge, Patrick hurried off to the kitchens to see how the food was coming along, leaving me to cope with a linen crisis: the crisp white cloth we had used to drape the buffet table had been in storage too long and it was smelling of the damp. We didn't have a replacement and it could hardly be hung out to dry in the gloom outside. I wanted to leave it where it was and hope that the fireplaces would dry it out before the guests arrived. But it really was smelling. Then, luckily, the Estate Officer, who had turned up to lecture us about how inflammable the Lodge was and the precautions we should take, stayed to show me a way out of the difficulty.

Fold it up and follow me, he said abruptly. I trailed after him across the gallery, right up to the entrance to the Morning Room, where he stopped and fished out a jangling bunch of oversized keys. Set in the panelling adjacent to the doors of the Morning Room was another door which I hadn't noticed. He opened it and we stepped into hot, mothballed darkness. I thought it was a kind of closet till he switched on the light. It was a long, narrow, windowless room, like a corridor that led nowhere. Fat metal pipes ran along the wall to my left, radiating heat. Boiler pipes, said my guide by way of explanation. This room runs along the length of the Morning Room. He pointed at several long, cloth-covered cylinders laid along the wall, close to the pipes. Carpets, he said. Keeps off the mould.

During the rains the room doubled as a gigantic airing cupboard to dry out the washing, but the clothes-lines strung across the narrow breadth of the room were too small for the table-cloth, so I and two others from the Cecil covered the floor with newspapers and laid the cloth over them.

You have an hour before the ball begins – it ought to dry by then, said the Estate Officer, and swept out of the room before I could thank him.

Patrick had set out the punch bowls by the time I returned to the ballroom. It was still half an hour to eight but an early guest was always possible and the punch could always be reheated.

There's some in the kitchen, said Patrick kindly.

It was good of him; after the long-brewed warmth of the airing room, the rest of the Lodge seemed even colder than before and it had been more than an hour since the last of the rum. So I hurried off to the kitchen and sampled the punch which tasted of nectar, mint and lemon peel. And rum. There was another bowl filled with warm red wine that smelt of cinnamon. After two glasses of each the sun blazed in my stomach once more and the horses neighed again.

Patrick had given me the job of running one last check to see that everything was in place. So, one item at a time, I inspected the festive paraphernalia of the Raj: silk flower arrangements; crystal punch bowls so large they looked like stranded chandeliers; the Cecil's crested Wedgwood service; hall-marked silverware; damask napkins; severally branched candelabras; Madeira and sherry glowing secretly in diamond-bright decanters; streamers, ribbons and Christmas baubles; the pianist and the string quartet in evening suits; Patrick parodically viceregal in tails – so many separate things, but some mysterious glaze of Englishness smoothed them all into a single scene – and left us on the outside, looking in. It was an authentic Old Master – Good Life with Waiters – large, assured, invulnerable: if I peed in those punch bowls I knew that it would turn into rum. And though we had put it together – shined the floors, decanted the drink, set the table, hung the bunting – it wasn't ours: we were apprentices filling assigned detail into our master's conception of the Good Life, priapic eunuchs in the king's hareem.

By the time the first guest arrived, I had been standing half-stooped for half an hour, trying to hide an erection that wouldn't go away. It wasn't a woman; it had something to do with the voluptuous formality of the ballroom, the thought that this minted perfection was about to be used.

Awkwardly rampant, I stood to one side and let the others

283

cope with the early arrivals. A dozen couples arrived within fifteen minutes of eight o'clock, soldiers and bureaucrats mainly, bred to punctuality. No one, I noticed, had actually run up a whole costume for the ball: the women had dug out their best long dresses, the men were airing their tails. The difference was that some of them had leafed through their Bibles while the others had been lazier. Heloise Kaufman, who had come on Tristram Greyly's arm, was wearing a velvet gown and a tiara; she was insisting in her girlish way that she was Mary of Magdala. Embedded on the points of her tiara was a row of devil's heads.

'Mary called Magdalene, out of whom went seven devils,' she recited and giggled. Luke 8:2.

Greyly was wearing a long beard and holding two slates which had been written upon with chalk. He was Moses.

There were already four Eves, each clutching an apple. Several stupid men had missed the point completely and turned up in fluffy white beards and Santa Claus caps. Elinor Armitage was one of the early ones in her role as hostess. She was wearing a deep blue gown made of stiff-looking silk. The décolletage went well past the first slope of bosom and long white gloves highlighted the rounded perfection of her arms. She looked much younger and, given my condition, unnecessarily sexy. Her biblical costume consisted of a doll's severed head which she held by the hair. It made me uneasy. Carrick placed her for Patrick and me. She's Salome, he explained. So? said Patrick challengingly. He disliked the dangling head even more than I did. That's John the Baptist she's carrying, added the Reverend. Patrick looked sick. He was beheaded by Herod, continued Carrick patiently. You mean she went around . . . ? Carrick nodded. Patrick asked no further questions. He poured himself a tankard of punch.

Elinor Armitage's husband, the Major-General, was wearing a leopard skin over his evening clothes without looking ridiculous. He was also carrying a swagger stick.

Where did you get the animal from, Charles? asked the oldest Santa.

The regiment's drummer, replied the Major-General,

looking pleased. He made fierce clubbing motions with the swagger stick.

Patrick looked a question at Carrick.

Cain, said the clergyman, shaking his head indulgently.

Byatt arrived a few minutes later, wearing a skull-cap and a straggly beard. The rest of him was wrapped in something that looked like a stylized dressing gown. The cigarette holder clenched between his teeth had never been more conspicuous. Picking up a glass of punch, he made his way towards Carrick.

Mother and child haven't arrived yet, he said.

It's early, said Carrick. You've done a wonderful job with the manger.

Byatt nodded. What d'you think of my costume? he asked, smoothing a hand over his dressing gown complacently.

Carrick looked at him doubtfully. Fagin? he offered.

Byatt laughed. I had planned to come as Jesus . . . only it is such a responsibility. Besides, with the manger next door, a grown-up Jesus didn't seem to fit. So I dug out the Shylock costume from last year's trunks and decided to be Judas instead.

Carrick looked reproving. You might have spared a thought for Mr Jacob's feelings.

I hadn't even thought of it like that, Reverend, said Byatt, sounding injured. Is it my fault that the apostles were Jewish?

Just then the pianist struck up a waltz in quick tempo and set couples whirling and bobbing on the huge dance floor. Byatt, I noticed, had claimed Elinor Armitage, while her husband gallantly led out the senior-most Eve. As the dance ran its course it became obvious that the numbers at this Christmas party didn't match: women outnumbered men two to one. By the time the third waltz wound down, this lopsidedness had become an embarrassment: there were more wallflowers than waltzers. Women, pretty, desirable women, were standing at the edges of the enchanted space churned up by the dancers, sipping their drinks or talking to other desirable women, and doing their best to seem unconcerned.

It was a sign of the times; in a normal year most of them would have left with their menfolk for the plains, but the rebellion last August, followed by the famine and the rumours of epidemic disease (that had sent Ammi scurrying upwards) had kept them from going down. So here they were – mothers, daughters, sisters, débutantes, wives – hovering like ghosts at the margins of the gayest whirl that Simla-out-of-Season had ever seen.

The Major-General took charge. For all wartime scarcities, there was one prescribed procedure: rationing. A word here, a look there and the pattern on the parquetry changed – each time the music started up, the men led out the ladies who had languished on the margins the dance before. He nobly set an example by partnering in quick succession the five ugliest women in the room.

By a little past nine, the dancing was in full swing. In general the women had drunk more than the men; under the Major-General's dispensation, they had to sit out every other dance, and they filled these intervals with punch. Some of the younger women, flush with drink and unwilling to wait their turn, had begun dancing with each other. The Reverend, who wasn't dancing, smiled indulgently at this spirited show of self-help; some others, including the Major-General, looked startled and uneasy but it was yuletide and there was innocence in the air – or there was meant to be – so giggling couples twirled about unchecked.

Byatt and Elinor Armitage had both disappeared for nearly fifteen minutes. They had left separately and they returned a couple of minutes apart. They stood in front of different fireplaces for a long time after returning, but I was certain that they had been trysting in a colder place. Her husband, though, didn't appear to notice anything, not even when Byatt led Elinor into a waltz and held her much too close. There were one or two women in that gathering whom I would have liked to hold like that . . . in fact except for the harridans that the general had picked for his duty dances, I would have given the gooseflesh off my back to hold any one of the women there in the legal lust-grip of a touching dance. But no one was about to ask Indian waiters to make up the numbers, so I wrestled with the tented-out front of my trousers till I was decent and wondered when this bunched-up ache would go away.

286

It took me ten minutes of rhythmic breathing to bring matters under control and I was about to resume my waiter's duties by fetching the table-cloth from the airing room (the buffet was scheduled for ten), when Delia Mulholland made an entrance. It was nicely timed to coincide with a lull in the dancing, so she had everyone's attention; then she let her coat drop and suddenly the air in the ballroom became thin as the assembled men sucked in their breaths.

My first impression was of white cloth and bare skin, of something pleated like a sari but worn without a blouse . . . or even a petticoat. Then I placed the costume; it was the fancy dress that Greek actresses wore for the torch-kindling ritual that inaugurated every Olympiad. She wasn't actually showing much – just arms and neck and collar bones and the pleats in front were quite obscuring – but she still managed to suggest a wanton Attic matron come to couple in an olive grove.

There was a rush to claim her and she was partnered for three dances in a row – but then wartime discipline won out and Delia found that she had to sit out every other dance like the rest. Some of the younger girls, like Esther Waters, had edged their beaux off the dance floor into screened-off nooks created by the wallpapered columns that bordered the ballroom. I saw Delia look longingly after them but she couldn't follow suit, not having a man of her own. As I watched, she filled and emptied her glass several times. Carrick, who had left the ballroom for a time, returned, and both Patrick and I asked him to identify the Biblical character Delia was impersonating in her toga outfit. Carrick looked her up and down professionally and made a few considering sounds, but all he came up with was Old Testament, of course, at which Patrick snorted contemptuously.

Why don't you ask her? he urged the Reverend.

All right, said Carrick tranquilly, and set off towards the window by which Delia had struck an attitude.

He returned blushing.

What did she say? asked Patrick beseechingly.

Carrick composed himself by swallowing a glass of punch. Then he wiped his face and began to chuckle.

Well go on, urged Patrick.

I asked her who she was meant to be, said Carrick. She said she wouldn't tell but she could show me where to look.

And? prompted Patrick.

She said the name was written in scarlet under her dress and over her heart!

Patrick gasped. I changed my mind about walking the breadth of the ballroom to retrieve the table-cloth. Instead I sat down slowly and crossed my legs again.

A little while later – it was coming on to dinnertime – I finally set off for the airing room. The toast-like warmth inside it had done the job – the table-cloth was perfectly dry. Making sure that I didn't kick up any dust, I folded it up and carried it out of the room draped over both arms like a medal cushion at an investiture. I used my bottom to push open the door and swivelled neatly, keeping the edges of the table-cloth clear of the potentially dusty door frame. Having completed the manoeuvre I allowed myself to look up . . . and saw Delia's face within kissing distance of my own.

I must have startled her, emerging like that out of the woodwork, because she involuntarily began to explain that she had come to take a look at the manger. But then she noticed my waiter's uniform and broke off – she didn't have to explain herself to a menial.

What's in there? she demanded peremptorily.

Still holding the door open with my bottom, I backed up further to let her look inside. Hitching up the hem of her toga, she walked in and inspected the room with great interest as if it was a mysterious, secret place and not just a stuffy, overheated hole, furnished with pipes, dust and mothballed carpets. Then she turned round, her eyes sparkling with inexplicable excitement, and headed towards the ballroom.

I followed more slowly, wondering when this evening would end and whether more punch would make it go faster. The crowd in the ballroom had been swelled by two wise men from the East whom I identified without any help from the Reverend, because they were wearing turbans and coloured skins. Besides, one of them was helpfully jingling a velvet purse to announce his gift of gold and the other had joss-sticks

288

smoking in the crown of his turban. I felt vaguely cheated that there wasn't a full complement of three – from my first Bible class at St Xavier's I had wondered about myrrh.

I didn't recognize them immediately because they had stained their skins till they were a deep shade of chocolate; I just assumed that they were painted whites. Then I saw the incense-bearing one comb his fingers through a Nebuchadnezzar beard in a gesture that I remembered from a speech in a mosque between railway tracks – and realized that this wise man wasn't a tinted white but a brown dyed darker. It was Masroor.

My innards clenched in a spasm of jealousy. What was he doing at the ball? I knew that he couldn't afford the fifty-rupee ticket. The answer lay in the identity of the second wise man, who, like Masroor, was authentically of the East: Cyrus Dastoor. It must have been his doing.

It was. Masroor swaggered up and made me ladle out a drink for him before he dropped the act and explained. Mr Jacob, he said, decided he was sick and gave Cyrus his ticket, who gave it to me. I had to see Parwana and the babies, he said earnestly.

Seeing the alarm on my face, he held up a palm in reassurance. I'm not going to talk to her; I'll just stand in a corner and look.

But she might see you, I objected.

Masroor shook his head. She won't remember my face, he said sadly. Even if she does, the turban and this varnish will hide me.

The music started up again and couples re-formed. Masroor and Cyrus drifted towards the dance floor, drawn by the excitement but uncertain of their reception – they were the only two Indians in the ballroom, not counting the waiters. Broodingly I watched them walk away. Each chore would be more oppressive, every minute longer now that I knew there were Indians in the room, enjoying themselves. As guests! Also, I could see that dinner was likely to be indefinitely postponed – no one showed any sign of quitting the dance floor.

Nothing happened for the first couple of dances. Cyrus

289

exchanged nods with Byatt and a few others he had known during his brief Gaiety phase. Masroor knew nobody, so he filled up the time with cigarettes, looking bizarrely pious as wisps of incense and streams of tobacco smoke haloed his head. No one asked him to dance – this could have been on account of prejudice; on the other hand, men were meant to do the asking. He stood there, watching the dancers, while drinking steadily and occasionally talking to Cyrus, and this was what he was doing when Delia captured him.

Which wasn't surprising. I had seen her watching him for a while and he was young, good-looking, and clearly unattached. She had been partial to him at Mowbray's too – I remembered Masroor complaining that she made him nervous when he showed her round the shelves. So I wasn't surprised when she manoeuvred him into a dance – just consumed by envy and the unfairness of it all.

He didn't know how to dance, so she taught him, holding him man-fashion at the waist, so she could lead. People looked but she ignored them, holding him close while dancing, hanging on his arm when they weren't. Twice they disappeared into one of the dark places into which Delia had watched other couples vanish earlier in the evening. Both times Masroor emerged looking mussed, flushed and a little hunted. For a moment I had the impression that he wanted to get away from her. It must have been a trick of the light: here he was being stalked by a steamy older woman – which ranked up there with being tongued by a naked lady vampire – why should he look oppressed?

Sighing, I turned away from them and concentrated on re-laying the table now that the cloth had been spread. There was so much to be grateful for, I told myself: it was hard having Masroor at the party, but how much worse it would have been if the Reverend had decided to invite Ammi or Asharfi or both.

Mulling over this as I set the table, I didn't immediately realize that Carrick was at my elbow, talking to me.

. . . a lemonade or something, mind you don't take her something alcoholic. Her mother will have my head. She only agreed to let her come because I promised that Sister

Magdalena or I would chaperone her every second of the time that she was here. And that too only for an hour after the dancing was over. He paused to look helplessly at the teeming dance floor. Well, it was meant to be over by now, he said defensively and half to himself. So mind you take good care of her and don't give her the punch or the wine by mistake. He mopped his face with a kerchief. It was hard work getting her here but I thought there should at least be one of them. After all, most of the peasants dying there, he said vaguely, are Muslim.

My head jerked up. It couldn't be. But there she was, sitting by the central fireplace, next to a nun, wide-eyed and lovely in a satin gharara the colour of peaches.

Asharfi.

Without thinking, I turned away to keep her from spotting me, and slipped out of the room. Suddenly the ball was a nightmare – with Parwana due in the manger, Asharfi and Masroor in the ballroom and all of them under one roof, the worst seemed possible: revelations, anguish, squalor. All I wanted at that moment was to be offstage when the curtain went up on this farce about a brother, a sister and the woman they loved.

Behind me, I heard footsteps echoing my own. Looking over my shoulder, I glimpsed Masroor sidling out of the ballroom – he was taking evasive action too. I didn't stop to compare notes with him: the last thing I wanted was company. Peace was a place without people where nothing happened. In the dark, windowless warmth of the airing room, I found it.

Time stopped. Light years later, footsteps pattered past the door and seemed to stop next door, near the manger. Seconds, ice ages afterwards, other? lighter? footsteps took the same route. Then, nothing. The noble silence of a geological epoch before life filled the room. Fishless oceans gurgled in the boiler pipes as continents drifted. Etna rumbled in my stomach. Were they ready for dinner now?

Patrick would be looking for me but I didn't want to return to sociable noise just yet. I would rest a while longer and when

I was ready to go back, I would switch the light on and let the here-and-now become visible again. I shut my eyes . . . it had been a long three days.

I woke to a medley of sounds: mewing, kissing sounds, a man's voice saying no, then repeating itself, a woman screaming for a coolie, a scuffle at the door . . . the door? The door to the airing room was more than half open. Silhouetted in the feeble radiance of the dimly lit gallery was a woman, her shoulders shaking. Wide awake but completely disoriented, I held my breath and tried to think. Had I slept through the party and were they looking for me . . . but she had called for a coolie, not a waiter. She was sobbing slightly, the silhouette woman, but in between difficult breaths she would say coolie! or bumboy! in a raging way.

I still hadn't got my bearings when she stepped inside and shut the door behind her, making the room pitch-black again. I heard her rustle as she leaned against the door and tried for control by breathing long shuddering breaths. Bastard, she hissed breathlessly. Eunuch! she shouted into the darkness. Cautiously I began breathing again. She wasn't looking for me.

I had placed the silhouette now: it was Delia. She had probably chased Masroor when he fled the ballroom, hoping to cuddle up with him. She must have found him in the manger mooning at Parwana. I remembered the gleam in her eye earlier in the evening when she first discovered the airing room. Had she stored it away in her mind as a cosy rendezvous? She had nearly got Masroor into it; perhaps the promise of Delia's Greek tunic had tempted him to the door, where true love triumphed and he found the will to flee? Perhaps. Anyway, here she was, draped against the door, weeping with rage, definitely a woman scorned.

For a while I sat perfectly still, breathing shallow, silent breaths, waiting for her to leave. Minutes passed with no change in the location of her ragged panting. I strained my ears to catch any shifting sounds which might indicate that she was planning to leave, but nothing happened. It was hard to measure the passage of time in a silent, pitch-black room: no clock went tick-tock, no shadows lengthened. I began counting her exhalations and got to one hundred and forty-four before panicking. Patrick would be frantic by now, what with the work of tending the buffet, then clearing things away.

According to the timetable Carrick had set out, half an hour was set aside for after-dinner drinks, then at eleven everyone would move to the manger for the carol singing. I had to get out . . . most pressingly because I needed to piss. All that punch I had drunk had seeped into my bladder and given me a late-night version of an early-morning condition: an erection. This had nothing to do with lust; it was simply a symptom of the urine dammed-up inside.

Then I heard her move and tensed, waiting for the light she would let in when she opened the door. The moving sounds continued but nothing relieved the perfect darkness. I listened harder – they sounded like palms sliding along a wall; she was looking for the light switch, not the exit. Which meant that she wasn't blocking the door! I quickly got to my feet and crept towards the door, arms held out and cautiously groping, like insect antennae. Luckily, I found the door handle at first grope and slipped outside, closing the door behind me.

I peeped into the manger to check if the carolling had begun and came away relieved. It hadn't; it was earlier than I had thought. Parwana and the baby were in place and fast asleep, warmed by a fire and tucked into an appropriately coarse blanket. The electric light had been switched off, leaving the room to tremble in the wavering light of the fire, like a nativity scene on a calendar stirring into life.

My bladder twinged a reminder and I started back along the gallery, headed for the lavatories. I had barely passed the airing room door on my right when I spotted a peach-pink gharara and a black cassock billow out of the ballroom at the far end. Asharfi and Carrick were headed my way – the meddling old fool was going to show her the manger.

Breaking stride, my feet side-stepped through the airing-room door into the refuge of darkness. Delia hadn't found the light switch yet. But the sound of the door thudding shut behind me stopped her shuffling. I heard her clothes rustle as she turned in the direction of the sound. Then footsteps, and suddenly I was pressed up against the door by another body. Two strong hands wrestled my head about while an invisible mouth buried in my neck husked indistinctly: you're back you're back you're back!

Even at that moment – with hot surges testing the limits to growth – I didn't let myself believe that she wanted me for my own sake. She probably thought that Masroor had changed his mind and returned to her. Mistaken identity. Then she stuck her tongue into my ear and I stopped thinking about false pretences. I was innocent: I hadn't tried to impersonate Masroor; he was inches taller and inches thinner. He was also wearing a beard and burning incense sticks in his turban. She ought to have been able to tell the difference. Unless she didn't want to. Which was possible; she was, after all, a woman who read Maugham, who knew that adultery was inevitable in the tropics, especially in a hot, black, faceless room, proofed against time, guilt and consequences by the embalming dark.

She removed her tongue from my ear and pushed it into my mouth, all the while pushing me down to the floor till she was sitting astride my hips. I forgot about peeing or breathing – the only feeling left in my body was a sense of squeezed excitement.

Driven fingers popped my fly buttons, tugged my underpants loose and reached inside. Her hand could have gone round twice with room to spare, so when she said, my Samson, in a breathy voice, I didn't believe her. I was blind in the dark and helpless with excitement: those bits fitted; did that mean that she was dressed as Delilah? It struck me that I was lying on my back, letting her do all the work. I didn't want her to think that I knew nothing about foreplay or that it was my first time, even if it was, so I aimed my hand under the hem of her gown and up her legs. My fingers met her underpants earlier than I had expected – I realized that she was wearing long drawers made of some slippery, satiny stuff. That was as far as I got before she slapped my hand away and tightened her fist threateningly, saying no several times as if she meant it. So I stopped. She pulled the drawers off herself. I couldn't see her do it but I could tell because suddenly she wasn't sitting on my thighs any more and there were sounds –

the tock of her shoes as she changed feet to step out of her underwear, the hiss of cloth slinking down its slidepath.

All the while I lay utterly still, willing myself not to flag. The thought of being half-masted when her palm returned had made my mouth go dry. I had been let down once, a long time ago, so now I thought of it in the third person and respected its autonomy. Luckily this time the stiffness was shored up with piss so when Delia settled her buttocks on my thighs again, she didn't have to go searching. I switched to breathing through my mouth as she leaned forward and grounded her knees on either side of me. Then, very slowly, with the caution natural to a person about to stab herself with a blunt instrument, she eased herself into a squat. It was effortless; at least the first inch was. I was neatly capped with warmth and I hadn't moved a thing. Then she stopped and for a while we stayed like that, fitted but unjoined. I stopped breathing; that is, I held my breath and waited for her to push down all the way. I could hear my heart beat strongly in my air-locked chest: dhup, dhup, dhup . . . proud visions streaked through my head and lit up the darkness: my manhood wearing a white woman on its head like a hat; my root holding up a Christmas tree.

Then she moved and the inches-thick silence was shredded with screams. Suddenly I was the one in a squat, cradling the ruins of my excitement. Through the rawness and the shouts of pain, my head echoed with a single question: if she's the one being stabbed, why am I screaming? Faintly, in some corner of my mind I could hear Delia curse and rustle but I didn't stop to listen. Pulling my trousers up I half-crawled to the door and stumbled out, looking for a private place where I could examine myself in peace. It felt like I had been skinned with a paper knife.

The lavatory was empty. I limped into one of the stand-up urinals and let my trousers drop. Moaning in anticipation, I gingerly checked the damage. Expecting to find my inelastic foreskin shredded, I found it in one piece. There was a bruise, though, a circular discoloration which ringed the top like a half-hearted black-eye.

Unluckily Patrick burst into the lavatory just at that moment and found me with my hands full.

Holy Jesus, he said in a trembling voice, averting his eyes. Didn't your bleeding mother ever tell you that it makes you blind? He paused and took a deep breath. You have one minute to get to the ballroom and start serving drinks, you frigging heathen. He turned on his heel and headed for the door. He was almost through it when he froze in mid-stride and spun around. First wash your frigging hands!

A bunch of bluff-looking older men were singing Auld Lang Syne with desperate, drunken feeling when I returned to resume my duties. Their women looked on, smiling coyly, supportive but too genteel to join in. There was no sign of Asharfi, so she was still closeted in the manger with Parwana. I didn't panic because Masroor wasn't with them; he was in plain sight in the ballroom, moodily nursing his coffee by a fireplace. He would visit the manger sooner or later since the Nativity tableau was meant to be the crowning highlight of the ball, and the carol singing was due to begin in fifteen minutes, but so long as he went with the others at the appointed time and not earlier or by himself, there was a sporting chance that Asharfi and he would be kept apart by the crowd.

From the corner of my eye, I saw Delia, dishevelled but decent, walk in. Instinctively I ducked my head and stared at the floor, and prayed for the parquetry to part and swallow me up. I sneaked a glance at her – she wasn't looking at me. Which wasn't surprising; she didn't know that it had been me with her in that blacked-out room. But I did . . . I could feel a hot blotch of shame discolour my face and ears like a virulent birthmark. I put the tray down and fled to the pantry, where I washed my face over and over again till it seemed the right colour. When I returned to the ballroom, Masroor was gone.

Everyone else was in place – Delia, the Reverend, the rest . . . only Asharfi and Masroor were missing. Even as my feet began hurrying me towards the door, I noticed, detachedly, Patrick bearing down on me from the other side. He looked as though he might bite. Ignoring him, I passed through the door, gathering speed, turning in my mind a puny, runtish plan of heading Masroor off in the gallery. The plan was still-born – the gallery was empty. I slowed to a walk; there didn't seem much need to hurry now. Unless I was wrong and Masroor had only stepped out for a piss, the siblings had been reunited in the manger. The worst had already happened. I wondered what they were saying to each other.

They were saying nothing; the manger was silent and in the fire-lit gloom it took my eyes a second to place them. Masroor was standing in roughly the middle of the room, a few feet from the Byatt-inspired bed of straw, his knuckles in his mouth, looking wrecked. Parwana was half-lying on the straw, propped up on her elbows, pale and frozen; crouched by her side, arm around her neck, face turned towards Masroor, stark with shock and guilt, was Asharfi. It looked unnatural – like actors posed for a publicity still. But it was real enough. I thought I had imagined the worst but nothing could be as bad as this; some clinical recess in my brain noted that both girls had their clothes on but that didn't mean much. The whole scene had a caught-in-the-act feel to it; rewound a few feet the frame would have shown them kissing. The room stayed still for a count of five – then the calf mooed and set the baby crying.

I discovered that I had been holding my breath and exhaled. In the distance I could hear the cheerful sounds of massed festivity – the carol singers were coming. They were coming down the gallery, singing Noel, serenading the infant who had saved their world.

I had just lost mine.

Again.

A Part of Myself

I SPENT THE NEXT nineteen months in Simla, learning at first hand the business of being alone. Towards the end of this year-and-a-half, when solitude became loneliness, I wondered how much of the story of that Christmas Eve had filtered back to Ammi and my grandmother. Their families left Simla inside a week of the ball. Dadi, Parwana and the Judge left the next evening; Masroor followed three days later, looking clenched and grim, curtly refusing my offer to see him off at the station. A waiter from the Cecil who happened to be at the platform that evening reported that Ammi and Asharfi had left by the same train, but he wasn't sure if they had been travelling with Masroor.

I didn't brood over their leaving. At the time, it was a relief not to have to fret about other people. For seven days between Christmas Eve and the New Year, the only things I thought about were the pain in my crotch and the unfinished business with Delia.

I spent hours in the lavatory working my foreskin up and down. It was useless – foreskins, unlike elastic knickers, don't go slack with use. My fantasies turned resentfully patriotic. One afternoon, during a restless nap, I dreamt of Delia wrapped in a Union Jack and hoist on me . . .

Then one morning it was 1944. New Year's Day. The world from my window was a square in black-and-white – everything that wasn't white with snow was black in contrast. The green of the leaves, the blue of the sky, the red of the pitched roofs on the valley's slopes were all frosted over; black trunks, dark clouds and grim, grey walls shaded the white into knowable shapes. The window's panes were double-glazed with ice, the water in my toilet bowl had frozen over and still I felt my spirits lift . . . because the world outside looked recent and unused like an unfilled outline in a colouring book.

My head was suddenly filled with clean slates and fresh starts. It seemed unthinkable that the years ahead should be haunted by an inflexible foreskin. Not just on account of sex; even romantic love in its most ethereal form was premised on the possibility of efficient junction. Shivering, I pushed both hands into my trouser pockets and found the tip of my foreskin through layers of cloth. I tweaked it cautiously. It didn't hurt. I had my New Year's resolution.

It was one in the morning and no longer New Year's Day when the train steamed into Kalka station. Snow on the narrow-gauge rail track had slowed it to a crawl. I managed to get a bed for the night in the Second Class Retiring Room. It was a long dormitory, furnished with ten beds, ten bedside tables and a fireplace. There wasn't a fire, but we were given two extra blankets over the regulation three to keep the cold out. The bedclothes smelt of coal and restlessness.

Sleep was fitful – I drifted in and out of shallow nightmares and napped in between them. The cold woke me up at four, my bladder hurting with the need to piss. I crawled out of the blankets, which were about as warm as sheets of tepid ice, wrapped a muffler round my ears, pulled on shoes and a long-sleeved sweater and then trekked fifty yards down the platform to the lavatories.

Bellied up to a tall white urinal called Shanks, I began to spray like a garden sprinkler, and had to skip about to keep my pajamas dry. Some pulling and tugging forged a single stream, and afterwards, I sat for a while on a bench overlooking the silent rail line. After tomorrow, this at least, wouldn't happen again. I had looked it up under 'C' in the Cecil's *Britannica*. Once it was done, the residual inflammation of the pissing slit would disappear and I would ever after produce a tight, clean jet. My teeth began to chatter in the cold but I stayed put on the bench till all the good reasons for going through with it had been itemized. Sex would be easier. Easier was the wrong word, actually – sex would be possible. I would be a whole man. It was an odd way of becoming whole but sometimes less was more.

299

I got to my feet and walked up to the edge of the platform from where I could see the just-visible glint of the track as it arrowed southwards to Delhi, leaving the frozen poise of Simla behind, for the changeable madness below. There, presumably, real life was being lived and history made. Some day, I would ride the Kalka Mail over these double lines, down to that definitive plain. But not yet. Right now I had more urgent things to do. Nothing earthshaking, nothing that would change by a hairsbreadth the future that real men were making in the flatlands; just a small personal alteration that would help me handle life in the 'forties, where I was tired of being the impotent spectator. The next time Delia (or Destiny) reached for my crotch, I'd spit her like a seekh kabab. On that surging thought, I went to my icy bed and slept dreamlessly. Outside, the sun climbed over wintry cloud to shine upon my circumcision.

On the morning of the second day of January 1944, I brushed my teeth, washed the gum from my eyes and went looking for a hajjam in Kalka. I could have found one in Simla but I didn't want gossip. Kalka was the logical alternative – far enough to be safe and less than a day away by rail. But that morning Kalka town looked too small to support a tea-shop, leave alone a barber-surgeon. Memory had misled me; the bloated little township of the 'eighties simply didn't exist. The Kalka I found was no more than a landing on a staircase – a halt on the way to higher places.

I exhausted its possibilities in under an hour and the only barbershop I saw was set up under a tree, which didn't seem private enough. I was about to give up and return to the railway station when I remembered that besides Simla, Kalka was also on the way to Kasauli, a small hill station less than two hours away. I had been there on assignment once, to take pictures of the Kasauli Club, which was notable only for having stayed unbendingly colonial in republican India. It was a military hill station, I remembered, more or less run by the army, and there was a residential public school near by. Soldiers and schoolboys needed regular haircuts. There was bound to be a good supply of barbers there. Perhaps one of them . . . ? When a friendly soldier on a khaki motorcycle gave me a lift all the way in his vacant sidecar, Kasauli began to seem pre-ordained. Barbers and sidecars had played a part in my life before.

By the time we reached Kasauli, the wind whipping past us had frozen me into numbness, so I found a tea-shop to thaw out in. Nursing my tea on a low wooden bench, I looked around to get my bearings. Kasauli was exactly as I remembered it. The road we had ridden up passed through a military check-post and ended in a large asphalted square which had shops on two sides and garages for lorries on the third. The square was the lowest part of Kasauli; the hill station rose steeply off its sides. I didn't try to look for a barber there, the shops were much too smart – more likely to deal in riding crops than haircuts.

I finished the tea and headed for Kasauli's Lower Bazaar, where the sahibs didn't shop but their servants did. The market was strung alongside a narrow, sloping road, surfaced with stones too irregular and worn to qualify as cobbles. I passed men milling flour, selling tops, weighing vegetables and talking briskly. I stopped a moment to stand in the warmth rushing out of a bakery where a man was sliding cake tins out of a room-sized oven. He sold me a selection of biscuits from a row of clouded glass jars, and I ate them on the move in place of breakfast and lunch. The shops had begun to peter out when I suddenly found a barber – not one, but three. Three shops in a row on the left of the lane, with mirrors, scissors and high wooden chairs, and signboards saying 'Saloon'.

I walked into the first one – Modern Hairdressing Saloon – and the barber sat me in a chair. My plan was to ask (at some point during the haircut) if he would do the other thing as well. Only I didn't get round to it after spotting a calendar picture of Shiva wedged into the top right corner of the mirror in front of me. A Hindu barber wasn't likely to be doing circumcisions on the side. It was too late to stop, though – he was already at work, scissors going kit-kit-kit, so I saved what I could by asking him only to trim.

I felt silly walking into the Military Hairdressing Saloon with talcum and stubble still on my neck but there wasn't a choice. In the interest of credibility, I commissioned a crewcut. Keeping to the plan, I put the further question to him halfway through, when he was spraying the left half of my head with the water pump. Not knowing the Urdu noun for circumcision, I tried to describe what I wanted him to do by using variations on the verb 'to cut'. He kept looking uncertain, so I pointed between the legs and made slicing motions. He tried to stab me with the scissors. It was a misunderstanding. Instead of pointing at my crotch to illustrate my meaning, I had in my nervousness, pointed at his.

I pacified him with money and apologies but he refused to complete the job, so I left his saloon with hair half mown and half overgrown into wild wet peaks, in a style ahead of my times. That is how I looked when, driven by a mechanical determination, I crossed the threshold of the Majestic Hairdressing Saloon and met its proprietor, Mian Fakhruddin Madar.

The name didn't fit because he looked like a wrinkled Nepali and I knew that Nepal was a Hindu kingdom. Then I saw the skull-cap and the wisps of beard. A little thread of hope unwound within me. Timidly, I asked if he would take off what was left of my hair. He nodded placidly. When he was hard at work with the miniature lawn-mower-type gadget that barbers use for backs and sides, I asked the second question and braced myself.

He shut the shop and took me home.

In a manner of speaking. He did take me home, but not the moment I asked him to circumcise me. First I saw his eyes widen and the clipper drop from his hand. Then he came round the chair so that he could look directly at my face instead of its reflection. Satisfied that I was serious, he raised his eyes and palms to the ceiling. Ya Allah, he breathed. I had seen it done before in the movies, but this was genuine thanksgiving, untouched by affectation. I didn't know why he was so deeply moved – even if he was a proper hajjam, one more foreskin hardly justified such heartfelt piety.

When he looked my way again, his face was split by a huge smile. Encouraged, I asked my question again. Beaming, he

302

reached out and caught my hand. He shook his head wonderingly:

There have been rumours for two years now but they were . . . just bazaar talk. But if you have come to me, they must be true. Jinnah Bhai's men were right – these hills will go to Pakistan!

And *then* he shut his shop and took me home.

It was a twenty-minute walk to where he lived, mostly uphill, and being too breathless to talk, I had time to puzzle over his reaction. The part about the hills going to Pakistan was easy – Jinnah and the Muslim League had, almost till the end, claimed the whole of the Punjab for Pakistan, and Kasauli, Kalka, Simla and the adjacent hills were all part of the undivided province. So it wasn't surprising that Mian Fakhruddin had heard talk about Kasauli going to Pakistan if the country was partitioned. But why did he think that my need to be circumcised made these rumours true? Why did the future of the Punjab hills hinge upon my foreskin?

We passed the Kasauli Club as we laboured up the twisting road. It was as I remembered it: pink roofs, green fence and trained climbing roses. Ahead, the road turned sharply round a spur and straightened out. Mian Fakhruddin stopped in front of the first house on the straight stretch. The oval wooden plaque on the gate said 'Pencarrow'. I followed him through the gate nervously; it didn't look like a barber's house.

It wasn't. Fakhruddin lived in one of its outhouses. To reach it we skirted the side of the house, crossed the back garden and went down a flight of cement steps cut into the hillside. The outbuildings were nearly fifty feet lower than the main house, but the view was still spectacular. Kasauli was built on the last range of the Himalayan foothills, so from where we stood, the hills rippled into the plains like a dying turbulence. The nightscape, I remembered, was even lovelier, with Chandigarh strung out in ropes of light – distance and darkness lent enchantment to even Corbusier's nightmare. There would be no lights tonight; Corbusier hadn't been commissioned yet to dream them up.

303

We entered a large, nearly empty room, which was warmer than it had any right to be in the middle of a hill winter. Then I noticed a banked bucket choolha smouldering in a corner. I sat on the only cot in the room and Mian Fakhruddin settled down on the neighbouring trunk. He smiled a welcome and gave me the use of his home with a courtly little wave of the hand.

I tried to smile back but the corners of my mouth wouldn't lift. Then my hands began shaking. I tucked them into my armpits and pretended to be cold. Suddenly I couldn't believe that I was sharing a room on this hilltop with a stranger, who, in a while, would flay the skin off my penis because I had asked him to. A stranger who had never worn a white coat or seen the inside of a hospital, who was going to take a knife to me without knocking me out and without a nurse in sight. Involuntarily my mouth opened and I heard myself laugh: a shrill, fluctuating sound, like a mynah being strangled.

My host watched in silence till this spasm passed, then he got to his feet and visited the corner of the room where the choolha was burning. He returned with a hookah, its bowl already glowing with embers borrowed from the choolha. He pulled at the mouthpiece a few times and made it bubble, then, still without a word, offered it to me. I took it eagerly, to give my hands and mouth something to do. I sucked cautiously and the cool smoke filled and soothed my insides like a balm. He didn't ask for it back, so I kept practising, inhaling smoke and exhaling languor. He let me fall into a gentle rhythm, then pulled his feet up and, perched cross-legged upon the trunk, told me his story.

He hadn't always had a barbershop or sold his skills to buy a livelihood. Once, he said sadly, he had led a simpler, truer life, where he had served and had been served in turn. He had been the hajjam of a community of bangle-makers in the western hills of Nepal. But – it was the old story – the market died when the glass bangles from across the border in Banaras swamped the bazaars – and gradually, so did the community. The men left in search of jobs, Mian Fakhruddin among them.

After months on the move, he found work with a Judge in Delhi. Not my grandfather; this one was a Punjabi, though he ate, dressed and spoke like a sahib and wiped his bum with paper. Mian Fakhruddin grimaced with remembered distaste. He was so pukka that he had the taps removed from his lavatories.

Mian Fakhruddin worked as the Judge's manservant by day and guarded the house at night. He was given a uniform because his master thought all Nepalese were potentially Gurkhas. He also assumed they were all called Man Bahadur, which annoyed Mian Fakhruddin, who was proud of his name. When the Judge retired, he couldn't take the boat home (being Indian he was home already), so he did the next best thing – he bought a house in the hills and named it Pencarrow. He took Fakhruddin along to his retirement home and had the outhouse built for him to live in. That was eight winters ago. The Judge had been dead three years now and his wife spent most of the year in Lahore with her son. Fakhruddin had been retained as caretaker and he had enough time on his hands to run the Majestic Hairdressing Saloon. He was using razors and scissors for a livelihood again – but this time round as a barber, not as a hajjam. There was no demand for his specialist skills in Kasauli; I was his first client in ten years.

He told me a great deal more, most of which I've forgotten, including a story about the time he saw his memsahib's half-English half-sister lying naked on the keyboard of the piano in the drawing room. There was a point to this story which slipped my mind as the smoke from the hookah gathered in my head like a swirling fog.

He never told me what he had burnt in that hookah's bowl or just how long it made me sleep, but it was dark outside when I came awake and I had been circumcised. I was lying spread-eagled on the cot with my hands and feet roped to its legs. My crotch hurt terribly but I couldn't see it because I was covered up to my chest with a quilt. I couldn't touch it either. I screamed.

Mian Fakhruddin materialized at once like a genie. Without a word, he untied the ropes, helped me sit up and arranged the quilt around my shoulders. I peeked underneath it. It was all there – or nearly. What had he done with the foreskin, I wondered.

It's buried in the rose bed outside, said Fakhruddin, without my asking. Where I come from, he said authoritatively, it's always buried.

He wouldn't let me pay . . . not even for his hospitality over the next four days. Coming down from Simla, I had, in my innocence, planned to return the same day by the night train. But when the muffling effect of the opiate wore off, the clean, sharp pain between my legs had me doubled up. If it wasn't for the fact that I could see it in the usual place, looking like a lewdly sugared confection (he had dusted it with boric powder), I might have panicked and gone looking in the rose beds. It hurt so much it felt like he had lopped the whole thing off. I wasn't going anywhere for a while.

It wouldn't be as painful if you were five years old, said Fakhruddin helpfully. The healing would be quicker too. But you're older and bigger and there's more of you to heal.

This was true, so I tried not to think of what Patrick would have to say about this unsanctioned holiday and gave myself up to time, that great healer.

Fakhruddin's style as host was that of next-of-kin. He lent me his lungis, which I wore loosely wrapped round my waist like a towel. They wouldn't, he explained, chafe my skinned knob as much as trousers or even pajamas might have done. He wouldn't let me go out for a walk and even cautioned me about moving around the room too much. So I spent most of those four days lying or sitting on the cot, while Mian Fakhruddin served up meals, distracted me with chess and, four mornings running, shaved my face. And since, despite the circumcision, we were strangers, I was overwhelmed.

But he wouldn't let me pay. I had given him a chance to practise his vocation, to confirm his skill – that was payment enough. He even apologized for drugging me. It wasn't something that he usually did; with children he just needed an assistant to hold them still while he distracted them with stories. There was a foolproof method: a pinch of foreskin pulled over the tip of the prepuce, a diversionary exclamation about a golden bird flying overhead and as the head jerked up, a single downward stroke . . . Boys were stupid; they believed anything. It was different with men, who were realists.

By the fourth day, the raw and tender feeling had faded into soreness – I didn't flinch each time the unprotected head touched cloth. It was time to leave. Mian Fakhruddin made one last examination and judged that it was healing well. Gingerly, I pulled my trousers on and drank a final cup of tea with him. We climbed the steps to the back of the main house where I paused by the flowerbeds for one last look at the loveliness of Chandigarh unbuilt.

He walked me down to Kasauli's main square and found me a lift in a lorry which twice weekly brought fresh vegetables up and ferried passengers down. The makeshift benches filled quickly and the driver honked the imminence of departure. Mian Fakhruddin embraced me ceremoniously – the head over one shoulder, then the next and back again. I climbed into the lorry and took my place, thighs carefully splayed. We started moving. I waved. My host raised his hand in benediction and farewell.

Send the others down, he called, just before we rolled out of earshot. I didn't know what he meant then, and I was too busy forcing down the lump in my throat to puzzle it out. I blinked hard and snorted into a handkerchief. Goodbyes were always a wrench but this one was special. I was leaving a part of myself behind.

The wound took another ten days to heal completely. The morning I returned to the snugness of underwear, the meaning of Mian Fakhruddin's parting words became clear to me.

Send the others down.

He'd said something earlier in the barbershop: that I was proof the Punjab hills would go to Pakistan. It had puzzled me then, but now I understood. Mian Fakhruddin had just put two and two together. Why would an adult kafir like me want to lose his foreskin? Obviously because I knew in some privileged, confidential way that the hills of East Punjab had been earmarked for Pakistan.

I felt vaguely humiliated. Did Mian Fakhruddin think I was

307

a weathercock Muslim currying favour with the Muslim state in the making? He obviously did. He also thought that I was a sign of things to come. That kind, pious man had visions of hundreds, perhaps thousands, of unbelievers in these hills, hiking down the trail I'd blazed, to make their peace with Pakistan.

Send the others down!

He was sitting in that outhouse, pulling at his hookah, waiting for the mountains to come to Muhammad. It might have been funny in another time, but this was January, 1944, and already half the month was gone. I wasn't laughing.

The moment passed – it was hard to feel continuously urgent in a frozen world. Frozen not so much by the winter, as by the global majesty of the War, for the length of which the local history of the Raj had been put on hold. Sometimes War seemed like another word for God: it was spelt with a capital, it transcended everything, affected everyone and despite that seemed so far away that it didn't matter.

Still, even in the frozen tranquillity of Simla, I had one personal connection with this God-like thing. When I returned to the Cecil after the surgery, there was a letter waiting for me, postmarked Dehra Dun. It was from Masroor: he had joined the army on a short-service commission. He was hoping, he wrote, to see action. I didn't write back. He had joined the army and was hoping to get shot. What could I have said?

But it wasn't the last I heard of him. Haasan wrote me a letter from Lucknow to report that Masroor had cabled his decision to enlist. His mother was worried sick. I didn't reply to him either. If I had I might have written that I was too far gone to be worried sick, that I was trying not to think of Masroor or anyone else that I knew, because between the end of the War, the death of the Raj and the division of India, I didn't know how many friends I would have left. Even Delia had left to holiday in the plains.

Alone on my hilltop, I replaced the missing people with routines. Every afternoon I took a walk up the hill to the Viceregal Lodge. Every other evening I spent a cathartic hour on the skating rink. Every Thursday, my day off, I cut myself sandwiches and picnicked in the Glen. Every Friday night I drank three shots of rum and wrote postcards to Masroor, Ammi, Asharfi, and Parwana – and tore them up on Saturday mornings. Time wasn't stilled in Simla; it did pass, only its measure was different and it moved in cycles, so nothing was lost and no one left behind. The seasons changed, the Season came and went, I was idle and busy, ill and well again.

Things changed elsewhere. The famine ran its course, helped along by the Vicereine's Christmas collection. The War was slowly won and the Japanese sent into retreat. With VE Day an era ended but from my mountain fastness it was a date from some foreign calendar. Sufficient in my routines, my red-letter days were reckoned differently – by the end of my second Simla winter, I could draw a figure-of-eight on a single skate, gliding backwards.

When the War ended, those days of peace ran out.

The fighting done, His Majesty's Government took India out of cold storage and found that the body hadn't kept too well. Tens of thousands of demobbed soldiers – Hindu, Muslim, Sikh – returned to their villages with their army surplus weapons and their war-honed killing skills. There was murder in the air, so the Viceroy did the statesman-like thing: he called a political conference. In the middle of June 1945 he sent off telegrams to India's notables, inviting them to sit together later that month and discuss with him the sub-continent's future. And since it was scheduled for June, he invited them to Simla.

So history came to the hills and nudged me out of limbo. I nearly took it personally because the Cecil was chosen as the lodging-place of the League delegation. The march of time was tramping up my doorstep. I was to wait on Jinnah again. Despite myself, I felt a prickle of excitement.

The representatives of the Congress weren't staying at the Cecil, though the management offered to make room for them. They were separately housed in bungalows spruced up for the conference. The Muslim Leaguers arrived on the evening of the twenty-fourth: Jinnah, Liaqat Ali Khan and Hossein Imam. Jinnah was wearing his two-coloured brogues.

Patrick was down with the 'flu, so I supervised the laying of their table. The vase at the centre had to be changed because the gardener had supplied an arrangement of red rosebuds, the flower patented by Nehru for his buttonhole. I had the rosebuds replaced with white carnations, which, so far as I knew, signified nothing. The walls of the private dining room were hung with large photographs of Viceregal picnic parties interchangeably captioned H.I.H. Lord Dufferin and his Household in Mashobra or H.I.H. Lord Curzon and the Fifth Foot in the Glen. They weren't exactly appropriate but removing them would have meant baring brilliant rectangles of colour in the faded floral wallpaper, so I let them be.

Dinner was scheduled for seven – as the clock chimed the hour, Jinnah led his colleagues into the room.

Where's Gandhi? burst out Liaqat Ali Khan, midway through the soup. Next to Jinnah's whippet leanness he looked more than ever like an overfed pug. He also looked worried.

In Simla, said Hossein Imam, dabbing at his mouth with a napkin. Manohar Villa to be precise, he added, finically centring his spoon in the soup bowl.

Then why isn't he attending the conference? demanded Liaqat aggressively, looking at the others in turn.

No one bothered to answer. The question was rhetorical. The Mahatma had been reiterating his reasons to the press for days now. He had written to the Viceroy explaining that he couldn't represent the Congress for the reason that he wasn't a member of that party. He wasn't partisan at all, or if he was, he was simply on the side of freedom.

Old hypocrite, offered Hossein Imam.

Why not Nehru, then? Why not him? This isn't Ludo or marbles, said Liaqat wrathfully. How can they be so . . . so non-serious? Azad is going to lead them into the conference. Azad!

Showboy! hissed Hossein Imam obligingly, and looked sideways at Jinnah for approval. But his Qaid said nothing. He had coined that sneering token-Muslim label for Azad some years ago and it had stuck; now he let his lieutenants chorus it.

Liaqat was still shaking his head. He wasn't the only one

puzzled. Leader-writers, Lord Wavell, Leaguers like Liaqat, laymen like me, even literate ladies, had all been wondering why the Father of the not-yet-Nation and his protégé weren't playing helmsmen for this critical meeting. At stake was the composition of the interim government which the Viceroy hoped would oversee the transition to a self-governing India. There was a lot to play for – why hadn't the Congress sent its champions?

What are they up to? growled Liaqat, worrying a chicken breast for its secrets. How can they afford to be so casual?

Because Nehru believes he has History on his side.

One sentence and Jinnah had their whole attention.

You must understand, he continued didactically, that Nehru is a Whig. All Socialists are. Take that Communist who was charged in the Cawnpore Conspiracy Case. His trial statement ran to five hundred and seventy-two pages. It began with the rise of capitalism and ended with the inevitability of violent class struggle – of which, he argued, the conspiracy for which he was being tried was but a single instance. If class struggle was predestined, his part in it was inevitable – not culpable. It was the most remarkable argument I've ever heard in court.

What happened to him? asked Liaqat, interested.

He hanged, said Jinnah absently. The point is, he believed he had History on his side. So does Nehru. He can send Azad to Simla without a qualm because it is written that the Congress will inherit an undivided country. Like he inherited Motilal's money. Because the Congress is Mother India's only son.

He leaned back as I served him the pudding, and steepled his fingers.

Like that Communist, Nehru *knows* he has History under rein. It wasn't an accident that he first called for complete independence while on horseback. You remember, Liaqat? How he rode to the Lahore Congress session on a white charger? That horse was History.

For himself, Jinnah favoured history without capitals. History not as live agent but as dead record which supplied precedents for his great political brief. When I returned with the coffee, he was patiently rehearsing his conference strategy for the creatures at his table.

The British own this country, he said, spacing his words, not the Congress. The Congress can give us nothing. Ignore it. The British can, but they won't until they're forced to. We're too small to force them to do what we want, but big enough to veto anything that doesn't suit us. When we sit at that table tomorrow, remember what we're working towards. Deadlock. Deadlock till they learn to listen, till they show their hands.

He paused to ask for cigars. When I came back with them five minutes later, Hossein Imam was picking his teeth and Liaqat had nearly nodded off. The Qaid had a job on his hands.

Deadlock it was. When the conference began, Jinnah dug his heels in about a Congress proposal to nominate a Muslim to the Viceroy's Executive Council. He insisted that Muslim nominations were the League's prerogative, that the Congress proposal was an insidious attempt to challenge the League's status as the sole spokesman of India's Muslims.

Typically, the rest of the country had got the details before we in Simla did, because the newspapers only got to the summer capital in the evenings. Patrick and I were sharing the paper after clearing up the debris of evening tea, when a large man with a walrus moustache drew up in a rickshaw pulled by four exhausted men. He disappeared into Jinnah's room and didn't emerge till two hours later. Basheshar, the head waiter, who was summoned to serve them coffee and cakes, reported that Jinnah's visitor was a Congress emissary, Gobind Ballabh Pant, one-time Premier of the United Provinces. He had come to help Jinnah change his mind.

Basheshar gave us bulletins every half hour. Jinnah for most of the meeting stood propped against the mantel, smoking his cigars and consulting his fob watch. Pant sat on the edge of the armchair and refused all refreshment: the cakes because of the taint of egg and the coffee because it inflamed the passions. Basheshar wasn't hopeful. When Pant emerged, he told the pressmen (who had appeared out of nowhere) that their talk was informal and private, so we knew it had failed.

The conference limped into the first week of July, but the hope had leaked out of it. At the end of twelve days when it became clear that the Viceroy's bid to draft the future around a table had failed, the leaders returned to the plains. Their holiday from History was over.

I had been cheated. Something big had happened in my neighbourhood, a conference on India's future had broken down. And yet, when Jinnah, Azad and the others left, Simla seemed eerily unchanged – almost as if the departed negotiators had packed the failure into their bags and carted it off to the plains. Simla, the sahib's sanatorium, had purged itself of the contagion of History. I should have felt safe; I felt sterilized.

Six thousand feet below, the world hurtled on. Three weeks after the conference the sky was split by a news flash: Churchill Wins War but Loses Election. Labour had come to power in England. British officialdom, civil and military, looked stricken: I overheard mutterings about Socialists in the Cecil's tea room, and Cyrus saw Byatt at Mowbrays, browsing through Gibbon.

Cyrus was back in Simla, chasing that elusive contract for the Viceregal Lodge's staterooms, but he didn't think it would come through now. They don't believe they'll be around to see the rooms renovated, he said gloomily. Of the white faces we recognized, only two resisted the general gloom: the Reverend Carrick carried on looking serene, but it was Delia Mulholland who glowed. Her husband was back from the wars, undamaged, and every evening she walked up the Mall, holding on to his arm, looking sated and full. Which she was, being six months pregnant.

The Japanese surrendered on the 14th of August, two years to the day from Partition. Then the countdown began: the Labour cabinet announced elections in India. Having decided to transfer power to the representatives of the Indian people, His Majesty's Government wanted to know who these tribunes were.

I knew what the results of the elections would be. The Muslim League would win nearly all the seats reserved for

313

Muslims, the Congress would win the rest and the stage would be set for Partition. Before that happened, before things became terminal, I wanted to return to Lucknow for a while to live in the Lalbagh house like a normal human being with a future.

That evening, my feet veered off the Mall and walked me down to the station, where I bought a platform ticket and watched trainloads of people begin their descent to the world of August 1945. It was probably raining in Lucknow. The channels that drained the courtyard in Ammi's house would be whistling with water. I pictured the cracked Chinese-looking vase in the hall stuffed with wet umbrellas, and the covered verandah overlooking the courtyard strung with clothes-lines. I could hear Asharfi complain that her clothes smelt damp . . . I could *smell* the damp! What was I doing in Simla? In this high, white ghetto peopled with brigadiers from Blighty? I wanted to go home again.

But I did nothing about it. I didn't think the Cecil would give me leave and I couldn't just quit. Jobs didn't grow on trees. And what if I did resign and reached Lucknow to find that they'd forgotten me? So instead of going to Lucknow, I did the next best thing – I took to reading the *Pioneer*, a Lucknow paper. There was never any mention of Ammi, Asharfi or Haasan, but I read the place names in the city news and obscurely felt in touch with them.

I would have carried on doing this for ever if the second Monday of October hadn't been my day off. Saturday's paper had just arrived in the afternoon, and with time on my hands, I was amusing myself with the *Pioneer*'s classified advertisements. That's where I saw it. That half-column inch of print which sent me home. The Lalbagh house was up for sale.

I must have read it a hundred times but classified ads don't often say why, and there were just three lines to read between. So the hundredth time round I still didn't know why Ammi was selling her home. But I was going to find out. In person. It wasn't just a house she was selling; she was selling my born-again birthplace. It was where I had come to life in 'forty-two; where Asharfi had nursed me and Ammi had fed me, where Masroor had helped me find a haircut. My memories needed a home to live in. I'd been robbed of my past and my whereabouts once, without notice or explanation. Not again. I circled the advertisement with a determined flourish. This time I wouldn't die wondering.

Ammi's Election

H AASAN OPENED THE door and shook my hand.
They were expecting me.

He's here, he called over his shoulder to someone inside.

I stood at the threshold for a long moment drinking the courtyard in. There were no umbrellas and it wasn't raining. Not that it was raining anywhere else in Lucknow – it was December and the monsoons were dead. Still, in the picture of the courtyard that I carried in my head, it was pouring. Having lived with that memory for more than three years, I had earned my disappointment. Weak winter sunlight and a matter-of-fact reception . . . my homecoming needed ambience.

The kitchen window that opened into the courtyard was smoking. Not wisps or plumes but clouds of dense black smoke were puffing out of it, darkening the sunlight and obscuring the arched façade of the drawing room. Ammi emerged through one of the arches, knuckling her eyes and coughing violently. Haasan took her elbow, sat her on the cot lying in the middle of the courtyard, then drew a deep breath and rushed indoors to investigate.

Why do you people make me cook? asked Ammi in a dying voice when the spasm had passed. Hissing sounds were heard from the kitchen – Haasan had doused the fire. Eyes streaming, he emerged holding a glass of water.

Nobody made you cook, he said exasperatedly, handing her the glass. You were the one who couldn't wait for Moonis to return. Who asked you to fry kababs without using ghee?

Ammi didn't bother to answer. She sprinkled her eyes with the water and blinked experimentally. When they didn't hurt she kept them open. That's when she first saw me.

It was more than a year and a half since she had left Simla;

she wasn't expecting me; she had smoke in her lungs and tears in her eyes but not for a moment did she look unknowing.

Her face softened – the lines on her forehead, the crowsfeet round her eyes, the sharply etched grooves that joined her nose to the corners of her mouth, blurred and disappeared, as if they'd been smoothed out by a magic iron. Abruptly she wasn't an honorary aunt or Asharfi's mother but a beautiful woman who was glad to see me.

Salaam aleikum, Ammi, I said grinning.

She raised an eyebrow. Very good, she said ironically. Then she smiled. Haasan Bhai was right. He was certain you would come.

I opened my mouth . . . then shut it again. Haasan was certain I would come? Unless he was God or the Cecil's administrative officer, I didn't see how. I hadn't known till the evening of the day before yesterday that my leave had been approved.

The courtyard door slammed open.

Ammi!

Asharfi rushed in waving a newspaper. I hadn't seen her in nearly two years. She looked much thinner and very striking in the flapping burqa with the veil thrown back. She homed in on her mother without noticing me.

Ammi, you're in the *Pioneer*!

I've told you one hundred and one times not to walk about by yourself, said her mother exasperatedly, plucking the newspaper from Asharfi's hand. Why is that Moonis not with you?

Because, said Asharfi with exaggerated patience, he is one hundred and one years old and you'd be holding yesterday's paper if I had waited for him. She snatched the rolled-up paper back and shook it out to the page where her mother was news.

The two-cornered contest for the Muslim Urban Women's seat (Lucknow City), Asharfi read aloud, has been enlivened and rendered triangular by an intriguing last-minute filing of nomination papers by Begum Kulsum Ganjoo (Independent), long-time resident of 1, Massaldan Lane, Lalbagh. Talking to our city correspondent, both Begum Amjadi Bano (Congress) and Begum Shakila Ara (Muslim League) were

317

confident that Begum Ganjoo's candidature would make no difference to their electoral prospects. The forthcoming election, they said, was a referendum on India's future, a choice between the Congress and the Muslim League. Independents were irrelevant. Begum Ganjoo clarified that she was only technically an independent candidate. She did represent a political party, but one too recently founded to be recognized by the Election Commission: the Anjuman-Bara-i-Tahaffuz-i-Haal.

Asharfi looked up from the paper, her eyes shining. She seemed thrilled but not surprised. Haasan, who reached out and took the paper to see for himself, wasn't surprised either. The courtyard stayed in focus, and took the announcement without rippling. So I tried to look unmoved. After all, I'd been away three years – it was unreasonable to expect this world to stay the same. It didn't work: my jaw dropped anyway. Ammi wasn't just selling the house; she was also contesting the elections, backed by a one-woman party with a gibberish name. It shook my faith in first things. Was the Lalbagh house the Lalbagh house? Had I come home or was I visiting strangers? Was Ammi a man?

Asharfi brought me back to earth. Her burqa smelt of sandalwood and her eyes were wide with recognition.

You're back, she said unbelievingly. Like the others! A huge smile enamelled her face. Just as Haasan Mamoo said. Ammi, she said turning to her mother, now we might even win.

I felt obscurely proud. I was sceptical about Haasan's second sight. I didn't know why Ammi was selling her house or entering electoral politics. And I had utterly no idea why Asharfi thought I could help her mother win. But I'd been claimed by an apsara and welcomed back – that was enough for now. I looked at Ammi and the others again, with proprietorial eyes. These weren't strangers. And I was home.

Home for Masroor was a barracks in New Delhi where he'd been allotted three rooms and a kerchief-sized courtyard. He would have waited much longer for quarters in the normal course, but his injury and his P.O.W. past helped him jump the queue.

He was shot in the armpit at Monte Cassino while raising his hands in surrender, explained Haasan that evening in the coffee house. He spent the rest of the war convalescing in Germany before being exchanged and shipped back to India two months ago. In October, he returned for a week to Lucknow.

Was he all right? I asked, abruptly reminded of Masroor standing by the Nativity manger, watching Parwana and Asharfi, joined at the mouth.

Well, he's bigger somehow. More chest, more weight, more beard. The Germans left the bullet inside, so his left arm curves out a little, like a close bracket, but it d——

No, not physically, I interrupted. How is he with . . . others?

Haasan shrugged.

He seemed the same at first, he said uncertainly. Not shell-shocked or depressed. We asked him about the war and how it was . . . and he told us. He told us in great detail – his blue-eyed German nurse, the food in camp, being a uniformed hero in London after VE Day – but you couldn't just chat with him any more. Each time I spoke to him it was like an interview. If I asked him a question, he answered it. Exhaustively. When he finished there wasn't a loose end left to pull the conversation along with – unless I asked a new question. He shook his head at the memory and signalled the waiter for another round.

I began to avoid talking to him alone, confessed Haasan, shamefacedly. Imagine. Masroor, Intezar's son, whom I knew before he knew his name: now I was scared to have a private word with him. A ten-minute talk left me spitless with the strain of asking relevant questions.

The coffee arrived. Haasan sucked his cup down in a single swallow.

That's another thing, he said, and stopped to light a cigarette.

I waited.

He wouldn't drink my coffee any more.

It wasn't just the coffee; Masroor couldn't bear to visit the coffee house. Haasan was bewildered: Masroor had virtually grown up within its walls. He had spent more time there through school and college than he had at the Lalbagh house. Haasan could remember a time when he had parked Masroor on the cash counter while he worked. One summer vacation, Masroor had bullied him into getting a miniature waiter's costume made up, complete with cockaded turban, and had then enchanted Haasan's world-weary clientele by serving them coffee, his eyes fixed on the trembling cups, his tongue stuck out in concentration. He had done this every day for two and a half months and Ammi had to drag him away in the afternoons for his nap.

But in October, when he visited Haasan the morning after coming home, he couldn't stay inside the coffee house for more than five minutes.

He said he couldn't breathe, said Haasan, frowning at the memory. He wanted to know why it was so dark, why the bulbs were so dim, why the chairs and tables were so broken down, why there were no pictures on the walls, or potted plants on the floor. And he didn't say this nicely. He said it like a man with an allergy.

I was hurt, said Haasan. Why did he want plants in a coffee house? Because he had seen plants in English tea rooms! We had things to learn from the English before seeing them off, he said. And one of these lessons was that the inside of my coffee house could be cheered up by living things. Living things! I told him my coffee house was full of living things – like my customers, who were better company than plants – even English plants.

But he kept feeling his collar as if it was too tight and when the coffee arrived he took a few sips – then suddenly gagged and ran outside to retch in the passageway.

He didn't actually vomit, said Haasan. Just made the sounds. I was so worried that I handed the cash box over and walked him home. He never visited the coffee house again in the six days he had left in Lucknow.

Masroor made his peace with Haasan that evening in the Lalbagh house by trying to explain. In the same way as it wasn't just the coffee, it wasn't just the coffee house. It was everything that was old, dirty, familiar and the same. The coffee house was all of these; the coffee simply helped him taste his feelings. It was weak, grey and chlorinated, exactly as it had always been, as if the same coffee had travelled down the years in a million greasy cups. Drinking it had been intimately disgusting, like sipping stored-up spit. That's why he wanted Ammi and Asharfi to sell the house and join him in Delhi, away from the nose-picking, Ganj-strolling, chikan-wearing, coffee-drinking habits of a lifetime. There wasn't a life for him in Lucknow any more, just death by bovine degrees, as he drowned in his cud while chewing it. Delhi was not the centre of the world – the war and London had taught him that – but at least it was a place where ambitious men were hatching India's future – not endlessly fingering their past.

Past! snapped Ammi scornfully. Future! she growled. Why do you people always talk about places that you've never been to?

Masroor, who had been talking to Haasan, looked up in surprise.

The last time I saw your father was fifteen years ago. So did he disappear in the *past*? She waited.

Her son said nothing.

Every day that he doesn't come home, he disappears. Every time I look for him, he disappears. He disappeared this morning when I got up. And when he does return, it won't be in your precious future – it will be today. Just as your children will be born today. And when you die, you will die today and then die every day for the lifetimes of the people who loved you. The young never understand that they aren't given a fund of days to spend . . . but just one, continuous life, where everything happens in the present.

Ammi, listen, said Masroor placatingly. Even if you're right, what is the harm in shifting to Delhi so that we can live together? What's left in Lucknow for you? Abba's gone and my job is transferable: I'll probably never be posted to Lucknow. And once Sharfu gets married . . . if you ever feel homesick, Lalbagh's just an overnight journey by rail.

But you said you wanted me to sell the house, said his mother warily.

Masroor sighed.

Yes, I did. But if it's going to keep you from coming to

Delhi, you can lock it up till you make up your mind about living there. Why don't you just think of the move to Delhi as a holiday? At least it will be a change.

But why did you want me to sell the house in the first place? persisted Ammi.

Because, said Masroor, with steely patience, the money from the house would give us the freedom to choose.

Choose what?

Masroor flushed.

Choose between India and Pakistan, he said defiantly. If Partition happens, he added, in a touch-wood whisper.

You want to sell the house to shift to this Pakistan? asked his mother incredulously.

I didn't say that, said Masroor hotly. He took a calming breath. There's nothing definite yet. But there has been talk that soldiers and civil servants will be given the choice, if the . . . if the need arises. It may not, but there's no harm being prepared. All I'm saying is that if we're living in Delhi with ready cash, and if the country is partitioned, we'll be in a much better position to cross the border – if we want to.

If if if, said Ammi dismissively. What about the most important if: if Intezar returns and finds his home sold to strangers? No, I won't move to Delhi. Because your father might come back. Because your reason for going to Delhi is absurd. You want to live in the future like the rest of them. Delhi's just your time-machine.

Her shoulders sagged.

Why should you want to wreck the only world you have for some day-after-tomorrow? You'll never get there – there's no such place. Throw the English out if you want – but why can't you leave the rest alone? Isn't it natural for people to be attached to their lives? You I can understand: the young always want to change the world. But Gandhi and Jinnah and Nehru? Experienced old men who want to sweep their lives away and live like strangers in brand-new countries. They must be mad. How do they know that the change will be for the better? That they won't yearn for things as they were before they were different? Why doesn't someone stop them?

Why don't you stop them, Ammi? asked Masroor evenly.

322

Try doing something instead of waiting. Waiting is all we've done since Abba left. It's your whole life now and it's the only life Asharfi has known. Left to you, I'd still be making a living out of the past: teaching schoolboys history and waiting for a ghost to knock. If I hadn't been . . . if I hadn't joined the army I wouldn't have known that there's a world outside where husbands and fathers disappear every day. Fifty million people died in Europe during the war, Ammi. Fifty million. But their families aren't waiting for their dead to rise. You won't go to Delhi, you won't even think about Pakistan. You can't bear Gandhi and Jinnah because you can't bear things to change. So stop them. Make a speech. Write to the papers. Win the elections.

Or sell this house. Not because I want you to. But because it's haunted.

Haasan winced and stole a look at Ammi. Her face was wiped clean of any emotion. He thought he saw her eyes glisten but it could have been his imagination. She had been sitting hunched in her armchair in despair at the world's recklessness – now she straightened, inch by measured inch, till she was upright, her hands clasped loosely in her lap, her elbows resting regally on the chair's arms, turning an argument into an audience, as Haasan watched in awe, by her bearing alone.

Haasan Bhai, she said, looking straight at her son, will the *Pioneer* print a notice advertising the sale of this house on Saturday if we give it in this evening?

Haasan nodded dumbly, feeling like a courtier.

Ammi, said Masroor worriedly, don't –

His mother cut him short with a gesture. Don't talk, said Ammi flatly. Just listen. I shall take your advice, she continued in that same toneless voice, and stand for election. If I lose, I will sell the house for the highest price that this advertisement fetches and shift to your quarters in Delhi. But if I win . . . she paused for emphasis and stared unblinkingly at her son, if I win, I'll withdraw the advertisement and keep the house – but you will leave the army and return to Lucknow. Then we'll wait for your father together.

She had staked her present against his future, her now

against his then. It was a strange wager but Masroor nodded: in late 1945, the oddest things made sense. It was a bet for the times.

The *Times of India*'s Lucknow correspondent interrupted the first meeting of our campaign team before it had properly begun. It was the first of many interruptions: in one morning Ammi received reporters from the *Hindustan Times*, the *Northern India Patrika*, *Dawn* and the *Statesman*. Yesterday's report in the *Pioneer* had obviously caught the attention of bored bureau chiefs. Haasan claimed that he wasn't surprised. Who wants to read the same Congress/League rubbish every day? he asked. Ammi makes much better copy.

He was wrong. Ammi by herself was of no interest to journalists. Binocular vision in 1945 meant special lenses: one tinted by the passion of the Congress, the other by the fervour of the League – like the red-and-green spectacles that cinema ushers once supplied for 3-D films. Without them the world was flat and far away, India was the name of a map, newspapers were almanacs, freedom was a transfer of power – and Ammi was just another old woman in a peeling house. But the reporters arrived with their glasses on and saw her in perspective: if the end of the Raj was scripted by the rhetoric of the Congress and the League, then Ammi in a walk-on part qualified as news. In this clash of titans set amid the mainly silent millions, Begum Kulsum Ganjoo (Independent) had bagged a speaking role. But the pressmen owned the questions and their manner suggested that they had the answers too. Except that Ammi's lines didn't often match their cues.

The interview with the man from the *Times* hiccupped even before he asked a question. The first thing he wanted to do was take a photograph of her. He had the frame worked out down to the smallest detail: Begum Ganjoo in a burqa sitting in an ornamental armchair with her husband standing off-centre behind her, his hand poised reassuringly on the chair's back-rest.

Ammi informed him that her husband was out of town and unavailable.

Don't worry, he said soothingly. What about this gentleman? he inquired, smiling kindly at Haasan.

Haasan's mouth opened and worked silently.

Ammi asked the man to leave.

The *Statesman*'s representative also wanted a picture. He came with a bellows camera which made my shutter finger itch, and an assistant armed with a huge magnesium flare.

This one wanted Ammi in a burqa-and-armchair too, but made better progress because he wasn't as committed to the husband prop. Since she was already wearing a burqa (with the hood and veil thrown back as she generally did inside the house) and since the drawing room had armchairs rubbing elbows, the scene was quickly set. When Ammi told him that the gallery running along the upper walls had once been part of the zenana, he insisted on posing her so that he could work it into the portrait. A high-domed Bengali, roughly contemporary with Haasan, he turned to him to share an inspiration:

From sheltered harem to electoral forum, he said happily.

Ammi overheard and her lips thinned but she stayed posed in the armchair. When he bent over to focus, she put on her camera face.

Yes, please, he said into the viewfinder.

Ammi stiffened into stillness.

The assistant touched a match to the magnesium.

Yes please, repeated the photographer urgently.

Ammi stopped breathing; the magnesium hissed – when it flared properly, the photographer would uncap the lens for a murmured count and then cover it again. I knew how it worked – it was just that I had never seen it happen.

Yes pleease wailed the Bengali as the magnesium whooshed into uninhibited brilliance, making Ammi start and scaring the pigeons from their gallery roosts into incoherent flight. Their wings beat a clumsy tattoo as they flapped overhead, shedding feathers and making strangled gobbling sounds. When quiet returned, nearly every surface, including the Bengali's baldness, was speckled with down and droppings, but despite the commotion that his flash had caused, he still hadn't taken a picture.

Madam did not cover her face, he said plaintively.

He'd been waiting for her to veil her face before he bared his lens.

325

Your paper wants a picture of a burqa? asked Haasan, his voice cracking with disbelief.

The thwarted reporter shook his head primly.

My paper wants a picture of a *Muslim* lady standing for election, he said.

All through the morning Ammi was stalked by the Muslim Lady.

She was at her shoulder when the dapper, Brylcreemed representative of *Dawn*, the Muslim League's mouthpiece, began asking questions.

Why do you . . . er . . . , he developed the pause by examining the super-fine blue of his blazer for dust, why should . . . *you*, he added by way of emphasis, shooting his cuffs to generate momentum, why did you as a Muslim woman set up a Muslim party when you already have the . . . umm . . . Muslim League?

What Muslim party? asked Ammi shortly. She had run out of patience with the press.

The . . . unn . . . , he said uncertainly, then peered at his diary notes, the Anjuman-ul-Hi . . . fazat-i-Islam . . . ?

Ammi snorted.

You've got Islam on the brain, she said scathingly. The Anjuman-Bara-i-Tahaffuz-i-Haal is what my party is called.

Exactly, agreed the reporter, brushing details aside to return to the big question. So why did you, a Muslim lady, establish another Muslim party?

Ammi stared at him.

Do you understand Urdu? she asked.

No, replied the reporter simply. *Dawn* is an English-language paper.

You'll do well in Pakistan, she muttered. Both you and your Jinnah. He doesn't know Urdu either. Doesn't need to considering he'll be surrounded by Punjabis. Look, I know it doesn't matter to you, but just write in your notebook that the Anjuman-Bara-i-Tahaffuz-i-Haal is not a Muslim party – it is the Society for the Defence of the Present.

But the reporter's nose kept tracking the Muslim Lady.

Yes but, he went on unstoppably, didn't she (as a Muslim)

want the Muslim League to win? Didn't she want to live in the Muslim homeland, in Pakistan?

What for? she said rudely.

It will umm . . . be the Republic of Islam, he ventured.

But it won't be Lucknow, said Ammi.

Ammi needs a good election poster, prescribed Bhukay, his voice thick and syrupy because he was eating jalebis at the same time. Slogan, symbol and name. Name in big letters. Green lettering on –

No, black, said Haasan, looking greedily at the new batch of jalebis that Bihari was nudging around in the bubbling oil. We were ranged around the temporary stall that Bihari had rented in the fairground to milk the circus crowds. The Great Raymond Circus had come to town.

No, green, insisted Bhukay. It's the Muslim women's seat that she's running for. She needs a Muslim colour.

But she isn't running as a *Muslim* Muslim, argued Haasan and the debate went on. The Muslim Lady was with us again.

After the press fiasco in the morning, Ammi had been in no mood to discuss campaign strategy, so the rest of us – Bhukay, Bihari, Haasan and I – arranged to meet later in the day at Bihari's stall. Asharfi had wanted desperately to come but Ammi didn't want her daughter seen at the circus in the company of four unrelated men; not before the elections at any rate.

I hadn't seen Bhukay and Bihari in more than three years, not since the night when we had gone looking for Masroor by the rail track in Unnao. Neither had been injured in the blast that had mangled the rail lines. Unlike Asharfi and me, their clothes and faces hadn't been singed by the bomb, so while we outran the police to the getaway car, they got away by losing themselves among the Mail's passengers. They found a couple of vacant berths, slept the night in the stalled train and walked back to Lucknow the next morning.

While they got home safely, both of them separately decided to leave town till the inquiry, the arrests and the related fuss inevitable in any case of sabotage was over and done with. Bhukay went east to Gorakhpur, his ancestral home town, where the family still owned land, and Bihari went westward to Rampur, to spend a quiet month with his uncle, who was employed in Nawabsahib's legendary kitchens.

Then the Quit India storm broke and months passed before it was safe to travel again. And when the trains became reliable, a rumour swept the United Provinces from east to west, whispering that the Raj was kidnapping able-bodied men, putting them in uniform and shipping them off to die in distant desert battles – this was around the time the Fourth Indian Division was giving its all at Alamein.

So Bihari stayed put in Rampur because he reckoned that he was safer in a princely state than in Lucknow, the heart of British India, where ruthless recruiting sergeants were probably rampaging up and down Hazrat Ganj. And Bhukay earned his astonished grandmother's dying gratitude by escorting her to every pilgrim town within a radius of two hundred miles – on the reasoning that if he didn't stay too long in any one place, he wouldn't get drafted.

They waited out the war in exile. Bihari would have returned earlier, some time in early 1944, but then he heard a fifth-hand account of Masroor's entry into the army. The story in this version related how Ammi's son had been brutally shanghaied. Bihari postponed his homecoming. Bhukay had got so used to a nomadic pilgrim life that he hadn't thought about going home at all.

Then, one week in October, they learnt of the advertisement announcing the sale of the Lalbagh house, the home of their childhood friend, Masroor. That made up their minds. They reached Lucknow within a couple of days of each other.

I knew they would come, said Haasan complacently, licking syrup off his fingers. Just as I knew you would, once you saw the advertisement.

So that was how. No crystal ball, no second sight – not that I believed in that kind of thing. Still, it was deflating to know that I had been just one of many. Till then I had felt like a maverick hero, impulsively racing to Ammi's rescue. Now I felt like Pavlov's dog.

Feeling depressed and unfree, I left them discussing the poster's colour and bought a ticket to the big top. The tent was

328

jammed with people and the loudspeakers were playing a waltz instead of the Hindi film songs I remembered from childhood visits to the circus. The place was alive with distracted chatter because onstage, spangled horses waltzed tediously in step. This at least was the same. Circus managements down the years had never discovered the simple truth that the paying customer only came to watch routines that were funny or dangerous. Dancing horses were neither – unless one of them broke a leg, and that was too slim a hope to fix the gaze of the cheap seats.

The last time I had been in a tent seemed a life ago, but I remembered every sight and sound of that Congress circus in Kashmiri Gate, lit by hissing kerosene lamps. It had been the one time when everyone I knew in this world had been present and accounted for under a single roof. That the roof had been temporary canvas seemed fitting now because after it collapsed on us we never came together again. Without closing my eyes I conjured up Parwana on that stationary tandem bicycle while the horses waltzed around her. Had Dadi kept her on or banished her to Nari Niketan? Alone, except for the horses, in that massive arena, she looked young and lost and vulnerable. I wondered how she was managing with the twins.

The music scrunched to an ugly halt and Parwana disappeared along with the horses. Their place was taken by two painted clowns hitting each other with wooden slats that made gunshot sounds. In between they pointed their arses outward and noisily farted great streams of chalk. The recently inattentive audience wept with laughter. The paying public had recovered its concentration, but I had lost mine. I tried to conjure up Asharfi working the pedal of her sewing machine – and couldn't. The clowns were too gross for nostalgia's ghosts.

The present seemed urgent again. If Ammi won the election and Masroor honoured the bet they had made, they wouldn't go to Pakistan, I wouldn't lose my foster-family and the Lalbagh house would still be home. Outside, Bhukay, Bihari and Haasan were working towards just that: they were arguing about ways to win votes for Ammi. And here I was, sulking in a tent because Haasan had consigned me to the common herd by predicting my arrival. Goosed by solidarity, I jumped up and began hurrying through a tangle of legs to the aisle.

Shhhh hissed a dozen voices though I wasn't saying anything. Some cursed, others yelled at me to sit, one asked me if I thought my arse was made of glass. All this because I'd come between them and two farting clowns. Shaken, I crept back to my seat. But when I looked up, the clowns had gone. The drapes of the performers' entrance had parted to reveal four men in velvet leopard skins pulling a gigantic cannon.

I could feel the inside of my mouth dry out . . . they were about to fire the Human Cannonball! Now I knew what the hissing and the fuss had been about; now I sympathized. Unlike the clowns and the interminable horses, this was a split-second act. Boom! and it was over. By moving across their line of sight I could have robbed them of the whole routine.

Ammi postponed, I settled into my chair and waited for the sequence that I knew by heart. Long trumpet sounds would climb the canvas walls and explode into a crash of cymbals; then a man in a silver suit would bound into the spotlight. This particular Silversuit was also wearing a black cape, a black hardhat and a silver Balaclava with the eyeholes picked out in black. He looked like an extra-terrestrial raccoon.

It was a front-loading cannon. The cymbals sounded as the Human Cannonball was lowered feet first into its muzzle – one jaunty wave of the hand and he was swallowed up entirely.

The music stopped and the audience stopped breathing. It was always like this before the gun went off; it was the reason I went to the circus: this breathless, smothering hush that filled my ears like jam. The Human Cannonball did it every time – no other act came close. Not the skill of the tumblers or the daring of the trapeze: just this single firework. I didn't know why. Perhaps the answer lay in the simplicity with which the act inverted real life. There, man fired gun. Here, gun fired man.

Sitting opposite the cannon, I was in the perfect position to

330

watch him fly – he would arc across the arena, land in the receiving net some twenty rows in front of me, then come upright in a single rebound like a trampoliner. Applause. That was the classic routine – but when the gun went off some childhood sensor told me that the script had changed. His flight-path was too flat. He landed ten yards short of the waiting net and didn't bounce.

Someone had blundered.

But not fatally. After a moment of sickening, immobile silence, Silversuit moaned and gathered himself on to his elbows and knees. The air shuddered as my neighbours exhaled their relief. When he weaved to his feet, someone began clapping and seconds later we were all on our feet. Lifted by the applause, he waved help away (the clowns had come on with a stretcher) and lifted his hardhat in acknowledgement. The clapping reached a pitch and showed no signs of ebbing, so he doffed his Balaclava too. There was a collective gasp because the left side of his face was masked with blood. But it was the other, unbloodied half that froze my clapping hands. I had seen this face before from my attic room in Banaras, advancing on a frightened, naked woman in the window opposite.

Opposite the flatbed litho press, Bihari was sitting at a stunted desk, writing Urdu backwards. His hand moved slowly from left to right, printing outsize mirror-image words, trying to get his fingers used to the unfamiliar motion before etching Ammi's manifesto on stone. This was the first time he had attempted lithography: Haasan had nominated him for the job on the grounds that anyone who could write Arabic on simmering oil with a jalebi bag could write Urdu the wrong way round on a firmer surface.

Bihari was game. He had already written and drawn the campaign poster and we had just finished printing five hundred copies. The last batch was still drying on the clothes-line strung for the purpose along the zenana's viewing gallery. Ammi wouldn't have them hung in the courtyard to dry – she didn't want casual visitors seeing them. Too public, she said. Haasan was exasperated. Election posters, he pointed

331

out unkindly, were meant to be public. Once they were pasted up, they would be seen by thousands of total strangers. That's different, said Ammi. But till the posters were in her keeping, she wouldn't have them shimmying in public like shameless dancing girls. So they were hung out to dry in the sunless seclusion of the zenana.

It wasn't just the posters – Ammi observed the strictest purdah on all election-related matters. Bihari made his début as calligrapher only because Ammi chose not to use the professional qatib who usually helped her with the printing of *Khatoon*. Only Haasan, Bhukay, Bihari and I (besides Asharfi and the faithful Moonis) had access to the materials being hatched in the zenana – the camaraderie of the campaign had made us kin. Other people were prying eyes; beyond us lay strangers.

But nobody had seen her manifesto yet, not even her campaign family. Haasan had been at her to detail her commitment to the present: as programme, plan, prescription, anything, but she hadn't got round to it. So Haasan was pushing her round to it now. Having cornered her in an armchair in the same room that housed the printing press, he was playing variations on his basic theme: we couldn't campaign on her creed alone.

Trapped and harassed, Ammi heard him out once, twice and again, then reached into her burqa and pulled out a rolled-up sheet of paper.

Here, she said abruptly. Don't ask me for more.

Haasan spread the sheet out and gave it to Bihari to read aloud. It was in Urdu.

There were no throat-clearing preliminaries:

For five years after the English leave
– no roads shall be renamed
– no statues removed
– no statues raised
– no republic constituted
– no Constitution written
– no coins minted
– no text books written

332

- no stamps issued
- no laws made
- no elections held
- no boundaries erased
- no frontiers drawn

till we sort out what we want to keep, from what they leave behind.

There was a moment of silence, then a rustling as Bihari turned the sheet over, searching hopefully for more. But there was nothing on the other side.

Haasan snatched the paper from Bihari and checked for himself.

What is this? he asked blankly, looking at Ammi. This no no no no business? You think people will vote for you if you tell them what you don't want? Do you ever send Moonis shopping with a list of things that he mustn't buy?

He looked at the paper he was holding and shook his head.

Jinnah wants Pakistan. Nehru tells the whole world twice a day that he dreams of a free, united, secular, democratic India. You have to tell people what you want – not what they mustn't do.

Why? asked Ammi simply. Nehru and Jinnah want to change the world so they need to give their dreams a name. But I don't have a dream – I like the world as it is. That's why I've listed a dozen things that Indians shouldn't do if they want to keep the world they know. What else could I have written?

Haasan opened his mouth, raised a wagging finger, wound himself up for argument . . . then said nothing. There was nothing he could say. The founder of the Anjuman-Bara-i-Tahaffuz-i-Haal had made an unanswerable case.

Bihari copied the twelve don'ts on to the litho stone and we spent the rest of the afternoon turning out one-page manifestos. It was routine, comforting work: each time I hung a damp sheet on the line, I was reassured by the calm certainty of Ammi's opinions. It didn't matter that she was in a minority of one, that she was a thousand-to-one outsider in the electoral stakes, that even if she won there was no chance of her manifesto being implemented. Her views were her own and she knew she was right. When the change-mongers won and Ammi lost her world, she wouldn't be an ambushed loser. Never having sleepwalked through second-hand dreams, she was safe from rude awakenings. Unlike Chaubey.

When I left the circus tent to rejoin Bhukay, Bihari and Haasan, I was still trembling from the shock of seeing the man who had raped Parwana. But gradually the cheery hubbub of the fairground put his reappearance in perspective. It was a coincidence Chaubey was here: he wasn't looking for me. That helped and I slowed down from a blur. Also I had just seen him fired from the business end of a cannon and injured. That helped too. So when I saw him much later walking stiffly towards our conversation, his head in a bandage, I beat the urge to hide behind Bihari, and stood my ground.

He walked right past us and stopped twenty yards away at a tea-stall. On a mad impulse I joined him. I had to tell him who I was three times before he recognized me. Then he smiled tiredly and apologized for his deafness. It was the explosion, he explained. It resounded so much in the bore of the cannon that his ears rang for hours afterwards.

He was reeking of some powerful liniment and the singed bits of his haggard face were shiny with salve. He must have caught me staring, because he wiped some off his cheek self-consciously.

I spend half the money they give me on ointments, he explained. More than I do on food, he said, looking sadly at the dirty bun he'd bought to swallow with his tea. Tiger Balm, mainly. I can't do without it. Especially on days when they shoot me off twice.

We talked about Guruji and Banaras, like friends exhuming the good old days. It even felt like that – there was no menace left to Chaubey any more – he looked too used up to be dangerous. His fall had begun when Guruji learnt about his sexual début. He threw him out of the akhara at once. Star pupil or not, celibacy was not negotiable.

Suddenly Chaubey was left with no moorings and nothing to do. His film career had ended with Parwana's escape. He couldn't go back to the Hindu University – he had put higher education behind him when he had hijacked a train in the name of the Nation, one distant day in a long-dead August. Then there had been the assault on the police station at Madhuban. Either would have been enough to get his name on a warrant – and he had starred in both.

When Guruji barred him from the akhara, Chaubey lost more than a training ground for his Mr India ambitions; he lost a world. Now he needed a job – and in the real world a loincloth wasn't nearly enough.

I had been hungry for two weeks when they came to Banaras, said Chaubey, nodding towards the big top. There was a vacancy. He shrugged. There's always a vacancy for the cannonball routine. People wear out.

His hands, wrapped round the warmth of the glass, shook a little and tea slopped over. He watched it trickle over his fingers.

I don't know, he said blankly.

And he didn't. He had tried to star in the dreams of others too long to even feel clearly. Gandhi's fight in 'forty-two; Guruji's muscular Ramlila; Gyanendra's deep blue fantasy: epic disasters each one but all they had taught him was tiredness. He had been so careless with the world he had once owned, that he couldn't even tell he had lost it.

The contrast between Chaubey and Ammi seemed starker the next afternoon, when I took down the dried-out posters and squared them into little stacks. There was her world, summed up in black-and-white in the name of her party. And there was her prescription for saving it, spelt out in twelve commandments.

Ammi knew what she had at stake – and she knew the odds. She was joining battle with her eyes open. Chaubey didn't even know there was a war on. He was cannon fodder where she was a bona-fide combatant. It was a comforting contrast – it made our campaign seem worthwhile.

There was a pot of sticky flour paste lying by the litho press which Bihari had boiled up as an experiment. The posters would have to be stuck all over the city soon – for a budget campaign like ours, home-made glue was a substantial saving. And there was the glue, just sitting there, all made up. The temptation was irresistible. It took me less than a minute to lather the back of one poster and stick it on to the middle of the wall just behind the press. It looked wonderful: sharp, potent, emphatic.

But it wouldn't help her win. Six months from now, this poster would bear fading witness to a doomed campaign. One way or the other, Ammi would be flattened by the road-rollers of history. Chaubey wouldn't seem so different then. In the sepia of hindsight, all losers look the same.

The same evening, Ammi lost her temper with me for the first time. It was the poster; the one I had stuck on the wall. When she saw it, she went tight-lipped with annoyance. Moonis was summoned and told to fetch a wash-cloth and a pail of water.

Rub it off, said Ammi.

When I owned up, she just looked at me for a time. This isn't a game, she said.

Then she pulled out a bunch of keys and told me to pick the posters up and follow her. The old zenana had three rooms, two of which I had always seen locked. Now Ammi opened one of them and let me in. It was a small room, hardly bigger than a storage closet, crammed with paper and junk. Ammi left me with the padlock and the keys; I was to find a corner for the posters and lock up afterwards.

I located the switch and turned on a ten-watt bulb well past its prime. There wasn't a single clean surface on which I could put Ammi's crisp, new campaign material. As my eyes got used to the gloom, the junk resolved itself into old news-papers, back issues of *Khatoon* and framed pictures stacked against the walls.

I didn't have a cloth to dust with, so I turned the top layers of the *Khatoon* pile over, clean side up, and put the posters down. When I took my hand away, they began sliding off – the top of the magazine stack wasn't perfectly even. Holding them in place with one hand, I picked up a picture frame, wiped the glass clean by passing it over my bottom, and began pushing it under the posters to level the base.

So when I first saw the long, half-naked gopis, they were disappearing inch by inch under a bunch of posters. I pulled them out quickly for a better look. The posters rustled and dived into the dirt. I let them be. They'd keep.

Held up to the bulb's ten-watt murk the picture divided into two main colours, brown and green: the skins all brown and the scene in green. There were six sad girls in gangetic-belle costume – long ghaghra-like skirts and gauzy dupattas draped over their heads and some other parts. In the bottom left and top right corners of the pictures two cows grazed on curly greens. It was a respectable subject, a staple of calendar art: gopis in Brindavan mourning the absence of Krishna.

Like the subject, the drawing was conventional. The figures were gracefully elongated – all flowing arms and legs, stretched fish eyes and endless fingers. The long, mannered line was broken only to make room for large breasts and buttocks and the one departure from the muted green-brown colour scheme was the emphatic red of the nipples.

The gopis' bereftness was simply conveyed: a single furrow between the eyebrows, one hand knuckled against the forehead or splayed against a breast, the other flung out in desolation, the head inclined towards a shoulder, impossible eyelids cast down.

I noticed that the girls had been paired off. The pairing was indicated not so much by proximity as by gesture. In every case, the outflung arm of one was drawn across the bosom of the other, the long pale fingers laid a hairsbreadth from a nipple. Unlike the fingertips of God and Adam, they didn't strain towards each other; it wasn't even clear if hand and breast were on the same plane since the artist's perspective lines were vague – but I could have sworn that a second ago, just before I looked, fingertips had trailed over nipples. Then I was certain that they had. The six mourning girls wore just two faces: Asharfi's and Parwana's, trebly paired!

I snatched up the other frames, sleeving the dust away. They were all the same. The number of gopis varied but the faces stayed the same. I didn't need to look for a signature. They were Asharfi's. She had chosen her theme cleverly; it allowed her to legitimately leave men out of the frame – even the cows in the corners had unmistakable udders and long, sinuous teats. I was faintly surprised that Asharfi should have chosen a Krishna theme to carry her meaning, but that could have been the fault of my post-Partition sensibility; perhaps things had been more eclectic before the great divide.

I wondered what the pictures were doing in the zenana. Most likely they had been banished there by Ammi, to help her daughter get over an unnatural obsession. Alternatively, they could have been a kind of therapy; perhaps Asharfi had painted Parwana out of her system and put the pictures behind her. Given the dust on them, they had been stored for some time. Either way, Parwana seemed to have been tidied into Asharfi's past.

Without my knowing it, my hands had wiped the pictures clean and propped them up wherever there was space. Suddenly I felt like taking them downstairs and hanging them up, six to a wall, in the drawing room. Moving things around had displaced great quantities of dust which spiralled to my nose and triggered off sixteen consecutive sneezes. They left me feeling irritable, teary and stirred up. I didn't want Asharfi to forget Parwana. Or file her away as a memory. Or book-press her into nostalgia. I wanted these pictures to be true, for Asharfi to pine for her vanished lover. I wanted her to worry about a future without Parwana, to dream about a reunion, to yearn for a fixed address and permanent friends. I wanted company.

I gathered the scattered posters, dusted them off and made them a stable perch out of old newspapers and ancient *Khatoons*. The papers began in 1931, the year Intezar set off on the Haj, and continued in an unbroken run till last week's editions. *Khatoon*'s inaugural issue was dated 1933; it had appeared, almost to the day, on the second anniversary of Intezar's departure. I realized that the store was an archive for Ammi's personal era – the Epoch of His Absence. The dead newspapers with their bustling headlines counted off the empty days. The old issues of *Khatoon* marked battles won in her epic campaign to fill that void with her imagination. Even Asharfi's pictures, those mannered studies in sundered love, seemed to echo Ammi's loss. Since all of them had women consoling each other in the conspicuous absence of men, it seemed proper that they were stored in a zenana.

338

It was time to go; Ammi would be waiting for her keys. I took the improvised exhibition down and put the pictures back where I had found them. All except one, which I hid under the folds of my kurta. I stole it for a very good reason – it was the nearest thing to a likeness of Parwana and Asharfi that I was likely to find. I wasn't supplied with snapshots of my friends.

I knew the one I wanted: the smallest one. It was no bigger than a Mughal miniature; even in its frame it slipped comfortably into the waistband of my pajamas. The others were the size of large tea-trays, or larger, impossible to smuggle out. If Ammi and her daughter ever moved to Delhi to join Masroor, freighting the pictures would be a proper headache. Immediately, inevitably, I thought of another, more ambitious move, of Asharfi in an endless caravan, headed west to a promised land, her framed canvases jolting behind her. Why couldn't she have made monumental statues instead? Or buildings. Or anything which didn't travel, which might anchor her to Lucknow. These pictures were no defence against Partition. Painting is a portable art.

Waiting for August

I N THE WEEK between polling day and the results, Ammi
took to the kitchen and produced seven dinners, the like of
which hadn't been seen since Lucknow's great days of
decadence. The last meal was staged the evening before the
results were to be formally gazetted. She invited everyone
she liked, generally the same people who had helped her with
her election campaign.

The hall was spread with mattresses covered with dhobi-
white sheets, and these were arranged around two low
tables, less than a foot high, which had been hired for the
evening by Haasan. Ammi had originally planned a
traditional feast, full of shorbas and kormas, biryanis and
sherbets of the sort that had illuminated her expansive
childhood, but the menu changed when Haasan argued
forcefully that the meal was meant to commemorate
not some vanished past but the eclectic present.

So under Haasan's ideological direction we had tomato
soup with croutons, jellied hooves, mutton dosas, biryani,
fish curried in mustard oil, prawns in coconut milk from
Haasan's time in Malabar, potatoes in a thin gruel of haldi
and dahi and water, free of garlic or onions – Haasan
generously wished to include a sample of vegetarian bigotry
– which no one ate, and finally, custard. Ammi and I were
against the custard but Haasan insisted. Not that he liked
custard – he was simply asserting our right to be Anglo-
Indian.

And everything on the menu was served up together.
Ammi would have served things in courses, but Haasan was
her conscience that night. Courses, he declared, were a direct
contradiction of her campaign, of her commitment to the
present. To eat by courses was to accept the tyranny of

chronological time. It was to allow that the past was an appetizer for the present, that the future was our just dessert.

Later, in the Fort, she told me that she had wanted the moment captured in a photograph, but Haasan had vetoed the idea. To photograph the present, he had argued, was not to make it permanent. It was merely to pander to posterity. So no magnesium flared and no shutters clicked, though Ammi later regretted giving in to Haasan's dogmatism. So did I.

Haasan had asked for all the papers the next morning just in case one of them got the result wrong. Long before *Dawn*, the *Pioneer* or the *Hindustan Times* flew over the wall, even before the sun had risen, there was a semi-circle of people sitting in the courtyard, facing the door, waiting for the news to come. From left to right, Haasan, Asharfi, Bhukay, Bihari, Moonis and I; there was an empty chair in the middle because at precisely eleven o'clock the previous night, Ammi pleaded her age and retired. Good news or bad, she warned us before going to bed, tell me only after I have had my tea.

The dak edition of the *Hindustan Times* arrived at a quarter to six, skimming over the wall and thump-landing like a novice bird. Asharfi got to it first. There was election news on the front page but no details, just the big picture. The Muslim League had won the Muslim seats and the Congress had swept the rest. Helped by several hands, Asharfi turned the pages looking for the seat-by-seat results. She found them on the back page, column after column of fine-print, but U.P. figured nowhere. There were scorecards for Bengal, Punjab, Madras, even Bihar, but not a word about us. Then we found a little boxed item which told us that results from the United Provinces were awaited at the time of going to press.

Then, at six-fifteen, came the *Pioneer* and Bihari caught it even before it hit the ground. He just undid the rolled-up tube – not even shaking it out where it was folded down the middle – looked at the headline half of the front page and threw it up into the air while shouting something that I couldn't make out. Asharfi burst into tears and Moonis went to comfort her because Haasan was somehow sitting on the shoulders of Bhukay and Bihari and they were all shouting in chorus what Bihari had been shrieking singly: Begum Kulsum Ganjoo, Zindabad!

It happened too fast for me to take in. In a film the paper would have arced up in slow motion; there would have been time to watch Asharfi's face crinkle into joy, time to savour the rough happiness behind Haasan's hoisting, and only then would the *Pioneer* have fallen in a shower of rustling sheets, like a blessing. As it was, the newspaper slapped the floor, still folded, and Ammi appeared at her bedroom window looking smudged and grumpy.

Arrey, what is this commotion? she demanded, her sleep-slurred voice breaking with irritation.

Everyone quietened.

Her eye fell on Moonis.

And where is my tea? she asked querulously.

We all burst out laughing, even the crying Asharfi.

Haasan picked the paper up and raised a hand for silence.

Begum Amjadi Bano, Congress, eight hundred and seventy-two votes, he read out formally, looking at Ammi in between words. Begum Shakila Ara, Muslim League, four thousand and twenty-three votes. Begum Kulsum Ganjoo, Independent – Haasan's voice wobbled on the last word and he paused to take a deep breath – Begum Kulsum Ganjoo, he repeated, his voice hoarse but steady, four thousand, three hundred and fifty-one votes!

The paper became airborne again, but this time I was watching Ammi. The newest member of the United Provinces Legislative Assembly, chosen by the electors of the Lucknow (Muslim Women's) constituency, had just enough composure to ask for tea again, before covering her face with her hands and letting the happy tears come.

But Begum Kulsum Ganjoo never took her seat in the Assembly . . . because she was disqualified on a technicality. Had we read the third paper that arrived that morning, *Dawn*, we would have learnt right then that Begum Shakila Ara of the Muslim League, who came second, had filed suit asking for Ammi's election to be set aside. Her lawyer submitted that Ammi had no right to stand for elections in the first place. He argued that Ammi did not own the Lalbagh house, and since all candidates for election had to own property of a minimum rateable value, her candidature was, as he put it, ipso facto null and void.

What do they mean by saying that we don't own the Lalbagh house? asked Asharfi indignantly. It's been in our family for generations. It was my father's house and his father's and his father's father's all the way back to 1857.

Rifaqat, who was the family advocate, explained.

They aren't saying that it is not your father's house. In fact their case is based upon that fact: that the house is still the property of your father, that your mother has no independent title to it and therefore doesn't meet the requirement that each candidate should own personal property of a certain value.

But he has been gone fifteen years, said Asharfi, bewildered.

Rifaqat nodded. That's what I told your mother. She just has to file a plea that her husband's property be transferred to her name on the grounds of prolonged absence and presumption of death. There are ways of making it apply with retrospective effect and her election would be perfectly legal. But she won't do it.

Asharfi wasn't surprised. Neither were the rest of us. Ammi hadn't waited for Intezar all these years to be the one to declare him dead. She ignored Rifaqat's urging and did nothing to contest the Muslim League suit. Consequently, she was disqualified.

The odd thing was that, as far as we could tell, she didn't mind. She seemed relieved at her rigged defeat; as though it had honourably discharged her from her lifelong vigil for Intezar. She even decided to leave Lucknow and live with Masroor. In the fortnight before she left for Delhi, Ammi grew younger before our eyes. It was as if, along with the house, she was casting off the years she had lived in it. Without fear or weaselling compromise, she had fought for her beliefs, kept faith with a world that everyone else wanted dead – and lost. Now she was radiant with the irresponsibility that came with honourable defeat, weightless with the freedom of the declared bankrupt. She was finished with causes: her goal in Delhi was to knit Masroor a woollen topi before the winter set in.

Ammi, Asharfi and I travelled to Delhi together. They needed an escort and I needed to report for work. Patrick had sent word that I wasn't to return to Simla before checking with the Cecil in Delhi; it was the off-season in the mountains while the capital was coping with the winter rush, so he thought I might be needed there.

We arrived at the Pandara Road barracks in the middle of the afternoon. I nearly missed the turn at the roundabout because the landmarks from a childhood lived near by were missing. Children's Park with its slides and swings and man-sized concrete mushrooms was still unbuilt. In its place was a wedge-shaped green planted with jamun trees. Pandara Road was too young for a signboard and the giant sheeshum trees that used to flank it were forty years smaller, just ambitious saplings. The great civil service bungalows of my time were gone: in their place, low, single-storeyed barracks ran along the road, like a mail train stranded on a platform.

Masroor was outside, waiting for us. He and I carried the luggage in. 'In' was three rooms in a row, that led into each other. They all gave out into a covered verandah which merged with a small courtyard. The courtyard was humid with drying clothes. A dozen clothes-lines were strung across it and hung with all sorts of clothes, including saris and a ruffled petticoat.

They aren't all mine, said Masroor.

I left them to settle in and took the waiting phut-phut across the city to Ludlow Castle and the Cecil. I wondered if I'd be able to get my old room back at the East India C——. It turned out that I didn't need it.

Captain Nazar, the Estate Officer, looked unhappy and embarrassed. Two-thirds of the rooms, he said mournfully, were empty. You chose a bad time to go on leave. He was really saying that business was bad and that the Cecil was retrenching. Also that I had been retrenched. He wrote me a wonderful reference, unasked. I put it into my tin trunk and carried it back to Pandara Road. I had nowhere else to go. When Masroor opened the door, I told him standing on the threshold that I didn't have a job. He pulled me in and opened a bottle of rum. The rest of the evening was a hospitable blank.

I was unemployed for that evening. The next day, I was

344

earning my keep again, thanks to Masroor's quiet word with the manager of the newly opened Ambassador Hotel and Captain Nazar's reference, in that order. I ought to have been ashamed that Masroor had pulled rank to get me a job but I wasn't. I was, in fact, warmed by a quiet glow of satisfaction. Someone, at least, thought me worth the bother and embarrassment of asking favours. I had never believed that friendship was only possible between self-reliant equals — it was a silly, bourgeois notion, too expensive for the working man.

I shared the servants' quarters in the left-hand corner of the courtyard with Abdullah the dhobi. The clothes on the lines were his. Ammi and Asharfi knew him because his father had done their laundry for years in Lucknow. Now he was in Delhi trying to make his way, and Masroor had given him the use of the quarters, plus the running water and the drying space he needed. In return he kept Masroor's uniforms starched and doubled as a bearer in the evenings.

We settled in smoothly. Asharfi even hung her pictures up without incident. When Asharfi began unpacking the frames, I pleaded diarrhoea and hurried to the remoteness of the lavatories in the courtyard. When I returned Masroor was standing on a lean-to ladder taking aim with a hammer. No, not in a row, said Asharfi. Masroor obediently descended two rungs and began tapping the nail in. Hanging on the wall, above and to the left of Masroor's present perch, was the group of six gopis that I'd first seen in the Lalbagh zenana. By the time the two of them had finished, there wasn't a room in the house which didn't bear witness to Asharfi's consummated passion for the woman that her brother had loved at a chaste mountain distance.

Neither Ammi nor Masroor raised any objection. Asharfi looked puzzled and a little thwarted. She had made her point fearlessly, she had declared as explicitly as was consistent with style that she would live with Masroor on her own terms, without air-brushing any part of her past. To be met with tame acquiescence must have been disappointing. There was only one explanation: neither mother nor brother had noticed that the gopis' faces belonged to Asharfi and Parwana.

Ammi and I went on long exploratory walks. Cornwallis

Road was just a step away, and built on either side of it were familiar places. Ambassador Hotel, where I worked, was five minutes down the road and facing it was a lovely court of red-brick flats built by Lutyens' main contractor, Sir Sobha Singh. The road ended at Lady Willingdon Park – Lodi Gardens by its proper name. There civilization ended and, according to Abdullah, scrubby jungle stocked with hyenas began. New Delhi in the 'forties was painfully new and it showed at every turn. Everywhere solidly built localities ended in wildernesses, as if the city had been patchily imagined in a dream.

Masroor spent all his time gardening the strip of dirt that fronted his portion of the barracks. Number 28 could be spotted from a furlong away because it was the only one with a hedged-off lawn and a façade obscured by creepers, shrubs and fruit trees. By the time we moved in, he had already planted raat-ki-raani, chameli, a fig tree, a pear and two custard apples. He bought most of his plants from the mosque at the end of Pandara Road which hadn't seen a proper congregation since the passing of the Mughals, so the current Imam had started a nursery in its grounds to make a living.

One evening, Masroor returned from a visit to the nursery, pushing a wheelbarrow loaded with four tiny date palms, looking triumphant.

Why date palms? asked Asharfi.

Because they grow so slowly and last for ever, he answered.

They took two hundred years to mature properly, he told us. He'd first seen them in Egypt in al Faiyum, the oasis town near Cairo when the Fourth Indian had been deployed in Alexandria. They had held back the sands for centuries. Planting them would be his contribution to the city's future. If they took root, he would feel like a proper Delhiwallah.

But you'll never live to see them fruit, I pointed out.

Yes, put in Asharfi. Why not roses?

Masroor snorted. Roses are for people who move on.

Well, so will you, I said. Soldiering is a transferable job.

Our jobs might be temporary, said Masroor haughtily, but we still have to live like permanent men.

Ammi, Asharfi and I made 28 Pandara Road a moated

fortress which the world outside visited only by appointment. Ammi spent all her time knitting till the heat of summer made wool untouchable. All of us read the newspaper but by unspoken consensus no one mentioned matters of state and Masroor soon learnt not to read the headlines out. The one time this rule was relaxed was during Lexicon games, when the only words we allowed were proper nouns from politics.

I worked the night shift at the hotel. I had discovered that daytime sleep wasn't host to the horrors that I saw at night. I dreamt in large clichés: acres of coffins, forests of pyres, rivers of blood, trains full of corpses, sacks of bleached or bloody skulls. None of this bothered me till a night in June, when one of a heap of skulls showed Masroor's likeness. I pissed in my bed that night but Abdullah rescued me by laundering the sheet discreetly. The next morning I asked for the night shift.

Asharfi spent her days painting. She found a subject in Abdullah's laundered clothes drying on the washing lines. White sheets, bright saris, sober khaki uniforms framed by the courtyard's whitewashed walls and backlit by the sun were stroked in with a palette knife. In between she played board games with whoever was willing, not Ludo or checkers but Monopoly if there was time and Lexicon if there wasn't.

Between March and October, that is, between the announcement of Ammi's election result and the setting in of the cold weather, we had half a year of home-bound contentment. The world elsewhere met crossroads, land-marks, turning points and tragedies, but in 28 Pandara Road we remained at peace with ourselves.

Then the first chill of winter set everyone worrying.

Ammi worried whether it would turn cold enough to vindicate the double-knit pullovers she had made for Asharfi and Masroor. Would it be cold enough for gloves? She didn't want to start without knowing because casting stitches for the fingers was so troublesome. Or could she do mittens, which would mean only doing the thumbs? Masroor worried about what the cold would do to his garden. Dressed in his territorial army shorts, khurpi in hand, he dug up his seasonal flowers to cut off their bulbs. These he stored away, happy that hope had been salvaged for the following season. Mostly he worried

347

about his date palms. It bothered him that he wouldn't have the house long enough to see the palms through their formative years. He fretted that the next official tenant might neglect them, or worse, tap them prematurely for their juice. Tapping stunted date palms. Left alone they were splendid trees, sometimes as tall as forty feet with a crown of leaves some thirty feet across.

He had been at some reference book. Masroor read too much and believed too much of what he read. A few days later he was pacing the garden in a frenzy because he had discovered that date palms were sometimes killed by cannibal banyan trees.

Ammi didn't bother to look up from her knitting. Asharfi laughed. He turned to me for solidarity.

Rubbish, I said.

It's true, he insisted. Birds eat the banyan's figs and spit the pips into the date palm's crown, where they sprout and send down aerial roots that hug the palm and smother it.

Rubbish, I said again.

All right, said Masroor hotly, I'll show you. It's in the *Cyclopaedia of India*. The great banyan in Calcutta's Botanical Gardens grew out of a date palm. *Phoenix sylvestris* is often prey to the *Ficus indica*, he recited, as if Latin names made stories true. The next day he covered the palms with a roof of fine wire mesh to shield them from bird-borne killer seeds.

I was worrying about other, more ominous things. Front-page bells had tolled all summer without worrying me. In May Nehru throttled the British Cabinet's plan for a con-federal India which, I remembered from the history books, had been the only alternative to Partition. At the end of July Jinnah called upon Muslims to celebrate 16 August as Direct Action Day. Nobody knew what that meant till the day rolled round and the killings began in Calcutta. Even that didn't disturb me much because Calcutta was a thousand miles away. Then some more were killed in Noakhali, but for me that was Bangladesh and someone else's country.

I only began to worry at the end of October, when the violence moved westward with the killings in Bihar. By November, there was a definite east-west trend. On the sixth, there was a riot at a fair in the pilgrim town of Garhmukhteshwar, just a hundred miles east of Delhi. I didn't remember it from my history lessons and that worried me. What else didn't I remember? Had there been riots in Delhi just before Partition? History lessons didn't help here. We had only been taught the big facts, not the minor killings. I knew there had been a pogrom of Muslims in Delhi – I just didn't know when. Up to now I had assumed that the slaughter had begun with Partition, on the fourteenth or fifteenth of August 1947, which meant I had ten clear months of peace. Unless the riots reached Delhi earlier.

November came and went, then December, without any violence in the vicinity. I had the vague impression that such killing as happened in Delhi had happened inside the walls of the Old City. That was reassuring. Dadi lived within the walls in Kashmiri Gate, but she was a Hindu and in Delhi it was mainly Muslims who had died. Still . . .

I caught myself worrying about Dadi and stopped. I knew she had survived Partition; I'd cremated her on the fiftieth anniversary of the Quit India rebellion. There were other things I knew: that I had a father in boarding school, who, twenty years from now, would sire his only son, that I'd be middle-aged before I was born.

I didn't feel giddy or scared thinking these thoughts any more; not only because there was no going back – if going back was the right phrase for returning to the future – but because I'd learnt from Ammi that there was no past or future, just one continuous life where everything happened now. Like the founder of the Anjuman-Bara-i-Tahaffuz-i-Haal (and for more intractable reasons), the present was time enough for me.

The days and weeks of 1947 drained away unnoticed as if they belonged to some other year. For me, each peaceful day just meant that the lull grew larger. It was a summer out of hell, the hottest hot weather anyone could remember in Delhi. Through May we stopped going out in the day; Asharfi, Ammi and I waited out the sun in long siestas and sluggish games of Monopoly.

349

Lying in bed through those sticky afternoons, I sometimes thought of my life in Kashmiri Gate. The East India C—— would rise before my open eyes and I found that I could remember the name of every noble patron on that double row of crests painted above the doors of the Imperial Tannery. That last blank crest in the second row would be filled in now, with Mountbatten's name . . . time was running out. Sometimes I thought of Dadi and wondered what she was doing now, or of Parwana, whom I had rescued once, so long ago. I worried about them but never enough to take the trouble to visit. I didn't even know if Parwana was still with my grandmother. It wouldn't have been difficult to find out, but I wasn't sure that I wanted Parwana in my life just when Pandara Road had come to seem like home. I couldn't take the risk of her upsetting Asharfi or Masroor again, not when I had less than three months left of family life, before the certain horror of Partition.

Partition became official on the third of June over the radio. Masroor had a Murphy radio set, large and almost perfectly round; its upper half, where the speakers were, was upholstered in shiny gold cloth. The broadcast had been announced in the papers, so five minutes before the time, Masroor gathered us around the radio and switched it on. A green pilot light came on and in less than half a minute the valves heated up and the speakers began crackling. Mountbatten came on first to announce, on behalf of His Majesty's Government, the decision to divide India, and then Nehru and Jinnah followed to say that they, and their parties, were agreeable. Neither said much but their voices rose and fell a lot as if they were addressing a crowd, which, I suppose, they were.

Family life was harder after that. Not that anything happened; no bombs exploded, no riots occurred . . . not in the neighbourhood, anyway. Life went on, but with a difference: it was like living on notice. Suddenly we didn't own our world any more; we were tenants living a rented life, the lease for which ran out in the middle of August.

The rains came to Delhi early; by the middle of June, two weeks before the monsoons were due, the avenues and vistas of New Delhi were under water. Pandara Road flowed like a river past our house and Masroor fretted because his garden was periodically submerged. For six days it rained and rained and rained, so hard and so continuously that moss greened the sunless courtyard. Ammi, Asharfi and Abdullah were miserable in the gloom, especially Abdullah, whose washing never dried, but I was grateful to the rains for breaking up the sinister calm of this Partition year.

Besides, the rains brought news of Dadi.

The report was buried in one of the inside pages of the *Hindustan Times* along with other news about the damage the rains had caused on the other bank of the Jamuna. Not much of Delhi's population lived on that side of the river but the fraction that did was found on trees, telegraph poles and other elevations after the floodwater had submerged their undrained bustees. The army threw a pontoon bridge across the heaving waters to evacuate the survivors, mainly lepers, lunatics, delinquent juveniles, hermaphrodites and repentant prostitutes – any group which needed to be quarantined by a river's width from Delhi's rate-paying citizens. Among these (according to the *Hindustan Times*) were the inmates of a female reformatory called Nari Niketan. I felt the electric thrill of recognition; I knew them. They were Dadi's fallen women.

Also, they were in my neighbourhood. The paper reported that now, after several attempts to house them in tent colonies pitched on open greens had been thwarted by solid citizens who didn't want lepers and prostitutes living next door, no matter how temporarily, the municipality had herded them into the Old Fort. The Fort was a good location because it had gates that could be closed, high enclosing walls which, though ruined, were hard to scale, and best of all, the nearest respectable locality was a mile or more away. That nearest respectable locality was our barracks on Pandara Road. Before the Partition announcement over the radio, I wouldn't have gone visiting, but given the inevitable, I had nothing to lose. So the next morning, a little after ten, I set out for the Fort to find my grandmother.

It was 22nd June, a Sunday. It had been a Sunday the last

time I'd visited the Fort four years ago, only now I was going alone. I hadn't shared my news with Masroor or Asharfi – they thought I was going for a walk. Ammi reminded me to take an umbrella. It was less than a mile to the Fort but getting there was slow work in the wet weather. There were puddles to be walked around and spray from the occasional car to be avoided and despite the umbrella I was damp all over and soaked in places by the time I arrived. I expected a guard at the gate but there wasn't one; perhaps the rain had driven him away.

Dadi's fallen women weren't hard to find. They were housed in a row of recessed arches set into the Fort wall, less than fifty yards from the gate through which I had entered. I couldn't see any tents – there probably hadn't been the time to pitch them. I took up position behind a column of the sandstone octagon which had once been Humayun's library, and spied on them from a distance.

They looked like bedraggled ghosts in their dirty grey saris that matched the gloom of the overcast sky. Nineteen fallen women, one to each hole in the wall, were being taught modesty. Six social-working matrons – I could tell them apart from the inmates by their starched saris in more than one colour – were moving from recess to recess, improvising curtains. They would stretch a string across the arch and hang a length of cloth on it with clothespegs; knowing my grandmother, it was probably khadi. Even from a distance, Dadi was unmistakable: erect, head tidily covered with a shawl, string bag slung over a forearm, umbrella in hand, tirelessly instructing repentant whores in decorum. She would have done more good in this miserable weather by giving them a cup of tea.

Then as I watched, five of the six social workers, including Dadi, left their charges and set off in a direction that took them deeper into the Fort. I had walked through a hundred puddles to see her and she was gone. Not that I had planned to walk up to her and start chatting; Dadi and I were strangers in this time and if it hadn't been for Parwana, we might never have met. Still, it was annoying to have her disappear like that. I wondered where Dadi and her friends had gone. Perhaps, having visited their charges, they had set off to inspect the lepers and the lunatics, wherever they were lodged.

Disappointed, I came out of hiding and walked slowly back towards the gate. The women were now in the care of the one starched matron who had stayed behind. She was wearing a plain white sari and I placed her as a respectable widow appointed by Dadi and the other trustees to manage the reformatory. She didn't seem particularly diligent because as soon as Dadi and the others were out of sight she abandoned her wards and found herself a sheltered niche to smoke a cigarette in. But it wasn't my business.

I stopped by the mosque where, four years ago, Ammi, Asharfi, Haasan and I had eaten bitter sandwiches. It had been in a good cause, to cheer up Asharfi, though I couldn't remember why she had been depressed in the first place. Then it came to me; not because I remembered, but simply because I heard a step and turned, and saw standing there, in a starched white sari, the cause of Asharfi's long-ago sadness: Parwana.

Why are you wearing white?

Have you come to take me away?

Our questions overlapped.

No! I said loudly in answer to hers. I wasn't there to take anyone away. Quite the reverse – I was just hoping that no one would be taken away from me.

She looked disappointed but not surprised, like a grown-up princess in a defective fairy tale.

Why are you wearing white? I persisted, partly because I wanted to know but mainly to change the subject.

Because I help her with them, she said, looking over her shoulder in the direction where Dadi had gone.

This was too cryptic for me, so I waited for her to explain.

Because of the children, she said impatiently. A dead husband is better than no husband at all.

The children. The twins! I had forgotten that Parwana was a mother. November 1943 . . . they would be three and a half now.

Dadi had made Parwana the warden of Nari Niketan.

Since a woman in charge of fallen women couldn't be one herself, Dadi had made her a widow as well.

You're living with her? I asked.

She nodded. But I don't want to.

Why? I asked, genuinely surprised. I wanted to know, since it appeared to me that Dadi, in her managing way, was being kind. Parwana had a job and she and her children had a place to stay. That seemed a lot for an unmarried mother in 1947.

Parwana looked at me incredulously.

Because I don't want to supervise prostitutes for the rest of my life, she said in a flat, certain voice. And I won't raise my children on someone's charity.

There was silence. I tried to think of a good reason for leaving quickly.

You won't help? she asked in a level voice.

What can I do? I countered defensively, my pitch higher than I wanted it to be.

You can marry me, she said, unfairly answering my rhetorical question. If you marry me, there will be two people to look after the boys. With a living husband I could practise my shorthand and get a real job.

Nothing about her expression suggested that she wasn't serious. I tried not to swallow but my Adam's apple bobbed on its own.

Then she relented.

It doesn't matter, she said briskly. Madam's husband has an English friend, also a judge, who is going back to England. His wife wants an Indian girl to go with them to help her around the house. Madam asked me if I wanted to go.

Go to England to be a memsahib's servant on the eve of Independence! She wasn't my business but I was appalled.

What about the children? I asked.

She just looked at me for a moment and smiled wryly.

Why do you think I asked you first? she said.

Then she looked over her shoulder again and stubbed her cigarette out. I must go, she said. Madam will be back any moment now.

She turned to leave, then stopped.

Do you know where Asharfi is? she asked abruptly.

I shrugged; it seemed a smaller lie than shaking my head.

She left without another word and I fled the Fort . . . trying not to feel guilty at feeling so relieved.

August came round and then the fifteenth of August, Independence Day. Pakistan had been inaugurated the day before. But the excitement, to my relief, didn't enter our house. Masroor half-heartedly suggested going down to the Red Fort to hear Nehru speak but no one was too keen and we all stayed at home. All of us except Abdullah, who had finished his washing for the week and wanted a look at the great man. I warned him about the possibility of trouble. He left his skull- cap behind.

He got home safely enough. Crores of people, he said, his eyes glittering. And Nehru had spoken without a note.

Any trouble? I asked, but he shook his head.

Would it never begin?

I couldn't sleep any more. On the twenty-fourth of August, Masroor took ten days' leave to think his future out. Each morning brought news of the massacres in the Punjab. Abdullah described a butchered train filled with corpses nearly every day as if he had actually seen it draw in.

Guests began to trickle into the house. One of Masroor's peons who lived in a village called Masjid Moth in the jungly suburbs south of New Delhi was the first to come. It was a Muslim village and everyone was leaving because the fields had begun to make odd sounds after dark. On the last day of August, Bihari and Moonis arrived from Lucknow. They didn't have a reason to give, just a kind of feeling.

They gave Masroor something to do. He pinned up a lavatory routine. He cleared the verandah to make room for our guests to sleep in. And somehow, through his quarter-master friend, he managed cots and rations for twelve. In between he found the time to assemble a waist-high summer house for his precious palms. The quartermaster had un-earthed a cache of redundant ventilator shutters with ground-glass panes. It was the rain and the coming cold he had to shelter them from, he told us.

On the morning of the second of September, Abdullah left

for his weekly round with his laundered bundle. It was the ninth day of Masroor's furlough and nothing had happened. The air was thick with news of gory death but the neighbourhood was quiet. That was reason enough for hope because it wasn't world peace we were looking for – just a little puddle of calm. So no one tried to stop Abdullah.

It was dinnertime before we thought of him again and though we put off eating by an hour, he didn't return. Neither was he there the next morning, the morning of the third. Bihari and I set off on bicycles to look for him. It was all a bit pointless, till it became strange.

We saw the smoke and heard shouting. The smoke was spiralling up from beyond the first line of government bungalows on the left. But what sent us home was the bicycle. It had rubber straps on its carrier like Abdullah's and it was lying at the end of the road, where Lady Willingdon's park began. It was just a fallen bike – no sinister stain or bloodstained skull-cap gave it menace.

But without a word we swerved our cycles about and pedalled furiously down Cornwallis Road. We must have been shouting with terror because we were hoarse when we braked in front of the summer-housed date palms.

Then we felt foolish because here there was normalcy. Across the road on the further pavement, a young man was reading a newspaper. The news couldn't be in our neighbourhood if he needed a paper to catch up with it. I even went up to him and asked if he had heard of riots in New Delhi. He turned a page of the *Inqulab* (I had enough Urdu to read the bold type of the masthead) before looking up unhurriedly and shaking his head. Feeling foolish, I went indoors with Bihari.

Abdullah hadn't returned in our absence. Masroor was in the garden reading the *Hindustan Times* and eating scrambled eggs and rotis (the bread man hadn't been by for four days). I tried to read the news over his shoulder, but it was difficult because he kept turning the pages. The paper rustled from right to left as he looked for the sports page. From right to left . . .

That's how the man on the pavement across the road had turned the pages . . . but pages in Urdu were turned from left

356

to right! I looked over the hedge where the man had been – there was no one there.

I told Masroor. He took one look at my face and ran inside the house to telephone. The phone was ringing by the time he got to it. It was Colonel Kardar, the quartermaster. Muslim families were being attacked in Lodi Estate, he told Masroor. Muslim officials and their families were being evacuated to the safety of the Old Fort. We were to stay inside the house with the doors latched till the trucks arrived.

Well, we didn't. We didn't because our neighbours' children found a dhobi bundle sitting in the service lane just by the courtyard door. Masroor opened it. It was a red-and-white dhobi bundle. A red-and-white dhobi bundle – with the dhobi inside. Abdullah was home.

Then we were running, all of us. No one locked up, no one packed, Masroor didn't water his date palms. No one called the police. Ammi, Asharfi, Masroor, Bihari, Moonis, the Masjid Moth family and I found ourselves running. Running running running down Cornwallis Road, running in the clear light of day to a ruined fort. Not for one step of the way did I forget that I was circumcised.

We reached the Fort at a walk because no one else on the road was hurrying and we began to feel conspicuous. We walked up that ramp of earth to the gate, as we had done four years ago on a Sunday morning. Only, this time we had company.

Home

FOR THE FIRST three days there was no refuge from the smell of turds churned up by rain. The first thing anyone running through the gates seemed to do was find a bush or shielding outcrop and shit. It was as if they were expelling the last residue of the country they had fled. Perhaps this was fanciful. Perhaps shit-scared was a better explanation.

Some never rose from a squat because they got diarrhoea, which was widely available. They shat so much and so often that they returned to the motherland the substance they had drawn from her. Many were buried in the Fort and in them the new Republic lost nothing – they had paid their dues in full.

There were others like us who, after the first hot surge of thanksgiving, became constipated. We walked about pent-up and farting, firing off little salutes to India or Pakistan or the not-quite-dead Empire. The ones who were undecided about their loyalties developed stomach aches from the wind trapped inside. Masroor suffered particularly.

A grotesque normalcy descended on the camp when, on the fourth day, it broke out into a rash of babies. Like any human settlement it was reproducing itself. Several of them died, choked by the smell of shit and its attendant hazards. Then the camp authorities – who didn't live there – improvised a maternity ward in the disused mosque and the death rate dropped. So more children lived to confront the dilemma of nationality. Patriots and traitors were born every hour. The newly minted Republic wasn't offering dual citizenship.

On the fifth day, a full twenty-four hours before the drinking water or the army surplus tents arrived, came the counters with their lists. Father's/Husband's Name; Sex; No. of Children; Place of Residence; Home Town; Preferred Nationality . . .

They came in the evening, just as Masroor had successfully got a fire going with rampart stones and balled-up newspapers, the only fuel available. We had tried burning turds on the analogy of cow-pats but it was impossible to set those nuggets of despair alight. We needed the fire to boil the water to make the tea that Mountbatten's wife had given us that morning.

So they came in the middle of a critical operation because we hadn't drunk tea since fleeing Pandara Road. Preferred Nationality, they said, and waited with an air of urgent boredom. They weren't so much putting questions as filling in blanks. Had it been another form, they might have said Preferred Gender:– or Preferred History:– in much the same tone.

Masroor just looked at them and there was such exhaustion on his face that they muttered something about coming later and moved off to the neighbouring huddle of intent tea makers.

But the fact remained that there were two countries now, and sooner or later the question would have to be answered. That night I stopped being constipated because anxiety moved my bowels. What would Masroor say? How would Ammi advise him? And where did Asharfi stand?

We had been forced to flee Pandara Road in shameful panic; Abdullah was dead, murdered, the Lalbagh house was gone . . . there was nothing left to keep Masroor from saying Pakistan. Long years ago, according to Nehru, he and some others had made a tryst with Destiny, but Masroor didn't have an appointment with anyone quite as grand. All he had were the date palms. Some weeks ago I made a date with date palms . . . he could have said – but it didn't sound like a good reason for staying.

Haasan arrived the next afternoon, bare-chested and bleeding. We had a tent by then, so we rushed him in, horrified, before asking questions. For a man with a gory chest, he was remarkably composed. He had arrived the day before, in the evening, having caught the first train to Delhi the moment he heard of the riots. Lucknow, he said, had been peaceful till the day he left. They had turned him away at the gate when he had come to search for us. The only Hindus allowed inside were civil servants, he was told.

It was too late to claim that he was actually Muhammad bin Qasim, so this morning he had opened the scars of the swastika that had been gouged on him a quarter of a century ago, by Hindus who thought he was a Mussalman. It had proved good for something after all those years: the bleeding lines convinced the guards at the gate. No Hindu was going to carve up his chest to pass for a Muslim. They let him in.

Haasan rounded off to twenty-five the number of people Ammi recognized in the camp in the first six days. They were all Muslims except for Haasan and me, which wasn't remarkable since the camp in the Fort was meant to shelter Muslim refugees from the violence outside. Some of them Ammi remembered from a youth spent travelling with her father – and Kamran Gulmargi had travelled a good deal, mainly to stay ahead of his creditors. Most of her father's contemporaries whom she spotted in the Fort were poets: Rizwan Monghyri from Bihar, whom she had recognized at once in spite of his beard and the fact that he arrived wearing a torn achkan and nothing else; Angrez Mashriqi, whose soul had always lived in London even as his body languished in Jabalpur; Javed Haryanvi, whose accent had so appalled her father; Masud Deccani, once, according to Kamran, the most promising talent of his generation, tragically drowned in drink – they were all there. Some of them she hadn't seen in twenty years, and suddenly they were gathered in one place, almost as if they had been invited to a valedictory mushaira.

Then there were her father's relatives whom she had lost touch with after marrying Intezar. The marriage had been a scandal: that she, a Syed, descended from the Prophet, through his daughter Bibi Fatima and Hazrat Ali, should have married a Hindu convert, a first-generation Muslim! It had provoked her kin to anger, embarrassment, pity and contempt, none of which had been welcome so she had put relatives behind her. But suddenly, there were kinsfolk at every turn: her cousin Khaleda who had married so well – a nawabzada distantly related to the Bhopals. Khaleda's sister, Sameena, relict of a minor taluqdar and mistress of a dozen mango orchards. Omar, her mother's first cousin's son, who had won a cricket blue at Cambridge, who had nearly played for England, then almost played for India, and had later turned out for Nawanagar when his duties as A.D.C. to the Nawab of Tonk permitted – he was there too, sometimes sitting on his hold-all, at others lobbying the camp authorities for a tent. His brother Shoaib – who had become a planter at the other end of the subcontinent from Tonk, in Assam – was wandering about the camp in long shorts, looking absurdly as if he was doing the rounds of his tea estate. One by one, they all turned up, aunts, uncles, and cousins, some long-forgotten and others several times removed. On their seventh night in the Fort, Ammi observed that the only one missing from this gathering of the clan was her great-uncle Athar, Pilibhit's only bar-at-law. He arrived the next morning in a black coat, striped trousers and starched white lawyer's bands, attended by his wives. It was uncanny.

And it wasn't just Ammi who kept seeing people she knew. The same thing happened to Masroor. In one day he met Saleem, Salman, Inayat, Rizwan and the incomparable Yousuf bin Ansoo. It was like a college reunion for the class of '42 – except that they weren't classmates; they were fellow-disappearees who had all done time in limbo. The only one he had actually met before was Saleem because they had both sheltered in the mosque between the tracks, but one face led to another. Saleem introduced him to Salman, his brother, who'd once been in love with Farheen, who had later married Rizwan, whose father had retained Inayat Sahib as his advocate for a land dispute. And Yousuf . . . who didn't know Yousuf bin Ansoo – the man who had made more Indians weep than Nadir Shah. And then one morning Maulvi Muin-ud-din arrived, the Imam of the station mosque, who had sheltered Masroor and Saleem, and the class of '42 had its teacher.

This place is full of people we know, said Asharfi for the fortieth time, looking bewildered. She wasn't the only one; Ammi, Masroor, Rizwan, Saleem, Javed, Masud – everyone we met – had said the same thing, in the same words, at one time or another.

The Fort is a sump, said Angrez Mashriqi, into which the Mussalmans of Hindustan are being drained.

That's a metaphor, not an explanation, said Haasan rudely.

But sooner or later everyone reached for metaphor as they tried to account for the rash of familiar faces in the Fort. Saleem, who was enthusiastic about Pakistan, decided that the Fort was an open-air retiring room in some mammoth railway station where everyone was waiting for the train to Pakistan. It's like going home, he suggested. You're bound to meet friends and relatives headed in the same direction.

Maulvi Muin-ud-din's explanation was simpler. Everyone knew everyone else because they were part of one large family and the Fort was our ark. Given how much it had rained in the recent past, this seemed literally true.

Ark or not, the Fort was a benign enough refuge once we got used to the rain, the mud and the open-air shitting. There were tented lavatories but only the women used those; Masroor and I went further and further into the interior of the Fort each day in search of virgin squatting space. We had a tent for the women and the rest of us slept outdoors, which was not as bad as it could have been because it was only the second week of September and the cold weather was a month and a half away. That was six weeks in the future, too remote to worry about – no one in the Fort was thinking more than a meal ahead. Mealtimes were depressing only because we had to queue to be served, but the food itself was edible. Bihari and Haasan had diarrhoea for a few days but no one fell seriously ill.

We even played games. There was a football and a badminton net supplied by the Y.M.C.A. which no one used for a while because there wasn't enough level ground for soccer and the Y.M.C.A. had forgotten to supply shuttles for badminton. Then Masroor put the net and the ball together and got volleyball matches going. It didn't stop there. Masroor became a kind of impresario. He got his army friends to provide a bat and a few rubber balls and improvised tennis-ball cricket. What was even more impressive was that he didn't just start people playing – he went further and organized them into a league. What might have been random evening recreation confined to a few enthusiasts developed instead into seriously competitive cricket, complete with knock-out rounds and a final. The rules, though, were changed halfway through the tournament when Saleem pulled a short ball over the ramparts. No one went to get it back and for a long moment there was a perfect stillness in both players and spectators, like the two-minute silence I remembered from school assemblies, when someone important died. Immediately after this Masroor ruled that all bowling would be under-arm and all shots were to be stroked along the ground. A lofted hit whether it was caught or not meant the batsman was out. These were harsh rules but everyone kept to them.

It didn't stop there. When the tournament was done, Masroor arranged for a team photograph. Colonel Kardar, his quartermaster friend, supplied him with a camera, complete with tripod, and when no one else came forward, I volunteered to take the picture. No one was in cricket whites but, that apart, it was a proper team picture: the players in two rows, one standing with Saleem, the captain, in the middle, the other sitting on the ground, ankles crossed, hands clasped, knees raised, and Masroor, by popular demand, in the middle. They could have just won the Pentangular.

When Colonel Kardar sent the prints back, they sparked off a passion for photographs. Everyone wanted to be in a group picture. The volleyball players followed the cricketers, then it transcended sport. Groups mushroomed on the flimsiest affinities: Moradabad Youngmen; Ladies in Purdah, Mothers and Sisters; Aligarh Old Boys; Friday Prayers (there were two or three of those with different faces showing); family photographs; one of *Khatoon*'s production team and a commemorative picture of the members of that short-lived party, the Anjuman-Bara-i-Tahaffuz-i-Haal. Perhaps everyone in the Fort wanted to be reassured that they still existed and these photographs ratified their existence. Or perhaps they just wanted proof that there had been others with them. Whatever the reason, the pictures had one thing in common: Masroor. He was in all of them, even Mothers and Sisters. Every group wanted him in their picture and though it embarrassed him, he was too considerate to refuse. The lowest common factor in these photographs was my absence – I didn't figure in any, not even the one of Ammi's Anjuman. Not that I expected to find my face in the photographs since I was taking them; still, I felt left out.

The only people in the Fort who avoided us were Ammi's relatives, who probably found it hard to accept that the riots had made them refugees, no better than the family's outcast daughter. Her father's poet friends, on the other hand, sought her out, invariably exclaiming how their little Kulsum had grown. Ammi would look embarrassed and offer them biscuits and tea. Not everyone had biscuits to offer – only those who were brought food parcels by visitors. Thanks to Masroor we were well supplied; he was regularly visited by a dozen brother officers. Only two of the twelve were Muslims but all of them offered Masroor, Ammi and Asharfi the safety of their homes. Masroor refused.

He refused in the name of his extended family, which now included more than kinsfolk. He told me this on one of our exploratory early morning treks for likely places to shit. He felt responsible for more than just his relatives. He had felt this way when we arrived in headlong panic at the Fort and the feeling had grown. First Saleem, Salman, Maulvi Muin-ud-din . . . and then the cricket matches and the group photographs – all of this had made him feel that he was part of a larger something. A larger Muslim something? I didn't ask and he didn't say, but it worried me.

The next morning, Masroor and I, this time with Haasan for company, went further than usual into the ruined Fort in search of private perches. We were still looking when we happened upon Parwana's charges in eight khaki tents pitched in an uneven clearing. Dadi's fallen women had found a fixed address.

They were sitting in a semi-circle chanting their prayers in chorus. Among the drab, dirt-coloured clothes, the bluish white of Parwana's sari was starkly visible. Even from a distance of thirty yards or more, Masroor recognized her at once. I wasn't surprised; he had had practice: all he had ever done in Simla was worship from afar.

What is she – ? was all he said. Haasan (who had spotted Parwana right away) and I waited for more but Masroor said nothing. Silently, he changed direction and found himself a bush. On our way back, Haasan tried to nudge a reaction out of him.

I wonder what she's doing in this place, he said aloud.

Masroor said nothing.

Masroor was noticeably taciturn through the week following our sighting of Parwana but it didn't affect his involvement with the life of the Fort. He was everywhere, head inclined, listening with the raptness of a campaigning politician . . . only, the elections that mattered were over. He helped get letters stamped and posted, he sorted out quarrels about stolen kerosene and disputed enamel mugs, he helped tidy up the departure of a family for Pakistan by getting Colonel Kardar to close their accounts at Lloyds, Connaught Place, and transfer the monies to Karachi – he became for all those who lacked access their postbox to the world outside.

People began to look to him. The volleyball games, the cricket tournament, those group photographs . . . for dislocated refugees any initiative was a passport to leadership. And Masroor had other credentials. He was young, therefore dynamic; a soldier, consequently trained to command; he had relatives and friends, so he was a respectable someone; he was the head of his family, which mitigated his youth. They gave him their trust and he repaid them by running their errands, answering their questions and hearing them out, eighteen hours a day. It seemed to suit him because he looked exalted. This had something to do with his glimpse of Parwana: cactus-like, he flowered in his desert of self-denial.

Why is he doing this? I asked myself for the hundredth time, watching Masroor poring over a stranger's problems by lantern light.

He's claiming his destiny, said Haasan solemnly.

I managed not to say bugger off but only just.

Silence didn't put him off. He had a theory. Haasan with a theory was a dog with a bone.

You remember his grandfather?

We were contemporaries in kindergarten, I wanted to say,

365

instead of which I just looked at him. It was wasted effort; his question had been rhetorical and he wasn't waiting for an answer.

It had all started, according to him, with that privately printed epic in two volumes: *The History and Destiny of the Ganjoos*. In this strange, hybrid book, part history, part horoscope, Kalidass had predicted glory for his infant son. The life of his only child, he forecast, would become synonymous with the history of his people. It happened exactly as Kalidass had written . . . but to another man's son.

Destiny could have been forgiven for missing her mark, so close was the resemblance between Intezar, once Charandass, and the usurper who got to play the part originally written for him. Both were the scions of expatriate Kashmiri brahmin families, both the only sons of ambitious, thrusting fathers, both born in the United Provinces and raised in similar cities – one the political capital of the state, the other the seat of its higher judiciary – and both owned degrees in law which they never used. They were of average height, light-skinned, and both had long upper lips and receding hairlines. To compound the confusion, they were also contemporaries, but Charandass was a year or two younger than the Nehru boy, Jawaharlal.

So much in common and yet – Haasan paused for drama – and yet Jawaharlal today is India's Prime Minister while Intezar is less than nothing – just a missing person, a blank. That's why Masroor spends his days and nights hearing them out. He is doing what his father should have done. He is claiming his people.

I looked across at Masroor, hunched over paper in a wash of yellow lantern light. There was a twisted plausibility to Haasan's explanation – the son redeeming his father. But who were his people? Nehru had the Indian end sewn up and the land of the pure was Jinnah's personal fief. Which left him the people in the Fort. A mainly Muslim people in the Fort. If he was claiming this people, where did that leave me?

Haasan's hypothesis began to look better over the next three days. I noticed Masroor helping families fill in forms – the same citizenship forms he had baulked at filling in for himself. He helped mainly by listening as they rehearsed the arguments for and against, which they must have gone over a million times in the silence of their minds. He offered no comments, no arguments; he just listened. That seemed to help because everyone who came to him completed their forms. Haasan asked him which way the tide was flowing.

Pakistan, he said.

If Masroor's people, his Fort constituency, were planning to leak across the border, was he going to leave with them? It began to seem likely. Ammi's relatives, who were going to Karachi in a body, made things worse by starting to cultivate her. Now that Masroor was a somebody in the Fort, his mother became a useful person to know.

Ammi was sceptical at first, but human enough to enjoy the attention of kinsfolk. It moved her in some abstract way to think that her children had cousins about them whom they could count on in this time of dislocation. Asharfi was particularly vulnerable to the comfort of owning an extended family; she had lost so much that seemed durable, like her home and her childhood friends, that blood-relatives, however remote, appeared in the light of permanent things. She dandled nephews she had never known, she laughed along with her new-found cousins, and words like Karachi and Qaid-i-Azam began to creep into campfire conversations. Aunts of all descriptions – phoophees, khalas, maiyas – sitting in the Fort, projected themselves effortlessly into the localities of Karachi that they planned to live in. Their fantasies made these places familiar.

Karachi is just like Bombay, said Omar casually. Ammi, who had never set eyes on Bombay, seemed to find this reassuring. She, who less than six months ago had found the thought of a changed Lucknow insupportable, was now contemplating Karachi.

As the violence outside the Fort became a fact of life, as normal as the rain, the population inside shrank a little as some families decided to return to the unguarded familiarity of their homes. Since Masroor knew everyone, they all came to see him before leaving. The menfolk embraced him, palmed their hearts and pledged, godwilling, that they would meet again. It sounded remarkably like goodbye.

Masroor showed no sign of quitting the Fort; the authorities began treating him like a prison trustee, as a reliable intermediary whom they trusted and whom their charges looked up to. Every day I watched dozens of people take their problems to his tent. Whether or not he was claiming his people, his people were definitely claiming him. Coming, going or staying, he touched the lives of everyone in the Fort. So it surprised no one when the superintendent of the camp sent the foreigner to Masroor.

They hadn't been able to sort out who he was or where he was from. They weren't even certain he was a Muslim. They thought he was, but only because the police had picked him up from Platform One of the New Delhi railway station to save him from the attentions of a knot of thugs, who had taken his trunk and were trying to tug his trousers off when they saw approaching uniforms and fled. When the police brought him to the Fort, the superintendent questioned him for half an hour before giving up. The man attended to the questions but his answers were in agitated sentences that didn't make sense to the people listening. Like Urdu spoken by the man on the moon, whispered the superintendent into Masroor's ear as he handed the problem visitor into his care and left.

We were sitting outside the tent, Bihari, Haasan and I, half-dozing, half-listening to the hum of an impromptu meeting centred on Masroor. Haasan called them Masroor's durbars. The durbar was crowded that morning because of a rumour that all unoccupied Muslim houses had been confiscated by the government as enemy property to be distributed to Hindu and Sikh refugees, driven out of West Punjab. Haasan was trying to calm them down when the stranger arrived. By the time the superintendent briefed Masroor, everyone had temporarily forgotten their threatened homes in a fever of speculation about this late arrival.

He looked about fifty years old and his face could have passed as Indian except for an angularity that suggested an origin farther west. His moustache looked foreign too – it was a dense, tightly cropped arc that neither tapered off at the ends nor did it part down the middle. It bristled on his face like a stub of rope.

He's an Afghan, said Shoaib-in-shorts, citing the moustache and the blue-green stubble on the stranger's face. Hairy, he explained in case someone had missed the point, and looked complacently down at his smooth, bare legs.

Masroor saw the superintendent off and turned back to the hairy stranger.

Assalaam aleikum, he said in formal greeting, holding out his hand.

Waleikum assalaam! exclaimed the other enthusiastically, shaking Masroor's hand with both of his. Masroor placed him at once.

Shoaib was wrong; he wasn't an Afghan, he was an Arab.

Masroor could tell; he had spent months in Alexandria during the war. Courteously he gestured to the Arab to sit down and told Asharfi, who was looking on, to fetch a cup of tea. He was buying time; we could almost see his brain whir, trying to work out the next thing to say and the language to say it in.

He settled on Urdu because it had so many Arabic words. You want to catch a train? he asked, seizing on the only fact he knew. His lips puckered as he made to mime a choo-choo train – then he stopped himself.

But the Arab nodded, appearing to understand.

Encouraged, Masroor asked the logical supplementary.

Where did you want to go?

Lucknow, said the man, with no hesitation and, oddly enough, no accent.

Asharfi returned with Haasan, all four hands holding cups of tea. Asharfi handed hers to Masroor and the Arab, so I called to Haasan to give me one of his cups before someone else claimed it. But Haasan didn't seem to hear. He just stood there, holding the cups, his eyes locked on the stranger.

Where are you from? asked Masroor intently.

Lucknow, said the Arab again.

Masroor looked disappointed. The Arab hadn't understood his question.

I still hadn't got my tea. Haasan was standing stock-still, tea slopping from the left-hand cup on to the ground. I made my way to his side and began prising a cup out of his hand.

Masroor tried again.

What, he asked, spacing out the words, is your name?

Haasan let go the cups without warning. One dropped and the one I was pulling at flew over my shoulder. Someone yelled.

Intezar? said Haasan, in question and answer.

The Arab's head jerked in the direction of Haasan's voice. His eyes searched . . . then widened.

Masroor was wrong too; the stranger wasn't an Arab – he was his father.

Talk of homecomings! The residents of the Fort did nothing else till the day we left. What an entrance! People were enchanted by the timing of the prodigal's return. So was I. For me he couldn't have picked a better moment. It changed everything for the better . . . though Masroor wouldn't have agreed.

But even he couldn't dispute the great, fat fact that Intezar was home. He only had to look at his mother; first she fainted in her tent, then wept in Intezar's arms as Haasan looked on, grinning to split his face, then laughed herself into hysterical tears. Even after the first shock of it, after her poise returned, she never let Intezar out of her sight; she went wherever he went, holding on to his arm. Not that Intezar was going anywhere. He was home.

For the first three days, nothing, no one except his wife and children, existed for him. He would break off in mid-sentence to hug Asharfi or Masroor. He even hugged Ammi in public a time or two and set her jealous old-cat relatives muttering about unseemliness. Mealtime conversation consisted of alternating monologues: either Ammi filling in the sixteen years he had missed with a potted history of India for that time, or Intezar, in his oddly guttural Urdu with every other 'g' gargled, describing his exile.

The exile had been as long as a life sentence but Intezar's account of it was summary. After the pilgrimage to Mecca, he had travelled to Cairo, believing in his innocence that

370

enrolling at Al Azhar was a matter of knocking at its doors. Well, he knocked; they told him to go to school first. Al Azhar was a university, not a primary school for Indians illiterate in Arabic. That was the first shock.

Depressed, and homesick for his family, he might have taken the first ship to Bombay, but the fear of going home a failure held him back. He decided to stay in Cairo for a few months to pick up what Arabic he could. At least he would have something to show for the journey when he returned to Lucknow.

Since he had just enough money for the fare but not enough to live on, he found himself a job at a hotel, the Hotel Beau Site. I heard the word hotel and listened more carefully with a sense of kinship, because hotels had been my refuge too. But Intezar never served as a waiter, he started higher up, as a receptionist. The Beau Site was a faintly shady, plainly shabby lodging house which catered to the poorer European traveller; Intezar was hired for his English.

Starting with ahlan! his Arabic improved, but side by side, a strange thing happened: his memories of home became less vivid. He didn't lose them altogether, not at first, but they changed from full colour into black-and-white and then began fading. Perhaps a life lived in Urdu didn't translate well into Arabic. And then, one day, the cable of the Beau Site's sixty-year-old lift snapped, and twenty passengers, including Intezar, hit the ground floor urgently. That was the second shock and it accounted for such brittle, sepia memories as remained.

But he still knew English, so when the concussion passed, he resumed his job at the desk and manned the Beau Site's reception for the next fourteen years. He might have gone on for ever if the management hadn't replaced the little bell on his counter with an electric bell-push. It wasn't properly earthed: the first time he pushed it he was nearly electrocuted. That third shock jolted him out of amnesia and brought him home. He stole the fare from the till in lieu of all the annual holidays he had never taken and took the first boat out of Suez. Urdu, which he hadn't thought in for fourteen years, came back to him slowly; the verbs came first and then the joining words –

he was still waiting for some nouns to return. From Bombay he had taken the train to Delhi and he had been looking for a day train to Lucknow when the thugs got after him. And here he was.

It was a good thing that the Fort's superintendent is a Madrasi, said Intezar more than once. Because if he had understood my Urdu, he wouldn't have taken me to my son!

His son. Masroor didn't know the part and Intezar had returned so abruptly that there hadn't been the time to learn. He wasn't comfortable being hugged and kissed by a grown man with people looking on mistily. But awkwardness wasn't the worst of it; harder to handle was the feeling that he wasn't the pivot of Fort life any more – now he was just part of a properly fathered family.

The family's world was defined by Intezar. Ammi's rediscovered relatives were immediately shed. Her cousins Khaleda and Sameena came visiting twice after Intezar's return but retreated, unnerved. Intezar wasn't rude – he simply didn't acknowledge their presence and, after being looked through and talked across for a while, they left, uncertain of their existence.

Then, slowly, the place names in our mealtime talk began to change. Out went cosy Karachi talk, that anticipatory fingering of the promised land . . . Clifton, Gandhi Gardens, McLeod Road . . . back came Hazrat Ganj, Chowk, Lalbagh, and after weeks of being taboo Lucknow became a familiar presence again. The change wasn't forced; it happened naturally, like a tide turning – Intezar, after all, was home.

On our lavatory treks, people began asking Masroor when he was going home . . . by which they meant Lucknow. Always the question was asked kindly, indulgently – they were happy for him, happy that the question of home had been settled for someone, even if they hadn't resolved it themselves, even if they were inclined towards the other place. The well-meant question never drew an answer from Masroor. He would shrug, looking grim and thwarted. Thwarted, not because he had wanted to move to Pakistan, but because he hadn't been given the chance to choose. That bothered him. A talked-out choice is what it should have been, but that hadn't happened. Jinnah's Muslim homeland had lost by default because Intezar, his father, was home.

Ammi was no help either. She spent every waking minute plotting her return to Lucknow. The house was still there because it hadn't been hers to sell. Since she didn't want Intezar to return after sixteen years to a dirty, disused home, she wrote to Bhukay in Lucknow (who had been left the keys to the house) and instructed him to have the rooms cleaned and aired, to buy new plants to replace the dead ones in the courtyard and to fill the living room with flowers. The next day this didn't seem enough. She worried that the post might be disrupted by the riots, that Bhukay, even if he got the letter might forget, so Moonis was nominated to leave for Lucknow and personally supervise the cleaning-up. Masroor arranged a ticket for him through Colonel Kardar, and Moonis was thus the first of us to return to India.

I was delighted by Lucknow's rising star, though sometimes, before dropping off to sleep, I felt sorry for Masroor and even a little guilty. I would think of the riots I had read about or heard described over the news in the years that I had lived in independent India, riots in places not far from Lucknow, places like Moradabad and Kanpur. Masroor was right: the family should have thought seriously about Pakistan, because whatever its drawbacks, at least no one there had died for being Muslim. But I needed Masroor and his family too much to think objectively about the decision to stay. Each night I told myself that people could die for a hundred reasons other than riots, and fell asleep.

Once Moonis sent word that the house was ready, the end came quickly. We left the Fort on a Friday morning. It was the third of October and the Fort had been home for a month. There were seven of us: Intezar, Ammi, Asharfi, Masroor, Haasan, Bihari and me. The superintendent was there to see us off and thanks to Masroor's military connections there were two jeeps and a truck waiting outside for us. The truck was loaded with everything that had been left behind in 28 Pandara Road, down to Asharfi's Parwana paintings and Masroor's date palms. The jeeps were there for us to ride in; we were going in convoy to Lucknow – Masroor's brother officers didn't trust the trains.

373

Intezar walked right through the great arched gate and sat in one of the jeeps with Asharfi behind him. They had been inseparable from the time he had returned. Ammi and the others trickled out after them. Masroor and I were the last to emerge because Masroor got stuck saying goodbye to Saleem, Salman and the other disappearees from 'forty-two. Saleem was off to Pakistan, so saying goodbye took longer. Masroor's eyes were already bloodshot with sleeplessness; now he clenched his teeth and wept. But he must have stopped when we finally walked out of the gate because he looks dry-eyed in the picture.

Ammi had learnt from her mistake after the election dinner. This time, no one, not Haasan, not God, was going to rob her of her memories. She hauled Intezar and Asharfi out of the jeep for a group photograph. Colonel Kardar had brought a roll of film and I, as usual, was the photographer.

Ammi told me to pose them with the Fort as backdrop, preferably framed by the gate we had walked out of. So that is how I organized the picture, with the camera resting on the bonnet of one of the jeeps to keep it steady. The way they are grouped, Intezar is in the middle, looking alert and impatient, with his arms around Ammi and Asharfi. Asharfi is barely smiling and Ammi (it must be a trick of the light) is looking sly. Haasan's face is turned away because he doesn't believe in photographs. In the top right corner, moving out of the picture, are two women in white saris, their heads cut off by the edge of the frame . . . I like to think that they are Dadi and Parwana, on their way to the fallen women. Bihari is kneeling in front of Haasan, obscuring him from the waist down. Also kneeling, in front of Intezar, is his son Masroor, looking young and serious. It's impossible to tell that a minute before the picture was taken he was crying. Between the two kneeling figures, at roughly the same level, is a swirling blur.

I had learnt some lessons too, from all the pictures I had taken and not figured in. The Colonel's camera had a self-timer and the jeep's bonnet was my tripod. After I lined them up, I twisted the timer and raced for the space between Bihari and Masroor. They were further away than they had seemed through the viewfinder and the shutter caught me on the turn.

But I am there – which is the important thing. In the kneeling row, between Bihari and Masroor, that turning blur is me.